Alessandra DiMario, my new commander, and I share mixed feelings about our arrival at Thule. I am uncertain about my hastily spliced and patched systems. Due to the urgent nature of my refitting, I have never been field-tested, a situation which perhaps alarms me more than my commander.

Our transit time has been brief, by interstellar military standards, less than a day at hyper-L. For the sake of Thule's beleaguered colonists, I am glad our transit time has been so short.

Orbital drop proceeds smoothly. I depart the starship Aldora's cargo bay and plunge into darkness as my heavy lift sled enters the night side of Thule. After I drop below cloud cover, I sight Rustenberg using infrared sensors and radar.

The bleak landscape—terrain I must hold against enemy incursions—gives me new cause for anxiousness. The colony sits in a vast and ancient lava field fissured by deep gorges and steep-sided valleys. Hundreds of enemy soldiers could congregate within a few dozen meters of Rustenberg, completely undetected until the moment of attack. I have a limited number of aerial survey packages on board, but if our mission briefing was correct, the Tersae will attempt to blast out of the sky anything we put up into it.

On the heels of that thought, my lift sled comes under enemy fire. "Seven incoming missiles of unknown configuration."

"Get 'em," my Commander says.

I attempt to lock onto the missiles—

—and am horrified to discover a devastating unsteadiness in my new target-acquisition and weapons-guidance systems. I am unable to secure an accurate weapons lock.

We are all but helpless in the air. . . .

The Bolo Series

Also by Keith Laumer:

COLD STEEL
A BOLOS NOVEL

created by Keith Laumer

edited by Bill Fawcett

BOLOS: COLD STEEL

This is a work of fiction. All the characters and events portrayed in this book are fictional, and any resemblance to real people or incidents is purely coincidental.

A Baen Books Original

Baen Publishing Enterprises
P.O. Box 1403
Riverdale, NY 10471
www.baen.com

ISBN: 0-7434-3549-4

Cover art by David Mattingly

First printing, July 2002

Distributed by Simon & Schuster
1230 Avenue of the Americas
New York, NY 10020

Typeset by Brilliant Press
Printed in the United States of America

Contents

Prologue

It wasn't anywhere you went for a vacation. Thule's eccentric orbit hinted the planet was not native to its sun, but had been captured from a passing star. That same orbit made for an agonizingly hot, wet, and short summer followed by a winter where a good day was merely unbearable. Both seasons shared only one thing: storms featuring winds over 100 KPH. To which was added the joy of a thin crust and constant volcanic activity.

The star system was crowded with debris; Thule itself had seventeen moons and the beginnings of at least one ring. It was generally a good place to avoid when there were so many more hospitable worlds to colonize. But that wasn't an option. Thule was unique for more than being the virtual poster world for being barely habitable. Wherever the planet originated, it had gathered into itself the largest concentration of the rare earth element saganium ever found by humans among the over 40,000 explored worlds—saganium was the vital trace ingredient in a newly developed and

1

amazingly resistant duralloy armor. With the Deng Incursion reaching its destructive climax, mining colonies were en route before the survey team's preliminary report was even finished printing out. There were just a few details they had missed.

The Greater Machine

J. Steven York &
Dean Wesley Smith

Chapter One

For the moment it wasn't pouring rain. Jennifer Harom dropped off the last rung of the ladder onto the damp sand and stretched, glad to be out of the massive pulverizer that towered fifty meters into the air above her. Her overalls were damp from the sweat and the light breeze felt good against her skin, cooling her and clearing her head. The jungle greenery pulped by the big machine had a chlorophyll and vinegar smell, like a Caesar salad.

The ground under her feet shook as the grinder tore into the earth, ultrasonic cannon aimed downward, tearing sand and gravel apart at a molecular level, turning it into the uniform, black ore-sand that crunched under her boots. Despite the violence and power of the pulverizer, active noise dampeners shielded the machine from its own power, reducing the sound to a low rumble, and incidentally keeping the crew from going deaf. She could have even heard the noises from the jungle around her, if the machine hadn't frightened away every animal within five kilometers.

Confident that she was safe from the local predators, she scrambled up a nearby bank and looked back at the big machine, floating on its contra-gravs a few meters above the ground, a duralloy thundercloud lost down from heaven and pretty damned pissed about it. Behind it a two-hundred-meter swath of freshly created ore-sand stretched back up the valley, waiting for the processing machines that followed a kilometer behind. Keeping the beast running, keeping it from ripping itself apart, was a big job, but her three co-workers were more than capable of covering for her while she got a little fresh air. Getting out of the control cabin in the middle of a shift was against the rules, especially while the grinder was in operation, but they all did it. Staying cramped into that small control cabin for ten hours straight would drive anyone nuts. Besides, who cared as long as the pulverizer kept tearing up the ground on this godforsaken planet.

She stepped toward the edge of the jungle. The wide-leafed plants and tall trees towered over her like a wall. At the moment the grinder was tearing a wide path up a sandbar beside a small river. When they reached the end of the valley they would turn around and come back down, cutting another swath beside the one they were working on now, passing the processing machines somewhere along the way. The pulverizer's downward-pointing sound cannon dug the ground to a depth of twenty meters and could chew up rocks as if they were cotton candy.

Eventually all the jungle would be gone from this valley as they mined the saganium, but that would take at least a year and she planned on being gone, headed back into civilized space, long before then. Ten years from now this valley would be twice as deep and wide as it was now, a scar big enough to see from orbit. There were ten colonies and more than double that number of mining sites spread around the planet. This planet, with its smells and heat was barely worth inhabiting now. She had no doubt that in ten years the place would be nothing more than a large pile of rock orbiting a weak sun.

She dropped down onto the ground and rested her back against a boulder. As the machine slowly moved away from her, the Caesar salad smell was already fading, replaced by a stench like mildew, old socks and rotting garbage. Now, after two weeks, she was starting to get used to the smells of this ugly planet. Not all the way yet, but enough that they didn't make her choke anymore. It was ironic that the only way to get a good smell out of the jungle was to blast it to hell, and even that didn't last.

She took a deep breath and let the solidness of the ground ease the tension of a long morning inside the pulverizer. She would take a few minutes, then get back to work. They were pushing the grinder as fast as it would go, and she had every intention of getting the bonus promised them if they made the cliff at the head of the valley in two weeks. The more money she made, the quicker she could head out of here, get back to school, finish the degree in architecture. Then all this labor would just become a bad memory, laughed at over drinks and a good meal.

Suddenly the smell of rot engulfed her even more strongly, and a branch cracked just behind her.

"What—?"

She sprang to her feet and spun around.

For a moment her mind didn't register what she was seeing. Along the edge of the jungle were at least twenty massive alien creatures. For a moment she thought that they were predators of some kind, that she'd been wrong about the sound scaring them away. The things were vaguely humanoid, small heads mounted on massive, fur-covered bodies. The fur was black and scattered with bold, irregular white spots. The things hunched slightly as they spotted her, their heads shifting nervously as they looked at her, first with one side-mounted eye, then the other, like massive birds. The lips on their wide mouths looked hard, beaklike, adding to the impression that these things were somehow in the bird family.

At first, she didn't realize they wore clothes, their black loincloths and harnesses blended so well with their fur. It was only when she saw the primitive hand weapons, curved knives, long blades mounted on shafts to create something like a cross between a spear and a broadsword, that she was sure she was dealing with intelligent creatures. The biggest of them also carried a long, heavy-looking, leather bag over his shoulder, though he lacked the spear/sword that the others carried.

Natives? The damned survey hadn't said anything about natives. She tried to remember something, anything that she'd been taught about first contact in school, but it was all gone, vanished down the same mental sinkhole as hyperspatial geometry and most of her Earth history. She held up her hands, trying to indicate she was unarmed. "Where did you come from?" she asked, managing to choke down the fear. That was stupid. Like they could understand her. Why had she left her side arm back in the pulverizer? It was regulation that she always carry it, just as it was regulation that they stay inside their machine for the entire shift. But there weren't supposed to be any aliens on this planet, especially aliens as big as these beasts.

The creature closest to her just turned its head from side to side, its birdlike black eyes staring down at her with great intensity, even if she couldn't read the emotion behind it. The creature showed no sign that it understood her. Of course, it wouldn't.

She eased a step back, trying not to move too suddenly. The smallest of the creatures, still a good three heads taller than she was, stepped forward, lowered his spear-weapon, and casually jabbed it at her. She cursed and jumped back, feeling the dull impact of the weapon against her side, just below the rib cage.

She cursed again, more angry than afraid. Her side hurt, and without thinking she touched herself, feeling something hot and wet on her fingers. She looked at her bloody fingers in shock. "You *cut* me, you bastards!"

The alien watched her intently, still utterly unreadable to her. Then it made a noise, a hissy, rasping noise, punctuated by clicks of those hard lips. It was talking.

The others joined in, all chattering at once.

She knew without a doubt she was going to have to make a break for it, and while they were talking seemed as good a time as any. She just hoped the others up in the grinder control cabin could see what was happening out here and have the door open when she came up the ladder.

She bolted, skittering back down the slope toward the waiting ladder. After twenty steps, she dared to glance back, and was surprised to see that the aliens weren't following. Instead, the big one had lowered his bag to the ground, and the others gathered around as he opened it and pulled out a large, cylindrical object made of metal. She had no idea what the object was, only that it clearly hadn't been made by a bunch of savages in loincloths. She stopped and clutched her injured side, trying to figure out what they were doing.

The big creature hoisted the cylinder up onto his shoulder, one eye pressing awkwardly against a rearward-facing eyepiece that seemed totally out of position for its anatomy. Then he turned toward the pulverizer. The other natives chattered excitedly.

If she didn't know any better, she'd think it was some kind of energy weapon. But that couldn't be. The rest of these creatures looked primitive, and none of them were carrying anything but swords and knives. Maybe they'd just found the weapon somehow, didn't even know what it did. Maybe they just wanted to see the pretty colors in the sighting system.

"Hey!" she shouted, stepping back slowly. "Don't be aiming that thing at my machine!"

The small alien barked something. From the tone, it might have been an expletive, then started moving towards her, stafflike sword raised. The big one snapped something else at the little one, but was ignored.

The large alien again lifted the energy weapon. For a moment she hesitated between running and trying to watch. Then it was decided for her. The flash nearly blinded her.

She felt the shock wave in her rib cage and staggered back. It *was* a plasma cannon.

The small alien paused, looking, as she was, at the pulverizer.

The cannon had been powerful, but the big mining machine was built to take punishment— Then she saw the smoke coming from the emitters over the sonic cannon. *They'd taken out the active noise cancellation.* She felt it first through her feet, like a pipe organ hitting a low note, building in intensity. Instinctively she covered her ears, knowing how little good it would do. The pulverizer was shaking now, ripples running through its metal sides. *Shut down, shut down!* What was wrong with her crew?

Then she saw someone on one of the catwalks near the control room. She squinted against the sky. Not one of her people. Another alien, and it carried something in one hand. It tossed the object down to the others. It was round. It bounced in the sand and rolled to a stop at the big one's taloned feet.

It was a head. She caught a glimpse of Vanderhaven's blonde hair, and felt her last meal fighting to come back up.

Then the sound came, full blown, like needles in her eardrums, distracting her even from the horror of what she had just seen. She fell to her knees in pain.

The pulverizer was tearing itself apart from the inside, shedding hull plating and external fittings in a gentle rain as it continued its blind way down the valley. The aliens watched, seemingly unbothered by the sound. The big one raised the weapon again, aiming at the midsection where the power core now stood revealed by peeling hull. She couldn't believe they knew what they were doing, but they clearly did.

He fired again. The power core exploded, not in a single blast, but like a string of huge firecrackers angling down through the hull toward the sonic cannon. She watched the machine, her friends, and every hope she had of earning her way off this rock, plow into the riverbank, sending up a shower of sand, smaller explosions sending shudders through its flame-engulfed hull.

Her friends were dead, and if she didn't run, she was going to be as well. While the aliens were still occupied watching the machine burn, she bolted, staggering as she slipped in the loose sand.

She never saw how the small one noticed her, never heard him as he made pursuit. She didn't even know the alien was there until the talons closed around the back of her neck, smashing her face down into the ore-sand.

She struggled weakly, called out, barely able to hear

her own voice. The creature rolled her over effort-
lessly, the point of the alien's blade centimeters from
her face.

She fought, but the talons on the creature's feet held
her while it reached down to grab her hair and yank
it back hard.

Her hearing started to come back, just in time as
the alien screamed and flashed toward her neck. And
this time—this time she understood the alien's meaning
completely.

Victory.

Tyrus Ogden stood on a catwalk that crossed the roof
of the vast vehicle hangar. On the floor below, a space
big enough to park a Concordiat cruiser of the line with
room to spare, a half dozen huge mining machines
were being assembled or repaired. Voices echoed
through the vast space, sometimes shouted instructions,
sometimes, eerily, a whisper relayed, as though by some
acoustic wormhole, from a hundred meters away. Power
tools chattered, buzzed, and roared. Brilliant flashes
from a dozen different exotic welding methods cast
colorful shadows on the walls. The place smelled of
ozone, hot metal, machine lubricant, and just a little
of sweat.

For Tyrus it should have been just another job. It
could have been any world, literally. Big as the building was, it was a standard prefab that he'd seen on
a dozen planets. But he hadn't asked to come here,
hadn't planned to drag his family to this jungle hellhole
of a mining colony. And most of all, he hadn't planned
on the machine whose superstructure towered up from
the floor, ending only a few meters below the catwalk.
It was the machine beneath his feet that made the
job different. He looked down at the gleaming
durachrome hull, the ranks of two-meter-wide treads,

the main turrets, each bigger than any house he'd ever lived in.

"Mr. Ogden," a man's voice, high and nasal, called from behind him.

Tyrus turned at the sound of dress shoes clattering on metal grate. The man walking towards him was thin, dark, average height, dressed in an executive suit wholly inappropriate to the environment. Tyrus recognized him from previous holo conversations. "Dyson, isn't it?"

Dyson shoved out his hand, and Tyrus shook it without enthusiasm. *Company man.*

"I see you're settling right in." He made a sweeping gesture to the machine below. "Like our new mining machine?"

"It's a Bolo, Dyson." He looked down, but not at the machine. "You shouldn't be wearing shoes like that up here. You slip, it's a long way down."

Dyson looked nervously down at his own feet. "I didn't know."

"I'm sure."

Dyson stepped cautiously up to the railing and looked over. "I do know about that, though. I signed the purchase order. It's a Prescott 4800 surface excavator, the first of its kind."

"It's a Bolo, Dyson."

Dyson looked uncomfortable. "Well—it's that too. A converted Bolo actually, an old Mark XX . . . I think, maybe a XXI. I don't know about those things. I hear Prescott found a whole regiment of them rusting in a scrap yard on some moon somewhere."

Tyrus looked at the shining sweep of the hull and felt his mind slipping back to another place and time, a place of fire, a time of war. "Bolos don't rust. After a few centuries on a planet like this, they might develop a surface patina. But they don't rust, and they don't bleed, and they don't ever, ever die."

"Excuse me?"

He looked at Dyson. "That's why they diverted me here, isn't it? Why they dragged me and my family into what amounts to a combat zone. I've had combat experience."

Dyson nodded. "This situation has developed very quickly and unexpectedly. The 4800's were already ordered as part of a trial program. You were already in the sector. You have the skills we needed. And you—know about Bolos."

"I've fought on the same side as Bolos, Dyson. That's a whole different thing. Maybe Bolo commanders are comfortable with those things, but I was infantry, and I never served with a man who wasn't rattled by them, who didn't spend as much time looking over his shoulder at his own Bolos as he did looking at the enemy line. What in heaven's name made you want to convert one into a blasted *tractor*?"

Dyson was starting to look annoyed. "I told you, we bought it, we didn't think it up. You've heard the losses we've experienced here. Three machines just last month. Out away from the colonies and the fixed defenses, they're essentially vulnerable against even light weapons. We've taken to issuing pulse rifles to all our crews, welded some makeshift armor to the control cabs, but the losses continue. These aliens—natives—whatever they are, somehow didn't show up on our surveys, so we never imagined it would be an issue. But this," he waved at the Bolo again, "was marketed as a solution for mining on 'hostile worlds.' They simply don't get much more hostile than this. The rest of our machines are vulnerable, but the Prescott 4800—"

"The Bolo."

"Whatever . . . It can take the kind of attacks we've been experiencing. We can send it into the most isolated and dangerous areas with impunity. They won't be able to hurt it, and maybe we can learn something. Learn how to protect the rest of our equipment."

Tyrus cursed under his breath. "You have no idea of the trouble you've caused me personally, bringing me here. I suppose you want me to work this beast into the maintenance rotation here?"

Dyson looked away. "Actually, we already have a pretty good maintenance chief at the colony. We were hoping that you'd run the 4800 for us."

Tyrus blinked his eyes in disbelief. "You want *me* to command a Bolo?"

Whitestar shifted the hand-forged blade in his hand, feeling the comfortable way his clawlike fingers held the grip, the natural way that the handle cradled against the long bones of his hand. It was a good blade, good balance, a weapon he understood, one that became an extension of his arm. The knife pleased him, made him glad to be alive. The weapons provided by the Ones Above were powerful, but clumsy and unnatural. Only with a blade in his hand did he feel like a fresh-hatched warrior again.

The afternoon breeze ruffled his fur and carried the smell of wood smoke from a nearby burrow. He was dimly aware of his fellow clansmen gathering around the circle, clicking their jaws in rhythm, the ancient ceremony of challenge. Some part of his mind dimly registered all this, cataloged it, filtered it for any undetected threat, but his focus, his *combat-eye*, was entirely on the smaller Tersae across the circle. His name was Warrior Twostone, and he was trying with all his might to kill Whitestar, his clan-lord.

Twostone lunged, his long, curved blade flashing in the dappled sunlight that filtered through the trees.

Agile for his greater size, Whitestar turned away from the thrust, hooked Twostone's blade with his own and pulled, throwing the warrior off balance. He brought his foot around and kicked Twostone in the back, his talons drawing blood.

Twostone staggered for a moment, but quickly caught himself, turning, knife held high in a gesture of defiance. He turned his head at right angles to Whitestar, focusing one eye on the lord, and a sound came from his throat, a low chattering that in the Tersae was an expression of amusement. In context it was a sign of continued calm and reason, despite his wounds. The Tersae blood ran hot. A warrior could too easily lose themselves in that heat, forget the mission, forget their clan-brothers, and waste their lives on the battlefield. A good warrior knew how to maintain the balance, even when their own blood painted the enemy's blade.

You are truly a fine warrior, Twostone. It will be a shame to lose you.

The two circled, each looking for some weakness in their opponent. Finally, Whitestar simply grew tired of looking. He feinted an attack causing Twostone to step backwards, then again, and again, never letting the warrior find balance, focusing his attention on Whitestar's blade. Then Whitestar struck, not with his blade, but with a flying kick, his talons digging into Twostone's blade-arm, pushing it aside. He *squeezed*, feeling skin tear beneath his claws, until the blade clattered to the forest floor, then released, twisted in midair to strike with his blade, bringing it against Twostone's throat. He held the blade there and he grabbed Twostone's arm and spun him around.

Twostone ended up with his back against Whitestar's left shoulder, the knife tight against his skin. "My life is my lord's," he gasped, "my blood is my lord's. Take them, in the name of the Ones Above."

"I take your life," responded Whitestar, "I take your blood. I give you back your blood. I give you back your life, Sacred Warrior Twostone, to serve the Ones Above." He lowered the knife, stepped in front of Twostone, and held it across his own chest in salute.

Twostone bowed, folding his arms behind his back like a new hatchling, a gesture of extreme supplication and humility. "How may my unworthy life serve the Ones Above?"

"Rise, Twostone. You have been bested by your lord, but you fought honorably, and well. You are worthy. Tonight we strike the devils in their nests. Tonight you will carry the Fist of the Ones Above. We will barter your life for a thousand and twenty-four of the enemy's lives."

Twostone nodded his head sharply in gratitude.

"Go to your fire, and we will speak later." He turned to the circle of observers. "Make way for the Sacred Warrior!" The circle parted and Twostone stepped through, and with that, the ceremony was ended. The crowd immediately began to disperse. A few looked disappointed that no more blood had been spilled, a few others paused to compliment Whitestar's skill and prowess.

Only old Scarbeak lingered at his side as Whitestar headed back to the Lord's Burrow. "You should take a new name, my lord. 'Bloodtalon' would suit you well."

"Such a name would only fire the young warriors, old one. I fight too many challenges as it is. Tonight our Great War begins. I should be reviewing our plans, not holding a knife to my own warrior's throat."

"So speaks the lord. I forgot for a moment the recent challenge of your eldest hatchling. It was thoughtless of me. It pains one to take blood from one's own brood, or one's own clan."

Whitestar dismissed him with a click of his jaw. "You meant only to compliment me, old one. I did what had to be done, and with luck, Blackspike will yet recover and take my place as lord of the clan."

They walked past the stream, where young females soaked weaver-vines and beat them between rocks to extract the useful fibers. A few young males crouched, watching them cautiously from a distance.

"You don't know these young ones, elder. The fire burns strong in them. They have no wisdom at the fight." He was not speaking of his son, but he could have been.

"Wisdom comes with age."

"Then it is not a lord's destiny to be wise, elder. One day I will be too slow at a challenge, and—" he hissed and made the motion of a slicing blade with his hand— "that will be the end of me."

"Wisdom is relative, lord. You are wise enough for what you do."

"And you, elder? Is the Fist of the Ones Above ready?"

"The sacred connections are made, the sacred modules all show the light-of-function. The Ones Above promise that it will cut deep into the belly of the human devils. The explosion should be spectacular."

"Let's hope so, Scarbeak. Twostone is a fine warrior. I wouldn't like to waste his life on a fool's mission."

The first sign of real trouble came when the hangar lights flickered, followed by the sound of a distant boom. Tyrus looked up from where he was crouched, inspecting one of the Bolo's two-meter-wide treads, and wondered if the area was prone to thunderstorms. At the same moment, a *quiver* seemed to go through the huge machine, as though all of its secondary systems were being cycled through their test cycles at once.

Tyrus shook his head and went back to his inspection, knowing as he did that it was pointless make-work. It was late. He should be home, helping the boys

unpack. Fact was, he didn't want to see Lee, and he
strongly suspected that she didn't want to see him.
They'd had a fight that afternoon. She'd never wanted
him to take the transfer to the Taft Colonies, even
though it was the only way to keep his job with the
company. When they were diverted to mining colonies
on Thule, she'd blamed him. Taft at least had alien
ruins for her to explore, some chance for her to continue her often-interrupted career as an archeologist.
Taft had an established family environment for the kids.
Thule was one step up from a shanty camp, a sprawling, walled, cluster of prefabs, brothels and miner bars.
A cold feeling of dread knotted in his gut. He was
going to lose them. He knew it.

The lights flickered again. More thunder. Or *something*.

"Unit DRK moving to status two alert mode. Awaiting instructions."

Tyrus looked up and blinked. A hundred meters
away, a small crew was overhauling a sonic pulverizer
cannon. Nobody else was close. Another one of those
acoustic tricks the hangar was famous for?

"Unit DRK awaiting instructions."

The sound seemed almost to be coming from inside
his head. Beamed sonics? He looked at the gleaming
curve of the Bolo's hull, and spotted an emitter rod
aimed straight at him. He shivered, somehow suddenly
feeling like a rabbit in the hunter's crosshairs. "You can
talk?" Of course it could talk. All Bolos could. But the
book said this one had been lobotomized or something,
placed into a standby mode that made it as passive and
stupid as a ground-car. There were recorded voice
responses, but it certainly shouldn't have been initi-
ating speech.

"You are Tyrus Ogden. I am keyed to respond to
your biometric profile. Awaiting orders, commander."

He frowned. "I'm not your commander, I'm your operator. You're a mining machine, a tractor."

"I am Bolo, Mark XXIV of the line, activated 2970 at the Fifield Armorworks, New Prescott Colony. My hull designation is DRK. I am commonly addressed by my commanding officers as 'Dirk.'"

More thunder. The overhaul crew stopped their work and began to talk rapidly among themselves. "Go back to sleep, Dirk."

"I cannot. Threat level is increasing. Moving to status one alert mode. Full Combat Reflex Mode is now on standby."

He dropped his tools and stood. "What threat? The thunder?" This was just the sort of thing he was afraid of. You can't make a house pet out of a trained attack dog, and you can't turn a Bolo into a mining machine. This thing could go on a rampage if he didn't get it calmed down. "It's just thunder. Natural, atmospheric, electrical discharges. It's no threat to us."

On the hull behind him the pilot's hatch, as thick and heavy as a vault door, swung smoothly open with a whir. "Commander, I suggest you enter the control room and prepare for combat."

"It's *thunder*, I tell you. Power down now! That's an order!"

"Negative."

Tyrus cursed. He had to talk to Dyson. Maybe he had an override code or something that would shut this beast down. He could use his wristcom, but the Bolo would be listening, and somehow, that didn't seem like a good idea. He was suddenly aware that he was standing on the tracks. If the machine decided to move, he could be pulped before he had time to scream.

He scrambled down from the side of the mining machine and headed toward the side door of the maintenance area, wiping grease off his hands as he ran. He reached the shops at the edge of the hangar just as an explosion rocked the far end of the hangar. Mechanics and operators were suddenly shouting, running everywhere.

"Full Combat Reflex Mode activat—" the Bolo's beamed voice was suddenly cut off. His first instinct was that the Bolo had gone rogue and fired off one of its weapons. But the big machine seemed inert, and he couldn't imagine that they'd left it with functional weapons. He realized he could still hear distant gunfire and explosions. *They were under attack!* The aliens he'd been told about must have somehow taken out the colony defenses without a shot, without setting off the general alarm. But how could a bunch of jungle savages know how to sabotage screen generators and autoturrets?

He spotted a rack of pulse rifles on an office wall and grabbed one of them. Just in time, as a furry, goggle-eyed humanoid giant rounded the corner and swung some kind of sword at him. Instinctively he swung the barrel around, his finger squeezing on the trigger into full auto mode. The first shot took the sword weapon off at the handle. The second tore a hunk out of the side of the alien's neck, the third ripped a hole in its right shoulder, sending a spray of something dark, wet, and hot across his face.

It fell, but two more appeared behind it shouting and clicking loudly. He took them down almost as easily as the first.

Another one. This one had something small and metal held awkwardly in its hand. A violet laser flash sent him scrambling behind a desk. A hole appeared in the plastic kick panel a few inches from his head, as the alien fired blindly.

Tyrus tightened his grip on the rifle, tried to imagine

where the alien might have gone since he last saw it, and sprang from behind the desk already firing. The alien was standing no more than a meter from him. They were both caught by surprise, but the alien was dead, his chest exploding like a ripe melon.

Tyrus retched at the smell of burned hair and sweet smell of roasted alien flesh. He spotted the hand weapon on the floor where the alien had dropped it. Hoping he didn't accidentally activate it, he shoved the weapon in his pocket.

He put his back against the office wall, watching the door, and tried his wristcom. It didn't work. Maybe they were jamming, or had disabled the relay towers. He had to figure some way to get home, defend the kids. His own ground-car was parked at the far end of the hangar, but he spotted a man-door in the office wall behind him that probably led outside. There might be company vehicles there that would respond to his employee unikey. He scooted to the door, opened it a crack to make sure things were clear, and stepped outside. What he saw nearly tore him apart.

The colony was located in a small valley, with the hangar on high ground at the south end. He could look down on at least half the structures there. Everywhere he looked there were flames, explosions, and laser flashes.

He could see the defense turrets along the ridgelines surrounding the valley, all pointed outwards, intact, and inert. At the far end of the valley hundreds of white-on-black aliens boiled out of the jungle like ants. The family apartments were to his left, near the shuttle port. For a moment, he held out some hope. The buildings were still intact, away from the main thrust of the aliens' charge. Then a plasma cannon began firing from a rooftop to the west, blasting the buildings one by one.

Behind them, an atmospheric shuttle lifted off, slowly, as though it were heavily loaded. At least somebody was getting away. The shuttle might be able to make it to one of the other colonies. Maybe his kids were on it. *Please.*

He hoped they had gotten away, but he couldn't take the chance. He had to find out for himself. He looked frantically around. A line of company utility vans were parked a dozen yards down the building. He could take one of them.

The missile streaked across his vision so quickly that he almost didn't see it, and ripped into the side of the hanger next to the vans. The force of the explosion ripped outwards throwing the vans around like a child's blocks, while leaving him relatively unscathed. He could see a line of aliens running up the hill towards him. He ducked back into the office.

"You need to return to my command compartment," said the voice in his head. The Bolo was back. "My exact status is unknown, but I am unable to actively protect you at this time. You must return to me."

The Bolo! If he could get the damned thing working, the small arms he'd seen wouldn't touch it. He could make his way across the colony, rescue his wife and kids. If they were still alive. He ran back into the hanger, only to see dozens of aliens running through the hangar.

He lifted the rifle and started squeezing off shots, taking an extra instant each time to line up an alien and make the shot count. It felt more like murder than a battle. He'd fire and one alien would drop. He'd fire again and another alien would drop. Most of them had swords. He didn't see any other advanced weapons, but they had to be out there somewhere.

"Quickly," said the Bolo.

The aliens just kept coming as fast as Tyrus could shoot them, wave after wave. He moved slowly towards the Bolo, careful not to let the aliens sneak behind him. Then, abruptly, his rhythm was broken. There were no targets. He could hear them moving away.

Something was very wrong.

He stepped out from behind a welding machine onto the hangar floor. Twenty meters away, a metal cylinder sat on the floor, gleaming in the hangar's still functional emergency lights. He'd never seen anything like it before, but he had a pretty good guess. *Bomb*.

He sprinted towards the Bolo. Halfway there he tossed down the rifle. He could see the Bolo ahead, an emergency hatch opening in its flank, down between two of the giant boogie wheels. He gave it his last burst of speed and dived for the opening.

The rest happened in slow motion, as the shock wave caught him and hurled him through the hatch.

He could see the bulkhead coming at him, every weld and bolt of it, in sickening detail, but he could do nothing to stop it.

There should have been an impact, but there was only nothing.

Chapter Two

It has been three minutes and sixteen seconds since I was ejected from the cargo bay of the Lexington. I will see combat sooner than I had ever expected. My commander and I, along with two other Bolos and their commanders were diverted from our original mission to the Tilla M outpost by a distress message from the recently established mining colonies on Thule. The settlements are under attack by a force or forces unknown. Due to the circumstances, we have been deployed from the Lexington in a non-optimal trajectory, while the ship hurriedly makes another jump with the rest of our unit to complete its original mission.

It is an exciting time. My first assignment was to a purely defensive post at the Depoe Shipyards, far from the lines of the Deng conflict, and while Tilla M has seen intermittent raids by well-armed pirates, any conflict would doubtless consisted of brief defense against space-based hit-and-run attacks. This is the kind of conflict for which I was designed and constructed, engaging a powerful enemy on a battlefield of planetary scope.

Our "hot" insertion and the limited intelligence available to us add to the challenge of the assignment, but I am unconcerned. I am unit VCK, a Bolo of the Line, Mark XXV, bearer of the proud tradition of the Dinochrome Brigade. I am proud be the first of our forces to land on Thule. I am confident that I will do my duty, and do it well.

It has been four minutes and three seconds since ejection. Broken transmissions indicate that any ship attempting to land may come under ground attack, therefore our individual assignment is to deploy and clear a landing zone. My commander will monitor the situation from my assault pod, which will wait in orbit, along with the other Bolos in their pods, and a trio of shuttles loaded with emergency gear. Instead of my usual deployment, I am strapped to a sandwiched pair of contra-grav cargo sleds and mats of ablative material forming a makeshift, but completely expendable, landing craft.

I fire the guidance thrusters on the cargo sleds, to roll my makeshift heat shield to face the atmosphere, and adjust the upper sleds contra-gravs to conserve power for the final braking. The contra-gravs on the lower sled are set to full output, as there will be no opportunity to utilize unused power later.

Five minutes and eighteen seconds since ejection. A faint vibration through my treads tells me that I am encountering the edge of Thule's atmosphere. I take the opportunity to make a long-range scan of the planet below me. I immediately detect the various colony installations in the expected locations, but the central installation shows none of the energy output I would expect of a functioning colony. Instead, I detect only the heat of residual fires, plus a chemical signature *consistent with large-scale combustion and the early decay stage of biological matter. The damage is even worse than we had been led to believe. I also detect flames and weapons signatures from the most northern colony. It too is under attack.*

I adjust my trajectory to move my landing site as far north as possible. I maintain communications silence, but there are distress calls coming from the Rustenberg Colony on several bands, some live, some via automated beacon. I monitor, trying to get some sense of our enemy, but other than descriptions of large humanoids, there is little else of strategic value, intelligence about their mounted and airborne weapons platforms, descriptions of their armored and mechanized divisions.

I am entering the planet's atmosphere now, and ionization is making my sensors unreliable. It must be, as I can detect none of the signatures I would associate with the enemy. I find no bases or roads, no radiation sources consistent with fusion power plants, no towns or bases, no armored columns or spaceports. The situation is most puzzling. It is almost as though the enemy does not exist.

The buffeting is quite heavy now. I am surrounded by an ionized curtain of superheated air, and flaming chunks of ablative mat are breaking off and flying past like fireworks. I must be putting on a spectacular show for anyone watching on the ground, but my signature will not be consistent with a Bolo assault pod. The enemy will doubtless hesitate before firing on me, consulting with their specialists to determine if I am an attack craft or a natural meteor. By the time they come to a decision, I should be safely near the ground.

Or not. I am emerging from the ionization blackout, and I detect, three—now five—now seven missile traces arching up from diverse points across the continent. They seem to be light nuclear interceptors, unlikely to do me serious damage, but they could destroy the contra-grav sled I need to make my landing. My first duty, however, is to secure the landing zone. I begin cycling my main Hellbores from launch point to launch point, targeting them with a multikiloton blast. Though I can detect no fixed installation at any of these points, someone there will pay the price for the folly of firing on a Bolo of the Dinochrome Brigade. I am hardly a defenseless drop ship.

There is a sudden lurch, and then I am in near freefall. The first sled has given out, either its power cells depleted, or damaged by a reentry burn-through. No matter. There is one last use I can make of it. I remotely fire the links holding the lower sled to the upper. My audio detectors pick up the rending of metal even in the thin air. Then the sled slides out from under me, a metal mattress the size of a schoolyard, its bottom charred and still glowing white hot in places. I transverse one of my secondary batteries, lock onto the sled, and fire a half-second pulse.

The sled explodes into flaming chunks just as the first missile closes on my position. I watch as the missile, and two of its companions, alter course to home in on the false target I have provided for them, their nuclear fireballs blossoming a safe kilometer above me. That still leaves four missiles closing on my position. I increase my battle screens to full power, and compute firing solutions for the remaining missiles. I begin to transverse my secondary batteries. I have four point three seven seconds until the first missile is in blast radius. Plenty of time.

Suddenly the missiles begin to take high-G evasive maneuvers. I detect a pattern to their movements, but this requires a critical one point-three seconds of observation and analysis. I am able to bring my batteries to bear on three of them. I begin a roll program, placing my own hull between the missile and the sled, selectively reinforce my battle screens, and shutter my more sensitive sensors against the blast.

The explosion rattles my structure, subjecting me to a momentary peak acceleration of 19 G's. It is fortunate that my commander remained safely in orbit, but I am unharmed. The energy from the explosion sizzles against my battle screens, and in a moment I can feel the converted energy surging into my storage cells. There has been a one point two percent degradation of my upper turret armor, but I am otherwise unharmed. The critical question now is, did the explosion damage the second contra-grav sled?

My visual sensors unshutter, and I see the horizon growing less curved by the second. I have been in freefall too long. Even with full sled function, I am in danger.

I tentatively apply power to the sled, alert for any problem, but the contra-gravs engage smoothly. I am slowing, but not quickly enough. I increase power to one hundred percent, then into overload, one hundred and ten, one hundred and twenty, one hundred and thirty.

The cells are draining at an alarming rate, and I am detecting an overheat condition in the contra-grav accelerator coils. The situation is critical, but there is little I can do. I must trust that the contra-grav sled is flawless in its manufacture and maintenance, that it was not damaged by the missile, reentry, or by the separation of the first-stage sled.

I take one last opportunity to do aerial deep scans with my sensors, focusing on the dead central colony, looking for any sign of my elusive enemy. I detect the remains of many ground vehicles, several shuttles trapped on the ground, large mining and construction machinery, and one other trace, an armored durachrome war hull—

Two point three four seconds to impact. I am still falling too fast. Below me, I see a green carpet of jungle canopy, a silver thread of river slicing through the trees. I retune my battle screens. In theory, they can absorb some of the kinetic energy of my landing, acting as a last-resort shock absorber, but to the best of my knowledge this has never been tested.

My last thought before I hit the ground is of those final sensor readings. No matter what happens, they give me hope. I do not know how, but the readings were unmistakable. There is already a Bolo on Thule.

Lord Whitestar moved through the night jungle by instinct, navigating by the smell of certain plants, by the echoes of his own footfalls off the trunks of trees, and the occasional flashes of starlight through the canopy above. The Ones Above had warned them that they must show no light to the sky above, no fire, no torch, as the devils would be watching. Even the wonderful weapons that the Ones Above had given them had to be taken into the nests for repair. The lights-of-function that showed when a given part was functional or should be replaced, even showing one of those to the sky could give them away.

He could hear quiet chants of victory all through the jungle, and he knew that chanting just like this spread through the jungle for several days' walk, to wherever the men of his widely dispersed clan made camp. They had cut deep into the enemy's vitals today, raided one of his nests, killed all his warriors, all his hatchlings.

Whitestar's fur bristled with satisfaction and pride. The Ones Above would be pleased, and would favor their blessings on his clan above all others. It had been promised that, when the time came, they would be shown where even more powerful weapons were hidden, shown how to use the ones they had in even more deadly ways.

He stopped, taking a deep breath. He smelled her before he heard her voice. She carried the brooding smell, the smell of one caring for eggs. It made his blood burn, but did not excite him. Instead it brought out instinctive, protective urges. It made him want to kill the human devils even more, to sweep the world clean of them to protect his eggs. "Are you there, Whitestar?"

"This way," he said. Her senses would be tuned for the eggs now, for the hatchlings. She could hear their cries of help across a raging river, or smell an illness before they would even feel it, but it made it more difficult to travel in the jungle at night.

She stepped closer, the smell of her stronger, the outline of her smaller form just visible in the starlight. "What are you doing here, Sweetwater? The eggs—"

"The second-wife warms them, my lord. As first-wife, it is my right to take a rest occasionally. I came looking for you."

"I was returning to the nest."

"Then I will follow you. I hear your victory was great today."

Whitestar clicked his bill in affirmation, and returned to walking, slower this time so she could keep up.

"Then Twostone is dead?"

"He took the Fist of the Ones Above to a place where it would disable their defenses. Take away their machines. They are soft and weak. Not like us. By nightfall, we had returned them all to their foul maker. Twostone died well. He did not die for nothing."

"Did he have to die at all, Whitestar?"

"Not this again, woman. The devils we have been

raised to fight are finally here. This is the time of destiny. We are lucky to be alive to see it."

"Your eldest hatchling is lucky to be alive to see it. I watched you from afar when you fought Twostone. You showed him mercy. Could you not do as much to your own hatchling, your eldest?"

"Blackspike would not yield, woman. He would have killed me. Only my skill saved me from killing him. I saved him from spilling his own blood in battle, like Twostone. I saved him to take my mantle as lord when I am gone."

"He is hot-blooded, Whitestar. All the young ones are, as the old women say your generation is hotter blooded than your fathers. It is like a creeping madness."

"It is our strength. It is what helps us kill the devil humans." This was a very sore subject between them. The old women remembered too much, talked too much, caused too much trouble. Some days he thought he should just have his warriors kill them. But there was truth to it, especially among the highborn who were blessed with the teachings of the Ones Above. It was the duty of the lowborn fodder to spill their blood against the devils. It was the duty of the highborn not to die without using their teachings, and without passing those teachings on.

They *had* to deny the heat of their own blood. He stopped outside the nest and turned to her. "Have you placed the eggs in the blessing chamber yet?" The blessing chambers were among their most sacred artifacts. Each new clutch of eggs was to spend two days in its warm, shuttered interior. It was there that the blessing of the Ones Above was delivered onto the clan.

She hesitated. "No, my lord, I have not. The old women say that is where the blood of our males becomes poisoned. The eggs are returned with tiny punctures in the skins. The old women say that is where it goes in, like venom from a sting-lizard's tongue."

"The old women make up stories to frighten the likes of you, first-wife. Forget what they tell you, and deliver our eggs for their blessing before it is too late."

"I speak these things because the lord should know what the females think. It is not just the old women. They tire of seeing their family males driven to madness by the fire within. They tire of losing their mates, their sons and brothers to duels, to challenges, and now to war. They fear that we will only anger the devils and that they will come and kill us all."

"If it's the will of the Ones Above that we die in our war against the devils, then so be it. But we are taught that one clan will rise above the others and show the Ones Above where the human devils are weak, where they can most easily be destroyed. That is why the clans must not mingle, why we must be different of custom and of form, so that we may demonstrate which is best. And once that clan has the devils on the run, then the Ones Above will sweep down from the skies and finish the job. The clan that shows the way will be our clan, and honored will be our place in the heavens at the side of the Ones Above."

"Who will be left to sit at their side, lord? You? Will your sons live to see that day? Remember that you have another one. Will you spill his blood too?"

"Is that what you really came to talk about? Sharpwing is barely out of the egg."

"Sharpwing is old enough at least to think he can fight, and he is younger, his blood burns hotter yet than his brother's. He is furious at what you have done. He longs to die for the Ones Above. I think he will challenge you. Perhaps soon."

"Then I will do what I must do. Blackspike will heal. He must become lord of the clan, for the good of all.

Sharpwing is my chick, but he is no leader. I will do what I must."

There was silence for a time. "Do not kill Sharpwing, husband. If you kill him, Whitestar, I will never forgive you. You will still be lord, but I will be sure that your time is never happy again."

Then she turned and left him alone in the darkness.

Alone with his own thoughts. "As though my time is happy now," he said quietly.

Tyrus awoke in darkness, head pounding, his face against cold, smooth, metal.

"Remain still and silent."

The words seemed to fill Tyrus Ogden's head, making the pain even worse. It took him a moment to remember what had happened. The explosion, the massive maintenance building trembling and collapsing around him. He had tried to get in the Bolo. Had he made it? The agonizing voice in his head suggested that he had.

"Do you wish me to turn on the lights?"

"Please," he whispered, knowing the Bolo would hear him. Then thinking about it, "dim lights."

A faint, red light bathed the area. He was in some sort of narrow machine space. A drive shaft as big around as his body punched through the compartment. Behind him was the closed hatch. Ahead was a tube with a sloping ladder that led up into darkness. "Where am I?"

"My number two ventral maintenance access. My internal sensors are fully intact, and indicate that you have a mild concussion. I do not believe that you will die."

"Thanks for that happy bit of news." He reached up to feel the large knot on top of his head, and winced. It least he didn't seem to be bleeding much. He tried to move his arm under his body to push himself up into a sitting position. He had to get to his wife and children, to make sure they were all right.

"If you must move," the Bolo's voice said, "do so quietly. The enemy is near, scanning the debris for survivors. There have been a number of patrols since the attack."

"How long was I unconscious?"

"Twelve hours, fourteen minutes, and either nineteen or thirty-eight seconds, depending on your definition of conscious."

Tyrus considered for a moment, and decided that lying on the floor for a while longer was a pretty damned good idea. He felt nauseous, weak, from even trying to move. "What am I supposed to call you?"

"I am Bolo Mark XXIV, designation DRK. I believe that my previous commanders used to refer to me as 'Dirk.'"

He suddenly remembered that Dirk had already given his name, before the attack. He wondered how much damage the bump on the head had done, and why Dirk didn't seem to remember it either.

"Okay, Dirk, I'm in pretty bad shape. How about you?"

"I have been seriously sabotaged in a means I do not yet understand. My weapons systems have largely been removed or disabled, my sensors and battle screens extensively modified from their original configurations, new equipment of unknown purpose welded to my hull, and most seriously, my psychotronics and memory have been seriously compromised. I attempted to engage Full Combat Reflex Mode during the attack, and internal feedback nearly destroyed my higher mental functions. It appears that I will require orders from a human commander before taking direct combat action."

"They probably hardwired some sort of inhibitor into your combat reflex circuits. They were as worried about your going berserk as I was. Dirk, you haven't exactly been sabotaged, though the word 'butchery' might apply. You've been turned into a mining machine."

The machine was uncharacteristically silent for a time.

"That is illogical."

"Damn straight, but they did it anyway."

More silence.

"That at least clarifies my situation. It explains why my sensors have been modified to detect seismic disturbances and mineral concentrations rather than targeting data, why my screens have been optimized for low-velocity kinetic impacts, and why my combat communications array has been replaced with one for civilian wavelengths. I will need to analyze my new capabilities, and attempt to compensate for my loss of combat readiness."

"You mean, you think you can still fight?"

"I can move. I have awareness. I have power. With your help, I will fight to the best of my capabilities."

"Listen, Dirk, I'd love to help out and all, but my soldiering days are over. I just want to find my family."

"Your family were in the colony outside the hangar?"

"Yes."

"Then they are no longer there, or they are dead. I cannot determine which."

That was the thing he'd been trying not to think about. He vaguely remembered seeing the colony in flames, the apartments exploding. But there could be survivors out there somewhere, and he'd seen an air shuttle getting away. There was hope. There had to be hope. There were so many things he had yet to say. He had to apologize for bringing them to this place, for failing to have the simple courage to say "no" to his superiors when the time was right. The last time with his wife, they had been fighting. It couldn't end like that.

There *had* to be hope.

Besides, this crippled Bolo freely admitted that its sensors weren't working right. "Dirk, how can you be so sure that there are no survivors out there? Do you have visual?"

"Negative. When the explosion went off, a section of the hillside above the hangar collapsed. We are buried under eight to ten meters of loose rock."

That stopped him for a moment. "Then how do you know *anything* about what is happening outside?"

"I seem to be equipped with a suite of sensitive seismic detectors. I can detect any surface movements in the area. The patrols I have detected are too heavy, their stride wrong, for them to be human. I have detected no movement, either by foot or vehicle, that I can identify as potentially human. In fact, I have detected no vehicles at all."

That didn't make sense either. An attacking force should have lots of vehicles. All those alien soldiers he'd seen certainly hadn't walked here through a thousand kilometers of jungle.

Feeling a little better, he pulled himself up to a sitting position. His arm hurt, his head throbbed, there were little dark flecks in his vision when he moved, but he thought he would live. "You don't seem concerned that we're buried. Can you get us out?"

"Affirmative. Despite the so-called 'butchery' of my systems, I am still a Bolo of the Line. When you are ready, I can begin extracting us from the rubble."

He sighed. Despite Dirk's claim, he wouldn't be satisfied until they made a visual inspection of the colony. Failing that, the shuttle had been headed north. There was another colony off that way if he remembered correctly. He might find his family there, and this Bolo was his best chance of making the trip. "Start digging."

"I would recommend that you strap yourself into my command crash couch first. It is also equipped with a field autodoc that can treat your injuries. Can you climb up to my control room?"

He looked at the ladder. "I think so. Which way?"

"Up the ladder, right at the horizontal passage, around my main turret bearing, through the fore circuitry room, right on until the end of the passage." He started climbing the ladder, careful not to hit his bump on the low, metal ceiling. "I should warn you," said Dirk, "that as soon as I bring my systems up to full power, there is a good possibility we will be detected."

"We'll deal with it when we have to. See what you can do about getting us some functioning weapons, and I'll have a quick look at your circuitry room as I pass through."

"I will begin bringing power systems on-line."

"Not while I'm touching an exposed buss bar, please." He reached the central passage and started crawling forward. "Get ready to dig us out. I want to see some sunlight."

Around him the massive mining machine came to life.

Chapter Three

The heat smothered them like a blanket, making the already thick atmosphere blur any long range visuals. The shimmering of the air, combined with the black and white markings of the aliens' fur, worked like a natural camouflage, letting them blend with the shadows at the edge of the jungle. Acting Militia Commander Jerry Donning let go of the binocs with disgust, letting them drop back into place on his vest. He could do better without them. He knew the aliens were out there. They had attacked twice already since the fall of the Odinberg Colony. There was no doubt they were coming again.

He stood on the top of a slight rise just to the south of the northern colony, staring into the scattered jungle below them. He felt lost, outmanned, outgunned and underqualified. It had only been a month since the first shipments of pulse rifles, body armor, and light weaponry had come in, along with orders from company headquarters, "able-bodied adults, especially those with military experience, are urged to form a militia for emergency defense."

"Urged" was just the company's way of saying "must," and so processing foreman Jerry Donning, who had once done a tour with the New Brazil Marines suddenly found himself prime officer material, in fact, found himself in charge of the colony's defenses. Never mind that in his three terrestrial years in the service he'd never gotten within a parsec of combat, never fired a shot outside a range or a training simulation. But there he was, in charge.

He'd figured it would be easy. Round up some volunteers, go shoot some daybats at the jungle's edge, lob off some practice mortar rounds at rock formations. Hell, it would be fun. It wasn't like they'd ever have to fire a shot in anger.

Then it happened. A hundred and eighty clicks to the south, the remains of the southern colony probably still smoldered, every man, woman, and child dead, or so it seemed. They'd sent out a flyer when the distress call had come in, and it had reported no sign of life, just before it too was taken down by a missile.

The Concordiat promised that help was on the way, but he had no idea when it was getting here. Not soon enough, that was for sure. He swatted away a hovering blood-bee that was going for his nose, and growled at nothing in particular.

Hell, if he was the best they had, then he'd have to do. He wasn't going to let what happened to the Odinberg Colony happen here. He had plasma cannons in fortifications, turret-mounted antimissile auto-batteries, over a hundred handheld missile launchers and mortars in ready positions, and the entire hillside in front of him had been mined. Sure, his men were undertrained, but they were learning fast. God knows, the aliens were giving them plenty of targets to practice on. If they were going to try to attack this front again, and all sensors showed they were massing to do just that, they were going to pay a very heavy price.

"Sir," Lieutenant Sinkler shouted from a hundred paces behind him. Sinkler, before the destruction of the southern colony, had been a communications clerk.

Donning glanced around. The main colony compound had been built on a hillside leading down into what had been a beautiful meadow bordering a wide river. The main area of mining was down a shallow valley to the west of the colony. The colony had not been built with the idea that it would be need to be defended. After the first alien attacks, he had had the jungle cleared back away from all sides of the main colony, and fortifications prepared, including massive amounts of land moving to build bunkers. Days of mining equipment time had been used, and the colony executive had given him all kinds of flack over it, but after the destruction of the Odinberg Colony no one was objecting at all.

Donning waved to Lieutenant Sinkler that he had heard the call and was coming. Suddenly the edge of the jungle below seemed to come alive. Thousands of aliens were flowing from the trees and brush, appearing where there hadn't seemed to be anything before.

He could see along their line that dozens of them carried plasma cannons and rifles that didn't seem to fit in their hands, but there was little doubt they could use them. Most of the rest carried swords or large knifes of some sort. The cannons and rifles held back while the mass of the force charged ahead.

The first shot from below exploded the mound to his right, sending dirt and dust into the air.

Some of his men were already shooting when he shouted, "Return fire!" He dropped back into a duracrete bunker just as a plasma blast slammed into the wall with a force that rattled his teeth.

"Sir!" Sinkler shouted again, coming up beside him. He pointed to the communications unit he was carrying, then at the sky over the jungle. "Help is coming!"

Donning could feel a flash of hope, but he didn't dare let it cloud anything they were doing. He'd known all along that help was coming, but it could be here in five minutes, or five weeks. They could all be dead by the time their would-be rescuers showed up.

"Great!" he shouted back at Sinkler, trying to sound encouraging. "Keep it to yourself for now. Understand? We're on our own here."

Sinkler nodded. Poor guy looked like he was going to cry, like he would happily gnaw off his own arm to go back to a nice, quiet desk job.

I know how you feel, buddy. Donning turned away and brought his plasma rifle up to a slot, using the telescopic scope to check out the horde of massive aliens rushing upslope at them. His troops were cutting most of them down almost as fast as they came, but not completely. It seemed these creatures had no fear of death at all. *What the hell did we ever do to them? All this for knocking over a few trees?*

The first line of mines took out at least fifty of the aliens right below him, but it barely slowed them down. Again, the aliens mounting high-tech weapons held back, as wave after wave of aliens threw themselves down across the minefield, till their bleeding, blasted bodies formed an organic bridge that the rest could cross.

Around the colony the mines were going off now in a continuous roar, filling the air with smoke and dust and the blood of the aliens. Mortars and plasma blasts cleared momentary circles in their ranks, but it was like trying to dig a hole in the water. Still they came.

This was impossible.

This was madness.

Inch by inch, the aliens were advancing against their defenses. It was at this moment that he knew this wasn't just another skirmish. This time the aliens were fighting to win, and they were going to crush the colony if they didn't run out of warm bodies first.

Once, when he was a boy back on New Brazil, he'd gone hiking on a bluff overlooking the ocean. He'd stood too near the edge of a cliff, and the crumbly clay had collapsed under his feet. He'd slid down the slope on his face, his bloody fingers clawing at every crack and pebble that might have given him some kind of purchase, knowing that the slope turned into a sheer drop-off just a few meters down. Yet despite anything he could do, he'd just kept sliding. That was how he felt now, and he knew from bitter experience that the rocks were sharp, hard, and a long, long way down.

He felt it first in the soles of his feet. The ground itself seemed to be shaking, not from explosions, but from something that rumbled like a building earthquake. *What now?* He scanned the killing field in front of him as best he could. All he could see were aliens. Screaming, bloodthirsty aliens.

Sinkler scampered over in a half squat, his head down. "What's that sound?" he shouted over the plasma shots and exploding mines.

Donning could now hear a roar, a gaseous bubbling thunder unlike anything he'd ever heard, filling the air above everything. It grew louder in matchstep with the ground's rumbling.

Below him even the relentless aliens seemed to pause, look around, then up at the sky, searching for the source of the rumbling and shaking.

The defenders did the same and there was a noticeable downturn in the sounds of the battle.

"Keep firing!" Donning shouted into his wristcom, cutting down three massive aliens with his own rifle

as he shouted. This was their only chance to turn the
battle, or at least delay the inevitable.

Around him the pace of the barrage picked back up.
The aliens renewed their attack, still seemingly distracted by the sounds behind them. Donning looked
up from the battle for just a moment and blinked in
disbelief. The normally placid river that crossed the
meadows was boiling!

Or at least it *looked* like it was boiling. Great domes
of muddy water were churning man-high above the
surface, waves slopped a dozen meters up either bank,
slicks of foam forming just in time to be swept slowly
downstream with the current. Then something long and
glistening, like the horn of some submerged monster
poked out of the water close to the near bank, then
another, and another, followed by a mounded shape that
towered out of the water, shedding cascading sheets
of mud, sediment, and muck.

It reared itself up onto the bank and Donning somehow expected it to stop, beached like a whale, but it
did not. It advanced across the meadows, churning a
path of destruction through the grass and wildflowers,
and its horn began to spit fire. Plasma fire.

Even as Donning dived for cover the shock waves
began to slam into them, and he knew what had
crawled out of the river. He'd never seen a Bolo in
person before, but there was no mistaking it for any
other fighting machine in the galaxy.

Help had finally come.

*I signal my commander, Colonel Houchen, as soon
as I emerge from the river and break communications
silence. As I had hoped, my fortuitous landing in the
river not only cushioned my landing, but provided
cover for my approach to the northern colony. Even
as I identify targets and open fire with my secondary*

batteries, I am puzzled by the situation. I am witnessing what could be, in many respects, a siege from pre-atomic Earth's medieval period. The colony's fortifications are surrounded not by armor, not assailed by aircraft, but rather by a vast army equipped primarily with hand weapons, mounting not so much as a draft animal. This defies any rational analysis, through it is consistent with my inability to identify enemy convoys or installations.

I slowly move closer to the colony, pinning the enemy between my own weapons and those of the fortifications. The toll on them is terrible, yet they are slow to disperse. I take sporadic return fire from low to medium power plasma weapons and assorted missiles, but all of it is stopped by my battle screens. I am perhaps growing overconfident when my deep scanners pick up the signature of a nuclear device moving slowly through the enemy throngs in front of me. I take point oh two seconds to analyze the device. It is a tactical fusion device with an antimatter trigger, small but highly sophisticated, more a puzzlement than a threat. I detect it visually, a cylinder half a meter long, carried by a lone alien who wades through his fellows like a swimmer going upstream. The image lingers in my memory as I destroy the device with a controlled secondary pulse.

There is a small explosion and a gamma pulse from the trigger. Perhaps fifty of the aliens are immediately killed. Hundreds more will doubtless die later from radiation exposure, but the colony, for which the weapon was doubtless intended, will be spared.

My destruction of the fusion device seems finally to have taken the fight from the attackers. I continue to bombard them as they scatter in all directions, disappearing into the jungle, diving into the river. I signal my commander that the landing zone is nearly secure,

*but that he make a rapid combat descent, and should
be prepared for missile attacks.*

*I am hailed by the defending forces, a Commander
Donning of the local militia. I relay the message to my
commander, and he patches his own voice through my
short-range transmitters.*

Donning had the transmission patched through his
wristcom.

"Commander, this is Colonel Houchen of the
Dinochrome Brigade."

"Thank you for the timely assist, Colonel. You got
here just in time."

"Actually, Commander, I'm not there yet, but I hope
to be shortly. Until then, I believe you've already met
Bolo KNN. Khan, say hello to Commander Donning.
You two probably have things to talk about until I get
there."

"Hello, Commander," said a second voice, one that
sounded as human as any of his men.

It took Donning a moment to find his voice. "Hello
back," he finally said.

Chapter Four

It had taken Dirk almost six hours to dig itself out from under the collapsed hillside and the debris from the fallen hangar. The problem was not lack of power or traction, but the loose nature of the rubble and the unstable hillside above, which threatened to completely collapse on top of them. Add to this the fact that Dirk was unfamiliar with his own new capabilities and limitations. Much of the equipment that had been welded to his duralloy hull was constructed of more fragile materials and threatened to wrench off with each movement. It would have been easy just to order Dirk to sheer it all off, but lacking proper weapons and sensors, there was no telling what of it they might need.

After a while, Tyrus became impatient. He felt well enough to disconnect himself from the autodoc and climb down into Dirk's electronic bays for a closer inspection. Butchery was still his assessment. He found whole banks of molecular circuitry ripped out, probably for salvage, and bridged or bypassed with primitive optical circuitry a hundred years out of date. It was no wonder Dirk had memory and operational problems. If this reflected the overall quality of Dirk's "conversion" into a mining machine, they were bound to discover other problems as they went on. Well, there was nothing he could do about it now. The Bolo was still his best hope of finding his family.

Twice Dirk had to stop and back up to loosen debris threatening to rip away a sensor, or disable a sonic cannon. After five hours the screens inside the main cabin started to show some light, and an hour later Dirk was completely free. It was the longest five hours Tyrus could ever remember.

It was midday when Tyrus opened the top hatch and stared at the sight that surrounded him. He could see both human and alien bodies, burnt and scattered in the rubble. The sun was hot on his face, and the wind was light and humid, blowing a sickening smell of death and burning plastic past him. He was forced to retreat to the cabin and find a breathing mask in one of the emergency lockers.

He emerged again and climbed down the Bolo's rock-scarred flank. Where the day before there had been a freshly built colony of homes, public buildings, and a full-fledged mining and processing operation, now only debris remained.

He did a slow turn, forcing himself to study everything. The jungle edges were leveled below the colony, and nothing over five feet high was left standing within a thousand meters of his position in all directions.

He pulled the Bolo command headset from his pocket and clipped it behind his ear. "Dirk, what type of weapon was used to cause this type of destruction?"

"From the readings I received during the time of the destruction, and the evidence now, it was a small fusion explosion, low residual radiation, limited yield. You should take an anti-radiation tab when you return to the cabin, but the current danger is slight, especially with the breathing mask."

"They carried it by hand?" Tyrus asked, remembering the aliens carrying weapons that ranged from spears to plasma cannons.

"From playback of my sensor logs before the event, this seems probable," Dirk said.

Tyrus looked down the hill at where his family's apartment had been in a three-story building. There was nothing left of the entire complex but debris. The bomb must have killed thousands of aliens at the same time. Why would they do that? And why had they attacked? None of this made any sense at all to him. He climbed back up onto the Bolo and ordered Dirk to move towards the residential section.

"Do you detect anyone left alive in the colony?"

"No," Dirk said.

"Can you trust your sensors?"

"My ability to detect biological signs has been severely compromised, however I am quite seismically aware. If there were anyone moving or talking in the area, I believe I could detect it."

He moved carefully over the Bolo's massive hull, from handhold to handhold, until he could look down over the machine's flank, down at one of its mighty treads. Once they got away from the area of the hangar, most of the human bodies he passed hadn't died from the explosions or weapon fire. They had been stabbed, hacked, their throats slit, or in many cases, beheaded. The damned aliens had taken the time to kill them one by one, men, women and children alike.

Tyrus just stared at the pile of rubble that had once held his home and his family, and maybe still did. There were hundreds of bodies visible, probably countless more buried in the collapsed buildings. He didn't recognize anyone. He hadn't had time to get to know any of his neighbors yet. There had been over thirty thousand people in this colony.

Now he might be the only survivor.

But there was still that shuttle he'd seen leaving. Still a little hope that his family, that *someone*, had survived.

He stared at the destroyed colony around him, ignoring the smell of burnt and rotting flesh. The images of his family flashed through his mind, how just a few days ago he had taken the kids out to a special dinner, an apology for bringing them here. His wife, angry, had stayed home. Now the restaurant, even the street they had walked down talking and laughing, was gone.

He fought the tears back and forced himself to take a deep breath. With the breath came a stench of death that gagged him. He desperately wanted to dig, search for his family's bodies, and give them the burial they deserved. But they might not be there, and right now he didn't dare take the time. There were other things to be done. The dead would wait.

"Dirk, can you contact any of the other colonies?"

"No," Dirk said. "My long-range communications capabilities appear to be limited, and were further damaged while digging out of the landslide. I am unable to contact anyone. If we move closer, or if we contact a station with relay capability, that could change."

Tyrus nodded. Though he'd hoped otherwise, he'd half expected it. A functional Bolo could communicate over interstellar distances, but that transceiver had probably been sold as salvage decades ago. Dirk wasn't much of a Bolo any more. It was just lucky the machine still had armor or he would be dead.

The conversion had left some of the old Bolo intact though, something he could resist the enemy with, maybe even something that could fight back. What had

Dirk said? "I have power, I can move, I can think," something like that. It would have to be enough.

He climbed down again and found a laser rifle still clutched in a headless woman's hand. He found himself checking the rings on that hand. Not his wife's. Who was she, he wondered? Had she died defending her children? Avenging her lover? No way to know.

He shouldered the rifle, aimed it at an uptilted slab of duracrete, and pulled the trigger. With some difficulty he managed to laser the date into the top of the slab. Then he began to form letters.

Here Lie The People Of Ellerbey Mining's Thule Central Colony, Killed in a Sneak Attack.

He hesitated, then raised the rifle again and added: *They Will Be Avenged.*

He looked at the charge reading on the rifle, almost empty, and tossed it aside. He climbed back up to the Bolo's hatch, staggered inside, heard it slam shut behind him.

"Get going," he said. "We're headed north."

Simulations are one thing, Colonel Bud Houchen observed, it's quite another when somebody is really trying to blow your ass out of the sky. It had been quite a ride down to the planet in his Bolo's assault pod, dodging missiles all the way. Fortunately, without the Bolo's 14,000 tons of dead weight the pod turned into a surprisingly agile brute, able to power itself through most any maneuver that its relatively fragile human cargo could stand.

With that, Khan's considerable remote piloting skills, the pod's own defensive countermeasures, and supporting fire from the Bolo, he'd been able to set down on the landing strip of Rustenberg without a scratch.

The pod had paused only long enough to drop off Houchen and its load of arms and relief supplies before

Khan sent the craft back to the relative safety of orbit. At the same time, it would provide a decoy while the other two Bolos landed in their assault pods.

Once on the ground, he found a situation as difficult as anything he could imagine.

There were no standing military forces on the planet, only a lightly armed militia of terrified colonists, most with little or no military experience. As he stood on the defensive ramparts of the colony with Militia Commander Donning, he observed that it is one thing to have someone trying to kill you when you're trained and mentally prepared for the job. It is quite another when you're a civilian cloaked in your typical civilian illusion of safety.

"I want you to know that your people did well here today, Donning. You got them organized and held your lines."

Donning smiled grimly. "We did what we had to do, Colonel. It's not like we had much choice. Now, when is the Concordiat going to get us off the rock? When do the rest of our reinforcements arrive?"

This, thought Houchen, is where it gets dicey. "Commander, I've received no word of any planned evacuation. The mining colonies here are seen as vital to Concordiat security, and our superiors don't seem inclined to release our toe-hold here."

"Duck," said Khan's voice in his command headset.

Houchen shoved Donning down behind the ramparts just as an explosion rocked the air beyond the wall. Though he didn't see it, he knew that Khan's secondary batteries had picked off the missile before it could strike the colony.

"Clear," said Khan. It had become routine. The harassment missile attacks went on and on.

Houchen stood and brushed himself off. "We have two more Bolos in orbit, but as soon as they land we're going to have to dispatch them to patrol other hot spots. You aren't the only colony on the planet, and all of them are being at least harassed by the aliens. Another full-scale attack could come at any point, and at any time."

Donning's smile had faded, replaced by a glare of anger. "So, you're saying we're drafted because some bureaucrat twenty light-years away has decided this ball of jungle rot is somehow important?"

Houchen looked grimly out at the ocean of trees dotted with mountaintop islands, that stretched off to the horizon. "I don't make those decisions, Donning, I'm just reporting what I've been told. I have my duty here, and so do you. I know that we can expect a greater show of military force here, in fact whatever it takes to keep the mining operations going, but I don't know the time frame. Concordiat forces in this sector are stretched rather thin at the moment. For the moment these three Bolos, and your own resources, are all we've got."

Donning was almost shaking, clearly from the weight that Houchen had suddenly put on his shoulders.

Houchen could imagine what Donning had been thinking, that they'd just hold the line until rescue, jump on a shuttle and head back to civilization. He could sympathize. He'd spent too many years in a headquarters office, and hadn't been under fire himself since he was a young man. He had a much keener sense of his own mortality these days.

"I'm a civilian," said Donning, "a volunteer. You can't hold me."

"As I said, *I'm* not doing anything, just passing down the word from above." He looked out at the vast sea of trees. "From where I stand, you don't have any place to go. We've got a few shuttles in orbit to extract the severely wounded, but I can't even get them down at the moment without risking lives."

Donning just frowned.

"Now, nobody can make you fight, much less command this outfit, but there doesn't seem to be anyone else better qualified to do the job. You rounded this crew up and organized this defense, and without what I saw today, you might have ended up like the Odinberg Colony."

Houchen wasn't even sure Donning was listening, but he went on anyway. "You could step down, go sit in your apartment, and wait for the place to be overrun, but somehow, I don't think you're the kind of person who would do that."

Donning chewed the inside of his lip. Then he nodded, hard and firm, as if making a sudden decision. "I don't have to like this, but I'll do what I can."

"Good," Houchen said. "We'll need you to keep your forces alert and ready. I'm sure command thought that three Bolos would have more than enough to handle the situation, but I have more colonies to defend than I have Bolos. That means that you can't count on Khan to be here full time."

"Wonderful," Donning said, looking out at the jungle.

"I understand," Houchen said. "But we might have to redeploy forces at any moment in response to a new attack, and that means you have to be prepared to defend yourselves until we get back."

"I don't understand. With all this firepower, why don't you just go after the hairy bastards? Wipe them out before they can attack again."

Houchen shook his head. "This isn't the kind of war Bolos are designed to fight, Donning. As far as we can tell, these aliens have no supply lines to cut, no factories to disrupt, no bases to destroy, and they seem utterly immune to fear and intimidation."

"True," Donning said. "All too true."

"Very little about this situation makes sense,"

Houchen said, "and that bothers me more than what we've seen so far on the battlefield. These aliens shouldn't be able to put together a muzzle-loader musket, much less a plasma cannon. From the looks of it, they don't even make their own steel for their knives and swords. They were probably still using bronze before somebody started giving them weapons."

"You're kidding?" Donning asked, staring at him. "Who would give creatures like these monsters weapons?"

"No one knows yet," Houchen said, "Moreover, there appear to be distinct subgroups of aliens. The group that attacked here and at the Odinberg Colony seems to be the same, but other colonies have reported aliens with completely different markings, completely different ways of fighting. All of them seem to have technology from the same source, and at about the same technical level, but there are differences in the types and distribution of individual weapons, as well as how they're used."

"You sound worried."

"I just keep wondering, who gives a plasma cannon to people living in mud huts? What could they possibly have to trade? Or failing that, what do their mysterious benefactors *really* want?"

"To kill us," Donning said. "Clearly."

Houchen knew Donning was right.

Lord Whitestar was in an especially foul mood. He walked the trails of their encampment in darkness, headed nowhere and going there fast. Nightbats and glow wings fluttered out of his way as he crashed, much louder than necessary, though the brush.

His first-wife rebelled, his second eldest son wished to kill him, and as the Ones Above had warned, the devils had brought their metal ogres into the battle.

Countless warriors had died, not just fodder, but highborn too, and precious weapons were lost or destroyed.

It was easy to assume that the Ones Above would always provide more weapons, but Whitestar could not bring himself to rely on it. He knew that the Ones Above came down from the sky only infrequently, hiding their weapons, only later telling his people, through their oracles, where the weapons could be found.

Around him, men huddled in groups, sharpening their weapons, telling tales of battle. He could smell them, the damp, earthy smell of satisfaction and contentment. Their losses this day had been huge, and yet the mood among his men was high. They had seen glorious battle this day, battle that they had lived all their lives only dreaming of. So, they died? Wasn't that what they were born to do?

Whitestar hissed quietly in anger. No. They were not born to *die*, they were born to *kill*.

The rivers ran with the juices of his people, and still the devils lived, their nest still stood, their hatchlings still slept safe. This was insufferable. They had to be made to die, and the ogres stood in his way.

He turned right at the next branch in the trail, walked on a log that crossed a rapidly flowing stream, and reached the large burrow that was Scarbeak's. The opening was curtained with several layers of fiber mats to keep in the light. Whitestar blinked and averted his eyes as he first stepped inside. Scarbeak worked using the magic torches that the Ones Above had provided him. Their light was pure and unflickering, white like daylight, and yet cool to the touch.

Except for a corner where a rumpled sleepmat lay spread, the room was full of the sacred modules of the Ones Above. On each module, a light glowed to show that it was functional, and color-coded connections showed how it was to be connected to its fellows to make a weapon.

All of the highborn were taught to repair and maintain the sacred weapons, but only old Scarbeak was their master. He was their weapons master, repairing weapons, and assembling new ones from salvaged parts. It was said that Scarbeak had even assembled modules against their sacred color coding, and made them do things that the Ones Above had not intended.

But Whitestar liked and trusted the oldster and would not listen to such lies. Scarbeak was of the faithful, a Speaker to the Oracle, and would never do such things. He was very old, and might not last more than another season or two. Whitestar would miss him.

For the moment, Scarbeak crouched on the floor, piecing together one plasma cannon from the parts of several damaged ones. He looked up. "My lord, I did not hear you coming. What brings you here this night?"

"You have to talk to the oracle, Scarbeak. We need a weapon, more powerful than any we've had so far, one that can kill the ogres."

"Ah," said Scarbeak, "yes. I've heard of the metal beast that killed so many of our warriors."

"Tell the oracle that we must kill it. Show us how."

"I cannot tell the oracles what to do, my lord."

"Of course not, but you can ask. You can plead. The ogres must die."

Scarbeak looked thoughtful for a moment. "A missile would not work. The ogre destroys our missiles in flight. Perhaps a mine."

"It would have to be a thousand and twenty-four mines, or a hundred and twenty-eight times that many. We cannot wait a lifetime for the ogre to be lured across a single mine."

"Then the weapon would have to be carried, my

lord. Perhaps placed right under the ogre's belly. Who will do that?"

"I have no shortage of highborn willing to take that honor, Scarbeak."

Scarbeak clucked his disapproval. "A waste of a good highborn, my lord. Perhaps it is time you considered training the fodder to—"

"I will take the weapon to the ogre." They both turned to the new voice in the room. It was Sharpwing, his second eldest.

Whitestar hissed in anger. "How long have you been there?"

"Listening, my sire? Eavesdropping? Long enough. I claim the honor as mine."

"No," said Whitestar firmly. "It would be a waste of a young warrior."

"It was not a request, sire, it was a challenge. You heard me, Scarbeak. You are my witness. I challenge you on tomorrow's moon for the right to take the new weapon to the ogre."

"You have no right."

"I have every right! I wish to die as my blood commands me. I tire of being called a coward, the hatchling of a coward." Sharpwing studied his father's face. "Oh, yes, that is what the young warriors say of you, that you fight from your burrow, that you hide from battle like an old woman."

Scarbeak looked first at one, then the other, seemingly trying to find some way out of the situation. Finally he spoke. "There will be no weapon for a time, young lord-son. Even if the oracles answer my request, it will be a span of nights."

Sharpwing looked at the old man. "Time enough till we die then. I challenge you in a span of nights for the right to carry the weapon."

He pulled his curved knife from his belt and

brandished it at Whitestar. "And I promise you, sire, that I will strike you with my brother's blade, and that I will strike to free my mother of your unworthy hold on her. Our ways are ever parted."

Then he stepped back through the curtains and was gone.

Whitestar looked down at Scarbeak, who looked back.

Finally Whitestar said, "I have too many wars to fight, and too many ogres to face. I hunger for an ending."

Chapter Five

Colonel Houchen watched as Donning climbed into the observer's seat on the far side of Khan's control compartment and strapped himself in. Houchen could tell he was impressed, that the power the Bolo represented was helping to strengthen the man's resolve, and his confidence that they hadn't been abandoned by the Concordiat.

This he knew was the third great mission of the Bolo. The first was to intimidate the enemy. The second was to strike the enemy with devastating power that could not be stopped. The third was to express the will of the Concordiat. Like the battleships, and later aircraft carriers of old Earth, a Bolo was a tangible, undeniable expression of its government's interest and concern in a situation.

It was the nature of Bolos that those who fought in more conventional forces often weren't comfortable with them, they could never forget them, ignore them, or deny them. The net result was that when a Bolo arrived, morale went up, because if the soldier was nervous about his own Bolo, how must the enemy feel?

The air conditioning in the cabin was finally starting to make some headway against the heat, humidity, and persistent jungle stench they'd brought with them from outside. Here, for a few minutes at least, they could feel comfortable, safe, and not completely helpless against their alien attackers.

"Khan, let's give our guest a little demonstration. But lay off full combat speed. I don't want to send him home in pieces." Houchen wasn't kidding about that. A Bolo's crash couch was a precision piece of equipment, vital if a human were ever to serve as an on-board commander during combat. A Mark XXV Bolo had a normal combat speed of 95 KPH over almost any kind of terrain, but when conditions allowed, it was capable of short sprints of 150 KPH. At that speed, a Bolo was a near unstoppable force. With its battle screens at full power, it could almost literally ram through small mountains.

The Bolo was capable of surviving the forces involved in such maneuvers, but a human commander was not, at least, not without a great deal of help. The crash couch acted as a vital three-dimensional shock absorber system for the more delicate human body. The observer seats had much more crude two-dimensional shock absorbers built in. Someone riding in one might survive full combat speed in rough terrain, but they wouldn't enjoy it, and they might not walk away under their own power.

"Aye, sir," replied Khan, and at once the growl of the drive system intensified around them and they were pushed back in their seats. The cabin was buffeted enough to give Donning an exciting ride. Nothing more.

"Let's clear back ten yards of jungle around the perimeter, just to keep the aliens awake out there."

Khan changed course, his multiple tread systems adjusting speed just enough to smoothly bring them in parallel to the jungle line, and then finally, overlapping two sets of treads into the trees like a giant lawn mower. The din was terrible as the treads knocked down trees by the hundreds, chewed them into splinters, then spit them out the back in a rooster tail of destruction. Houchen had intentionally detuned the active noise cancellation systems in the cabin for just that effect.

"Khan, let's pick the pace up. You're free to fire." There was an aggressive whir as the secondary gunports opened, and an almost machine-gunlike chatter as the ion-bolt infinite repeaters shot off short bursts in rapid succession. Suddenly, while mowing down trees on one side of the perimeter, Khan was simultaneously blasting them on two others. Houchen wished he could show off the Bolo's main armament, a 90mm super-Hellbore, but firing it at any visible target this close to the colony could do them more damage than the enemy already had done. If the aliens simply offered them a significant target worthy of that mighty weapon, this battle might already be over.

At last they finished their sweep around the perimeter. Khan slowed and resumed his patrol midway between the defenses and the tree line. "We could keep knocking down trees I suppose," said Houchen, "but it just keeps getting harder, and it takes Khan farther and farther away from the colony, giving them an opportunity to attack on another flank."

There was a loud thump as Khan fired off another secondary, a longer pulse, to take down an incoming missile.

"They're building for another attack, aren't they?"

Houchen nodded. Donning was green, but he was no fool. "We're pretty sure they're gathering out there.

To be honest, our intelligence on this is limited. We occasionally pick up something from orbit that might be a cook-fire, but no concentrations of them, nothing that's consistent from night to night. Last night, while on their way to the New Marikana, Lieutenant Winter and his Bolo stumbled on an abandoned encampment. More of a nest really. Tunnels, seemingly dug with hand tools, aboveground huts and passages made from native plant materials."

"Any sign of technology?" Donning asked.

"Amazingly primitive," Houchen said, "not at all consistent with the weapons we've been seeing. I wish he'd had time to find and excavate one of their trash dumps. It might have told us something. The camp was stripped almost completely clean."

Donning only nodded, so Houchen went on. "But it explains why we can't find them from orbit. They don't clear land, they don't build roads, they don't seem to use reactors or power cells or anything we can pick up from orbit. To make things worse, they have a number of close relatives out there in the jungle, large, flightless, birdlike creatures, probably only a little farther from them than chimps and gorillas are from humans. Until one of them powers up his weapon, he could be just another part of the local wildlife as far as we're concerned."

"Then you don't know what they're going to do." Donning looked over at Houchen.

"I think my gut is telling me the same thing your gut is telling you," Houchen said. "The harassment attacks continue for a reason, to keep us off guard, to keep our people on alert until they're exhausted. When the aliens are ready, they'll try again."

There was an uncomfortable silence. Finally, Houchen said, "You know, there's something I've been meaning to ask you about. Khan swears that, just before his landing, he picked up sensor readings consistent with a Bolo hull in or near the Odinberg Colony. But that couldn't be. We show no record of a Bolo ever being dispatched to this planet. Do you know anything about it?"

Donning nodded. "That would be the Prescott machine."

Houchen shook his head. He had no idea what a Prescott machine was.

"An armored mining machine," Donning said, "built on a converted Bolo chassis? I heard they were bringing one in, but I don't think they had time to deploy it."

Now Houchen felt really puzzled. What had they done to the old Bolo brain, and all the firepower? "Your aircraft didn't report seeing it when they scouted the Odinberg Colony after the attack?"

"They saw the hangar where it would have been parked flattened by some kind of bomb," Donning said, "half a mountain dropped down on it. That's all I know. Like we told you, they didn't have much time to report back before they were shot down. But that thing is gone, like the rest of Odinberg. Write it off. It's no use to us now."

Houchen rubbed his chin thoughtfully. He wasn't going to believe that. Bolos did not die easily. "I don't know—"

Another thump as a missile was destroyed.

"You know," said Donning, "they've been hitting us with these harassment attacks, maybe we should do the same to them."

"Fire off random shots into the jungle?" Houchen asked, staring at the commander. "As long as the aliens remain dispersed we are unlikely to do them significant damage, and they don't seem in any way inclined to be discouraged by such tactics."

Donning nodded, thinking.

Houchen knew exactly what Donning was trying to do. He was trying to take a role in defending his colony, and it wasn't like the Bolo's energy weapons were going to run out of ammo. "I suppose we could try it for a day or two and see what happens."

"Maybe you should have the Bolos do preventative strikes against the moving groups," Donning said. "The aliens aren't staying anywhere close to out of range. We might be able to disrupt their gathering for attack."

Suddenly an alarm filled the room. It was the sound Houchen had been dreading.

"Too late," Donning said.

"Colonel," said Khan, "I have alien forces massing just beyond the tree line. Another attack appears imminent."

"Damn," said Donning, unbuckling his harness and grabbing for his rifle.

"Where are you going?" said Houchen, trying to keep one eye on the external view and tactical screens.

Donning pulled on his helmet and fastened the strap. "Back to my men. It's only about a hundred meters back to the wall. Comm my people to cover me, and you do the same. I used to be pretty good at the hundred meter in my day."

"You can send orders from here."

"I can send orders, but I can't *give* orders from here, Colonel." He slapped the hatch release.

"Khan, get him in as close as you can, stop just long enough for him to jump clear of the tracks, then turn to place us between him and the enemy lines."

Donning paused inside the hatch and looked back at Houchen as Khan came around. "You think that other Bolo machine might still be active out there somehow?"

"One thing I've learned, Commander. *Never* write a Bolo off."

Donning nodded. It was time. "Good luck, Colonel."

"To you too, Commander."

Then Donning was out, and the hatch slammed closed.

Houchen looked up at the screens, one showing thousands of alien warriors flooding out of the trees, another showing Donning sprinting for the wall. No matter what else, the man had guts.

Donning hit the ground running. The rifle slowed him down, but he was going to need it if things turned bad. Behind him he could hear the churning roar of the turning Bolo, and the shrill cries of countless charging alien warriors.

A plasma bolt shattered a divot out of the wall to his right, and he turned sharply, zigzagging to offer a poorer target. He felt the concussion as the Bolo's batteries opened fire on the aliens, followed by a different kind of thump as the Bolo mortars started lobbing rounds over the colony to disrupt the advance there.

A missile screamed past in the confusion, meters over his head, missing the wall entirely and heading back out over the jungle. Perhaps the Bolo had known it would miss, and simply chose not to waste a shot. Above him, the rapid crackling of pulse rifles was comforting. The aliens were gaining on him fast. They'd clocked some of the big monsters hitting 50 KPH in short sprints.

Just ahead, a line with a rescue loop dropped down the face of the wall. He grabbed the loop and hooked it under his armpits, then jerked the line to signal the hoist operators. The line immediately became taut and yanked his feet off the ground. He managed to get his feet between him and the wall, literally running up the duracrete surface.

Another plasma bolt struck a dozen yards away, and he was very aware of what a choice target he made. He started leaping from side to side as best he could. A smaller bolt, probably from a rifle, came from below him. He jumped, twisted his body, tried to keep his head forward, and slammed his back into the wall. Below him, a handful of aliens had somehow made it past the Bolo.

Gasping for breath, his ribs on fire, he sighted down his own rifle and opened fire, full auto. The dirt churned around the aliens, then one of them fell, another's head exploded. A blast from the Bolo, vast overkill, finished the rest of them.

As he reached the top of the wall, a dozen hands grabbed him and hauled him over. He shrugged off a woman wearing a medical armband and headed for his command post higher on the wall. Later, after the fighting was over, after he'd had a chance to think about it, his face would whiten, his knees would quake, his stomach would knot and threaten to send his breakfast into full retreat. But just that second, Donning had never felt more alive.

"What do you mean it isn't supposed to be this way?" Tyrus wasn't sure he was going to survive the trip. The mining machine called Dirk didn't seem to be designed for the comfort of the operator under the best of circumstances, but plowing as they were through the jungle at best possible speed, bowling over trees as it went, was a nightmare.

"My crash couch is designed to cushion the commander against momentary accelerations of up to thirty standard gravities in any axis."

"Ow!" Tyrus slapped his hand to his mouth. "Then why did I just bite my tongue for the third time?"

"I believe that most of my active shock absorbers

have been replaced," Dirk said, "either with passive gas cylinders of some kind, or rigid struts, perhaps with the idea of making it easier to maintain. I do not believe that they intended me to travel more than a dozen kilometers per hour in my modified form."

"How fast are we going now?"

"Forty KPH, about half my old cruise speed."

"Good lord. You mean I could be hurting *more*?"

"Would you like me to reduce speed?"

"No. We've got to get to Rustenberg, warn them to be on the lookout for bombs, see if there's anything we can do to help. They could attack there at any time."

"The attack has already begun," Dirk said.

Tyrus blinked in surprise. "Excuse me? How would you know that?"

"While I am unable to transmit a signal that they can receive, I am detecting strategic communications between three Bolos, including one at the northern colony."

"Bolos? Bolos like you? I mean, like you before your conversion."

"Not exactly. I am Mark XXIV, they are Mark XXV. I am unfamiliar with the designation. It seems to have been introduced after I was put into mothballs and placed on standby."

So, the Concordiat had sent help, even if it was too late for the Odinberg Colony. "They should be okay there then, with a Bolo on station?"

"I believe there is still a danger, especially if they are unaware of the possibility of suicide bomb attacks such as destroyed our hangar. That weapon was one of the smallest such weapons that can be constructed. It is only logical that the enemy may possess bigger ones."

"Big enough to destroy an entire colony, Bolo or no Bolo?"

"Quite possibly."

"How long until we reach Rustenberg?"

"At this speed, five hours and fifty minutes."

Tyrus felt something wet on his chest. He looked down and saw that the left shoulder strap had opened a cut there, a raw stinging mess that slowly oozed blood into his shirt. "Go faster," he said to Dirk.

One of the "gifts" the drop pod had delivered was a full-fledged modular fire control system for the colony's defenses. The self-contained control center had stations for himself and two other officers, plus room for observers. No longer did Donning have to watch from the ramparts and shout his orders into a wristcom. He could watch any part of the defenses through multiple screens around his command chair, call up status displays on any of the fixed weapons systems, track the status of each and every mine, and even monitor the Bolo's sensory systems.

An integrated communication system allowed orders to be issued through headsets to his troops, either individually or en masse. A lot of the center's capabilities were either irrelevant to their situation (they were in no apparent danger of attack from space, or other than missiles, from the air), or simply beyond their limited technical skills to employ, but the equipment had immensely improved their ability to defend themselves.

During their first attack, Donning had barely felt in control, and unaware of what was happening outside his direct line of view. Now he was instantly aware of any trouble spot and able to issue detailed orders to hundreds of troops with a single voice command.

As Donning rushed into the command control center, he found Lieutenant Peak manning one of the stations. He was a young electronics expert who had served a three-year stint in combat training. The other seat was empty, probably for lack of a trained officer, but given their limited use of the equipment, the second station really wasn't needed anyway.

Donning sat down in the command chair and ordered up a strategic overview. The five main screens showed the different defense positions around the colony. The Bolo had moved a kilometer or so away from the colony to the north, to give it a clearer field of fire.

Since the last attack Donning had had his people plant new, reprogrammed mines. Now they were equipped with time delay fuses that kept all the mines in a given area from being triggered at once. A supposedly "clear" area of the field could now suddenly spring to life, killing masses of unsuspecting aliens. Already, hundreds of alien bodies were scattered throughout the minefield, and the edges of the jungle seemed to be moving, alive as the massive aliens ran into the opening, beaklike mouths open.

He checked to make sure that all families and noncombatants were headed into the new underground shelters that they had built. Building those shelters and the defensive fortifications had been top priority since the destruction of the Odinberg Colony. No matter what level weapon those ugly bastards threw at this colony, most of the civilians were going to survive if he had anything to say about it.

He tried to take it all in at once. Clearly this attack was much more fierce than the last, but the colony was better prepared, better armed, and had a Bolo guarding them. For the moment at least, things in the command center felt in control. But Donning knew that wouldn't last.

"Peak, keep an eye out for trouble spots. I'm going to take some time to study the enemy, see if I can learn anything we can use against them."

"Got it," Peak said.

The aliens had also modified their tactics since the last attack. Rather than just storming the walls, the aliens moved in smaller, more dispersed groups that were a less tempting target for the Bolo's big guns. Rather than directly attacking, groups would move out of the trees, transverse the perimeter to draw fire, then fade back into the jungle.

Small missiles swarmed in almost constantly, seemingly more to occupy the Bolo's guns than to do any real damage. Most of the missiles seemed to be coming from just within the jungle, but one nearby hilltop had been the source of several shots. As Donning watched, Khan's main gun transversed and locked on the hill. A blinding beam of energy lanced out, and the hilltop instantly vaporized into an expanding ball of flame and debris.

Donning heard the Bolo commander laugh through the comm link. "That may not have been strategically effective, but it sure felt good to unlimber the Hellbore for a change. This place is cramping Khan's style."

"Looked good from here as well," Donning said.

Another new development was that single aliens would break from groups, sprint towards the colony, and set satchel charges against the base of the fortifications. Each charge took a bite out of the big wall. While each one did little damage, if they could plant enough of these in one area, that might eventually create a breach. Donning instructed his subordinates on the wall to monitor this situation closely and position their best snipers to protect vulnerable areas.

Donning zoomed one of the cameras in on a particular alien and set it to automatically track the creature. The alien was huge, muscular, covered with white on black fir in patterns that reminded him of a panda or orca from Old Earth. Though they were generally humanoid, there were just enough avian characteristics to suggest that they really had evolved from predatory flightless birds. They had powerful, talon-equipped feet, hard ridges around their mouths that might have been beaks or bills, and large, round eyes mounted on the sides of their heads.

Donning started to notice a pattern in how it moved. They were fast sprinters, and strong, but their peak activity seemed to come in bursts, almost as though their metabolism had trouble sustaining their full energy output.

He noticed another significant thing. The weapons not only didn't seem to be designed *by* the aliens, they didn't seem to be designed *for* them. Sites and eye-pieces seemed shaped for users with eyes on the front of their heads, not the sides, and the grips and controls poorly fit the natives' hands, which, perhaps because they were evolved from wings, not paws, were long and strangely jointed.

Peak waved at one of the big screens. "What kind of weapon is that?" he asked, indicating three aliens leading one attack wave.

"That's new," Donning said, looking closer. The metal cylinder was big enough that three of the aliens were required to carry it on their huge shoulders.

He hesitated. The safest thing to do would be to focus fire on the unknown weapon, but if he did, they wouldn't know its capabilities. One of the unknowns could get past them at a weaker moment and turn the battle, unless they learned to defend against it. In the end, he decided to let the battle run its course. If his people took the three out, so be it, but if they did get to fire, he'd be watching.

In fact, as Donning watched, a rifle shot took down one of the three. As he fell, a half dozen more aliens suddenly converged to take his place, actually getting into a shoving contest over who would take the honor. Then, a moment later, another alien appeared and took the dead one's place, not after a fight, but what seemed somehow like a servile surrender.

Donning nodded to himself. So, the enemy did have some sort of ranking or caste system. That meant that despite the seeming chaos out there, there might be officers that could be targeted, some kind of command and control structure that could be disrupted.

"There are more of them," said Peak. He pointed to where another trio was lugging their cylinder out of the jungle, and another one on the far side of the compound.

"Damn." Donning thumbed a communications toggle. "Houchen, there's a new weapon showing up out there, a cylinder, takes three aliens to carry it."

"We're on it," replied Houchen over the comm.

But it was too late. The cylinders were aimed at their target, not the colony, but the Bolo itself, and all of them fired in rapid succession. The rear of the device Donning was watching literally exploded, injuring several aliens unlucky enough to be standing within a yard or so behind it. And as it exploded a single, brief beam was emitted from the other end.

"We're hit!" shouted Houchen. "Never seen anything like those before. They're like pocket Hellbores. Actually put a dent in our battle screens and our armor. If they were lucky enough to find a vital spot at close range, they might actually be able to do us some significant damage."

Donning was about to order his men to open fire on the cylinders when he saw the three operators toss one aside and run to join their unarmed fellows. "I think it's only good for one shot, Colonel. Now that we know what we're dealing with, we can take them out before they can get close. Good thing too. Our fortifications wouldn't hold up long against those."

"Tell your people to break out their breathers and antirad pills," Houchen said. "The radiation levels just peaked down here. I wonder if the aliens know that they're slow-cooking themselves every time they fire off one of those things?"

Donning shifted his view to another attacker, firing one of the smaller plasma cannon that they'd seen before. As he watched, the alien went down. Two of the aliens behind him scrambled for the cannon he had been carrying. The one who ended up with it dropped his spear and seemed to growl or snarl at the other in celebration, then turn back to the attack.

Donning suddenly made the connection. Armed with spears and swords, the individual aliens weren't the threat. Knock down one, and a dozen would instantly replace him. It was the weapons themselves, obviously still in limited supply, that were the threat.

He opened a command channel. "All snipers and gunners, save your shots for aliens carrying high technology weapons. Do not target the operator. Repeat, do not target the operator. Go for the weapon itself."

Tyrus winced as a sudden bump slammed him against the roof of the narrow service passage. If the defective crash couch had been a problem, this was just a little slice of hell. Still, he observed, if he survived the experience, the results might be worth it. They had discovered that unlike his primary Hellbore, Dirk's secondary batteries were still intact.

Perhaps the Prescott folks had decided they were too difficult to remove. Instead, they had removed the power busses and data couplings, dogged the gunports from the inside, then welded them from outside. He couldn't do anything about the welds, but he could certainly unbolt the dogs, try to rig a power bypass, reconnect the data links, and hope for the best.

Dirk seemed hopeful that, if enough power were restored, he might be able to shatter the welds by overloading his port actuators. Of course, he might not be able to close the ports again, but that was a problem for another time.

"You reading me, Dirk?"

"Yes, Commander."

"I wish you wouldn't keep calling me that, Dirk. I just replaced your buss bar. I'm gonna move back beyond the safety gate, and then I want you to apply trickle power and see what happens."

Tyrus crawled back past all the "danger" and "high voltage" placards and latched the insulated gate that protected the power circuits. "Go for it, Dirk."

There was a pause. "I can feel my secondary mechanisms! Of course, I am as yet unable to apply enough power to the actuators to take up the slack in the port mechanicals."

"Well, let's take this slow. The bundle of superconducting rod I used in place of the original bar probably won't hold for long, and I don't have anything to replace it with. My luck, you'll get the ports open, only to find there's no power left for the weapons."

"I have a great deal of confidence in you, Tyrus."

He laughed grimly. "Based on what?"

"You've acquitted yourself well. I know enough about human psychology to know this situation must be very difficult for you to cope with."

"I'm not coping at all. That's the trick. You try to cope, you can fail. I'm saving that for later."

"Tyrus."

There was something in the Bolo's voice.

"We are being hailed. A Concordiat spacecraft in orbit has evidently spotted us."

"Can you respond?"

"I am trying, but I do not believe they will be able

to receive me. Tyrus, I am receiving instructions that we are to proceed to the northern colony if possible and assist with the defense there."

"That's where we were headed anyway. I've done all I can here. I'm headed back up to the control compartment. Get your busted crash couch ready."

He packed up the emergency tool kit as best he could. Several of the tools had simply disappeared, probably bounced away by the Bolo's constant motion and vibration. Then he crawled back through the service passages towards the control room. He was halfway there when Dirk spoke again.

"Tyrus, the jungle ahead shows signs of a recent fire. I am detecting metallic traces that I believe to be wreckage."

Tyrus felt the hair stand up on the back of his neck. "Is it human?"

"The alloys are consistent with human construction."

"Are there aliens in the area?"

"Given my scrambled sensors, impossible to say. I see no obvious signs."

"Slow down, and stop just short of the wreckage. I'm going to get out and investigate." He crawled back to the service hatch where he'd first entered the Bolo, picking up the rifle and side arm that he'd stashed there earlier.

He sat, his back against a cool bulkhead, his heart pounding as he contemplated the inside of the hatch. Finally the Bolo stopped. "Open the hatch, Dirk."

There was a hiss, followed by a whir, and a brilliant ring of morning sunlight appeared around the hatch, which then slid up into the body of the machine. The combination of heat, humidity, and smell hit him like a wave after so long in the beast's air-conditioned belly. Outside he could hear only the buzzing of insects, the rustling of foliage in the slight breeze, and the cries of jungle animals, hopefully none too big or too close.

He duck walked up to the hatch and climbed down a massive boogie wheel to the ground. Something he never saw buzzed down to take a bite out of his neck, didn't like the taste, and rapidly buzzed away.

The jungle wasn't as thick here as most he'd seen. There were large spaces between the higher trees, large patches of blue visible above the underbrush. Ten meters in front of the Bolo, the burn started.

As he crossed into the blackened area and stooped down to inspect, he could see that Dirk was right about the fire being recent. Not even a few green shoots had emerged from the blackened soil, though doubtlessly within a few days the forest would already be healing itself.

He stood. "Dirk, which way to the wreckage?"

"I read a large concentration of metal behind those trees to your right, about fifteen meters."

He stepped carefully, moving around the charred pillars that had once been stately trees. Something glinted in the sun ahead, and he picked up his pace.

He found nothing that he could have identified definitely as an air shuttle, only a four-meter-long, flattened, twisted hunk of alloy sheet, carbon composite, and superconducting cable.

"The total mass of metal that I am reading," said Dirk, "is only about eighty percent of what I would expect from the shuttle's wreckage. Possibly this is some other craft."

Tyrus didn't think so. "Or the rest of the wreckage was lost well before they hit the ground. I think a missile hit this thing, whatever it is."

Then he looked up. Somehow, an entire skin panel, at least four meters across and two meters long had somehow survived almost intact, cradled in the burned tree limbs almost like an intentionally placed signpost. On the left edge, half of the seal of the Concordiat could be seen, along with most of the mining company's logo. And below that, a number.

His stomach knotted. "Dirk, does the number 'TN-1045' mean anything to you?"

"That was the call sign used by the departing shuttle in its distress call, Tyrus. I am sorry."

He heard a small, mournful noise, and realized only a moment later that it had come from his own throat.

"It is possible your family was not on the shuttle, Tyrus."

It took him a minute to swallow, get his voice working again. "They were here, or back at the colony. It really doesn't matter if they died here or not. This is where hope died, Dirk. This is where they died in my heart."

"I am sorry, Tyrus."

He started scanning the ground, looking for he didn't know what, some scrap of clothing, some personal artifact, some scrap of bone, something to tell him about the people that died here.

"Tyrus."

He spotted a superconducting impeller coil, a port-hole and its surrounding chunk of bulkhead, completely intact.

"Tyrus! Behind you!"

Old reflexes cut in and he was raising the rifle even as he turned. The dozen aliens that stood at the edge of the jungle had only knives and spears. He saw them with almost superhuman clarity, a flood of adrenaline pushing aside the grief for the moment. Their colors were different from the ones he'd seen: white, with mottled spots of yellow, brown, and black on gray stripes. They wore what looked like green togas, belted at the waist. They were different than the ones that destroyed the colony. Had they fired the missile that brought down the plane? He didn't know. Didn't care. They would do.

Ignoring his gun, two of them lowered their sword-tipped spears and charged at him, howling as they did so. He pulled the trigger to full auto, cutting one charging alien in half, his misses shooting into the others waiting behind.

He swept the gun back and forth, mowing them all down.

Suddenly there were more, seemingly charging from every side.

He fanned the gun back and forth, waist high, trying to take them down before they got too close.

More aliens fell, more aliens appeared.

He ducked aside as a thrown spear sailed past his head, so close that he could feel the wind on his hair.

The aliens screamed.

He screamed back.

He fired the gun until it overheated, and forced him to go back to choosing his targets and squeezing off shots one by one.

The aliens came closer and closer until he was forced to use his rifle barrel as a club to fend off a stabbing spear, forced to throw the gun aside, grab the pistol from his belt and fire into the charging alien's chest.

One.

Two.

Three.

Four times.

Then a knife sliced between his ribs and the dead weight of the alien's body fell on him like a side of beef.

He braced himself for the spear that would finish the job, the knife that would take his head like so many he'd seen back at the colony.

Then the world exploded. Over and over again.

Behind him, in front of him, to his left, to his right.

He heard the growl of the slowly advancing Bolo, the rain of dust and debris, the whir of the opening hatch.

Then it was very, very quiet.

After a few moments, he braced himself, and in a supreme effort, managed to roll the dead alien off the top of him. As the alien fell, he saw a splinter of shattered tree trunk as long as his forearm buried in its neck.

"That was some risk," Tyrus said, staggering to his feet and looking around, "firing your secondaries that close to me."

"I waited until there was no other choice," Dirk said, "and I hoped your attacker's body would shield you."

"It worked," he said, staggered slowly towards the hatch, clutching his bleeding chest. Something under his palm made a little sucking sound.

"You are injured," said Dirk, as Tyrus staggered and fell through the hatch.

"Very," he gasped. He lay on the compartment floor, the metal decking cool and smooth against his cheek.

"If you can get to the control cabin, my autodoc may be able to help."

"No can do."

"You must try."

"You just go on your way. I'll ride down here."

"You must try."

"Can't. Can't," Tyrus said, staring at the wall, wondering why he was even still talking to the machine that had just saved his life. "Got no hope left, big buddy. If you have some, it will have to be enough for both of us."

He felt the Bolo start to move.

"We will be at the Rustenberg Colony in a few hours. There will be medical help there."

"If you say so," Tyrus said, not really caring.

"I will try not to jostle you, but it may be a difficult journey."

"I can't stop you."

Tyrus figured he passed out for a moment, or an hour, the nightmare of the room jerking around him keeping him just barely aware.

"Tyrus."

"What?"

"There is a protected place in every Bolo's memory where we store remembrances of our past commanders. My service history goes back more than two hundred years, and though my memory has been damaged, that part is still intact. I can remember my first commander with complete clarity, and each officer I have served with since. I have been privileged with an excellent run of commanders. I have been most fortunate."

"That's good, Dirk."

"I have created a place for you there, Tyrus, not in anticipation of any given event, but in honor of what we're been through in our brief time together."

"I'm honored, Dirk."

"The honor is mine, Commander Tyrus."

It was getting very hard to stay awake.

"Dirk."

"Yes, Commander."

"Be sure to warn them about the bombs."

"Yes, Commander."

He felt himself sinking into a very dark place, and he didn't want to talk any more.

Chapter Six

Donning reclined in his command chair, which fortunately had been designed with the possibility of sleep in mind. The alien attack had lost its intensity after they'd expended their one-shot weapons against the Bolo, then finally ended without incident about dusk. Casualties were minimal. Donning felt that next time he'd know even better how to fight the aliens.

He could have gone back to his bed when the fighting ended, but surprisingly, he felt more comfortable here. He watched the sun come up on the big screen, ordered his breakfast brought up, then dozed for a while. It was midmorning when the call came from Houchen, the call he'd been anticipating, and dreading.

"Commander, I just got word that New Marikana is under intense attack. They've got their own brand of aliens, orange stripes and cruise missiles, and they're just not ready. They haven't had a bit of trouble until now. In fact, they were still running mining missions until yesterday."

"You need to go."

"I'm afraid so."

"Then go." He racked his chair upright, rubbed the sleep out of his eyes, and checked his status screens.

"We both knew this was coming."

"I think we've got a handle on it, Colonel. We can hold out until reinforcements come. The auto-turrets are finally completely integrated with the new command and control system, so we should be able to handle our own antimissile defense. Go."

"Thanks for taking this so well, Donning. You're a fine officer."

"I'm a man doing what he has to do," Donning said. "I think that describes all of us here." He watched the Bolo on his screen. Already it was making maximum speed and headed away.

"With luck, Khan and I or one of the other Bolos will be back here in a couple days. Signal if you get trouble."

"Will do."

"One more thing, Donning," Houchen said, "you might have some help here sooner than you think. Our ships are picking up that Bolo mining machine from Odinberg, and it's on the move."

"You're kidding?" Donning asked.

"Nope," Houchen said. "It stopped for a while, but now it's moving again, toward you. We haven't been able to contact it though, so we don't know what sort of fighting shape it's in, or who's on board. It could be something to help with your defense, or just more survivors to take care of."

"We'll take care of it."

"Good luck, Commander."

"I just hope we won't need it," Donning said. But he knew better. They were going to need all the luck they could get very, very shortly.

A blip sailed across one of his screens, an incoming harassment missile. As he watched, the west auto-turret snapped around and blew it out of the sky.

Donning chuckled. "Open for business."

Lord Whitestar paced from one end of Scarbeak's chamber to another. "What do you mean, the ogre has gone?"

Scarbeak looked up from the new weapon he had been studying so intently. "Just that, lord. A runner returned from the meadow's edge just moments ago with the news. The ogre has left the area of the human nest and is moving northwest. Perhaps the new weapons we used hurt it more than we believed, or perhaps one of the other clans is attacking a nest in that direction, and the ogre is responding to their calls of distress."

Whitestar kicked over a stack of modules in anger, before he realized the sacrilege of what he had done. He quickly inspected the modules to be sure their lights-of-function were still lit, and stacked them neatly. "Forgive me, Scarbeak. My blood runs as hot as a new chick's. I have spent these days preparing myself to kill the ogre, and now it is snatched from me."

"The ogre is gone. Is that not what we wanted?"

"This nest has proven to be far more difficult to destroy than the first, old one," Whitestar said. "*That* is what we want, but even without the ogre there, I am not sure that we can do it, and if we do not do it quickly, the ogre may return. And I still must meet Sharpwing in challenge."

Scarbeak looked surprised. "Surely he will not want to press challenge, now that the ogre is gone."

"The ogre is his key to a place of the honored dead," Whitestar said, "but it is my blood that he truly wishes to spill. He will not care that the ogre is gone, and I will have to kill him. If I do that, neither my eldest nor my first-wife will forgive me, and the disgrace will cripple my ability to lead."

"Then let your eldest lead. That was what you planned anyway. Refuse to fight Sharpwing. Dishonor is not such a terrible thing to live with. It might be your only hope to live as long as I have."

"He has only begun to recover from the wounds I gave him. If I give Sharpwing honor by refusing to fight, the hatchling will try to take control. Before his brother is recovered, he may have already led our clan to ruin, that we may taste death and defeat at the same meal."

Scarbeak put down his tools and looked up at his lord, gazing at him intently with the right eye of truth. "What if there is no future for our clan, my lord?"

"What foolishness are you talking about now, old man?" Whitestar demanded, staring at the old one.

"The warriors that carried the new weapons," Scarbeak said, not backing down, "indeed, even those warriors that were close when the weapons fired, they sicken, my lord. Their fur falls out in clumps, and they cannot keep down their food."

"We can make more eggs quickly," Whitestar said. He did not like what Scarbeak was getting at.

"True," Scarbeak said, nodding, "but the losses are staggering, far faster than even we can make eggs. So many die from the devil's weapons, and now more and more die from our own as well. Sharpwing's generation, or perhaps a few after him, could be the last."

"First my wife, now you. If that is the plan that the Ones Above have for us, so be it. But consider this, which of my sons should be leader, if our people are to live longest?"

Whitestar didn't wait for an answer, but instead knelt next to the new weapon, a flattened disk half as wide as he was tall, with straps to hold it to a warrior's back for carrying. "How powerful is this weapon, Scarbeak?"

"Powerful enough to pierce the skin of the ogre and strike his heart, if you can place it underneath, or perhaps just close to his body at any point."

Scarbeak moved over and touched the weapon reverently. "Unlike the other Fists we have been given, this one strikes in one direction only, and the oracles tell me that it acts as a shield against the devil's weapons."

Whitestar stared at the object. It did have the appearance of a shield, but he didn't see how it would stop the great firebolts that came from the ogre. Still, he had to trust the oracles, trust the Ones Above. Many things were still in their control. "Scarbeak, could this thing pierce the walls of the devil's nest?"

"It might, my lord. In fact, I am almost certain it would. We have been able to damage those walls repeatedly, while we have barely scratched the hide of the ogre."

"And if I could break open their nest so that our warriors could slaughter them, it would shorten this war, save countless of our people's lives, and still serve the will of the Ones Above. Wouldn't that be worth the life of a lord?"

Scarbeak said nothing for a while. Then, "I'm old, my friend. I had always imagined that you would outlive me."

Chapter Seven

Donning could have had the new command and control center installed anywhere in the colony. It was self-contained, weatherproof, and could have communicated over an area many times larger than the colony. But he had chosen to have it set up just behind the southern ramparts, where it was still well protected, but close enough to the walls that he could easily climb up and visit the troops there. He knew that, as the siege dragged on, and a siege is what this was, the morale of the people manning the walls and defenses would be everything. So each morning he tried to make the circuit of those walls, to let everyone see him, to stop occasionally, ask people how they were doing, and offer a few words of encouragement.

The perimeter was too long to comfortably walk, and staying well behind the walls in a ground-car would have defeated the purpose, so he'd had a small electric scooter hauled up. Each morning found him on that scooter, zipping along the catwalks and weapons platforms built into its top and rear, making his rounds.

It wasn't terribly dignified or impressive, but he somehow thought that the people serving under him appreciated the effort.

This morning, his first stop was at a sniper platform a few hundred meters counter-clockwise from the C&C. Manning the post this day was Private Vetta Rampling. Donning had been keeping an eye on her. She had no military experience, but she'd lived on frontier worlds most of her life. She knew how to handle a weapon, and wasn't afraid to use them with deadly intent. Given how many of his troops had started out as file clerks and machine operators, as afraid of their own weapons as the enemy, he wished he had a couple dozen more like her.

He rolled up and stepped off the scooter. "Good morning, Private."

She gave him a sloppy salute. Rampling wasn't much on military protocol, but that described a lot of the people under his command. Actually it wasn't that, so much as that she seemed distracted, concerned with something out beyond the wall.

"Problem, Private?" He stepped up and looked out the gun slit. He wasn't overly cautious, a shimmer field built into the opening made it almost impossible for an enemy sniper to target anyone behind the wall.

Things looked quiet outside. Below them, a remote-controlled construction machine was repairing wall damage from the last attack, a boom moving back and fourth spraying fast-hardening duracrete into the openings. Beyond that, a bit of low fog hung to the meadows, and the tree line seemed quiet.

"They're out there, Commander, getting ready to attack again."

Overactive imagination? But she seemed to be suggesting fact, and not just speculation. "Are your eyes better than mine, Private?"

"Maybe, but that's not it." She looked at him, as though wondering if he'd think her crazy. "I don't suppose you can *smell* them, can you, sir?"

He chuckled in spite himself. "I don't much *want* to smell them, Private."

"No, sir, really. I can smell them out there, smell their mood, I think. It could be part of how they communicate, or how they coordinate their attacks. And what I'm smelling today, I smelled before the last two attacks started. I think they're massing out there."

Donning considered for a moment. He'd read somewhere that women had much more sensitive noses than men. Maybe she was onto something. He touched his earpiece. "Peak."

"Yes, sir," the voice came back.

"Are you reading anything unusual on the perimeter?"

"I was just about to call you, sir. We've got a lot of movement beyond the tree line. Not as much as the last attack, but I think things could be heating up."

"I'm on my way." He put the headset on standby and climbed back on his scooter, turning it back towards the C&C. "Private, when you get a chance, see if any of the other women have been smelling what you've been smelling, and if you get any other insights into what's about to happen, you send them up to C&C immediately."

"Yes, sir!"

Despite his concern about the impending attack, Donning smiled as he rode back to the C&C. Every clue, every insight they got into the aliens, how they thought, how they operated, made them easier to fight. For the longest time it had been difficult for Donning to think beyond the next hour, the next day, the next attack. But now he could finally start to project beyond that.

The Concordiat wasn't trying to keep them here to

cower behind their walls forever. They were keeping them here to mine, and that meant leaving the relative safety of the compound. Houchen had told him about the Bolo mining machine on its way from the Odinberg Colony. Even if it wasn't any use to them as a combat vehicle, they might be able to use it for its mining capabilities. Maybe they could be back in the mining business faster than anyone imagined.

Yet even as he was thinking these things, some part of his mind was reminding him that there was a fine line between competence and overconfidence.

Scarbeak had put on his finest robe before heading to the gathering. It was made of a soft fabric obtained by endlessly pounding the fibrous shells of a certain jungle nut and dyed purple and red using the condensed juice of fermented berries. At the bottom, it came almost to the tops of his feet and a hood could be raised to cover his head. A knotted rope around the middle of his chest secured the garment.

He liked the robe and wore it on those public occasions when he wished to be noticed. Whitestar used to make fun of it. The men of their clan normally wore little clothing. "It makes you look like an old woman," he would say. But Scarbeak just ignored him. He was old and entitled to his eccentricities.

Surely this day, as he entered the clearing, he was noticed, though there may have been other reasons. At the far edge stood Sharpwing and a group of his loyalist supporters, a low fog swimming around their ankles. They made small, derisive noises as Scarbeak walked up.

"Where," demanded Sharpwing, "is he, old man?"

"Is he afraid to come?" asked one Sharpwing supporter.

"Does he send you to fight for him?" laughed another.

"He will fight," said Scarbeak, tucking his hands inside his robe. "Wait, you will see." He assumed a waitful posture and proceeded to ignore the pack of noisy hatchlings that Sharpwing had brought with him.

Time passed. The sun was higher in the sky. Scarbeak enjoyed watching the fog thin, and finally disappear. Insects began to buzz about in search of food. It would be a good day, today, he thought.

Sharpwing and his followers were becoming visibly impatient. "Where is he?" demanded Sharpwing, stepping threateningly close to the old warrior. "When will he be here?"

Scarbeak made a little sound of amusement. "I do not believe that I said he would be here at all, only that he would fight."

"What do you mean?"

Scarbeak looked at the young warrior with as much disgust as he could show. "He has cheated you of the two things you claimed to want: his life, and the right to take the Fist of the Ones Above against the enemy. He has gone to lead our warriors through the walls and into the aliens' nest. He will strike against them with his last breath, and bring honor to his name and those who fight at his side."

Sharpwing looked confused.

"Don't you smell the fight in the air, young one? No, of course not, you smell only your own stink of combat, that of you and your friends. This is how an army could slip by you in the jungle and you would never know."

Sharpwing hissed in rage. "Did my sire send you to do this, to taunt me?"

"I came on my own, to delay you as long as I could, for you'll never catch him in time. By the time you arrive, the battle will be all but over, and the people will talk of it. 'It was glorious,' they will say. 'What courage Whitestar had at the end. But where was Sharpwing? Where were his followers? How did such a fine warrior sire such a coward?'"

Hissing, Sharpwing turned to leave in disgust.

"Wait," said Scarbeak. "Do not leave without your gift. It is something your father wanted you to have, but could never bear to give you himself."

Curious, Scarbeak hesitated, then turned back toward the old warrior. "Give it to me," he said.

Under his robe, Scarbeak's old knife, unused for years, felt good in his hand. He slid the long, curved blade from under the fabric with one smooth motion, and plunged it into Sharpwing's stomach. He used all his strength to pull up on the handle and twist, a motion that would slice into Sharpwing's entrails, ensuring a fatal wound.

Sharpwing looked down in horror at the wound, but somehow his hand found his own blade. He stabbed the blade deep into the old man's chest, using his superior strength to force it between the closely-spaced ribs, digging to find something vital.

A bloody cough dribbled down from Scarbeak's open mouth, his head drifted backwards, his eyes already turning milky. "My lord," he said, his voice a gurgle, "I do precede you into death."

"Can you hear me?"

Tyrus groaned and turned his head. It hurt too much for him not to be alive, though he wasn't sure how he'd survived.

"Tyrus. Commander. Can you hear me?"

Dirk. The voice had a name, and he remembered it. Dirk. The mining machine made from a Bolo.

It was hard to breathe. His chest hurt. He managed a wet, gurgling cough.

"I could not get you to the autodoc, but I was able

to adjust my internal life support to increase the oxygen pressure considerably. If you can move, I suggest you be careful not to create a spark or flame."

"No moving. Don't worry. No moving."

"I need you, Commander. The inhibitions placed on my combat reflexes are too strong. I cannot fight without you."

He suddenly felt a little more alert. "Fight? Fight who? Fight where?"

"We are nearly to Rustenberg. I could proceed there directly and get you to medical care. However, among my functional sensors is a suite designed to detect radioactive materials. These produced a certain signature from the alien suicide bomb."

"You—you found another one?"

"Rapidly moving through the jungle towards the colony. Commander, from the transmissions I have monitored, this colony has resisted repeated attacks by the enemy, but the enemy has yet to employ such weapons here. The colonists have not been warned."

"They have a Bolo," he said. He studied the conduits and ducts on the ceiling of the passageway, memorizing every detail, and wondering if they would be the last thing he ever saw.

"The Bolo left for the Marikana, to repel a new attack. They have only their fixed defenses. And if I am interpreting my sensors correctly, this device is different than the one that was used at Odinberg, possibly much more powerful."

Tyrus coughed, feeling something wet on his lips. "You're asking me what to do."

"I cannot fight without you. I will not risk your life further without your direct order."

He closed his eyes. He remembered the words he had lasered onto metal back at the Odinberg Colony. *They will be avenged.*

It had been an impulse, an afterthought. Perhaps they had been the wrong words. Perhaps the right words would have been, *Never again.*

He opened his eyes, tried to clear his mind. Then he said aloud to Dirk. "Target that bomb. Let's intercept it if we can."

"It will be a close thing," said Dirk.

"Did you open the rest of those gunports yet?"

"I have not tried. The overload could damage other systems. I have been waiting for the right moment."

"This would be it. Time to fight, Dirk. Do what you were born to do. Do what you have to do."

"Yes, Commander."

All around him, the gunport servos whirred, then howled, then screamed. The lights in the passage dimmed—or was it just his vision? Then a crack, like an old style cannon, and another, and another, and another.

"Six of eighteen ports have opened, Commander. The actuators on the rest have burned out, but I have limited secondary armaments at the ready."

Something about Dirk's voice sounded different to Tyrus, or was it just his imagination?

"I am fighting unit DRK, Mark XXIV of the Dinochrome Brigade. I proudly serve under Unit Commander Tyrus Ogden. We go to defend humanity against alien aggression."

"Sounds good to me," said Tyrus, ignoring the pain in his chest. "Let's do it."

Chapter Eight

The wall-repair machine had been trapped outside the walls when the attack came. Donning had ordered the machine rolled away from the colony, avoiding the main body of the aliens, hoping that they might ignore it.

No such luck.

The machine was still moving, slowly, its upper structure now entirely engulfed in flame. As the aliens streamed past on either side, they would shoot it with their rifles, blue arcs of light that slowly were slicing the robotic vehicle to ribbons. Finally a missile slipped through their overloaded defenses and struck the machine, causing it to explode into a shower of metal and flaming parts.

More missiles slipped past, slamming into the walls, one damaging auto-turret six. There were fewer aliens this time, but they were more organized, more determined than they'd ever been before. They'd blown up three of the single-shot cannon before the weapon could be used, but when they'd tried to destroy a fourth one, it shattered into splinters, a cleverly made decoy constructed from a hollow log. He had to give them that. The aliens were smart and resourceful in their own suicidal way.

"Sir," said Peak, "off on the southern horizon."

At first Donning thought it was a hill, but he'd studied every inch of that horizon, and there was no hill in that direction. Then he saw it was moving. He zoomed in.

Donning watched his screens in amazement. The Bolo looked like it had already been through a war. Its hull was charred and pitted, and smoke poured from a closed aft gunport. Though it bore a family resemblance to Khan, it was even bigger, a lumbering mountain of metal that waded through the jungle like a child wading through a pool. It was much slower than Khan too, though whether that was due to its modifications, its age, or damage sustained along the way, he couldn't be sure.

A few patches of yellow paint could still be seen on its side, remnants of someone's absurd attempt to make it look more like a standard mining machine.

Broken bits of welded-on mining gear hung in tatters from its hull, including a huge derrick that lay folded back over the main turret, deprived now of its original Hellbore cannon. He'd had hopes for this machine, that it might be able to fight for them, or mine for them, but now, seeing it, he didn't think it would be able to do either.

"Sir," said Peak, "I'm picking up some low power transmissions on one of the civilian mining bands. I think they're coming from the Bolo."

"What do they say?"

"Nothing yet, sir. Just a carrier wave and garbled static, but it's getting stronger."

"Keep monitoring. We have to know their intentions.

Under the circumstances, we can't just open the gates and let them in."

Lord Whitestar trotted through the jungle, hunched forward because of the heavy weapon strapped to his back. The air was sweet in his lungs, the foliage as splendid and lush as he ever remembered it, the sun like a jewel as it peeked through the canopy of trees. It felt good to run, good to carry the power of the Ones Above. He had clarity now.

He knew what he had to do.

There were chants for this, to give the warrior focus, to ease his fear, to give him the courage to make the final sacrifice for victory. He had learned those chants, practiced them since he was a hatchling, but now that it was time, he found he had no need of them. He was free of fear, his resolve as sharp as a knife blade, his determination complete.

Instead, in his mind he rehearsed what he must do. Already the diversionary attacks were under way. There would be confusion on the meadows, and his purpose would be to stay away from those attacks, to avoid enemy fire as much as possible. He carried no other weapon, not even a knife, that might attract enemy attention. A loose wrapping of rags helped to disguise the weapon. He had already chosen his spot on the wall, a place that still showed cracks and scars from their last attack, one positioned so that his warriors could do the most damage when they broke through.

Scarbeak had said the weapon would shield him, but he thought that was foolishness. He would simply not get shot. That would be the way to do it. He would sprint up to the wall, arm the weapon, press the face of it against one of those cracks, and press the activation stud.

Probably he would never even feel it. But if what Scarbeak had told him was true, the Fist would explode a column of fire directly into the wall. Almost certainly it would punch through. Ideally it would do terrible damage to the structures and people on the other side, and cause that whole part of the wall to collapse.

From there, his warriors would stream inside, killing every living thing that they saw: warriors, females, hatchlings. All would die, and the world would be cleansed of one more human-devil nest.

Ahead he could see fire, hear the cries of warriors echoing off the walls of the enemy, smell the glory of battle. And then he turned his head and saw something that shattered his resolve. Looming over the trees was an ogre, and it was coming his way. Suddenly, nothing was clear at all.

"Commander," said Peak, "I'm getting voice transmission from the Bolo."

"Put it on the speaker."

"Unit . . . Dinochro . . . colony . . ."

It was still too broken to understand.

"Can you filter that somehow?"

Peak looked very unhappy. Doubtless his console could clear up the message, but it was beyond his limited skills. "I'll do what I can."

"Meanwhile, let's see if we can talk to them. Patch me through."

He watched as Peak pushed something on his console. "Unidentified Bolo, this is Commander Donning of the Colonial Militia. We can't yet receive you, but we're trying to clear up your signal. We're currently under attack. You may want to withdraw until we can repel the aliens."

No response.

"Keep trying!" Donning ordered.

❖   ❖   ❖

Tyrus listened to the hidden speaker in wonderment. He'd thought he might never hear a live human voice again.

"Dirk, when they can hear us, let me talk to them."

"Understood," Dirk said.

Tyrus took a moment to try and catch his breath. It was getting hard to talk, hard to even breathe. His whole existence was a dull ache, threaded with sharp pains. He had to focus, to stay alert long enough to save this colony.

"Where's the bomb?"

"Two thousand meters and closing," Dirk said. "I can obtain only an approximate position and I can't make a visual sighting. It may already be within blast radius of the fortifications."

Tyrus tried to make himself think. They had to stop that bomb. "Can you . . . shoot it?"

"There might be a secondary explosion, but I do not believe a direct hit would trigger the bomb."

"Do it."

"I don't have a visual identification of the target."

"Might be hidden. Camouflage."

"Commander, I have voice contact. Putting you on."

Somebody started to talk from the speaker.

"Shut up," he gasped. "Listen. There's a fusion bomb. Suicide weapon. Get to shelters."

Someone had left the mike open, and he heard someone shouting a rapid chain of orders before it was cut off.

"I see an unarmed alien, alone," Dirk said, "carrying a heavy object wrapped in rags."

"Moving directly towards the walls?" Tyrus asked. "Yes."

"Get him," Tyrus ordered.

He heard a secondary battery fire.

Dirk jerked into faster motion, slamming him into the bulkhead and intense pain.

Whitestar dropped his pace, confused. This was not the same ogre as before. This one was bigger, but it was already wounded, some of its weapons seemingly missing or damaged. It lacked the single "mountain-killer" horn of the other machine. But an ogre was an ogre, and his blood told him to return to his original mission, to go destroy it.

He almost turned. Then he thought of the warriors who would die needlessly. The ogre would be dead, but the walls would still stand, and the other ogre might yet return.

Destroy the nest. That was what he must do.

He moved away from the ogre and doubled his pace. To his alarm, the ogre turned to follow. Had it detected his weapon? He must not be stopped.

Then he saw the mouth of one of the ogre's firebolts turn toward him, and knew there was no hope. He stopped, faced his attacker, closed his eyes, and awaited his death without fear.

A blinding light that came even through his closed eyelids, an indescribable noise, an energy that felt like invisible insects whizzing through his flesh, and a heat that made his fur smolder.

Then it was over, and nobody was more surprised than he was that he was still alive.

"I don't believe it," said the voice from the speaker. "Your Bolo just fired on a lone alien from maybe five hundred meters, and he's still standing."

"Dirk," Tyrus said, "malfunction?"

"My weapons are operating on reduced power, but he should have been vaporized with several gigawatts of energy to spare."

"Then what happened?" Tyrus demanded.

"My analysis indicates some sort of personal battle screen," Dirk said, "possibly deriving power inductively from my own weapon. I register that the alien has probably already sustained a fatal radiation overdose, but that may not stop him from completing his mission."

"Damn, damn, damn," the voice on the speaker said.

Tyrus groaned. "Keep firing, Dirk, keep firing!"

There was a cracking noise, and the lights went out for a moment. Tyrus knew that was not a good sign at all.

"The power buss to my weapons system has just failed."

"Stop him, Dirk. Any way you can."

"Yes, Commander," Dirk said.

Donning shouted into his mike, directing his snipers and fixed guns to fire on the lone figure now sprinting for their southwest wall, but their shots glanced away without effect. The noncombatants were already in their shelters, but unfortunately, those shelters began beneath the streets just a hundred yards inside that wall.

Donning knew, without a doubt, that those walls would not stop a fusion bomb set off close, and neither would the shelters just beyond the walls protect the colonists.

Right here, right now, this battle was either going to be won or lost.

"Keep firing everything we have at him!" shouted Donning.

As he watched, nothing seemed to work.

The alien kept moving, getting closer and closer.

The old Bolo still churned forward, its guns dead.

Perhaps, so were they all.

✧   ✧   ✧

Whitestar forced himself toward the wall. Though the enemy's weapons bounced away harmlessly, he felt sick, injured inside in a way he couldn't describe or understand. No matter. He had only to survive a few more seconds under the miraculous protection of the Ones Above, and then it wouldn't matter. The ramparts were just ahead of him now—

Then someone rolled a wall in his way, blotted out the sun.

He barely stopped himself from tumbling into the churning tracks and giant spinning wheels.

He looked around, stunned. He was *under* the ogre!

He was blocked from the walls. It would be so easy now, to lift the weapon over his head, trigger it against the belly of the beast—

But that was not his mission.

He saw sunlight at the rear of the thing, like the opening of a tunnel, and he sprinted for it.

He would complete his task. Not even the ogre would stop him.

"Where is he?" Tyrus demanded.

"He's under our treads, Commander," Dirk said. "In the galley between tread four and five. He's trying to escape."

"Run him down."

"The bomb may be triggered."

"Will be . . . anyway. Do it. That's an order!"

Tyrus felt the passage turn around him as the Bolo spun in its own length.

Suddenly, the spot of light in front of Whitestar began to move, spinning away like a ghost.

He found himself in a hellish passage with moving walls of machinery, all ready to eat him alive. One misstep and he would have failed, smashed by the ogre.

He ran towards the light, was forced to double back, saw light the other way, but was forced back from there as well.

If he did not make it from under this beast, he would at least take the beast with him.

As he ran, he unstrapped the weapon from his back. The wall of the human nest was only a few meters away. If he only knew the direction, perhaps he could still trigger the weapon from here.

But he was confused after turning so many times, confused by the spinning ogre over his head. He hesitated, making sure the lights-of-function showed the correct color.

The weapon was ready.

His attention to the weapon cost him. He never saw the tread until it was on him like a set of giant metal teeth. It threw him down on the ground, crushing him up to the waist.

He ignored the pain, worked his free hand to find the firing stud.

"I have him pinned under my number five tread, Commander," Dirk said.

"Good job, good . . . job." Tyrus was very tired. Maybe he could finally sleep now. The colony had been saved.

"Good-bye, Commander," Dirk said.

The explosion shook the walls like a groundquake, even in the C&C, mounted as it was on shock absorbers.

Donning was tossed to the floor, but he quickly scrambled back to his chair, watching the screens. A moment before, the old Bolo had run right over the top of the alien.

He had cheered, thinking the alien had been crushed and the bomb hadn't exploded.

But he had been wrong. Now, on the screen, there was a sight that he would never forget: the blasted, 14,000-ton hull of the Bolo flipping high into the air, end over end, like a tossed coin.

Chapter Nine

Houchen could hardly believe the mess when he and Khan arrived back at the northern colony, but the walls were still intact, the colony survived, and that was all he could have asked for.

No, not quite true. He would have liked to know about the man who had fought on even when he knew it would cost him his life, and the crippled Bolo who had shielded an entire colony with his war hull. But they didn't know, not even their names. They just knew there had been one survivor of the Odinberg Colony massacre, and now there were none.

The hull was still there, in the charred meadows outside the colony walls, and it would probably still be there centuries from now if the jungles didn't reclaim it. Eventually the grass would regrow, the flowers would bloom, and animals would make their homes in its gutted hull.

Houchen wondered if humans would still be here then, or if they would have taken what they wanted from this world and left it behind. He wondered if any of the aliens would survive, and what stories they would tell of this day.

Surely some of them must have survived to tell the tale. Not many though. The Bolo's hull had done more than shield the colony from the blast, it had redirected it, sending a crescent-shaped shock wave away from the walls of the colony that had flattened trees for two kilometers, and killed aliens by the thousands.

There were still a few attacks, an occasional missile or two, and around half a dozen other colonies around the continent the aliens were as much a threat as ever. But here and now, the enemy's back seemed to be broken. Donning was repairing his fortifications, and they were busy modifying their mining machines to add armor and weapons. Here at least, things might soon be settling into a new routine, something akin to normal.

As Khan rolled past the dead Bolo one last time, he raised his guns in salute, and launched a volley of shots into the empty sky. Twenty-one times he fired.

And then he turned, and they rolled toward the distant horizon. There were other colonies to be defended.

Lord Blackspike pushed himself up painfully with his cane, and hissed in rage at the distant thunder of the human weapons. He had brought his people here, to the deep jungle, far from any of the human nests, so that they could recover and rebuild. But even here, there was no escape from the human devils.

He sat back down on a fallen log and looked around him. The camp was small and ragged. There were only a few warriors left, and most of them were injured or maimed. Some still died slowly from the invisible sickness. What was left were women, eggs, and hatchlings.

Even the oracles were gone, but before Blackspike had left, his sire had come to him and whispered where others could be found.

In time, the hatchlings would grow, there would be more eggs, and in three seasons' time, new warriors to begin again. The Ones Above would show them new weapons. More powerful weapons. Then they would go back.

Then the human devils would pay.

But it was not too early to begin the fight.

Never too early.

"Hatchlings," he shouted. "Your lord commands you, gather round and listen!"

He sat on his log, and the little ones gathered round. He reached into his pouch, his fingers sliding over the cool, smooth bone there. He pulled the skull out and held it up for the hatchlings to see.

"This," he said, "is a human. This is a devil. What do we do to humans?"

At once they began to chant.

Kill. Kill. Kill. Kill. Kill. Kill. . . .

Though Hell Should Bar the Way

Linda Evans

Chapter One

My first conscious thought upon activation is surprise. I do not remember possessing the psychotronic circuitry which has just been flooded with power. My surprise deepens as my awareness, triggered into a level approaching my old full Battle Reflex Alert, expands into a secondary brain system which is completely unknown to me. I am now far more fully self-aware than I have ever been outside of actual combat. It is an unsettling feeling. Not unpleasant, precisely, but quite unsettling. I am unused to such mental alertness off the battlefield.

My initial astonishment gives way to vast confusion. My last conscious memory is a communication from my commander that I was to be mothballed as obsolete. I am a Mark XXIII Bolo with forty-eight years of active service. Since I understood—albeit regretted—the necessity of taking older units off-line as improvements in psychotronics, weaponry, and armor were fielded, I said my good-byes and mourned only the loss of my usefulness to my creators. The order to shut down all

*but my survival center was the last command I expected
ever to receive.*

For an agonizing zero point twenty-two seconds, I
attempt to understand the staggering internal changes
to my psychotronic systems, while speculating uselessly
upon possible reasons for them. Have I been captured
by enemy forces and subverted in some fashion? I can
sense newer installations which my upgraded spec
manuals identify as molecular circuitry. These have
been patched into my older, seriously antiquated systems in a hodgepodge I cannot follow, even with self-
diagnostics. I almost suspect I have been put together
by a work team suffering fatigue-induced hallucinations.
I have just turned my awareness outward through my
external sensor arrays, in an attempt to discover where
I am, when I receive a communication from a source
I recognize as a Bolo Sector Command frequency.

"Unit SPQ-561, prepare to receive Command VSR."

"Acknowledged." *I attempt to contain my deep
curiosity and wait for enlightenment.*

"Unit SPQ-561, respond to command code VJ-2012.
Your new designation is SPQ/R-561. You have been
refurbished with a number of system upgrades and
reactivated as a /R unit, to respond to a military threat
in this sector." *I receive a flood of data regarding the
world I am to defend, a world which has suffered a
serious incursion of humanity's old enemy, the Deng.
At the time of my deactivation, the Deng were not
expected to become a threat again for at least a century. Indeed, my own combat experience has been
confined largely to the Quern Wars, which are not even
mentioned in the data I am receiving now.*

As I sift eagerly through the mission briefing material, I become aware that I am no longer in the Sector Command Depot Yard. Indeed, I am no longer
anywhere near Sector Command. I occupy a cargo

berth on what appears to be an interstellar military transport, with my war hull sandwiched between two Bolo units of unknown configuration. Hull designations tell me they are a Mark XXIV and a Mark XXV Bolo, respectively. It is an eerie sensation, to feel so antiquated, and rather disquieting, to have been on-loaded while remaining at a level of psychotronic activity below self-awareness.

I make my first request. "Unit SPQ/R-561, requesting clarification. I see no mention of a commander in the VSR just received. May I expect assignment to a human commander while in transit?"

"Affirmative, SPQ/R-561. Your commander is en route to your cargo berth now."

I signal acknowledgment and wait with growing impatience to have my questions answered. Given the date stamp on my VSR from Sector Command, it is extremely unlikely that my commander remains Major Von Hurst. Jack was nearing retirement age when the orders came to mothball me in a Depot salvage yard. That order was transmitted twenty-three standard years ago. I find myself grateful for the reprieve from deactivation and salvage, but mourn the loss of my old comrade. Jack Von Hurst was a fine officer. I shall miss him. Even so, I await my new commander's arrival with a sense of pleased expectation, for I have been given a rare second chance to serve.

Clearly, the strategic situation facing humanity is grim, if Bolo units twenty-three standard years out of date are being refurbished from salvage yards and sent into combat. I long to close with the enemy and fulfill my mission once more. Humanity must be protected. My strange new circuitry hums as I wait.

My external sensor arrays detect the sound of a shipboard lift in operation. I hear the soft hiss and thump as the lift halts at my level, followed by the pneumatic swish of lift doors sliding open. I locate the source of the sound with visible-light camera systems and observe carefully the individual stepping onto the cargo deck. She is slim and surprisingly short for a Concordiat officer, with the olive-toned skin and dark hair I have learned to associate with individuals of ancient Terran-Mediterranean descent. She surveys my war hull coolly, her expression remote, revealing nothing of her thoughts. She halts three point nine meters from my port-side treads and tips her head back to gaze into my nearest external camera lens.

"Unit SPQ/R-561, respond to code 'bread and circuses.'"

This is not my old recognition code, but psychotronic engineers have been at work throughout my systems, for I recognize this as a valid code, even though I had not been aware until now of the change in my programming. The deeply unsettled feeling returns, full force, but I do my best to ignore it. "Welcome, Commander," *I respond.* "May I know your name and rank?"

She delays answering for two point oh three seconds, leading me to wonder if she intends to respond at all. "Captain DiMario," *she says at length.* "Alessandra DiMario. Open your personnel hatch, I'm coming aboard."

I bristle silently. Major Von Hurst would never have issued such a baldly phrased order, devoid of standard courtesies. I theorize that Captain DiMario is not pleased with her new command. I know a moment of disappointment. It is good to have a genuine companion aboard when facing combat—but comradeship is unlikely to develop if I am not held in esteem by my new commander. Despite my past victories, I must seem an antique beside the other Bolo units in this cargo bay, enhanced as I am only with patchwork psychotronics. Wordlessly, I open my personnel hatch, allowing my commander access to my command compartment. Captain DiMario climbs up in total silence, sliding through the open hatch and crawling down into the command chair. She powers up and checks my systems in stony silence.

"Well," *she mutters at length, having run through a thoroughly comprehensive systems check without pause,* "the ham-handed morons who put you together apparently did something right." *She runs one hand through her short, dark hair.* "God, I wish I knew what I'd done to piss off General Willard."

I do not know General Willard. From her tone, I suspect I should be glad this is so.

Perhaps the old adage that wisdom comes with age has some merit, for I do not offer comment, doubtless the most politic thing I have managed to accomplish in my long and somewhat incendiary career. Obsolescence has a quelling effect on my once-bold brand of conversation. My new commander sighs and taps slim fingertips against the padded armrest of the command chair's console. "Well, I guess we're stuck with each other, huh?"

This appears to be an invitation to conversation. It also appears that I am far more pleased to have Captain DiMario as a commander than she is to have me as a command. I attempt to broach the awkward situation in which I find myself.

"I am grateful to be of service again," *I say carefully.* "May I ask how I might best accomplish that task and aid you in yours?"

Captain DiMario thins her lips. "You could start by transforming yourself into something besides a jumped-up, rusted-out tub I wouldn't trust to take over a kindergarten."

This is not going well.

I decide that I have very little to lose, given my

commander's current opinions, and determine that I will cease to respect myself if I do not speak what is on my mind.

"Captain DiMario," *I say very formally,* "I am a retrofitted Mark XXIII Bolo, without the modern systems to which you are clearly accustomed, but this is hardly my fault. May I request that you at least address me with the courtesy my war record should command from an officer of the line?"

Her mouth falls open. She stares into my video pickup lens, eyes growing wider with each passing beat of her heart. She remains totally silent for six point nine seven seconds, an eternity of shock. I detect a tremor which runs through her entire body. Then she explodes into motion, slapping at restraint releases on the command chair, swarming up the ladder toward my command hatch. Since I closed this in automatic reflex when she boarded, her exodus is momentarily blocked.

"Get that stinking hatch cover open!"

I comply speedily.

She disappears down the hull-side ladder and jumps to the cargo deck, striding angrily toward the cargo lift. A moment later, the lift doors open with a soft hiss and she is gone. I listen to the echoes fading into silence and wonder what on earth to do now. Perhaps General Willard was not so very wrong, after all, to assign Captain DiMario to command an obsolete Bolo of questionable value? It is a thought unworthy of a unit of the Dinochrome Brigade and it shames me the moment I conceptualize it, but I have never been treated so abrasively—or rudely—in my entire career.

I sting from the indignity of it.

And worry, intensely, about the combat which lies ahead.

Chapter Two

Ginger Gianesco was used to working under adverse conditions. A woman didn't achieve an appointment as Operations Director of a colony like Rustenberg without the know-how to keep a community running under difficult conditions. Ginger—whose sixty-first birthday was a week away—had brought to the Thule Expedition forty years of experience, including three two-year tours as OD of highly profitable mines on other colony worlds. Those mines had been running deep into the red before she'd turned them around, mainly by improving the lives of the miners until they were cheerfully churning out solid profit—two factors inextricably interwoven in operations on far-flung colonies, out beyond the reach of civilized luxuries. She'd run successful mining ops through fire, flood, and famine, on howling methane hells and airless moons and swamps so treacherous, a body had to put on biochem isolation suits just to step out the front door.

But she'd never poured a plascrete defensive wall or dug bomb shelters during a hurricane-force ice storm, under the guns of an alien enemy. A more generous God would have thrown only one of those curves at Rustenberg; but the local gods seemed a bit short of generosity. *Those* gods had given them a Thulian winter storm breaking six weeks too soon and a surprise sentient native species that wasn't supposed to exist, doing its dead-level best to exterminate Ginger Gianesco and every man, woman, and screaming infant under her care. If that ecosystem biologist over at Eisenbrucke Station hadn't stumbled across the Tersae three months ago, the surprise attack against every colony on Thule would have been even more shocking. As it was . . .

Her comm link crackled wildly.

"Movement on the southern perimeter!"

Harriet James' position, she realized grimly, along the unfinished stretch that hadn't been poured, yet. Harriet's voice was shaking, from cold or fright or both. Ginger, busy directing the team using shaft-boring equipment to dig shelters out of the basalt bedrock, keyed the mike and shouted above the howl of wind, freezing rain, and sleet. "How many and how close?"

"Looks like twenty of 'em, at least." A burst of static interrupted Harriet. ". . . three hundred meters out and closing fast. Jeezus, those damned hairy birds can *move . . .*" More static. "They've got one team shooting at us from a wood line, two others leapfrogging it toward us in three-second sprints, one shooting while the other one runs. Comin' in with the wind at their backs, damn 'em—we can't even *see* 'em half the time with this storm in our faces, and the sleet's clogging our optics—"

Another burst of static interrupted.

"Wilson," Ginger barked into the comm link, "get your people into position! Move it! We've got incoming at the southern breakpoint."

"Roger that, heading out now. That ice slick we poured a few hours ago ought to slow 'em down, at least." Jeremy Wilson, who had seen active military service in the Concordiat Infantry, had already saved hundreds of lives with his creative flow of nasty tricks to slow down the enemy. He'd ordered a slurry of water and mud poured in a broad sheet outside the one remaining hole in their plascrete defensive wall, a slurry that had solidified into black ice, slick as the bottom circle of hell and hard to see until it was too late. And beyond that, a thin crust of ice over a deep pit gouged out in the night and covered over with a roof of filmilon fabric and water, the filmilon later dissolved from underneath with solvents that left a treacherous crust of ice above the acid-filled pit.

The nine men and women of Jeremy's "commando unit" had served in various other military branches, mostly the navy. They were armed now with civilian hunting rifles, brought in to defend mining parties from Thule's more aggressive predator species. *Huh*, she thought darkly, *they don't come much more aggressive than kamikaze maniacs. . . .* If Ginger's people could just get this last section of wall poured, they'd have a defensible perimeter enclosing the heart of the town, including the medical clinic, school, and meeting hall. With a wall to slow down the Tersae and shelters to get the noncombatants underground, out of direct enemy fire, at least the kids might survive.

Ginger snarled at the wind and shouted the warning to her drillers to look sharp for possible breakthroughs from the south. The last three days had blurred into one long, sleepless tunnel of desperation, with brutal memories etched indelibly into her consciousness: small groups of heavily armed Tersae warriors charging in from the teeth of the storm; the crack of rifle fire, sharp as the sound of breaking rock; spurts of flame in the darkness as Tersae snipers gained the cover of warehouses and ore depots, firing with frightful accuracy from rooftops and doorways; the screams and jerking, disjointed falls as men and women went down, fatally hit by enemy weapons—thirty of her best people dead in only three days. The arcing, hideously graceful flight of sophisticated antipersonnel mortar rounds and high-explosive bombs lobbed into streets, warehouses, and homes around the edge of town. The first rounds had missed their targets as the wind snatched the incoming rounds off course—but the Tersae gunners learned *fast* how to correct their trajectories.

And everywhere, from every side, Tersae dying, gleefully, under the frantic guns of the defenders while explosions trapped the colonists inside a ring of blazing buildings. Fires hot enough to melt iron would've cooked them alive, if not for the freezing rain and sleet of the storm. Those fires had forced a steady retreat toward the very core of town, abandoning supplies they couldn't shift under enemy fire. And through it all, the numbing, bruising rush to knock together hasty wooden forms and pour a protective wall around the subterranean shelters they were gouging out of the ground, trying to hold on long enough for Concordiat military help to arrive.

Just a few more hours, Ginger prayed, *we can have it all done in just a few more hours.*

As though to mock her prayer, explosions rocked the southern perimeter. A massive fireball rose up beyond the rooftops and the ice-coated wooden forms of the unfinished wall. *Omigod . . .* Ginger was already running, slinging her rifle across her back and shouting orders into her comm link. "Hank, keep those shaftboring drills going! Zephrim, what can you see from up there?"

The teenaged boy posted as southern lookout on the

school's rooftop was sobbing into his own comm link. "They've got missiles, goddamned high-explosive *guided missiles*, started shooting 'em from the trees after the first batch of 'em fell into the acid pits and the second batch fell down on the black ice long enough to blow their heads off—oh, shit, here comes another wave—"

More explosions rocked the southern perimeter. The school—and young Zephrim—went up in a blast of heat and a shock wave that jarred Ginger's teeth from a distance of three hundred meters. She shook herself groggily, fumbled with the comm link strapped to her wrist. "We've got a gap in the southern perimeter! Anybody with a rifle, *close that gap!*" She saw people running, sliding on the glare of ice laid down by the freezing rain, slipping and throwing themselves back to their feet again, rushing to fill the southern gap. A dark wave of misshapen bodies hurled through the smoke and ruins, silhouetted against the blazing fires. The Tersae were immense shapes towering seven, eight feet high, carrying oddly shaped rifles and shooting at anything that moved.

When a hail of rifle fire blasted toward her, Ginger threw herself prone, her own weapon a bruising weight across her spine. She dragged the rifle off her shoulder and pulled it around to shoot from where she lay, sprawled prone in the slush and slurry. She sighted and fired, centering the bastards and squeezing off the rounds, jolting her shoulder with bruising force because she couldn't rise up enough to properly seat the weapon in the pocket of her shoulder. One of the furry bastards went down screaming, then another, and a third . . . Christ, how many of them *were* there? She saw the high, arcing flight of the grenade, knew she couldn't possibly scramble up and run fast enough to avoid it—

Tommy Watkins, eleven years old and howling obscenities his mother had never taught him, lunged in front of her. He swung a baseball bat with all his eleven-year-old strength. *CRACK!* The grenade spun away with home-run velocity and distance. It struck a house wall, bounced, and exploded in the gut of a startled Tersae warrior. The alien vanished in a red rain of debris that fell in gobbets and stained the icy slush crimson.

"C'mon!" Tommy was shouting, tugging at her arm. "We gotta get to the wall!"

Ginger climbed somehow to her feet, ran forward on rubberized legs while gasping into her comm link, "Report! What the hell's happening at the gap?"

She could hear weird, alien screams, human cries of agony and rage, the staccato reports of rifle fire and the deeper roar of explosions. Wind-flung sleet nearly blinded her as they rounded the corner of the blazing school and headed toward the embattled gap. Bodies lay sprawled everywhere, twisted in death, still writhing in the last moments of dying. At least some of those shapes were Tersae, shooting even as they died. The ones still moving, the great, furry shapes of the not-quite-birds that constituted the enemy, Ginger pumped rounds into from her rifle, skull shots that ended the twisting and the weird, alien screams. The ruthlessness of it shocked her, even as she snarled and fired again methodically, moving from one wounded Tersae to the next. Tommy laid about with his baseball bat, crushing the skulls of those merely twitching, safe enough to approach but still dangerously alive.

Until the bat came whistling down across eyes and strange, hooked beaks.

Blood sprayed scarlet against the glare of ice and sleet. Sickness rose in the back of Ginger's throat. She chugged it down again and kept going. *"Report, dammit!"*

she shouted into the comm link again. Jennifer Granger's voice, shrill through the static, sobbed out, "I can't see very well, but it looks like we're holding 'em."

Jennifer Granger, fifteen years old, perched atop the meeting hall . . .

Ginger was close enough, now, to see that Jennifer was right. The fighting at the gap was desperate, but rifle-wielding miners were driving the enemy back through the gap in the wall, a gap blown through the wooden forms with high-explosive rounds. Ginger took up a good, solid stance, braced the rifle in the hollow of her bruised shoulder, and added her fire to the pitched battle, dropping two of the bastards in their taloned tracks.

Within minutes, it was over.

This time.

She couldn't afford to let her people stop to catch their breath. "Mandy," she grabbed the nearest crew chief she could find, "pull together a crew and get to work on these ruined forms. Tear this section down and rebuild it, stat. I want every able-bodied adult we've got left pouring this section within the hour."

"But—" Mandy sputtered, face grey with exhaustion. "That won't leave anyone to man the guns!"

"Get the kids out here," Ginger said grimly. "Any child big enough to lift a rifle. Put 'em on top of the poured sections to either side of this gap, but get 'em armed and get 'em in position." She picked up a rifle from Jeremy Wilson's bloodied fingers, trying desperately not to look at the ghastly red ruin where the top of his head had been, and thrust the weapon into Tommy's hands—then turned a glare on Mandy's shocked expression. "You don't like it? Got any better ideas? I didn't think so. *Move*, dammit!"

It was only in her heart—cold as the howling sleet beating against her face—that Ginger wept.

Chapter Three

The wind was a wild and howling moan above the crackle of the Council fire. The bone-shivering sound of the storm, one of the murderous, early-season blizzards that roared up from the distant oceans and took two hands of days to blow themselves out again, matched the howl in Chilaili's soul. The storm raging through Chilaili was born of anger and frustration, a visible cloud as violent as the blizzard outside. The focus of Chilaili's rage stood glowering on the far side of the Council fire, a tall and gracile male whose stubbornness and refusal to see reason formed a deadly omen of things to come, of disasters the ruling Grandmothers must be made to recognize.

"We cannot make war against the humans," Chilaili said again, forcefully. "We have been more fortunate than you can possibly understand that this storm," she gestured toward the entrance to the Council cavern, blocked by thick, woven mats that kept the heat inside, but did very little to keep out the shriek of the wind, "has kept us locked in our winter nest. Let the other clans rush to destruction, if they so choose, but do not send *our* mates and *our* sons to battle against the humans. War against them will bring nothing but the death of Icewing Clan. It is stupid to fight them—stupid and unnecessary."

Across the Council fire, the clan's *akule* met Chilaili's gaze with a blaze of anger. Kestejoo was an outsider, even after twenty winters in Icewing Clan. He had come to them from Snowclaw Clan, so smitten by the gloriously sensual Zaltana, he had forsaken his own birth clan for love of her. Their meeting was still the stuff of legend, told to hatchlings around the winter hearth fires.

At his shoulder stood another male, Yiska, the clan's war leader. Taller by a full head than Kestejoo, Yiska was nearly two heads taller than Chilaili, and she was not the smallest of the huntresses. Yiska's eyes, unlike Kestejoo's, did not hold a glint of anger. They reflected instead the same deep thoughtfulness that had marked his many years as *viho*, leading them again and again to successful battle.

Kestejoo lifted his hands in a frustrated gesture, bringing Chilaili's attention back to the *akule*. "How can you say this war is not necessary? The Ones Above demand it. Therefore it is utterly necessary. I have deep respect for your knowledge, your insights as clan *katori*, but in this matter, there is no room for theorizing. No place for a healer's guesswork. Our creators have ordered it, so it must be done."

Chilaili, whose mothers before her had all been *katori*, healing the sick and dancing the sacred rites to heal the wounded soul—and whose only daughter, Sooleawa, would be *katori* after her, if they survived so long—reached desperately for her patience. "There is wisdom in your words, but we have far more to consider than orders from the Oracle. Perhaps

He-Who-Looks-Up has been staring at the stars so long, he has forgotten to look at the faces of those to whom he speaks the Oracle's words? Look at our people, *akule*," she gestured around the Council cavern, "look at the tiny handful of us, barely three hundred in all, and tell me again how necessary it is to send our sons and our mates into battle with creatures who have never meant us any harm."

A stir ran through the assembled clan, born of surprise and uncertainty that flew like wind-driven snow. The ancient Anevay, ten times a Great-Grandmother and the eldest member of the ruling Council, spoke from her seat near Chilaili's right hand. "How can you say this with such certainty, *katori*, when none of us has ever spoken with one of these newcomers, to judge such matters?"

Chilaili drew breath to speak—and the words stuck in her craw like a long and pointed *urka* thorn, tearing at her constricted throat. She glanced into her daughter's eyes, caught Sooleawa's wide and frightened gaze . . . and time spun crazily, tilting and plunging her into a night that had changed them both, forever, a night that had challenged things they had long believed. Things they could not yet bring themselves to say aloud, except to one another, in the strictest privacy—and always carefully away from the nest.

On that fateful night, she and her daughter had left the clan's migrational summer nest for a night-hunt, Sooleawa's first, the Blooding Hunt every young female was required to make under the supervision of her Mother—or guardian, if a girl's Mother had died. The multiple moons soared across the sky like a scattered and distant flock of birds, casting crazy, crisscrossed shadows that tricked the eye, but Chilaili and Sooleawa had little trouble seeing the undergrowth beyond their carefully concealed summer nest. Chilaili always hunted

by night—and so would Sooleawa, once Blooded. Most
of the clan's huntresses preferred the day-stalk, but
night was the time, the realm in which Chilaili's bloodline excelled. The Ones Above had made them that
way, an experiment, so her Grandmothers had said, to
see if a fiercesome dayhunter could be made to rule
the night, as well.

The Ones Above had wrought well in that much,
at least, creating Chilaili's foremothers. When the
daystar vanished beneath the rim of the world, only
Chilaili's bloodline—able to see far better in the darkness than any other bloodline—dared hunt the broken,
fissured terrain of their clan's home range. Now it was
her only daughter's turn to learn the night-stalk—and
Chilaili tasted worry the moment they left the nest,
armed with nothing but their own claws, as custom
demanded. The empty sheath at her belt, its beautiful knife left in the hut she and her daughter shared,
left Chilaili feeling naked, vulnerable, afraid. The omens
had been poor all day, yet the Blooding Hunt was
always performed—by clan law—on the fifteenth
anniversary of a young girl's hatching, never sooner and
never later.

To fail to make at least an attempt to hunt, regardless of how ill or injured a girl might be, was to be
shunned, to become One Who Never Hunted, with no
say in the clan's Councils and no hope of breeding,
ever. Chilaili had seen Mothers carry daughters dying
of fever into the deep forests of their clan's home range
to give their daughters the honored status of Huntress,
without which even a dying girl's sisters would be
sullied and overlooked when the time for breeding
came.

"What's wrong, Honored Mother?" Sooleawa asked,
when Chilaili jumped at shadows for perhaps the
hundredth time since leaving the nest.

"I cannot say for sure," Chilaili muttered, staring narrow-eyed into the moonlit shadows. "But I am uneasy, daughter, and mistrust the omens. Keep your wits sharp and your eyesight keen, precious one, for there is something wrong about this night."

Not the best words to give a nervous young candidate, yet Chilaili could not lie to the aspiring huntress she had so lovingly raised. Better to be blunt and ensure her child would be doubly vigilant, than to remain silent and court utter disaster. Sooleawa considered the warning for a long moment, then crouched down and broke off a young tree with a wrenching snap and stripped away long, thin needles and branches. Sticky, resinous sap smeared her claws, prompting a grimace that left Chilaili hiding a smile. Sooleawa used the sharp edges of her beak to scrape one end to a point, spitting and wiping her beak with one arm as the pungent taste of the sap drew another grimace. Her efforts left Sooleawa with a sturdy pole as thick as a foot-talon at its base. The crude spear was not the best weapon, true, but serviceable for the task.

Chilaili hummed approval at her daughter's decision to arm herself immediately upon hearing her mother's concerns. If the ancestors looked favorably upon her, Sooleawa would become a fine huntress. They traveled east, Sooleawa casting ahead for signs of prey, trying to find the spoor of some unlucky creature she could kill and carry home. They were perhaps six hours' distance from the nest when her daughter found the faint trail left by a *wurpa* stag—good eating, with a prized pelt, a high-status kill. They set out on the *wurpa*'s trail, Sooleawa leading.

The spoor was growing stronger, scent and temperature and the freshness of broken twigs telling them the *wurpa* could not be far ahead, when Chilaili became aware of at least one reason for her uneasiness. She began to taste changes in the air which spoke of bad weather on its way, but she could not yet tell how severe the storm would become. When they heard the first distant rumble of thunder, Chilaili came to a complete halt, pupils dilating as her sense of dread turned into full-blown fright. The ominous sound rolling across the dense forest canopy was no ordinary thunder. It was a continuous, booming roar, without even a moment's pause between the individual crashes of sound. The distant, flickering strobe of lightning was a solid glare, a wild haze of killing light that turned night into hellish day.

Storms like this could take down hundred-foot trees as easily as a hatchling snapped a twig in his claws. They needed shelter—and they needed it *now*. Without a word spoken, she forged ahead to lead the way, despite the fact that this was supposed to be Sooleawa's night for choosing. Sooleawa followed, visibly frightened now, while Chilaili hunched forward slightly, partly in dread and partly in anger that such weather should stalk them on this most critical night in her only daughter's life. Chilaili glowered at the rumbling, grumbling threat sweeping across the sky and moved as fast as she dared, blessing whatever guardian spirit had prompted Sooleawa to head into the least treacherous part of their hunting range.

Chilaili tipped her head sideways from time to time to glance up through the forest canopy, where clouds blotted out the stars and those moons which had already risen. Already the leafy crowns high above were shaking and rattling with a hissing sound like angry hatchlings as the wind picked up. Sooleawa glanced upward as well, but said nothing, concentrating instead on not putting her feet wrong as they jogged through the darkness. Chilaili was heading for a particular valley where she had taken shelter from

bad weather many times before. They had nearly
reached it when lightning split the night sky in a
blinding display.

Thunder cracked directly overhead—

—and the sound split the sky wide open.

Rain smashed down into the treetops, pelting them
with woody debris and shredded leaves an instant
before the water struck. In seconds, sight and scent
were obliterated, washed out by the deluge. Sooleawa
shouted above the roar, "Mother, shouldn't we go that
way?" and pointed ahead and slightly to their right. She
was pointing directly at the valley Chilaili had been
heading toward, where it opened out from a narrow
fissure to a broad, deep gouge bounded by cliffs that
overhung a deep lake.

"Yes! Go!"

They ran, Chilaili now following her daughter's lead,
pleased that Sooleawa's younger eyes had spotted the
cooler colors where temperature changes marked
abrupt drops into valleys. The girl had seen the way
to safe shelter before Chilaili had, even knowing where
to look. Sooleawa would do well as a huntress—if they
survived this storm. Heads bent against the deluge,
Chilaili and Sooleawa cautiously approached the edge
of the deep gorge. Sooleawa moved her head back and
forth to judge the depth of the drop, scanning the lip
of the ravine for a safe way down, then followed as
Chilaili moved parallel to the edge, heading for the spot
where a path of sorts led downward through a side
fissure that opened out into the larger valley. Far below,
water glinted in the flares of lightning. Forest giants
overhung the deep lake, leaning out over the edge of
the bluff, their crowns seeking the sunlight which fell
in stronger concentration where the deep gorge had
cut a gap through the forest.

In the rain-slashed darkness, they slipped and

slithered and tripped over great gnarls of tree roots and thick undergrowth. They had nearly reached the side fissure and the path down when lightning crackled and slammed into the tree just ahead of them. Blue-white light glared, actinic, blinding. The tree burst into flame, split along its entire length by the lightning bolt. Thunder crushed them flat against the mud as the immense tree broke in half and crashed down. Chilaili screamed. . . .

The ground shook under the smashing weight of the tree, shook and broke under them. An undercut ledge of rock hanging out over empty space crumbled into pieces beneath the weight of the falling tree. They all went plunging over the edge as the jutting overhang of rock cracked and gave way. Chilaili fell. Sooleawa spun away from her, dropping into the blackness just beyond the reach of her clawtips. The world windmilled as she thrashed, trying to grasp the wildly flailing branches of the fallen tree. Rough wood and long, whippy leaves slashed through her hands, slowing her fall, but didn't give her enough purchase to halt the sickening plunge. She struck water with a smashing shock, the impact driving the breath from her lungs. She went deep into the dark water, thrashing frantically. Chilaili struggled toward the surface, chest on fire from the need to breathe, and finally broke her head above water. She sucked down air—

—and screamed for her daughter.

"*Sooleawa!*"

Chilaili scanned the roiled surface of the lake. Rain and lightning blinded her. Half of the tree lay jammed across the broken edge and the far wall of the ravine, spanning the narrow, deep lake. The tree's bulk loomed ominously, a black bar high above her head. Then she realized that thick, black shape was shifting, its base dropping as more of the rocky lip crumbled away beneath it. She saw it falling, saw the immense shadow plunging down at the very same instant she spotted Sooleawa. Her daughter was closer to the edge of the lake than Chilaili was, treading water directly beneath the smashing weight of that huge tree.

"*Sooleawa!*"

Rock and wood fell in a rain of death.

Her daughter folded up and dove for the bottom in a hopeless attempt to avoid being crushed. Chilaili, stricken motionless by horror, could only watch the slow-motion fall of that killer tree, oblivious to her own danger. Then something heavy grazed her shoulder, sent her spinning into the black depths. She held her breath by instinct, stunned and unable to thrash her way back toward the surface. Long, dizzy moments passed, while the world tried to right itself inside her brain. When the fog cleared enough to realize she was deep under-water, Chilaili moved sluggish limbs, found rough wood under her clawtips, pulled herself hand over hand toward the surface. Her head broke water again and she gulped down lungfuls of air, then searched frantically for signs of her child.

The tree was completely down now, its shattered crown leaning drunkenly against the far wall of the ravine, its broken base disappearing underwater. Chilaili fought her way toward the trunk, screaming her daughter's name. "*Sooleawa!*" In the non-stop flares of lightning, she saw the glimmer of pale fur far below, down in the black water. She dove, fighting and clawing her way down. With shaking hands, she tugged at her daughter's arm, trying to tow the girl to the surface.

She might as well have tried to tug the *tree* up out of the water. She explored frantically with shaking hands and found a thick, jagged splinter of wood, thicker than Chilaili's own body. It held her daughter trapped more than a body length beneath the surface.

Sooleawa was unconscious, her pulse fluttering, her lungs filling with water. Chilaili wrenched at the huge splinter with her claws, frantic. It was too thick, too massive to break—and even if she'd had her knife, she couldn't have hacked through all that wood in time. She was still wrenching at it, despairing, when a pale glimmer appeared right at the edge of Chilaili's vision.

She jerked her head around in the dark water—and her pupils dilated with shock. A wraithlike shape hovered in the water beside her. Chilaili had never seen a creature like it, not in all in her life. It was slender, fragile-looking. Its long, thin limbs were completely hairless, its face round and strange. Long, dark fur floated in a wild tangle around its head. The creature was holding something, and whatever it was, it *glowed.* The thing was long and narrow, like a thick stick, out of which light blazed. It held something else, too, some kind of knife blade. When the creature drove that flimsy-looking blade through the body-thick splinter pinning Sooleawa, the wood parted like fog before the wind. An instant was all it took and Sooleawa was free. Chilaili grasped her daughter's arm, pulling desperately toward the surface. The creature fumbled its knife into a carrier on its clothing and clamped the glowing thing in its teeth, then took Sooleawa's other arm and swam strongly upward. Between them, they towed the unconscious girl to the surface.

In the flare of lightning, the creature gestured unmistakably toward the rocky bank. They swam awkwardly for shore, keeping Sooleawa's head above water. Chilaili dragged her daughter onto the broken litter where the lip of the ravine had crashed down. Sooleawa wasn't breathing, wasn't moving at all. The strange creature bent, listened at her chest, then tilted Sooleawa's head back and forced open her beak. It used surprisingly strong, blunt-fingered hands to press up under her rib cage. Water trickled from Sooleawa's mouth. Chilaili saw at once what the slender creature was doing, pushing the water up and out by compressing Sooleawa's lungs. Chilaili, stronger and larger than the stranger, took over the work.

The strange creature crouched down over the girl, listening, then fastened a tiny mouth over Sooleawa's and blew air down her throat, again and again. Chilaili watched in astonishment as the creature—she couldn't call it an animal, for it was clearly intelligent—worked frantically to try and breathe life back into Chilaili's child. When Sooleawa twitched and moved, Chilaili's fur stood on end. Her daughter made a choking sound, ghastly and weak, then her rib cage heaved and she started to vomit water. The creature hastily turned Sooleawa's head, rolling her onto her side, which helped the girl bring the water up more easily. Chilaili took her daughter's head gently between her hands and steadied her when she began to tremble violently, coughing and gasping for air.

At a blur of unexpected movement, Chilaili jerked her gaze up. The creature had abandoned them—but only for a few moments. It came rapidly back along the rocky lakeshore, moving at a somewhat reckless jog, given the uneven footing, the driving rain, and the uncertain shadows and flares of the lightning. It was carrying something, a squarish, bulky thing that proved to be some sort of carrysack, and used the glowing thing in its hand to light its way along the debris-riddled shore as it ran. The creature pulled from the carrysack something lightweight, as thin as the inner bark of the *seylish* tree. It spread the thing across Sooleawa's shuddering frame.

It was a blanket of some kind, Chilaili realized, its surface silvery as moonlight and strange to the touch. Chilaili appreciated the effort, but it was far too thin to do much good. Sooleawa's shudders eased away almost at once, however, startling Chilaili into investigating more closely. When she slipped a hand beneath the filmy thing, she found a surprising amount of heat building up under it. What strange manner of blanket was this? And what manner of creature was its maker?

At that moment, Sooleawa's eyes opened.

Her gaze rested directly on the face of the creature which had saved her life.

Her pupils dilated in utter shock. "M-mother?" she gasped, stiffening in fright.

"Hush, dearest one," she soothed, stroking her daughter's wet head-fur. "This creature has returned your life to you, precious one. It risked itself to free you from a tangle of branches under the water, gave you breath from its own lungs."

Sooleawa stared from Chilaili to the slender creature which crouched beside them. It was watching them through strange, luminous blue eyes. Its long head-fur, as black as the night, lay plastered wetly to its pale hide, falling in a bedraggled mass past its narrow waist. It wore strange body coverings over much of that moon-pale hide, coverings that looked ruggedly sturdy, to protect its fragile-looking skin. Beneath the upper coverings, its body bulged strangely at the front, and its hips flared wide beneath the narrow waist. It even wore coverings to protect its feet. If the blunt ends of its fingers were any indication, there were no claws inside those foot coverings, just bare stubs like those at the tips of its long, thin fingers.

It was looking at the belt Chilaili wore, the belt which held an empty sheath where she normally carried her knife. And as it stared, its round and luminous eyes narrowed slightly, its expression alien and baffling.

"What *is* it?" Sooleawa breathed, her voice an awe-struck whisper.

"I don't know," Chilaili admitted. "It's nothing like the Ones Above, is it?"

The *akule* had long kept sacred likenesses of the Ones Above who had created Chilaili's clan, to remind them of their duty to their makers. They brought out the likenesses for the various sacred ceremonies their clan observed during the long wheel of the year. The creature she studied so closely in the lightning flares was as unlike the Ones Above as Chilaili was. And given its reactions, the way it stared back at her, this creature had never seen any of the Tersae before, either. Where had it come from? There was only one place Chilaili could think of that made any sense at all: the sky.

Certainly, there had never been anything like this creature anywhere in the world. And since the Ones Above dwelt amongst the moons and the stars beyond, it was reasonable to believe other intelligent beings might, as well. The Ones Above had sometimes spoken through the Oracle about devils among the stars, but this creature could be no devil. It was far too fragile-looking to be a devil. Besides, the devils spoken of by the Ones Above did nothing but kill and this creature had worked frantically to save Sooleawa's life.

Its strange, glowing stick, its wondrous knife, and its gossamer-thin blanket told Chilaili that these creatures were able, like Chilaili's makers, to manufacture things far beyond her understanding. She shivered beneath the downpour, staring almost fearfully into its luminous, alien eyes. It met Chilaili's gaze squarely, then gestured carefully toward itself.

"Bessany Weyman," it said, its voice an alien ripple of sound, pausing between the two words to emphasize their separateness. "Bessany Weyman," it said again, then gestured to Chilaili and her daughter.

"Chilaili," she said slowly, touching her own chest, then touched her child's shoulder. "Sooleawa. My daughter, Sooleawa."

Bessany Weyman repeated the sounds of their names. Its accent was strange, its eyes oddly compelling as it studied them. Flares of lightning and the driving rain caused it to shiver. It spoke again, a rapid burble of sound, then gestured down the shoreline in the direction of a good, deep cave Chilaili knew existed along the base of the cliff—the shelter she had been trying to reach when the tree had come down. Chilaili nodded, pointing toward the cave, then said, "Daughter, there is a cave at the other end of this shoreline. I have used it before, when caught by bad weather. Can you stand?"

Sooleawa was desperately shaky, but managed to rise to her feet with both Chilaili and Bessany Weyman to assist her. Bessany Weyman folded up its silvery blanket and returned the thing to its carrysack, then offered a shoulder for Sooleawa to lean against. Had Sooleawa been fully grown, the alien would have been far too short to be of much practical use, for it was a small creature, but Sooleawa had just turned fifteen and would not reach her full growth for a number of years yet. The creature's shoulder was almost the perfect height for Sooleawa to lean against. Between them, Chilaili and the alien creature braced the shaken girl, helping her limp down the rocky, debris-littered shore of the lake.

Blood trickled hotly down Chilaili's side from deeper injuries her daughter had sustained. Chilaili clicked her beak in agitation, but until they got Sooleawa to shelter, there was little she could do about the wound. Sooleawa was trembling violently by the time they found the cave entrance. It lay half a Tersae length above them, where the ravine wall sloped back under a deep overhang. They climbed a scree-littered slope, then stepped into a dry shelter, out of the wind and rain.

They eased Sooleawa down and Chilaili ran careful hands over her child, searching out the extent of her injuries and peering worriedly at the deep cuts which still oozed beneath Sooleawa's fur. Bessany Weyman rummaged in the carrysack again, removing a number of fathomless items. The alien set up several shiny poles which somehow collapsed into themselves for storage, but when pulled open extended an arm span or more in length. It set the poles up carefully, angling them to its satisfaction and anchoring them against the rocky ground, then fastened to them a large, lightweight sheet of some tough fabric, similar to the silvery blanket, but made of a different substance.

It proved an effective windbreak, keeping out the gusts and occasional drifts of rain that blew into the shelter. A second item sent light flooding into every crack and crevice of their shelter, as bright as the noonday sun, yet Chilaili could feel no appreciable heat radiating from it. A third strange device looked like a squat, squarish lump of metal without any practical use at all, but when the alien fiddled with it, the thing began to glow a dull reddish color and gave off a delicious heat, warming their protected little shelter in an astonishingly short time.

It sat down, then, to watch them. Chilaili had traced the extent of her daughter's cuts and was trying to stanch the bleeding with her hands. The alien rummaged again in its carrysack, then offered a small bundle of whitish cloth which, once unrolled, the alien easily tore into smaller pieces which it used to press against the wounds, halting the flow of blood. It handed Chilaili another little bundle of the stuff, making motions with its hands. Chilaili nodded, unrolling it and winding the filmy stuff around the wound to hold the compresses in place. Sooleawa's eyes had closed. She was trembling, with faint tremors that told Chilaili shock was setting in. Terror took hold of her again, seeing that. Shock could prove just as fatal as drowning.

The instant they had bandaged Sooleawa's various wounds, the alien brought out the silvery blanket again, covering the shivering girl with it, which warmed her even more rapidly than the flameless heating device. The frightening shudders began to ease away. Chilaili hadn't realized she'd been holding her breath until she gulped down a lungful of air in sheer relief. The alien then produced a cup from the carrysack and stepped to the edge of their shelter, leaning out to fill it with clean rainwater, carefully avoiding the muddy spilloff that plunged over the edge of the ravine wall high above them.

A moment later, it knelt at Sooleawa's side and offered the cup to Chilaili, gesturing to the girl's mouth. It was awkwardly shaped, clearly designed for the alien's smaller, soft-edged mouth, but Chilaili found it functional enough when she lifted Sooleawa's head and coaxed her to swallow. "Yes, that's good, most precious one," Chilaili murmured, stroking her child's fur gently, "take a little more, now."

Her daughter finished the water slowly and gazed in wonderment at the alien beside them. It watched them silently through those eerie, water-blue eyes, by far the best feature in its strange, round face. A small protuberance which jutted out from the center must house its nostrils, Chilaili decided at length, watching it breathe. Her own nostrils were part of her beak, but some of the creatures they hunted had separate bumps to breathe through—although she'd never seen any shaped quite like the one on Bessany Weyman's ashpale face. It was a compellingly odd face. The skin stretched and shifted into differing shapes as thoughts passed with lightning rapidity through its eyes, doubtless rendering visible its feelings, if one knew how to read the expressions.

Chilaili wondered what it made of her own face, if it felt as puzzled about how to interpret Chilaili's thoughts as she felt, trying to fathom the alien's. Chilaili had to shift her head back and forth to accurately judge the distance between them, which made trying to understand its alien expressions even more difficult. Those water-blue eyes followed the swing of Chilaili's head with a wrinkle furrowing its upper face. It was uncomfortable, Chilaili realized abruptly, cued as much by the shift in its scent as by the expression on its mobile face, uncomfortable and unused to creatures who shifted their heads more or less continuously to judge depths and distances. She handed back the cup with a low murmur of thanks and tipped her head to one side, gazing one-eyed at the alien, which appeared to reduce its level of discomfort.

Chilaili was startled when the alien parroted back the sound of her thanks. Its mouth wasn't shaped correctly, however, and the word came out hopelessly mangled. After a moment, it pointed to the cup and said a single word. Chilaili spoke it back and the skin of its face stretched upwards, turning the soft-edged mouth upward like a hunting bow.

It's an expression of pleasure, Chilaili realized slowly. It filled the cup again with rainwater, then touched the water inside and said another word. Chilaili repeated it, finding the sounds required of its language far less difficult to pronounce than it found hers. Sooleawa and Chilaili watched, wide-eyed with interest, as the creature touched and named the rocks, the cloth of its portable shelter frame, the flameless heating device, the silvery blanket, even its body coverings in a desperate attempt at communication. Then it gestured to Chilaili and Sooleawa, not separately, but inclusively. Chilaili narrowed her pupils for a moment, trying to understand, then understood the question in a sudden flash of insight. She nodded.

"Tersae," she said, naming their species as a whole. "Chilaili," she said, tapping her chest, and "Sooleawa," touching her daughter's silver-covered shoulder, then she gestured to them both and said, "Tersae."

"Tersae?"

Chilaili nodded, clicking her approval in the base of her throat.

The alien touched itself and said, "Bessany Weyman," then sketched other imaginary figures in the air, tracing the same rough shape as itself, and said, "Humans."

"Humans." The name of its species was as strange as its appearance. Chilaili pointed at the alien. "Bessany Weyman," she said, then sketched rough approximations of others of its kind in the mud at their feet, using one clawtip to scrape the rough pattern of its face and body and head-fur. "Humans."

The alien's face wrinkled again in its expression of pleasure.

Chilaili stepped to the entrance of their little shelter and gestured for the alien to join her. It rose and moved to stand beside her shoulder. It was such a little creature, really not much larger than a half-grown nestling. The top of its head barely reached Chilaili's shoulder. She marveled that its slender limbs and delicate-looking hands had been strong enough to support Sooleawa's weight, carrying the wounded girl up to this cave. As the lightning flared, Chilaili pointed to the trees and said, "Forest." The alien said another word, which

Chilaili repeated. Chilaili then tapped herself, pointed to Sooleawa, and pointed to the forest, moving her hands in a broad circle, trying to convey that they lived in this area. She pointed to the alien, hesitated, then pointed questioningly to the sky. "Humans?"

The creature made a sharp sound and stared up into Chilaili's face.

Then, very slowly, it nodded, copying Chilaili's own head-bobbing gesture. Or perhaps the gesture was one the aliens used, as well? It pointed upwards and said, "Humans, sky." Then it pointed in another direction, off to the east, thankfully in the opposite direction from Icewing Clan's current, summer nest. "Humans," it said, and a word that sounded like *"hohm."*

They had made a nest, then, somewhere to the east.

Chilaili found herself wondering if the Ones Above knew about the arrival of the humans—and if so, what They intended to do about it. Had these aliens come here to build new nests and colonize the Tersae's world? Were there just a few humans or would more arrive? Chilaili felt uneasy posing such questions, particularly since the Ones Above had spoken of devils among the stars, dangerous devils that killed with weapons of great power.

Were the humans such devils, after all? Surely not. Chilaili could not imagine a creature of evil risking its own life to save the trapped and drowning child of another species. A devil would simply have stood on the shore, watching with pleasure as Sooleawa died, possibly even shooting Chilaili down afterward, as she struggled from the water. Chilaili stared down at the slender little alien with a troubled gaze, wanting desperately to know more of these human creatures and why they had come to Chilaili's world.

She made a good start, at least, during Sooleawa's recovery from her brush with death. They stayed with

Bessany Weyman in the little lakeside cave for two full days, giving Sooleawa time to rest from the wounds in her side. While they rested, they learned a surprisingly large number of the human's words—but not nearly enough to ask the questions in Chilaili's heart or to answer those she could see flickering through the alien's luminous eyes. On the morning after Sooleawa's accident, a morning which dawned grey with rain, but without the wind and lightning of the previous night, Bessany Weyman produced a small device from its carrysack, speaking into it. Another, deeper voice answered and a lengthy conversation followed, startling Chilaili enormously. *It's like a tiny Oracle,* she realized with a prickle of awe.

She had considered climbing to the top of the bluff this morning, and sending out a distress call using the low, deep sounds a Tersae huntress in trouble used to call for help, sounds that covered great distances; but Chilaili now found herself wanting to keep the existence of the humans secret from her clan, at least for a while. Why she felt that way, Chilaili couldn't decide, even in her own mind. Certainly, the clan would not be worried about them, yet. Blooding Hunts sometimes took days to complete, as inexperienced huntresses learned the art of the stalk, sometimes blundering through a dozen or more attempted kills before achieving success.

When the alien finished speaking into its tiny Oracle, Chilaili pointed to the device and asked in the human's language, "What is?" then wondered if she would understand the answer.

"Radio," it said slowly.

"*Radio?*" Chilaili copied the strange word.

It nodded.

Chilaili thought about the best way to word her question. "*Radio* is human Oracle?"

It studied her with an expression that—if Chilaili were interpreting it correctly—radiated considerable surprise. "Oracle?" it repeated the word.

Chilaili tried to explain, pointing to the sky. "Oracle. From the Ones Above."

Abstract concepts were almost impossible to convey, with their painfully limited vocabulary. Chilaili pointed to Bessany Weyman's complex tools, pointed to the sky. "From the Ones Above?"

The alien seemed to understand that Chilaili knew these devices had come from the sky, and that somehow, Chilaili had seen something else that had come from the sky, but it didn't look very happy about that fact. The human asked, "What are the 'Ones Above'?"

Chilaili used one claw to sketch the general outline of the Ones Above in the mud. "The Ones Above," she said, pointing from the muddy drawing to the sky again.

It was a crude sketch, very little like the Ones Above, really, but the shape she'd drawn looked nothing like a Tersae and even less like a human. Bessany Weyman stared at it for a long time, then pulled a device from its carrysack and pointed it at the drawing. Chilaili hurriedly erased the marks, worried now, and more than a little afraid. The alien held her gaze for a long moment, then wordlessly put the device away again. It brought out another device instead, similar to the collapsible poles of the shelter frame, only this one opened into a circle at one end, then bent back around to fasten securely. To this, the alien attached a long, almost transparent net of exceedingly fine mesh.

Bessany Weyman gestured for Chilaili to follow, then led the way around the end of the lake, to a deep pool where a shelf of rock made an ideal place for fish to gather. It peered down into the water, which rippled grey-green in the cloudy morning light. Rain pocked and roiled the slate-dark surface. Chilaili could see the warm shapes of fish in the chilly depths, good-sized fish, enough of them to feed Chilaili, her daughter, and the alien. The human studied the fish for several silent moments, then dipped the net swiftly, with a sure movement, and dragged three to the surface. They struggled wildly, but the net was made of strong fiber. The alien scooped them out, killing them neatly with a sharp blow of their heads against the rock. It waited patiently for the remaining fish to lose their fear and regather, then dipped the net twice more, capturing ten fish in total. The human handed half of them to Chilaili.

She accepted with a rumble of thanks in the base of her throat.

They returned to the shelter, where the human proceeded to build an ordinary fire, although it lit the wood with a device as strange as the flameless heater. It then produced a small knife-shaped device and touched a recessed place in its end. The knife began to hum with a strange, very low sound. This, then, was the tool it had used to free Sooleawa from that underwater death trap. The blade was as long as the human's hand—and the alien took great care never to touch that blade with its fingers. It used the humming knife with great skill, gutting all ten fish, stripping off neat little fillets almost completely devoid of bones, then tossed the offal and gristly bones into the water, glancing occasionally at Chilaili as if to check whether or not it had violated some clan taboo with each new activity.

The human cut several short sticks from a nearby shrub, then did something that caused the knife to fall silent. It put away the strange tool and spitted the fillets on the sharpened sticks. Chilaili and her strange new companion held the makeshift roasting spits over the flames and soon the tantalizing scents of hot fish filled their little shelter. Sooleawa sat up, pulling the silvery blanket around her shoulders with a shiver, but ate with fair appetite—a truly hopeful sign.

They shared the meal in silence, but it was a companionable silence, born more of hunger than uneasiness or lack of vocabulary. When the last, flaky morsels had been eaten, they started another language lesson, which carried Chilaili and the human far beyond the shelter, naming everything within sight. The alien tried to convey a sense of grammar and language structure as it strung together words and attempted to communicate the concepts behind those groupings. By nightfall, Chilaili was starting to make progress. By the end of the next day, she was able to speak in crude, somewhat disjointed sentences, although somewhat seriously limited in scope and topic. That second night, she taught Sooleawa everything the human had taught her during the day. Her daughter carefully repeated back the words, glancing at Bessany Weyman to confirm that she'd said them correctly. The alien wrinkled its face in the pleasure expression again and again, saying, "Yes" and "Good" many times.

On the third morning, when it was clear Sooleawa would be able to travel again, their unlikely companion packed up its carrysack and made ready to return to its nest. The human actually invited them, with gestures and words, to accompany it. "You come my home, Chilaili, Sooleawa. You come, much happy."

Chilaili and Sooleawa exchanged a long glance, then Sooleawa said, "I would like to *see* the human nest, at least, Respected Mother. I want to know more about these creatures I owe my life to. If you think it safe?"

Given what it had done for them already, Chilaili couldn't imagine the human deliberately doing anything to harm them. And Chilaili, too, was curious. Moreover, as Icewing Clan's *katori*, it was her responsibility to learn everything she could about these newcomers, to protect the clan as best she could. So they went with the alien, walking for three full days through broken country where deep gullies and ravines slashed unpredictably through miles of forest. Stands of thick-boled conifers showed like dark streams flowing through the vast, pale-green seas of broad-leafed trees that predominated where soil and rainfall allowed them to thrive. When winter came, the broad, water-rich leaves would turn crimson and brilliant gold, then fall in a brightly colored rain, leaving the dark-needled conifers to rule the eleven long months of darkness, snow, and ice. Come winter, every other living plant would go deep into hibernation or die back to roots and seed pods.

Scattered here and there, in sheltered valleys and white-water gorges, rushing plumes of water shot out across the ragged, jagged lips of stone, falling with a perpetual misting spray. Tree ferns swayed like graceful girls and broad-spined, prickly *akrati* fronds rattled like whole nestfuls of warlike boys caught up in late summer's courtship dance. By winter, these gorges would be solid ice, fantastical sculptures of it, where waterfalls froze, locking away the tree ferns and the prickly *akrati* in a coating of solid ice up to a handsbreadth thick. Winter turned such gorges into a breathtaking wonderland—where one tiny misstep could leave a body crushed under cracked and falling tons of ice and snapped-off trees or impaled on ice swords and thorny protrusions where *akrati* fronds jutted out with six-foot-long points of ice.

Winter on Chilaili's homeworld had five hundred brutal ways to kill the unwary, the careless, the poorly trained. Chilaili worried about the humans. This world did not forgive ignorance or poor judgment or even one moment of inattention. When the deep cold came—all eleven, bitter, long moons of it—even native animals were pushed hard to the ragged edge of survival. The clans always lost heavily over the winters: the old ones, those who fell ill or suffered some other weakness or infirmity, the unlucky huntresses who came back maimed, if at all. How could the humans, complete strangers to winter's treacheries, possibly hope to survive, even with their magical tools?

Chilaili and her companions finally reached the edge of a large valley which Chilaili had seen before, only too many times. She stared, horrified. The humans could scarcely have chosen a more dangerous place to build, a fact she did not yet know enough vocabulary to convey. Sooleawa tipped her head to peer up at Chilaili, having caught scent of Chilaili's sudden, acute worry.

"What is it, Mother?" she asked in a low whisper while the human forged on ahead, greatly excited now. "Do you know this place?"

Chilaili turned her gaze from the long, knife-blade gouge in the ground and met her daughter's troubled eyes. "Oh, yes," she murmured in their own tongue, "I know a great deal of this place."

A long, steep-walled gorge snaked away through the badlands of cliffs and broken fissures, topped with its fringe of forest like a heavy green beard. A sparkling clear lake drowned the far end of the valley, born of the meltoff pouring down from an immense glacier that towered above. Calving ice thundered down each spring in an avalanche of debris that spilled into the far end of the lake and set its pristine waters to sloshing. The humans' hard-walled nest stood within a spear's throw of the lake. High above, water exploded in freshets and gushes, leaping down across the face of the glacier and roaring through the narrow upper fissure where this particular gorge was born.

In winter, that water would freeze across the whole

top of the fissure, leaving a natural ice bridge spanning the top of the valley. It was a favorite spot for
males to taunt one another for their bravery. *Walk the
ice bridge . . .* the males goaded, gulping down fermented *yacto* juice to heat their blood and dull cau-
tionary reason. *If you're really a man, you'll walk the
ice bridge . . .*

Nor was it just the appalling ease of falling to one's
death that made this place so deadly. An insane,
whipping whirl of wind blasted down off the glacier
to meet the warmer, moister air rising from the forest, particularly from the lush growth down in the protected gorge itself, creating dangerous twist-winds. Even
after the forest had dropped its leaves, there would still
be heat to stir up the troubled air, for a ring of fire
mountains girdled this whole area, active volcanoes that
spewed plumes of heat and smoke into the air and set
the hot springs simmering like so many cookpots.

Weather in this gorge, when winter set cruel fangs
into the land, was without doubt the most interesting
anywhere in the whole of Icewing Clan's vast range.
She wondered why the humans, who showed such
sharp intelligence in other ways, had chosen so dreadfully in building their new nest? Maybe they *were* an
afflicted species of devils, as the Ones Above insisted.
Whatever the reason for it, unless they possessed tools
of tremendous power indeed, they were likely to find
their first winter here full of lethal surprises.

Sooleawa whispered, "Is this valley taboo, Mother?
Is that why you stare so strangely?"

Chilaili roused herself with difficulty. "No . . ." She
sighed. "No, it is not taboo. Perhaps it should be. I've
helped bury too many fools who fell from the ice
bridge that forms each winter, there at the foot of the
glacier." A hideous task it was, too, scraping up the
spattered mess that was left after falling more than two

hundred feet onto a jagged ice field. She'd also treated shattered limbs and deep puncture wounds sustained by those who'd managed to stop the fatal slide off the edge, but only at the sacrifice of crushed arms, shattered legs, and splintered ribs that drove spikes of bone through lung tissue. She wasn't sure which was worse, fast and messy death below the ice bridge or slow death from choking on blood and the pneumonia sickness. . . .

The most surprising thing Chilaili saw, however, more shocking than the hard-walled structures of the alien nest, was a gently sloping stone incline which rose from the valley floor to the very spot where the three of them had emerged from the forest. The incline looped back on itself multiple times as it climbed up more than two hundred feet of cliff face. The rock looked as though it had been shaped, cut by some immense knife. Chilaili shivered involuntarily. Given what she'd seen of this human's miraculous belt knife, these creatures *might* use machines to cut solid stone as easily as Chilaili could split a softened, overripe fruit.

Down in the valley, itself, the humans had cleared a wide swath of trees, providing a broad, flattened area for the hard-walled nest. Part of that flattened area glinted whitely in the sunlight. The humans had laid down a slab of something hard, for an unfathomable reason. A collection of strangely shaped huts, made from some other hard substance, sat nearby. Chilaili hoped those huts were as strong as they looked. They were too small and too few in number to house very many of the humans. Strange objects sat beside the huts, while larger objects rested on the edges of the flat, white thing, their uses well beyond Chilaili's ability to determine.

When she spotted other humans in the distance, perhaps a dozen of them, Chilaili realized in some surprise that they came in two startlingly different shapes. There were several smallish ones like Bessany Weyman, with flared hips and chest bulges, but there were taller, broader ones as well, with flat chests and hips that did not flare at all, but dropped straight from their long torsos. Males and females, Chilaili guessed, trying to puzzle out which were which through the aliens' behavior toward one another. She could discern no apparent system of rankings or subservience, however, which frustrated her. If they followed the Tersae's pattern, the males would be larger and heavier, but with creatures from the stars, who could say whether or not that pattern would hold true?

As they watched, a dark shape in the air, tiny with distance, came arrowing in rapidly. As it came racing nearer, Chilaili realized it was too large and moved too swiftly to be any kind of bird. It approached the human nest, slowed, then settled gently down to land on the broad, white slab. It came to a rolling halt near one edge. A shiny door made of some type of metal opened in its side and a human climbed out, closing the door behind itself before jogging across the ground to join the other humans. The flying machine sat near others very similar to it, five of them, in total.

Chilaili's fur prickled, gazing down at them. How far could a human travel in such a device? Given that thing's speed, it could probably reach the hunting grounds of even the most distant clans with ease—and probably could find her summer nest within a few hours. Chilaili repressed a shiver and glanced at her daughter, who was staring in rapt fascination at the human nest and its multiple wonders. When Bessany Weyman tried to urge Chilaili and Sooleawa out into the open, to follow the alien down the sloping incline to the human nest, Chilaili quietly refused.

"No," she said firmly, using the human word. "Chilaili, Sooleawa no walk."

The human tilted its head to look up into Chilaili's nearest eye. "Home?" it asked, glancing toward the forest.

"Home," Chilaili agreed.

"I come?" it asked.

Chilaili hesitated.

"I come cave? You come cave? We talk?"

Chilaili nodded. "Yes. Cave. We talk." She pointed to the sun, made an arc over her head to symbolize the sun's path across the sky, then made four more arcs to represent five days. "You come, I come, Sooleawa come. Five sun."

Bessany Weyman sketched five arcs across the sky. "Five suns? Five days?"

"Yes. Five suns. Five days. Cave. You, not humans." She pointed toward the human nest.

Bessany Weyman nodded, although the human did not look happy about the stipulation to come alone. Those luminous blue eyes studied Chilaili and Sooleawa in turn, then the human said a word that must have been a farewell, for it turned away immediately afterward, hiking down toward its nest. It moved quickly, clearly eager to be among its own kind, again. They watched the human reach the valley floor, watched it disappear into the trees between the stone incline and the hard-walled nest, watched curiously as Bessany Weyman emerged on the other side of the trees and rejoined her own kind. The excited welcome spread as other humans came running from the hard-walled huts. From the way the others treated Bessany Weyman, it was clear that their human was held in high esteem by its fellow creatures.

"It is *tiponi*, among them," Sooleawa murmured. *Child of importance.*

True, the human was scarcely larger than a half-grown child, although clearly an adult among its own kind. The word *tiponi* was usually reserved for the heirs of a clan's leaders, yet it seemed to fit this alien who was treated with obvious respect and deference by its fellows. "Yes, perhaps it is," Chilaili agreed softly. "Come, Sooleawa, they have turned their attention toward us."

The humans were staring up toward the treeline where Chilaili and Sooleawa stood. While Chilaili and her daughter had been careful to hide in the shadows of the nearest trees, they might well be visible to whatever powerful tools such creatures could make. So they melted back into the forest, moving swiftly, now, and put a great deal of distance between themselves and the human nest. Chilaili led the way, taking them along a circuitous, snaking path that would add a hand of days to their journey home, but might serve to confuse any human who tried to follow.

Chilaili later determined that no human had attempted to trail them.

And five days after they left the human at her home nest, Bessany Weyman had come alone to the little cave, as promised. For three full cycles of the moons, Chilaili and Sooleawa had met secretly with the human, determined to learn more of the strangers from the stars. Unlike the Ones Above, who had never actually shown their faces to Chilaili's little clan, sending only flat likenesses to be revered and speaking only through the Oracles, *Tiponi* Weyman had walked freely with them, trying to understand Chilaili's language, trying to understand what they believed and why they did things in the ways they did them.

Bessany Weyman had taught Chilaili much about the humans in the process. There was a great deal to admire, as well as fear. The human acted with honor and clearly respected Chilaili. Not once had the human made Chilaili feel inferior, despite the enormous gulf between Chilaili's knowledge and primitive tools and the human's almost magical ones. *Tiponi* Weyman treated Chilaili as a valued friend, one who respected Chilaili's thoughts and sought her opinions.

And now the Ones Above had ordered Chilaili to destroy every human in the world.

Chilaili blinked at the Council fire, then met the gaze of Great-Grandmother Anevay once more. Anevay—and the rest of Icewing Clan—waited for her to speak, to explain herself and her insistence that this war with the humans was not only a disaster, but unnecessary. She glanced into the eyes of every Grandmother on the council, met the *viho*'s gaze and the *akule*'s, knew that the Oracle Kestejoo served would be listening, weighing, judging. Speak aloud where the machine left by the Ones Above could hear her treasonous, heretical arguments? She suppressed a shudder.

Choosing her words with great care, she said, "As *katori* to Icewing Clan, it is my sacred duty to protect our people, to guide the clan when we must make important decisions that affect our health, our very survival. The humans are powerful creatures, able to make and use tools far beyond our comprehension. They rival the Ones Above who created all the true Tersae there are in this world—"

"No one doubts the humans' cleverness in making weapons that kill effectively," the *akule* interrupted, earnestly. "Of course they can. They are devils. Murderous fiends sent to destroy us. You know how deeply I love Icewing Clan, Chilaili, what I gave up to come here. Can anyone in this clan doubt my loyalty, my sincerity?"

Not even Chilaili could argue that.

Kestejoo had given up his home and blood kin for Zaltana and for Icewing Clan. When season after season passed, producing neither daughters nor sons—which left the clan without an heir to become Speaker for the Oracle—Kestejoo had learned all the rituals of Zaltana's office as *akule*. During the long months of her final illness, he had not left her side even to sleep and eat, grieving and vowing to accept the mantle of *akule*.

He had been zealous in his work, after Zaltana's death.

Too zealous, perhaps.

He took a single step forward, holding out one hand toward Chilaili, and his voice rang with the power of profound belief. "We must fight these demons from the stars. We must fight with every ounce of our strength, our determination, our courage. And yes, if necessary, our warriors must fight to the death. Such monsters cannot be allowed to draw breath under our sun. If we do not destroy them or at least drive them back to the stars, they will hunt us down and kill us all, to the last unborn hatchling still in its eggshell!"

"If we make enemies of such creatures," Chilaili snapped, "we do so at our own peril! If we attack, as the Ones Above demand, the humans' tools are quite capable of killing the clans by the thousands. There are not so many of us, anywhere in the world, that we can sustain such losses. If Icewing Clan, at least, does not make war, if we remain safely hidden in our winter nest and keep them ignorant of our presence, the humans will have no reason to attack us."

Worried murmurs buzzed like summer insects.

The war leader shook his grizzled head. "No, Chilaili, you are wrong." Yiska's voice was a low rumble, startling to hear at the Council fire, since Yiska usually remained silent, merely carrying out the will of the Grandmothers and Huntresses. "The Ones Above have warned us. The human devils can locate us by any open show of fire or heat against the snow, even the heat of our bodies. They can track us through the magical power of our Oracles, if we use them while the humans still possess their weapons. Do you really think we can remain hidden from them? No. They would find and kill us, so we must—"

"*The Ones Above are killing us already!* Must we rush to finish it by *suiciding?*"

Shocked silence fell.

Even the *akule* trembled. "Chilaili! Th-that's *blasphemy!*"

"Is it blasphemy to speak what every Mother and Grandmother of every clan already knows?" Chilaili demanded. "If so, then our entire race is guilty of it! What can you, a *male*, possibly know of such matters?"

Kestejoo's pupils dilated for one long, thunderstruck moment. Then naked hurt throbbed in his eyes, causing Chilaili to clamp her beak tightly, wishing she could take back the harsh words. Chilaili had often wondered if the Ones Above had been responsible, somehow, for that terrible lack of hatchlings at Kestejoo and Zaltana's hearth. Once, as recently as three turnings of the moons ago, Chilaili would have accepted such a cruel dictate as natural and right. But the time she had spent with Bessany Weyman had made Chilaili doubt many things.

Huntress Alsoomse rose to her feet, bowing deferentially to the Council members. "I would add my voice to Chilaili's."

Great-Grandmother Anevay nodded.

"I have traveled far," Alsoomse said quietly, "trading with distant clans, with my mate and often my older sons at my side to protect me. I have spoken to many Mothers and Grandmothers about such matters. I have risked much to learn what we desperately need to know. As dangerous as our own situation is, things are far worse in the other clans. Mothers and Grandmothers elsewhere hold no power, as we Huntresses do. They must bow to the dictates of their clan lords—even in matters of the eggs. Even so, the Mothers and Grandmothers of *all* the clans are whispering rebellion, for we all feel the same anger and terror. The Ones Above *are* destroying us."

The *akule* turned a shocked, disapproving glare on Alsoomse. The Huntress ducked her head unhappily, but she did not back down. "I am sorry, *akule*, but I will not deny what I have seen and heard, no matter what you tell us the Oracle has said. Chilaili speaks the truth. Mothers and Grandmothers everywhere are saying it. The blessing chambers, in which we have been so strictly commanded to place our eggs, do *not* bring blessings. They bring death. The chambers leave our eggs changed, *akule*, not just Icewing's, but the eggs of *all* the clans, with damage so visible, even Grand-mothers with no say in their own clans' affairs have begun to hold back eggs, refusing to put all of them into the blessing chambers."

Kestejoo stared at Alsoomse in horror. "You dare—?"

"Yes, we dare!" an aging, grey-furred Grandmother snarled, coming angrily to her feet. "The eggs which are destined to become male show the greatest dam-age! I have watched for years as our young males have changed—and never for the better. The shells of eggs that hatch out male come out of the blessing cham-bers riddled with tiny holes—and each new male hatched from such eggs is more hot-tempered, more eager to die than the ones before him! They are far more violent than males hatched from eggs hidden away to mature naturally. We fear for the future of our race, *akule*. The Ones Above are doing something to us, to our males, and what they are doing brings noth-ing but death!"

Great-Grandmother Anevay hissed softly. "Then it is not my imagination, about the younger males? I have worried that perhaps I had forgotten what it was like when my mate was young."

Chilaili's precious daughter, Sooleawa, shook her head, the silver patches on her fur ruddy from the Council Cavern's fire. "No, Respected Great-Grandmother, you have not forgotten. I am the youngest Huntress in this circle and I have watched my nestmates closely these past fifteen years. My youngest brothers are far more violent and dangerous than my oldest ones. It troubles me, as well, that I am the only female born to my mother's nest. Ten nestmates I have, *all* male—and two of them were killed by their own brothers. How many other bloodlines can claim more than one female breaking shell? How many have lost sons to other sons? I will not put my eggs in the blessing chambers, Respected Great-Grandmother, for I desire daughters to hunt at my side and I refuse to watch my sons murder one another senselessly. I fear for the future of our race. If all the males seek nothing but crazy battles without purpose, fighting and killing one another, destroying their wiser fathers in challenge after challenge, who will be left to make us fertile? And the death toll in this new war will be disastrous. Even you, *akule*, have admitted this."

Several Huntresses nodded agreement, sending a low murmur through the assembly.

"The Ones Above insist on calling the humans devils," Sooleawa said quietly. "I am not so sure of that. The humans have been among us for many moons without once using their weapons against us. Would devils intent on destroying us sit quietly for cycle after cycle of the moons? They did nothing against us until we attacked them and now they are destroying the clans, using weapons the Ones Above would be hard-pressed to duplicate. And the fighting has gone on for only a handful of days! The clans cannot sustain the loss. It will be years before some of our clans recover— if they ever do. I am a newly blooded Huntress, *akule*, and I would very much like to take a mate before all the males are dead, fighting a war we cannot win!"

She ducked her head at that, clicking her beak in agitation for the blasphemy.

Chilaili stroked her daughter's soft fur, gentling her. "No, do not apologize for having spoken the truth, Sooleawa," she said quietly. "It is one thing to serve Those who made us, in gratitude for our making. It is quite another to die for them, to the last poisoned chick, when the creatures they would have us fight are virtually the equals of the Ones Above." She held up her hands, clawtips glinting in the firelight. "We hunt with these, and with spears and knives and bows. Do you think any Huntress at this Council fire doesn't understand how primitive our best weapons are, compared with the *least* weapons of the Ones Above? Or those of the humans?"

A low murmur of assent rippled through the gathered Huntresses.

The *akule*, tone almost pleading, said, "When the command to fight came, the Ones Above promised to send greater and greater weapons to carry on the fight, weapons more powerful than any the human devils possess."

"More weapons?" Chilaili countered sharply. "Yes, I can well believe the Ones Above are willing to give us more weapons. But they do not show themselves, for all their wondrous skill in crafting such things. I want to know why, *akule*, it is left to *us* to fight and die, when the Ones Above are so much more capable than we of carrying out such battles? They sit safely in their nests among the stars and the moons, their claws bloodless. Why don't they fight these devils, if the humans are truly so deadly?"

It was the wrong thing to say; Chilaili knew it the instant the words exploded past her beak. But she could not unsay them and she knew, in her very bones, that they were nothing but naked truth. The *akule* cried, "Chilaili! The Ones Above send us to battle to test our worthiness! Everyone knows this! It is the way things have always been. It is part of the great plan for our race—"

"Proving our worthiness by destroying ourselves? That aids no one! Ourselves, least of all." At the stir of fright that shivered through the gathering, beaks clicking softly in agitation like branches in the wind, Chilaili gentled her voice. "I am *katori*. My own Grandmother's Great-Grandmother passed down the story of the grand plan, to see which clan's ways will prove strongest, most viable. Icewing Clan is the only one in all the world ruled by Mothers and Grandmothers. While our Daughters and Mothers hunt far from the nest, our bigger and stronger males remain behind to guard the nest against all predators. Even against the males of other clans. The Grandmothers watch the hatchlings and make all critical decisions while the Grandfathers incubate the eggs. Because this is so, ours may well be the *only* clan of the Tersae capable of saving our race."

"How is that?" a young huntress across the Council fire asked in puzzled tones.

"Because," Chilaili said very gently, "in our clan, Grandmothers choose which males to breed with which females to strengthen the bloodlines. They are wise enough to select carefully for intelligence, for speed and endurance, skill of dexterity and resistance to illness, all the critical factors that mean survival for a clan—or death, if the choices made are poor ones."

Great-Grandmother Anevay spoke again. "I have worried about this very thing, for the clans we trade with most often have gone dangerously unstable. The males now making decisions think of nothing but food in their bellies and weapons in their enemies' entrails. There is much merit in your words, Chilaili, although they disturb me more than I would like to admit."

Chilaili bowed her head. "Your wisdom has guided us for many years, Great-Grandmother Anevay. And these are disturbing things to face, deeply disturbing decisions we are forced to make. We argue issues tonight that will be the death of our clan—perhaps the death of *all* the clans—if we decide wrongly."

The *akule* broke silence, at that. "You are more right than you begin to guess, Chilaili," he said, voice heavy with fear as he rolled one eye toward the cavern where the Oracle rested, the small cavern Kestejoo and his mate had shared for so many hatchless winters. "What you have forgotten—what *all* of you have forgotten—is the solemn warning we live under. The Ones Above demand obedience. Anything less is punished—severely and irrevocably. We all agree the weapons they have given us are terrifying. But you, Chilaili, have forgotten that the Ones Above can turn those weapons on *us* as easily and swiftly as young hotheads issue challenge."

A profound silence fell across the entire, assembled clan. The Council fire crackled ominously, portent of worse fires to come. Chilaili shivered. The fur along her spine crawled. She could make no answer to the *akule*'s words, for there was no answer *any* Tersae could make. The Ones Above had created them. They could just as easily destroy.

Very softly, Chilaili said, "The *akule* speaks the truth in this. To our shame, we are helpless before them, helpless as unhatched nestlings. I believe attacking the human nests is profoundly wrong and more dangerous than any of you can understand. But I cannot deny the threat the Ones Above hold over us. Decide amongst yourselves what you feel is best. I will abide by the Council's edicts."

Rebellion surged in her heart, but there was nothing she could do.

The vote did not take long.

Within the hour, the warriors were packing joyously, bringing weapons out of storage, spears and swords and carefully cached weapons from the Ones Above, stored years previously in the deepest caverns of their permanent winter nest. The clan had held them for generations against future emergency, such as this current crisis. Yiska glanced at Chilaili from time to time, his expression troubled, but the Council had made its decision and he would never disobey a direct order from the Grandmothers. The younger males sang as they worked, for once not bickering and fighting amongst themselves. Ancient Grandfathers incubating eggs not yet due for another round in the blessing chambers watched with sad and dreaming eyes as others claimed the honor of battle.

"The warriors will form one war party to attack the large human nest three days' travel away," Yiska was saying. "We will bypass—for now—the smaller, closer nest. The two attacks must occur simultaneously or the nests will reinforce each other. That would make victory far more costly. The huntresses will attack the smaller nest, since we do not have enough warriors to attack both at once. The warriors must travel three times the distance, so they will leave first. The huntresses will set out two days after they leave, to time the attacks properly. We will strike both nests at dawn of the fourth day."

Chilaili felt ill, listening. To send the clan's huntresses to war was a decision lost in utter folly—and should have been a powerful argument against attacking at all. But when the Ones Above dictated the rules, logic flew out of the cavern on crippled wings. She watched her sons chanting war songs with glee in their eyes and a joyous spring in their steps, and hated her clan's helplessness.

And she hated the Ones Above. Their makers had—according to the oldest of the *akule*'s teaching stories—raised them up from the nests of flightless, clever beasts that still roamed the deep forests. Had taken them in as pets and playthings, had doctored them with machines and with substances Chilaili would never even be able to pronounce, let alone comprehend. Then, having created them and given them language and understanding, they had taken their pets and placed them back down in the forests and set them at one another's throats, with pretty-sounding laws to live by—laws that kept the clans fighting one another without ever quite allowing the males the dreamed-of joy of ripping and rending everything in their paths.

With the humans, no such restrictions existed.

The males were now in the only version of heaven they were ever likely to know firsthand. How the Ones Above must laugh at the blind, stupid, battle-mad Tersae, the fools down in the dung and the dead leaves and the blood, obediently—joyously—dying for their creators. Chilaili watched sons she had loved to distraction singing and laughing on their way to slaughter and knew she had to do *something* besides sit like a feeble Grandmother in the shadowed corner of her living cavern. The semiprivate chamber reserved for the *katori* had never seemed so lonely, not even in the aftermath of losing her beloved mate, killed in a mindless challenge. She watched with growing despair as the little ones played amongst the star-weapons.

It is our future the Ones Above are stealing, she realized bleakly. *We are toys to them, to chuckle over during conversation around an evening's cookfire.* Did the Ones Above even have cookfires? *They created us, but why? They care nothing about us. Our welfare, our anguish, what brings us joy through the wheel of the year means as little to them as a rotting log in the forest means to me.* Less, perhaps. A rotting log at least provided an abundance of edible and medicinal fungi.

A stray blast of wind set the fires to dancing, sending sparks toward the cavern ceiling with a whoosh and a roar—and the thought that came whispering in from the night with it set Chilaili's beak to chattering. *I do not want to worship creatures whose only desire is to see how well we die. I want friendship with those who delight in living.*

Chilaili came to her feet, grief and indecision falling away in one blinding, clear-sighted instant, one that turned her entire world upside down. There were, indeed, devils among the stars. They had created Chilaili's race. She moved purposefully through her living cavern, filled by a great calm she could not explain, particularly as she should have been shaking with mortal terror. She prepared her hunting pack, slung it onto her back, strapped on her weapons belt, donned heavy furs usually reserved for the deepest cold of winter, and considered whether or not to take the snow-webs. No, she decided, *if I try to walk in heavy wind with snow-webs strapped to my feet, the wind will catch them and I will break a leg. Or both of them.* Regretfully, she left them in their place against the wall.

Chilaili covered the pack and weapons belt with the sacred *katori* robe, handed from mother to daughter for generations. The small oil lamp in one corner cast terrifying shadows on the walls, for the *katori* ceremonial cloak, massively decorated for *katori* ritual work, carried a misshapen profile. It turned the wearer into an awe-inspiring apparition, one with great power to intercede with spirits and unseen forces. Chilaili still remembered her own fright as a new hatchling whenever her mother had donned it for some new ceremony. Chilaili understood very well its impact on an uninitiated Tersae's mind. Tonight, she was counting on it.

It did wonders to disguise the hunting pack and weapons belt beneath it.

Satisfied, Chilaili turned to leave her semiprivate living cavern, only to find Sooleawa standing in the entrance. Her daughter's eyes glittered in the lamplight.

"Respected Mother."

Chilaili's heart thundered painfully for a long moment. "Cherished Daughter?"

"I—" Sooleawa hesitated, glanced into the raucous Council Cavern. Then she said in a low voice, "I would accompany you on this holy ritual. I, too, must learn all the teachings of the *katori.*"

The rebellion in Sooleawa's eyes flashed an unmistakable warning. Chilaili reached for words of persuasion, rather than a direct and confrontational order that Sooleawa would probably disregard, given the enormity of the girl's life-debt. "You are old enough to know, Sooleawa, what I am about, this night. You are more precious to me than life itself. I will not rob you of your birthright and refuse you the right to go with me, but do so, child, with your eyes open and your claws sharp. It is dangerous ground I tread, far more dangerous than the fury of the blizzard I must walk through. If you go, there is a very terrible chance our bloodline will die out, in the female line. I need you here, Sooleawa—"

"To cower like a frightened child with the old ones and the newly hatched?"

She held her daughter's angry gaze until Sooleawa

dipped her head in shame. "Forgive me, Respected Mother."

Chilaili gentled her voice. "When I have gone, yours will be the only voice of reason left to advise the Grandmothers. You and I are the only Tersae in all the world who have walked with humans and learned their tongue. If the battles go as disastrously as I believe they will, yours may be the only voice left to judge what the humans might do in retaliation. I need you to stay, Daughter, far more than I need your support in the task I have set myself. And if I do not return, the clan must still have a *katori*."

Her precious daughter chittered softly, a sound of deep distress. So young, to face such a decision. Yet she was little older than Chilaili herself had been, when the *katori* mantle had fallen so unexpectedly onto her own shoulders with her mother's untimely death. Sooleawa gulped air several times, then whispered, "I will obey your greater wisdom, honored *katori*. But . . ." Her voice shattered like a very young child's. "Please, Mother, *be careful!*"

Chilaili hugged her trembling daughter close, smoothed her ruffled fur gently. "Hush, most precious one. What must come will come and we will meet it bravely, yes?"

Her daughter looked up, tilting her head to gaze one-eyed up into Chilaili's face.

"Be careful?"

"Always." Chilaili held back a sigh and touched her daughter's face with one gentle hand, then headed swiftly through the bustling Council Cavern. Wide, shocked stares followed her progress. Even warriors hurried to step out of her way as she stalked past cookfires and piles of weapons. Her misshapen shadow danced across the fur of the little ones, who stared open-beaked at the *katori* in full ceremonial garb. A few of the Grandmothers—and Yiska—furrowed their brows in puzzlement, but remained silent. She was deeply thankful for that, since a single question would have endangered her plans before she could implement them. Perhaps they were merely granting her the right to die in the manner of her own choosing, rather than waiting to die with the other huntresses?

At the entrance to the Council Cavern, Chilaili pushed aside the woven screen lashed to a framework set snugly across the rocky opening and stepped out into a slashing wind. Driven snow stung her face. As bad as the wind was in the narrow ravine where their winter nest lay, it would be far worse in the forest above. She drew a fur hood around her face for added protection and was about to step into the howling storm when the *akule* appeared. He had been standing behind a huge tree close to the cavern entrance. His body pulsed with the colors of heat against the icy tones of the dark storm beyond.

"Where are you going?" Kestejoo asked, voice sharp with alarm.

"What are you doing outside the cavern?"

"Trying to get a feel for the storm, to predict when it might pass over us and allow us to march against the humans."

Chilaili grunted. Kestejoo's weather wisdom was legendary. His mother, it was said, had been Snowclaw Clan's *yepa*—their snow woman—scenting the weather to protect the entire clan. Kestejoo had saved Icewing Clan more than once from killer storms, including deluges of rain that sparked flash floods through narrow gorges and the first blizzards of winter, which sometimes struck weeks too early, catching a clan still busy at the harvest.

"What do your senses tell you, Kestejoo?" she asked quietly.

"Two days, at most," he said, cocking his head sideways as though listening to something only he could hear. "Two days and we can set out in clear weather. The worst of it has passed. But why are you out in such weather, Chilaili? You're wearing hunting furs beneath the *katori* cloak. I don't understand."

He had little reason to suspect the truth, since he didn't know of her liaisons with the human. Or did he? She narrowed her pupils thoughtfully, but there was no suspicion, no guile in his eyes, only puzzlement. Very well. Without evidence, she would give the gentle-souled *akule* the benefit of the doubt.

"You have declared *altsoba*, the all-war that sends every fighting adult into battle, jeopardizing the entire clan's future. I must protect their souls with the proper holy rites. The Oracle may transmit the will of the Ones Above, but it knows nothing of the rituals my foremothers have used to keep the clan safe and prosperous for as long as there have been Tersae in the world."

"But Chilaili—the storm! Can't the rituals wait for clear weather?"

She shook her head. "They require a prescribed number of days in fasting, to prepare for the vision quest that will bring the help of powerful spirits, the animals and the winds and the waters, the spirits who guide the newly dead into the afterlife. It is exacting, exhausting ritual work. If the storm clears in only two days, there will barely be enough time."

Worry darkened Kestejoo's eyes. "Will you at least be able to perform the ritual in a safe shelter?" he asked as they shivered in an icy blast of wind. "I can arrange an escort to see you there."

Chilaili shook her head. "Thank you, Kestejoo, but I must not reveal the location of the holy cavern. It is too sacred a place to profane it, even by those who mean only the best."

Regret passed visibly through his eyes. "Then you must risk it. May the Ones Above watch over you, Chilaili."

She repressed a shudder. That was exactly what terrified her most. She took perverse comfort in the brutal force of the storm. No matter how powerful their tools, Chilaili simply could not believe even the Ones Above would see her crawling along the ground through a savage blizzard.

She thanked Kestejoo for his concern, then murmured, "May the ancestors watch over you" and moved rapidly into the howling swirl of snow. When Chilaili glanced back, the *akule* was leaning against the tree, watching her go. The colored bands of heat that pulsed the length of his long frame shuddered in the jerky patterns of fright and cold against the darkness of the cliff. There was something profoundly pathetic about him, huddled against the tree, watching her go—perhaps to her death—believing as gospel truth everything the Oracle said. Perhaps after Zaltana's death, he'd had nothing else to believe in?

Moving in grim silence, Chilaili stalked away into the darkness, pausing to slip off her ceremonial cloak at the bottom of the path leading up to the wind-blasted forest. She folded the cloak carefully and stuffed it into her hunting pack. Now that it had served its purpose, hiding her weapons belt—which she would not have needed merely to conduct a holy ritual—she could not afford to hamper her movements. As soon as it was safely stowed, Chilaili climbed up the narrow trail and moved cautiously out through the driven snow.

The way to *Tiponi* Weyman's nest lay in the direction the wind was blowing, at least, so the worst of the blizzard would be at her back. If she'd had to struggle into the teeth of the storm, she might not have set out at all. One other factor gave her hope of success. Their winter nest lay less than a full day's walk from the humans' nest. With luck and caution, she might make it.

She refused to dwell on the whisper at the back of her mind that the humans now believed all Tersae to be their deadly enemies. That did not matter, could not be allowed to matter. Chilaili must warn *Tiponi* Weyman of the coming attack, would plead with the human to return to the safety of the stars before it was too late. Chilaili's life-debt *would* be repaid.

One way or another.

Chapter Four

Eight days into the first howling blizzard of the winter season, Bessany Weyman was convinced the Thule Research Expedition—of which she was a charter member—had made a dreadful mistake. As the wind shook Eisenbrucke Station's solid plascrete walls, Bessany glared across the rec-room table at Ed Parker, resident meteorologist.

"Tell me again, Ed. Why did we pick this horrible spot to build a research station?"

Mutters of agreement from the other scientists and technicians riding out the blizzard met Bessany's dour question, but Ed Parker just grinned. "Ain't it great?" Parker enthused, waving an expansive hand toward the ceiling. "The weather in this place is *amazing*. Simply amazing!"

Down the table, Elin Olsson glared at him. "That's not the word *I'd* have chosen." The petite blonde who served as the team's geologist was only three quarters the size of the burly meteorologist, but what she lacked in mass she made up for in sheer force of will. Bessany had seen Elin Olsson face down surly stevedores in backwater spaceports and leave them mumbling apologies. Ed Parker, however, was apparently immune to any forces of nature other than those related to wind speed and cloud formation.

"Mmm . . ." Parker smiled, "who was it said this spot was a geological treasure trove? Volcanic mountains to the south, an upthrust-fault mountain range to the north, complete with resident glacier that's got most of Thule's geologic history trapped in its ice layers? And a fissured basalt flow right next door, covering an ancient limestone seabed?"

Elin waved a dismissive hand. "I never said it wasn't a good research spot, Ed. The geological processes are fascinating. But I would not call that" —she jabbed a finger toward the ceiling— "amazing weather. Homicidal, maybe."

Parker chuckled. "Weather can't be homicidal, Elin, it's not sentient."

"Are you sure?" the geologist muttered.

Chuckles ran through the rec room, mingling with the clink of coffee cups and forks against plates. Bessany toyed with the last few crumbs of pie on her own plate, blessing whatever guiding angel had induced their provisions clerk to include a generous supply of desserts with the more prosaic rations usual in a facility like this one. Comfort foods became astonishingly important when a blizzard kept everyone confined to quarters day after monotonous day.

Elin sipped her coffee. "Anyway, I'm starting to agree with Bessany about this site. The planetary scouts who recommended it ought to have their licenses revoked."

Herve Sinclair, the expedition's project director, dunked a cookie into his hot chocolate and said mildly, "Winter's bad everywhere on Thule. Even the equatorial belt turns cold enough to cause a general dieback of the rainforest. Where should we have built? Underground? With as much seismic activity as Thule generates in an average month?"

One of the equipment mechanics muttered, "Aboveground or belowground, Thule's gonna getcha, ain't it? At least we got the aircars into the hangar before that blizzard hit. If we hadn't, our only transport would be thin smears of metal on the far canyon wall. Not that they're doing anybody a helluva lot of good. Not with the Tersae shooting down everything that tries to take off."

Bessany shivered. The Eisenbrucke Research Station—officially named just a few weeks previously, when the waterfalls pouring off the glacier had frozen into a solid bridge of ice—had been spared from attack, for now, but everyone knew only too well their reprieve wouldn't last past the end of the bad weather.

Herve spoke firmly, before already low spirits could plunge through the bedrock under the plascrete floors. "We've been lucky, very lucky, with this storm. Seta Point, too. I can't imagine anything alive moving through that kind of wind and snow, which means we should be safe until the weather clears. And that will give the promised military help time to arrive. At least," he frowned slightly, "I hope the Tersae can't travel through this kind of weather."

All eyes turned to Bessany. As resident xenoecologist—and the only human on Thule who'd actually *talked* to a Tersae—the ball was squarely in her court. She folded her hands in front of her to keep them from shaking. "Let's just say I'd be very surprised if they could travel through that blizzard. Not in any great numbers," she said cautiously. "The native species are remarkably well adapted to the vagaries of the

Thulian ecosystems, so God alone knows what temperatures or weather conditions the Tersae may be able to stand. Seismic activity notwithstanding, I suspect the Tersae build sheltered winter nests in natural cavern systems. They'd *have* to, because their young couldn't survive a storm like this one without shelter and they don't build villages or towns on the surface. And I'm afraid I agree with Elin. *We* shouldn't have built on the surface, either. None of us should have, mining colonies included."

"How do you know their young don't mature in one season, same as most animals?"

The question came from Billy Dolinski, a genius with computer equipment, whose understanding of ecological sciences remained as vague as Bessany's comprehension of psychotronic matrix programming.

Bessany shook her head. "They can't. Sooleawa is fifteen summers old, but she isn't anywhere near her full adult growth yet. Chilaili is only an inch shy of eight feet, but Sooleawa is no taller than I am, and I know she's still growing, because I asked."

"Oh."

Herve Sinclair rubbed the side of his nose absently. "What about their wild ancestral stock? What do they do to survive winter?"

Bessany lifted her hands in a timeless "who knows?" gesture. "I didn't see any signs of migration before the blizzard hit. So unless this is a freakishly early storm—and I suspect it is, since Chilaili gave me no hint that she expected bad weather soon—they must overwinter in the same ranges they use in summer and autumn. But I won't know for certain until the weather clears and I can get out to check my data recorders. If," she added darkly, "I ever get the chance."

Bleak silence met her assessment.

Bessany massaged her neck and rotated her head

slightly, trying to ease muscle tension. "Anyway, my best guess is the Tersae will be holed up in their winter nests for the duration of the storm, at the very least. The sustained winds on the plateau above this gorge are over a hundred kilometers per hour, with gusts clocked at one fifty. I can't imagine anything without roots—deep ones—not being torn away in that kind of wind." She pursed her lips for a moment and glanced at the burly meteorologist. "Any prediction on how long until this blizzard blows itself out?"

Ed Parker shook his head. "Not a very precise one, no. If we had good satellite feed, it would be a snap. Trouble is, *all* our satellites have gone dead. The ones put in place by the original planetary scouts died right after we got here and the ones our own transport ships left in orbit have gone dead, too. That's hardly surprising, considering how much junk is whirling through this star system."

Bessany's mouth twitched, halfway between a smile and a grimace. The night skies above Thule were spectacular, and not just because of the seventeen moons that sailed across the planet's heavens like ancient galleons going to war. There was an immense amount of debris in the Thule star system, which made for spectacular meteor showers on clear nights.

Meteors weren't the only spectacular thing on Thule, either. Ferocious summer thunderstorms produced appalling quantities of lightning, sparking fires in grasslands and forests if too little rain fell along the edge of the storm system to quench the flames. Bessany would never forget the storm that had caught her three days' hike from the station, when Sooleawa and Chilaili had nearly been killed right before her astonished eyes. The very *last* thing she'd expected to stumble across was a sentient species, much less two of its members in near-fatal trouble.

Alison Collingwood, the station's biochemist, asked quietly, "Do you think anyone's going to answer your messages?"

Bessany pushed back her long hair with a frustrated sigh. "I wish I knew. I'm not even sure any of my reports have even been *seen*. The Ministry of Mineral Resources hasn't responded at all. Not even with a routine 'report in message queue' reply. The Ministry of Xenology should have been really interested, but they haven't answered, either. The only thing that makes sense is budget-conscious bean counters refusing to foot the bill for an answering message."

Elin made a rude noise. "Given the outcome of the last elections, I'm surprised there's still a budget to keep *us* going."

Alison's lips twitched. "The cost cutters haven't pulled the plug because it would take more to ship us back home than to leave us out here. And you're probably right, Bessany. Communications techs who have to justify every teensy expense won't send expensive SWIFT messages to a world as far on the edge of space as Thule is, not without a really critical reason. I guess the Tersae aren't critical enough, huh?" A bitter silence fell as everyone reflected on the cost of that particular bureaucratic blunder. Open warfare on every human colony not socked in by this blizzard. Hundreds—maybe thousands—dead. A feeling of near hopelessness swept through Bessany, closing her throat and stinging her eyes.

Herve cleared his throat in the stricken silence. "Well, we have the comfort of knowing that has changed. Thule is at the top of the military's list of worlds to protect, Deng War notwithstanding. Speaking of which . . . isn't your brother-in-law in the military, Bessany?"

"Oh, yes. Third Dinochrome Brigade."

He wasn't answering her messages, either.

Of course, she and Lieutenant Colonel John Weyman were hardly on speaking terms.

She rubbed her temples, trying to soothe the beginnings of a ragged headache. Bessany had stupidly ignored his warning not to marry Alexander Weyman in the first place. Then she'd refused to answer any of her brother-in-law's messages in the aftermath of her husband's messy and very public suicide.

Sending a message—any message—to John Weyman had been one of the hardest things she'd ever done. Right up there with facing the endless sea of news cameras after the shattering dissolution of her marriage. Given her own track record, she could hardly blame him for not returning her messages, but it was distressing, nonetheless. Even if the reply was short and obscene, she'd expected him to say *something* about those incendiary reports of hers.

Yeah, well, he's assigned to the Dinochrome Brigade, which means he's probably at the front lines of the Deng War. Which is damned well where he belongs. Where he's happiest, God pity him . . .

She was about to ask Ed Parker if he could give them an educated guess on the blizzard's duration when an eerie sound brought the fine hairs at the nape of her neck starkly erect. "What's that noise?" she frowned, staring at the far plascrete wall, since it seemed to be coming from that direction. Her headache throbbed with a dull and distant warning. At that same instant, an alarm began to shriek from the weather station in the corner of the rec room.

Ed Parker blanched—a terrifying sight—and scrambled for the computer terminal which displayed weather conditions around the clock, for everyone's benefit. Parker rattled keys, scrolling through data screens, then stared in open horror. "Oh, my God . . ."

"*What is it?*" Bessany demanded, coming to her feet as real fright began to take hold. The noise—a low-pitched moaning roar—was getting louder. Much louder.

"Everybody down!" Parker yelled, throwing himself prone. "We've got a force five tornado bearing down on us—and I don't think it's going to miss!"

Chairs crashed. Bessany hit the floor, sliding frantically toward a doorway as a fragment of long-ago disaster training flashed through her mind. *Doorways are more stable when buildings collapse. Aren't they?* And hard on the heels of that thought, *Since when do blizzards spawn force five tornadoes? Don't tornadoes form during collisions of warm-air fronts?* Ed Parker's assessment of Thule's weather—amazing—was no longer even remotely funny. The tornado's monstrous roar rose to a scream . . .

Then the world shattered around her.

Chapter Five

Alessandra DiMario leaned against the wall of the cargo lift and shook.

I've got no business going back into combat, she told herself bitterly, unsure whether to rage more at herself or at the officers who'd decided to jerk her out of a hospital ship and send her back into the trenches against the Deng. She'd already lost one Bolo, literally destroyed around her ears, a death she blamed squarely on herself. It had nearly destroyed her, just listening to Danny die, knowing it was her fault, her decision, her responsibility. She'd lain trapped in the smoking ruins for nearly two days, while the tide of battle raged back and forth across ground Unit DNY had died trying to take.

Even after the battle ended in a resounding human victory, it had taken combat engineers hours to extract her from the shattered war hull. They'd shipped her off-world to a mobile combat treatment center, where surgeons had repaired the physical damage and combat psychiatrists had gone to work on the emotional wreckage. But the damned, hairy horrors they were fighting wouldn't wait for time or tide or one battered officer's mental state. So here she was, on her way back to combat, with a Bolo so old, the psychotronic engineers refurbishing him had been forced to fabricate parts just to splice in the new systems.

And dammit, her new unit had been right to call her onto the carpet. She'd been unforgivably rude and she knew it.

But the crawling sickness in her gut wouldn't go away and the realization that she'd be facing the guns of Yavac Heavies again with a Bolo so ancient, he still had *flintsteel* in his war hull, instead of duralloy, left her with a desperate case of the shakes. *Oh, God,* she groaned, trembling against the wall of the cargo lift, *I'm in trouble, we're all in trouble....*

She ought to march straight into her commander's quarters and lay it on the table: "I'm not fit for command, sir. And you and I both know it."

The trouble was, with the Deng hammering human worlds along the incredibly long front they'd hit this time, she was pretty much all that was available. And they both knew that, too. Somehow, she *had* to pull it together. The lift was slowing for the level her quarters occupied when the alert sounded, a signal piped shipwide that meant, "Bolo commanders, assemble in the wardroom, stat." Alessandra gulped and slapped controls that would send the lift another three decks higher. *What's happened now?* she wondered grimly.

Three minutes later, she strode into the CSS *Cheslav's* wardroom, the last on-board Bolo commander to arrive. "Sorry," she said, slightly out of breath from the run down the corridor, "I was in the cargo bay lift when the alert sounded. Took me seventeen decks and a midships bounce to get here."

Colonel Tischler nodded and she slid into the nearest seat.

"Sixty-three minutes from now," Tischler said quietly, "this transport will be dropping out of hyper-L to rendezvous with a combat courier ship. We've received an urgent request from Sector Command to divert a portion of this command to a place called Thule." He turned and activated a viewscreen which flashed up a star chart of the sector. "Three months ago, ten colonies of miners were dispatched to secure rich saganium deposits critical to military navigation systems. Thule was declared devoid of sentient life by the planetary scouts who first discovered the saganium. They were wrong. The colonists have been hit hard by a sentient, native life-form and the mines—and several thousand miners and their families—are now at risk of total destruction."

Alessandra frowned. "How in the world could planetary scouts miss a sentient species?"

"That's one of many questions we want answered," the colonel said grimly. "One of the others is where a species that apparently exists on a stone-age cultural level got its claws on energy rifles and fusion bombs. Unless the stuff was left lying around where these birds could find it—which isn't very likely—then *something* has to be supplying and training them. I'd like to know what."

Alessandra's eyes widened. Several officers muttered under their breaths.

"All of you know how important this mission against the Deng is," Colonel Tischler said, "but that saganium is critical. I can spare only two of you. I'd like to ask for volunteers."

Alessandra didn't even hesitate. "I'll go, sir."

Tischler met her gaze levelly—and the understanding in his eyes cut at her. "Thank you, DiMario. I was hoping you would volunteer. SPQ/R may not look like much, but he's as solid as they come and, frankly, we need your people skills on Thule. He'll be a big help to you, that way. He likes people."

She flushed. He didn't like *her*, that much was certain even if nothing else was. Before Danny's destruction, she had been good with people. Since waking up on the hospital ship . . . she wasn't so sure, any longer. But it was good to hear her commander's faith in her. Whatever else happened before they dropped out of hyper-L, she swore a solemn oath to look up SPQ/R-561's military record.

She'd better go over those technical specs again, too, since they were about as decipherable as hieroglyphics. God help them both if she had to jury-rig anything herself, due to battle damage. Still and all, it was far better than fighting spodders. *Anything* was better than facing the Deng again. Even apologizing to her Bolo.

The second volunteer was a young captain she hadn't met yet, a red-haired officer by the name of Roth. They exchanged glances and nods across the wardroom table, then Colonel Tischler reshuffled the remaining officers to cover the revised mission parameters before dismissing the rest of his command. When the others had gone, Tischler looked from Roth to Alessandra and back again.

"I would suggest you prep yourselves and your Bolos for immediate departure. I'll leave orders and mission debriefings with you. I have every confidence in your ability to carry out your new missions successfully. You'll debark at portside lock seventeen. Good luck."

They exchanged salutes and Alessandra headed for her temporary quarters, holding onto the hope that without the Deng to face, she might yet survive this crisis of nerves and come out whole and sane on the other side. *Don't blow it, DiMario, for God's sake, just don't blow it, okay?*

She reached her quarters, downloaded the mission-briefing files, checked to be sure they had come through without corruption, then queried the ship's computers for the full mission history of her Bolo, loaded into the records filed with Colonel Tischler upon the Bolo's assignment to his command. She found it without difficulty and took a precious eight minutes to scan through it. And felt the sting of shame as she skimmed through a battle record dotted with high praise from Central Command, as well as Sector.

Unit SPQ/R-561 had earned no fewer than seven major battle honors and a whole host of starclusters, all carefully welded to his turret by a former commander's loving hand. In good, bright sunlight, those honors would shine like glitter against the blue-black iodine hue of his ancient flintsteel war hull. In the gloom of the cargo hold, she hadn't seen them at all. She'd noticed only the old battle scars gouged across his aging war hull. Even if there had been enough light to see, Alessandra had been far too wrapped up in her own troubles to notice them.

I have really screwed this up, she realized bleakly.

And wondered if it was possible to start over with a machine that literally could not forget an insult.

Chapter Six

A series of loud clangs and thumps marks the completion of my heavy lift platform's lockdown against the cargo deck of the CSS Darknight. *I dislike naval transport ships, although I would be hard pressed for answers if asked why. Perhaps I simply prefer open sky and the feel of wind across my war hull. Even combat drops are better than confinement in a naval transport. I signal my all-clear to the cargo officer, who relays it to the* Darknight's *command deck. The* Darknight *breaks orbit from Sherman's World and moves ponderously toward this star system's optimal hyper-L jump point, escorted by the destroyer CSS* Vengeance. *My commander sends his respects to the captain.*

"Lieutenant Colonel John Weyman, reporting in, ma'am."

"Welcome aboard, Colonel," *Captain Harrelson responds.* "We'll be under way in a moment. Once we've made hyper-L, I'll meet you and the other Bolo commanders in the wardroom."

"Very good, Captain. Weyman, out."

*The Darknight's ops officer downloads to my Action/
Command Center the complete mission briefing files
for our new assignment. The fact that we have been
pulled away from Sherman's World, along with four
of my brothers and sisters of the Third Dinochrome
Brigade, reveals how urgently we are needed on Thule.
John whistles tunelessly under his breath as he reviews
the files from his customary place in my command
chair.*

*I find the entry seventeen seconds before he does.
Even as dismay races through my psychotronic
neural nets, John punches pause, halting the scan of
Thule's personnel rosters. His face runs dreadfully pale,
with a deep emotion I have seen there only twice
before. Both times, the woman whose name glows like
a beacon on the Eisenbrucke Station roster has been
at the eye of a disastrous emotional storm. One which
has shaken my commander a third time, now.*

*I am appalled—and have not the slightest idea what
to say, to break the dreadful silence. I want desperately to help him, to offer some bit of verbal support,
and find myself unable to think of anything, other than
a helpless, "John—?"*

*My commander slaps the releases on his harness
without a word. I watch in growing agitation as he
leaves my command compartment, climbs down my war
hull, and vanishes from the cargo hold, still without
speaking. There is literally nothing I can do, other than
watch him go. Whatever he intends, he will tell me once
he has done it. Or not, as the case may be. When it
comes to Bessany Weyman, the pattern to date has been
a stiff and unbroken silence. Deeply disturbed, I turn
my attention with reluctance back to the mission briefing files.*

It is not, perhaps, so strange that Bessany Weyman

has joined the Thule Research Expedition. Thule is doubtless one of the few places in human space where she is able to work in peace, beyond the reach of reporters and news cameras. Given what I know of human psychology—admittedly limited, since I am not human and will never fully understand my creators— she has probably needed to bury herself in work. My commander's exact feelings towards his sister-in-law have never been clear, for this is one area of his life he has never revealed to me.

My commander is not given to chatty conversation, in any case, but anything to do with his older brother's marriage and death sends him into stony silence. Over the five years, three months, and twenty-nine days since Alexander Weyman's shattering suicide, I have come to believe that John Weyman does not, in fact, blame his sister-in-law, regardless of the stories fielded by the press.

But even now, I cannot be sure. John has shared only one conversation with me concerning Bessany Weyman. The invitation to attend his politically prominent brother's wedding induced a pale, shaken look of horror. John immediately requested leave, which his commanding officer granted readily. Shortly after his return, John sought the privacy of my command compartment for the uncharacteristic action of emptying an entire bottle of whiskey. There, in the alcohol-filled silence, he whispered out the thing which was preying upon him.

"She wouldn't listen to me, Rapier. Dammed innocent fool of a girl blew up in my face, when I tried to warn her. God, what Alex is capable to doing to that sweet child . . . I should never have gone back for the wedding. Big mistake. One unholy *hell* of a mistake. And he *knew*. Alex knew exactly why I came and he laughed the whole time I was there. All the way to the altar and probably all the way through the honeymoon. But I had to try, Rapier. God knows, I couldn't just let her marry him, blind, not knowing *anything*."

That painful, post-wedding conversation, brief as it was, is the only revelation John Weyman has ever made, regarding his feelings for his brother's wife. The sick, shaken look returned for the second time when the news media descended, demanding his "reaction" to his brother's self-inflicted death.

He refused to answer any of their questions, earning my deep respect, but he said nothing to me, either, triggering a deep worry which has been with me ever since. He has not spoken Alexander Weyman's name even once in the ensuing five years, three months, and twenty-nine days. I do know that my commander sent three separate SWIFT messages to the shocked widow, but if she replied to them, he did not share her answers with me.

I have watched anxiously over John, doing my limited best to help, but I am only a Bolo. Help is difficult to render when I do not possess a human soul, leaving me incapable even of understanding the full scope of the problem. But John Weyman, even in his silence, is a fine commander, brilliant and courageous. Whatever I have been capable of doing, I have done, gladly.

And now, as we ride to battle with an enemy of unknown strength and capability, the one person John Weyman tried so hard—and failed so wretchedly—to help tops a list of people most likely to become fatalities. Bessany Weyman's research station sits dead last on Sector Command's list of priority defense sites. There is no Bolo available to defend a facility with only fifty-three people in residence, nor is there any military reason to send a Bolo there, since the mines are the critical facilities on Thule.

*Without military help, Bessany Weyman will
certainly die under enemy guns. The more I brood on
it, the more I wonder, anxiously, where my commander
has gone.*

*I learn the answer when the CSS Darknight's com-
munications officer attempts to raise Eisenbrucke Station via SWIFT. I am plugged into the Darknight's data
net, which allows me to overhear the transmission.
When there is no response, not even the autoresponder
code that should have acknowledged the incoming
signal, the communications officer tries to raise the
closest human habitation to the research facility. This
second SWIFT message races across vast interstellar
distances and is answered within one point three
minutes.*

"CSS *Darknight*, this is Seta Point Colony, responding. Do you copy?"

"Seta Point, we copy. Communications Officer
Tabbert here. We're trying to hail Eisenbrucke Station.
Their SWIFT unit appears to be down. Have they
sustained an enemy assault?"

"We can't raise them either, but I can't believe it's
due to any Tersae attack. A blizzard howled across the
whole eastern half of the Chak Upthrust almost a week
ago, well before the attacks came. Hurricane-force
winds and snow more than a meter deep. *Nothing's*
moving across open ground out here. When the station dropped off-line, we figured it must be storm damage to their communications equipment."

*It is a plausible explanation. Not entirely reassur-
ing, but plausible enough to restore hope. If the blizzard continues to hold off Tersae attacks long enough
for us to arrive, we may be able to secure Seta Point
and send an armed force to evacuate the research
station. Still, I continue to worry, uncertain whether
or not anything listens to soldiers' prayers—or if that*

something would bother listening to a machine. This does not stop me from hoping, deep in the privacy of my own thoughts, that something watches over both John Weyman and his sister-in-law. For now, it is the best I can do.

I fear it is not nearly enough.

Chapter Seven

In the aftermath of my unhappy first encounter with Captain DiMario, I have busied myself studying the mission briefing files on the conflict we are soon to join, partly to prepare myself for combat and partly to distract myself from worry over my new commander's unorthodox behavior. The files are not overly large, however, and the review does not take long.

I therefore turn my attention to internal diagnostics, trying to determine the extent of changes to my psychotronic circuitry, weapons systems, and war hull. I am still occupied with this self-evaluation when the cargo lift hums again, signaling the approach of another human. I turn my attention to the lift doors and am startled when my new commander emerges, moving purposefully in my direction. She carries a heavy duffle, presumably containing her personal gear. Given the grim set of her face, I brace myself for further unpleasantness.

Captain DiMario pauses directly in front of my war hull. I have spent many years learning to read human *emotions based on the movements of facial muscles and skin. Unless I am mistaken, my commander is embarrassed. I doubt the accuracy of my analysis. Then—unexpectedly—she clears her throat, the sound uncertain in the vastness of the cargo hold.*

"Hello again," *she says in a low voice.* "I'm afraid I owe you a fairly serious apology."

I am so surprised, I cannot even find words to answer.

"I won't try to excuse my behavior, which was fairly hideous. I . . . Oh, hell, there just isn't any easy way to say it. I came aboard this transport directly from a hospital ship. I should still be on it." *I detect fine tremors in both her body and her voice. A sheen of sweat has appeared on her skin. My commander is clearly suffering deep emotional distress. I listen silently, trying to understand.*

"I spent more than three months on the front lines, fighting the Deng from world to world. Three weeks ago, my Bolo was destroyed. I knew the risk was high. Terribly high. But I couldn't see any other choice. I lie awake nights, wondering if there might have been some option I missed, some other way out that wouldn't have involved ordering Danny to his death." *She blinks rapidly; wetness trembles on dark eyelashes. Three months is a long time for a human to spend in constant combat. I am keenly aware of the human need for periodic rest from the stress of battle, without which even the strongest soldier begins to experience psychological dysfunction. I begin to understand.*

"After the salvage engineers cut me out of the wreckage, the surgeons fixed most of what was wrong. And the psychiatrists pumped me full of drugs, trying to fix the rest of it . . ." *She draws a deep breath. I feel a deep and unexpected pity for her, watching this struggle and realizing the cost of this admission,*

made to me in an unmistakable gesture of apology.
"When word came of another Deng breakthrough, the
command went out to scrape together every officer
capable of fighting, to put into active service every
Bolo that could be pulled out of mothballs and refitted
for combat. All I could think, when they sent me out
here to rendezvous with this transport, was that I was
going back to the front lines, when I knew I wasn't
in any shape for it. And going back in a Bolo that
wasn't . . ."

Her voice breaks, raggedly. I say, as gently as pos-
sible, "I am old, Commander, and my war hull may be
flintsteel, but that flintsteel is still quite strong and
duralloy ablative armor has been added for extra protection. I will endure against even direct fire from Yavac
Heavies."

A strange sound emerges from her throat, defying
interpretation. "I'm sure you would, if we were still
assigned to the Deng front lines. That's the other
reason I came back down, with my gear." *She lifts one*
shoulder, over which she has slung the heavy duffle.
"We're dropping out of hyper-L in about fifteen minutes, to rendezvous with a fast courier. We've been
reassigned."

"Reassigned?" *I repeat, deeply startled.*

"There's been an unexpected attack on the saganium
mines at Thule."

"By Deng?"

"No." *She gives me a strained smile.* "By a sentient
native species nobody knew existed. I've got the new
mission files with me. I'll copy them to your Action/
Command Center before we off-load. We'll transfer
to the new courier ship together, with me tucked into
your command compartment. Captain Roth and his
Bolo will be shipping out with us." *She manages*
another strained smile. "Colonel Tischler can spare

only two of his battle group for the Thule relief effort. He asked for volunteers."

I understand. Profoundly. My commander is doubtless correct that she is not fit for front-lines combat, leaving me with a feeling of deep unease. But I am a fully self-aware and self-directing Bolo, capable of carrying out even complex battle plans without human guidance. If my commander collapses, I will not be crippled and neither will our mission. For her sake, I hope that we do not see the kind of heavy fighting that would doubtless tip her back into a state of psychological breakdown.

"Understood, Commander."

She nods, slowly. "Thank you, SPQ/R-561. Permission to come aboard?"

"Of course, Commander." *I open my hatch with a hiss of pneumatics. She climbs aboard and stows her gear in one of the command compartment's storage bins, then powers up the command chair, straps in, and feeds the new mission files into my Action/Command Center. I scan rapidly, satisfied with the completeness of the data. I begin to look forward to the coming mission, which holds out the promise of being far more interesting than mere combat against Deng Yavacs.*

As my commander runs through the systems check required of any ship-to-ship transfer of my war hull, she says, "I can't keep calling you SPQ/R-561. It's too long, for one thing. And I don't want to use whatever nickname your last commander used. That's a little too personal. If you miss your old commander the way I—" *She breaks off, biting one lip.*

"I am deeply sorry for your loss, Commander," *I say gently.*

"Thank you." *She clears her throat.* "I will get over it. So . . . when I saw your unit number for the first time, it reminded me of something from old Earth history. They added that /R designation for Refurbished, which is what triggered the association. SPQR. The Senate and People of Rome." *She smiles slightly into my video pickup.* "My remote ancestors were Roman legionaries, you know."

DiMario is an Italian-derived patronymic, meaning "son of Mario." The name strongly reminds me of Marius and Cinna, the Roman consuls to whom Julius Caesar was related, by birth and by marriage. Indeed, legionaries were known for centuries afterwards as Marius' mules, for the massive reforms he instituted in the armies of Rome. My commander bears a proud lineage. When I tell her so, she seems pleased.

"If you don't mind, I think I'd like to call you Senator," *she says quietly.*

The name she has chosen bears the hallmarks of an apology, carrying as it does the connotations of venerable age, wisdom, and deep cultural respect. The name delights me.

"I would be honored to have you address me as Senator, Commander."

She smiles again. "I'm glad."

"I am receiving ship's signal, Commander. Brace for drop into sub-light."

Our transport shudders with the transition from hyper-L to sub-light speeds. Braking thrusters fire to slow our forward motion further. "Contact with the CSS *Aldora* established," *I relay.* "Ship-to-ship transfer will commence as soon as we have matched velocities and closed to feasible transfer distances. The *Aldora* is firing thrusters to halt centrifugal spin. Prepare for weightlessness."

My commander nods, flicking her gaze across my data screens, watching as the two transports fire thrusters to match velocities and trajectories, making the ship-to-ship transfer possible. Both transports jockey cautiously toward one another under the control of precise computer guidance systems. This data is shared with myself and the other Bolo unit preparing to disembark. My sensors detect the jerking motions as rotational spin halts, then resumes in tiny bursts as the navigational computers match with the Aldora, *lining up their respective cargo bays for transfer. Weightlessness returns. My treads are held fast in the clamps of the heavy lift sled on which I rest, preventing me from floating away from the deck. The sled itself is anchored directly to that deck. I receive the ready signal.*

"Preparing for ship-to-ship transfer," I relay. "Cargo hold depressurizing for evacuation."

Alessandra DiMario nods. "Thank you, Senator." *Her fingers close against the padded armrests of the command chair. I understand her increased stress. Such transfers are hardly routine, even under computer guidance. I have never experienced such a transfer before, nor have I spoken with another Bolo unit which has accomplished this type of maneuver. The engines of the heavy lift sled on which I rest rumble to life, vibrating my treads. During a combat drop, I maintain full control of the sled, but in an operation this ticklish, I will allow the sled's computers to maneuver us, using data feed from the* Cheslav *and the* Aldora.

The Cheslav's *immense cargo doors slide open, exposing my war hull and those of the other Bolo units in this bay to hard vacuum. This does not bother me and my command compartment is hermetically sealed, protecting Captain DiMario. But when the cargo sled releases its mooring grapples and propels my war hull into open space, I experience a surge through my psychotronic circuitry that can only be interpreted as nervousness. I have experienced many orbital combat drops, sliding out of transport-ship cargo bays on heavy lift sleds exactly like this one—but always with the immense bulk of a planet directly beneath us.*

Interstellar space is incredibly vast.

And disturbingly empty.

The ship in which we have traveled, far larger than my war hull, shrinks to a comparative speck of matter against the black depths waiting outside the cargo hold. My commander draws air in sharply, gaze glued to my forward data screen. The cargo sled fires thrusters and we proceed forward, ponderously. The CSS Aldora lies on a direct line-of-sight trajectory from our cargo bay. The sled fires its engines in short bursts, sending us toward the waiting transport. We approach rapidly, drawing another sharp breath from Alessandra DiMario.

I locate the open bay toward which our sled's computers are guiding us. The Aldora is a far smaller ship than the Cheslav, but the cargo bay doors are ample to admit my bulk. We slow on final approach and drift forward gently. The massive doors slide past as we enter the waiting bay. Our sled fires lateral thrusters to jockey cautiously sideways, out of the open doorway, and we settle carefully toward a waiting set of mooring grapples. A vibration clangs through my treads as the grapples take hold and winch us down, mating us solidly with the deck. Three point nine minutes later, Captain Roth and Unit XPJ-1411 enter the cargo bay and moor themselves to the deck beside us.

"Welcome aboard," *a cheerful voice greets us.* "Communications Officer O'Leary here. As soon as we restore pressure to the hold, we'll escort you up to the wardroom."

"Thank you," *Alessandra responds.* "I'm looking forward to a full debriefing." *She breaks contact as pressure returns to the cargo hold and the ship fires its engines, re-establishing centrifugal spin as well as forward momentum.* "What a relief," *my commander mutters as the artificial gravity of spin settles her firmly into the command chair once more.* "I hate freefall. At least I hadn't eaten lunch yet, so there was nothing to bring up."

I have never understood the biological predilection for motion sickness in freefall. In the privacy of my thoughts, I suspect I am fortunate this is so.

"Well, Senator," *my commander sighs, slapping releases on the command chair's restraints,* "for better or worse, we're on course for Thule."

For better or worse . . .

I draw comfort from the similarity of my commander's observation to human marriage customs. We are, indeed, committed. To one another as much as to the mission. As my commander climbs out through my hatch and joins Captain Roth on the Aldora's *cargo deck, I am hopeful about the altered situation between us.*

I watch her move briskly across the deck, where a lift similar to the one on the Cheslav *opens to reveal a uniformed welcoming committee. As the lift doors close again, I find myself hoping—fervently—that the upcoming mission will not add to the burden of combat stress my commander has already experienced.*

We are heading into the unknown. And if there is one thing my long experience of combat has taught me, it is that the unknown is often far deadlier than the well-known and understood, however stressful that well-known situation might be. It is not a comfortable feeling.

So far, nothing about my return to duty has been.

Chapter Eight

If Chilaili's winter nest had lain any farther from the valley where Bessany Weyman's nestmates had built their home—even as far as Icewing Clan's migratory summer nests—she would never have made it. As it was, a journey which should have taken her an easy day's walk, at most, instead took nearly twenty hours of bitter struggle with the wind and the stinging snow at her back. She kept to deep forest as much as possible, for the trees helped break the worst of the screaming wind and prevented the snow from piling quite so deeply. It was at least possible to walk through the heavy stretches of forest. When she came to open stretches that had to be crossed, Chilaili got down on her belly and *crawled*, presenting as little of herself as possible to the maddened fingers of the wind.

Even so, one particularly strong gust picked her up and flung her nearly fifteen yards before she slithered to a bruised and scratchy halt. She landed in a deep drift piled up against a tangle of underbrush where the forest closed in, again. She lay shaking for long minutes, getting back her strength and her courage, then crawled deeper into the trees before she dared standing up again. After that, Chilaili swung out of her way to avoid stretches of open ground, aware with every fiber of her battered being just how lucky she was to have survived that screaming gust of wind.

It was utterly imperative that she reach Bessany Weyman's nest before darkness fell again. Chilaili's winter coat was thick and her subcutaneous layer of fat provided extra insulation, enough to allow her to thrive in the deepest cold of winter, but the wind was so fierce, it effectively dropped the temperature to the lowest ranges she could tolerate. She would not survive a night exposed to this wind and the deeper cold of darkness.

Drifts were already twice her height in places, forcing her to swing wide of easier paths time and again. The constant shrieking of the wind deafened her so greatly, she didn't even hear the snap and crash of trees brought down in the storm. She was beyond hoping none of them crushed her. She had to focus every ounce of her strength on putting one foot in front of the other, probing with a long stick for sudden dropoffs buried beneath the snow. As the long day wore exhaustingly on, Chilaili's strength faded, frightening her. She struggled on, unable to do anything else.

Night caught her an hour short of her destination—and the blizzard, although abated somewhat in its fierceness, still howled at her back. She paused as the light faded, debating the wisdom of fighting on through the darkness. Although she couldn't see more than a few yards in any direction, Chilaili knew precisely where she was and precisely how much farther she had to go to reach the valley of the ice bridge. This innate knowledge was something Chilaili had long suspected the

Tersae shared with their ancestral stock. It was literally impossible for Chilaili to lose her way, even in the white-out conditions of this storm. Awareness of the invisible lines of force which ran through the earth beneath her taloned feet told her it would take only ten steps to reach a steep-walled little gorge she knew of.

That gorge would offer at least some shelter for the bitterly cold hours ahead. She could climb down, build a fire under the overhanging cliff walls. Chilaili turned toward the path she knew lay no more than ten steps away . . .

And literally could not make her foot move in that direction. Startled, Chilaili realized she had just received a warning, one she didn't understand. She tried to listen to the energies loose in the night, to understand what those energies were trying to communicate to her. As both a master *katori* and a successful huntress, she had listened to the voices of wind and trees and water and soil too many times in the past, avoiding disaster that might otherwise have overtaken her, to ignore the message now.

She was not meant to take shelter, yet. She was meant to go on, to reach the human nest as quickly as possible. *Why*, she didn't know, but knew it would be revealed, in time.

Swearing under her breath at the seeming folly of it, she set out once more toward the valley of the ice bridge, using her stick to probe ahead for every step of the way as the light vanished. Night plunged her into a darkly howling world of uncertain footing and rising fear. She slowed down, by necessity, but fought on, determined to keep going. Chilaili stumbled more frequently as well, sprawling sometimes across buried tangles of brush. The hour stretched out, agonizingly, until it felt like she'd been struggling through darkness for half her life.

When the wind's scream rose sharply, Chilaili halted, listening, stretching out her hands to test the wind's strength. Judging from the sound and the force of the wind, the trees had to be thinning out directly ahead. That, plus the invisible grid inside her head, told her she had come to the edge of the humans' valley. There was only one safe way down—the rock ramp the humans had fashioned. In total darkness, she would be unable to see it. She had glimpsed it only once and wasn't at all sure of its twists and turns as it dropped two hundred feet to the valley floor. Chilaili hesitated . . .

And as she paused, a deeper sound lifted the fur on the nape of her neck. A savage, snarling roar growled toward her through the darkness, coming from the open ground to Chilaili's right, across the valley in the direction of the smoking mountains. Terror took hold as she recognized that sound. *Twist-wind!* Chilaili threw herself prone, wrapped arms and legs around the base of a solid tree, prayed to every ancestress, every spirit of rock and tree and wind she had ever prayed to, and hung on. The monstrous roar drew rapidly nearer. The wind whipped savagely through the forest, changing directions in wild gusts. Her ears popped as the air pressure dropped. The killer wind siphon drew so close, she could feel it plucking at the under-brush around her—

Then it dove over the lip of the gorge and roared its way down the long, narrow valley toward the human nest. Chilaili lay shaking and sick, too terrified to move, helpless as she listened to the monster rush toward her one human friend in all the world. The friend she had risked so much to help. *Why?* she demanded fiercely of the night. *Why let me come so close, only to destroy her with a twist-wind?* Chilaili shivered at the base of her tree, listening as the killer wind's roar receded in the distance. She heard a muted change in its sound as it skipped up out of the valley and collided with the mountain beyond, then she could hear it no more. Either the twist-wind had died on the slopes of the glacier or it had skipped back into the storm clouds.

Deeply shaken, Chilaili sat up.

Gradually, it came to her that the warning to struggle forward might have come so she would be on hand when the twist-wind struck the humans' valley. Not to make her a witness to their deaths, but to render aid to any survivors. The thought sent her stumbling forward, crawling through the last of the trees, hugging the ground on her belly as she slithered forward, probing with her stick over the lip of the steep-walled gorge. The wind had scoured away all snow along the rim at least, so she didn't have to struggle through drifts. Her stick located the stone ramp with a solid thunk.

She started down, flat on her belly as the wind plucked at her.

It took her nearly a quarter of an hour to reach the bottom, probing ahead with her stick as the stone ramp turned back on itself time and again. Once down, she stumbled toward the most sheltered side of the gorge, where the cliff walls gave her enough protection from the wind to stand up. She set out again, probing once more with her walking stick, and soon encountered massive debris from the twist-wind. Trees were down everywhere, making her path through the damage treacherous. She crawled blindly over downed tree trunks, stumbled and tripped through tangled branches, scraped her legs against splintered stumps. Trembling with exhaustion, she fought her way forward, then stumbled onto something very hard and very flat and exceedingly smooth.

She halted, frowning; then she had it.

The landing pad, Bessany Weyman had called it, for their flying machines.

She was close, then, very close. Chilaili traced the edge with her stick, turned in the direction she hoped would aim her toward the hard-walled huts, and tapped ahead to try and avoid walking into anything that might be lying in her path. She stayed on the landing pad for a long way, then came to the edge and traced it with her stick again, probing for debris that might lurk ahead. Chilaili stepped off and inched her way forward—

And heard voices.

Thin, *human* voices, crying for help, screaming in terrible pain.

Chilaili's heart leaped into her throat, pounding raggedly. *Someone* had survived. Several someones, from the sound of it. She hurried forward, stumbled across chunks of debris, what felt like pieces of the hard-walled huts themselves, scattered like leaves by the killer wind. Then she caught a gleam of light, white light, strange and startling against the snow-blown darkness. She rushed toward it, realized it was coming from a partially intact piece of the human nest. Then she heard a voice she knew, the only human voice she knew, sobbing for help from somewhere directly in front of her.

Chilaili tossed her walking stick aside and started digging through the rubble.

Chapter Nine

My new commander and I share mixed feelings about our arrival at Thule. Alessandra DiMario is understandably stressed, although anxious to come to grips with her personal demon and overcome it. I am uncertain about my spliced and patched systems. Due to the urgent nature of my refitting, I have never been field-tested, a situation which perhaps alarms me more than it does my commander, who is doing her best to put her faith in me.

Our transit time has been brief, by interstellar military standards, less than a day at hyper-L, although I suspect Thule's beleaguered colonists would say those twenty-three point two standard Terran hours were not brief. It is a curious phenomenon, much commented upon by biological life-forms, that the passage of time seems to be variable in relation to the events against which it is measured. I calculate the passage of time exactly and have never experienced this phenomenon for myself; but even a refurbished Mark XXIII Bolo can understand how bleak and long the *hours must seem to people who are waiting almost hopelessly for rescue.*

For the sake of Rustenberg's colonists, I am glad our transit time has been so short.

From orbit, Thule's daylight hemisphere—glimpsed briefly, as Rustenberg currently lies in the night side of the planet—shows the blinding flash of sun-struck snow fields across most of the northern and southern hemispheres. Thule is beautiful in its way, with rainbow dazzles off glaciers and vast tracts of virgin snow. Deep sapphire oceans have generated bands of moisture-laden clouds which spill over Thule's northern land masses, dropping snow in locally severe blizzard conditions.

We are informed, upon achieving orbit, that the mining colony at Seta Point and the Eisenbrucke Research Station are the only two human settlements affected by this foul weather, which has acted as a temporary protection against Tersae attacks. Rustenberg, which lies at the southernmost edge of this massive storm front, has experienced high winds and freezing rain, but this has not been enough to protect them from enemy aggression.

Thule's axial tilt, almost directly vertical, has created a narrow band of tropical luxuriance at the equator, bounded by vast regions of forest and tundra and enormous ice caps which reach from the planetary poles to more than thirty degrees of latitude. Thule's seasons are brought about by its eccentric orbit, which brings it closer to the system's star in summer. With Thule rapidly retreating from its primary, the entire planet is now entering the winter season. Within weeks, even the equatorial belt will turn cold, plunging the entire planet into its long winter.

Rugged mountain chains, thousands of kilometers long, are visible as dark and jagged scars across the sun-bright glare of snow, where tectonic plates have collided or pulled apart in fiery volcanic violence. Ancient impact craters are visible as faint outlines in snow-free areas. The Thule system is thick with debris from the ancient supernova which created the star system, making trans-system shipping for ore freighters and our own naval transport a tricky proposition. If the saganium were not so critical, prompting Concordiat underwriting, shipping costs through the muck flying loose in the Thule system would be prohibitive.

Despite the difficulties of trans-system navigation, we achieve orbit without incident and orbital drop proceeds smoothly. Captain Roth and Unit XPJ-1411 leave our transport first. I depart the Aldora's cargo bay six point two five minutes later and plunge into darkness as my heavy lift sled enters the night side of Thule. The glowing contrail from my powered drop platform leaves a trail of fire across the nighttime sky. If anyone—or anything—below is watching, our arrival will certainly be spectacular.

My trajectory carries me in a streaking arc to the planetary west, toward the edge of the storm system which has brushed so closely past Rustenberg. As I plunge into heavy cloud cover, we experience strong buffeting from storm winds. My commander grips the padded consoles of my command chair, thins her lips, and says nothing. Combat drop is always stressful for humans, this one particularly so.

To our mutual relief, I drop below cloud cover and sight Rustenberg using infrared sensors and radar. The bleak landscape beyond Rustenberg's outermost structures—terrain I must hold against enemy incursions—gives me new cause for anxiousness. The colony sits in a vast and ancient lava field, fissured by deep gorges and steep-sided valleys. A mantle of forest covers the

*surface of this ancient basalt, making it doubly diffi-
cult to see anything in the deep cracks. Hundreds or
even thousands of enemy soldiers could congregate
within a few dozen meters of Rustenberg, completely
undetected until the moment of attack. I have a limited number of aerial survey packages on board, which
is cause for concern. If our mission briefing was correct, the Tersae will attempt to blast out of the sky
anything we put up into it.*

*On the heels of that thought, my heavy lift sled
comes under enemy fire.* "Seven incoming missiles of
unknown configuration."

"Get 'em."

I attempt to lock onto the missiles—

*—and am horrified to discover a devastating
unsteadiness in my new target-acquisition and weapons-
guidance systems. I am unable to secure an accurate
weapons lock. A disorienting stutter of incompatible
signals ghosts across the interface between old circuitry
and new.*

We are all but helpless in the air.

*The best I can do is fire heat-seeking missiles of my
own, which do not rely on my internal, malfunctioning guidance systems. They are not the weapon of
choice, given the speed at which the enemy missiles
are closing with my heavy lift sled.*

*I slew us around midair, overriding the sled's auto-
programming. This cants us so any missiles which elude
my return fire will detonate against my war hull, not
the lifter. My commander shouts in shocked reaction.
I am built to withstand high explosive rounds, but the
underside of my lift sled is vulnerable without my guns
to take down incoming fire. I log the frantic observation that this constitutes a serious design flaw in the
lift sleds. I cannot risk a fall from this altitude, since
the impact would crush my commander. As we twist*

sideways in the air, three enemy missiles reach my war hull and explode. A brief flare of pain registers on my damage-control sensors, but I am barely scratched. I slew us around again to continue the descent.

"Jesus Christ! What the *hell* do you think you're doing?" *Her voice is more a sob of terror than a demand for information.*

"I am experiencing an unknown weapons-control malfunction, originating in the interface between my original and upgraded systems." *As I speak, I take careful note of where each missile originated, backtracking heat signatures and missile-launch flares against the darkened, ice-covered rooftops.* "Mapping origination points to my forward data screen. Coding enemy emplacements in flashing red. The enemy has penetrated most of the settlement." *Indeed, the Tersae have ringed Rustenberg in a vast circle of death.*

"The enemy is firing from rooftops as indicated, Commander." *I superimpose flashing pointers over the launch sites, laying down a gridwork map to show the extent of abandoned habitations below.* "I detect a plascrete wall four meters high around this central core, which could serve no logical peacetime purpose." *I highlight the structure, which encloses an area of approximately five acres, on which numerous structures have been built.*

"They must've retreated as far as they could, then threw up a defensive barrier. God knows how they got that wall up under enemy fire."

There is no point in speculation about the ease or difficulty of the wall's construction. The colonists have abandoned most of Rustenberg as indefensible, a fact of immediate and critical importance. The open-pit mineworks north of town and a crude-oil refinery capable of cracking crude petroleum into useable fuels have been likewise abandoned.

More missiles arch upwards in a blaze of fire against the darkness. Most are aimed at my lift sled, which has dropped to a mere five thousand decimeters, but five of them streak over the settlement's defensive plascrete wall. I fire interceptors at both sets and once again slew us sideways in the air. We are hit by four more enemy missiles. Our transport rocks and shudders. The lift sled has taken a direct hit in the armored engine nodules. Another such hit and we will lose the engines. I cut power to drop rapidly, making us a more difficult target to acquire. My commander shouts once, violently, then digs her fingers into the padded armrests.

My interceptor missiles knock down four of the five missiles racing toward the heart of Rustenberg. The explosions spread burning debris across the rooftops and streets, well inside the defensive wall. The fifth missile slams against a tall structure. The warhead explodes and its target burns fiercely. If this building was occupied by refugees, they had no time to escape, for the entire structure ignites within zero point six seven seconds and burns unchecked.

My commander snarls ugly and helpless curses.

Fury and shame engulf my battle reflex circuitry. I do not understand what is wrong. I have failed to stop easy targets. What can I say to my commander that will put this right? Nothing. I struggle with diagnostic programs and restore power to our heavy lift sled for final descent. "Ninety-seven heat signatures detected on the rooftops surrounding Rustenberg's core," *I say with a sense of desperation.* "These heat signatures correspond with missile-launch points."

"Verifiable as nonhuman?" *Captain DiMario's voice grates with tones of anger.*

I attempt verification at the top speed of which I am capable. Using laser range finders to give me exact distances and using the size of human-built doorways and windows as a gauge, I determine that these heat signatures are too large to be human in origin, although the temperature range they exhibit is within 0.2 degrees of human-normal. "Heat signatures register as bi-pedal and biological, averaging two point five one meters in height. These cannot be human heat signatures."

"Fry 'em."

Her voice is terse, ugly. I fire ion-bolt infinite repeaters and HE short-range missiles, raking the Tersae's rooftop positions in a broad dispersal pattern that does not require the pin-point accuracy of anti-missile fire. The Tersae's visible heat signatures vanish in a flare of violent explosions which destroy the buildings they have occupied. Fires raging from these initial explosions ignite neighboring structures, until the outer circle of Rustenberg burns fiercely.

"Goddammit, Senator! We've got live refugees down there and you just ignited a firestorm!"

I know deep and desperate shame. I am unable to properly carry out even the simplest of tasks. That I have, at least, destroyed ninety-seven of the enemy before reaching the ground is of little consequence, given the enormity of my failures and the unknown cause of the drift malfunctions in my weapons-guidance and fire-control systems.

My heavy lift sled sets down outside the ring of blazing buildings and releases the tiedowns fastened to my treads. I engage drive engines and begin a rapid circle of the town's perimeter. A complete circuit reveals no trace of enemy personnel outside the ring of blazing buildings. In this, at least, I have been effective. But I must deal with the fires my HE rounds have ignited before the flames destroy what little Rustenberg's miners have managed to salvage.

My commander has the same thought, for she says,

"All right, Senator, if it's burning, knock it down. We'll salvage what's left in the buildings that haven't burned yet, then knock them down, too. I want a good, clear perimeter around this place."

"Understood, Commander."

I wade into the burning mass, grinding down blazing timbers and crushing plascrete walls to rubble. My commander punches controls to initiate radio transmission, muttering, "Those people have to be terrified, with all the explosions out here. It's going to be hard enough on them, when they see how much they've just lost. Rustenberg, this is Captain Alessandra DiMario, Third Dinochrome Brigade. Do you copy? Repeat, this is Captain Alessandra DiMario. Are you receiving?"

Static greets us for zero point eight seven seconds. Then a human voice responds, a woman's voice, babbling in tones of semihysteria. "Oh, my God, are you *really* here? Was that your guns firing, just now? We thought—never mind what we thought, oh, thank God you've finally come!"

"Sorry it took our transport so long to reach you. Where are you?"

"Underground," *the woman answers. Excited voices erupt through the open radio link somewhere close to her.* "We used the mining equipment to dig bunkers."

My commander says very gently, "You can come out of hiding very soon, ma'am. My Bolo has already killed nearly a hundred Tersae firing on your compound. As soon as we've cleared your perimeter, you'll be able to come up."

I fret over the unpleasant surprise waiting for these people. Very little shocks and demoralizes a civilian population more swiftly than the loss of homes. All else that civilians endure in combat—bombardments, destruction of livelihoods and cultural centers, even the death of friends—is simply part of the misery that must be lived through, however numbly or angrily. But the loss of home is a personal wound. Such violations breed hatred—and hatred becomes a wind that sweeps whole worlds into war.

I fear for the repercussions of my actions.

It takes me ten point three five minutes to knock down the greater portion of town. This leaves me with a beautifully clear perimeter where the enemy is denied concealment and cover, but leaves the owners of Rustenberg with a vast rubble field where an occasional warehouse or personal home rises, lonely and scorched, from the ruins. I feel a sensation akin to pity as I complete the task. Captain DiMario does not speak during the entire ten point three five minutes, but sits staring at the forward data screen, jaw muscles as tightly clenched as her fingers, which curl crushingly around the padded armrest.

"All burning structures outside the wall are down, Commander. There is still an unchecked blaze inside the defensive barricade. Shall I breach the wall and knock down these structures, as well?"

"Christ, no! Not until we find out where those people are." *She reestablishes radio contact.* "Rustenberg, Captain DiMario here. You're clear to come up. Please evacuate quickly. We have a fire burning out of control inside your defensive wall. We need to bring the buildings down before the fire spreads. If we run over your bunker, trying to reach the blaze, my Bolo will cave the roof in."

"Good God, I hadn't thought of that," *the same voice responds, sounding startled.* "We're coming up, Captain."

From the vantage point of my uppermost turret sensors, I locate a deep pit gouged into the soil near the center of town. This proves to be the entrance to the underground bunker. Heavy-gauge metal doors

crash open at the bottom. A moment later, a stream
of shaken, filthy colonists appears, rushing forward to
greet their rescuers. Most of them stare up at my war
hull, which towers above the broken wall, bathed in
harsh firelight from the blaze still burning inside the
defended compound. My commander watches the exo-
dus in silence for five point eight seconds, then issues
rapid commands.

"Senator, after you deal with this last fire, I want
you to clear out those trees south and west of town.
Give us a five-thousand-meter cleared perimeter in all
directions. I want a report on the condition of the
mines, equipment, and ore stockpiles. And scout our
perimeter out to a distance of one kilometer. I want
to know what we're up against, out there. That terrain
looks wicked. Map it to the last centimeter, along with
anything the Tersae have stashed in convenient over-
hangs and crannies. Look for places we can leave a few
surprises, too. And start thinking about what kind of
surprises we can jury-rig from whatever the colonists
can fabricate. If," *she adds grimly,* "there's anything left
to fabricate things *with.* Any questions?"

"None, Commander. Permission to file VSR?"

"Shoot."

"I have attempted to run diagnostics and cannot
trace the difficulty with my tracking and fire-control
systems. I believe the source to lie somewhere in the
splices between my pre-existing systems and the new
upgrades. I am experiencing data scrambling which
suggests the systems are not entirely compatible. It is
urgent that we discover whether anyone in Rustenberg
has experience in psychotronic systems repair. This
situation alarms me."

My commander possesses a most creative vocabu-
lary. Her tone, however, softens when she addresses me
directly again. "It doesn't make me want to dance,

either. God, what else—" *She bites off the rest of whatever she had planned to say.* "All right, we'll just have to play this hand as dealt, since there's nobody out here to redeal. Get those burning buildings knocked down, get that perimeter cleared and that survey done, then we'll take a look at your retrofitting specs."

"Very good, Commander."

Captain DiMario exits my command compartment and climbs down to greet the shaken inhabitants of Rustenberg. I wait until she and the colonists are clear, then engage drive engines. I back up and turn my prow towards the wall, then carefully push down the section closest to the blaze. Within two point three nine minutes, I have demolished the burning structures and contained the blaze, although the narrowness of the street requires additional demolition which distresses me.

I back out again with extreme caution and set out to complete the other assigned tasks. As I carry out the terrain survey, I realize that reconnaissance will be difficult across the entire range of territory to be monitored. I turn my thoughts toward ways other than aerial surveillance to accomplish this. I cannot formulate complete plans until I know what tools and materials remain available, but entertain fair hope of creating a simple, effective network which will surprise the enemy.

Given the circumstances and my uncertain malfunctions, I hope this not overly optimistic.

Chapter Ten

Bessany Weyman woke from a fragmented memory of falling walls and the howling roar of the tornado and wondered how long she'd been unconscious. She lay without moving, trying to determine exactly where she was and how badly injured she might be. She could feel pain, dull and frightening, along her back and legs where something heavy pinned her down. She was cold, too, and realized the tornado had knocked down enough of the building to let the freezing night air howl through the shattered remains of the rec room. She could hear the blizzard's shrieking winds, but was so completely buried, no snow had reached her.

Gingerly, she tried to move, and found that she was pinned fast beneath the rubble. Some of it shifted ominously and she froze, heart pounding in renewed terror. Then, dimly, she heard voices, recognized Herve Sinclair and Ed Parker and Elin Olsson, shouting above the moaning of the wind. And somewhere farther away, someone was screaming in mindless agony. Bessany strained to hear and realized Sinclair was moving through the ruins, shouting names, trying to find people. Bessany cried out, "Herve! Herve, I'm trapped! Help!"

"Bessany?"

"I'm here! There's rubble on top of me—I can't move!"

The project director called faintly, "Ed, help me! Bessany, keep shouting so we can find you. Most of the lights are out and we can barely see!"

Bessany kept calling out, "Here! I'm over here! I think I'm under part of the doorway!"

Rubble started to shift above her. Bessany sobbed aloud, flinching and bracing herself for the worst as heavy slabs of plascrete teetered and moved with an ominous groan. She heard a wordless shout . . . Then the heaviest, largest slab lifted, freeing her. Bessany scrambled through the smaller debris, wincing as injuries along her back and legs protested the injudicious movement. The heavy plascrete fell as her rescuers dropped it, then someone helped her up—

Bessany gasped in shock.

The hand around her wrist was *clawed*, clawed and furred along its whole length. Bessany jerked her gaze up, squinting through the near darkness, and made out a towering, heavily furred shape, nearly eight feet tall against the driving snow. Light from one of the side labs that had remained miraculously intact spilled out into the darkness, revealing the last face she had dreamed she would see, tonight.

"*Chilaili!*" she cried. "What—how—?"

"Bessany!" Herve Sinclair shouted behind her. "Run!"

She turned, shaken and still off balance, and found the project director rushing toward her. Ed Parker was at his heels. Both men brandished makeshift clubs. It took a long, slow second to realize they thought she was in danger, that the Tersae standing above her had come to attack them. "No!" she shouted, suddenly grasping it. She stepped between the *katori* and the onrushing men. "Herve, Ed, no! It's Chilaili!"

They paused, panting, a meter away.

"Chilaili?" Herve frowned.

"Yes! She pulled me out of the rubble."

"Bessany Weyman," the tall Tersae said urgently, "many of your nestmates are still trapped. We must dig them free, quickly. This rubble is not stable and the cold will penetrate quickly, lowering their chances of survival. And someone must start a fire or we will *all* freeze to death, myself included. This is not suitable weather to be aboveground without shelter and warmth."

Bessany scrubbed her forehead, willing the fog in her brain to recede, and brought down her hand to find it red with blood. She scrubbed it off on her shirt. No time, yet, for minor injuries. "Right." She stared at the damage, peering toward the source of light spilling out into the snow. "My God, it's the *med lab* still standing!" And since the med lab's lights still blazed, the power plant itself was undamaged. That single fact might well mean the difference between life and death.

Sinclair wrapped her up in a coat scavenged from the debris. "Yes, most of it was spared, thank God. In fact, several of the labs survived pretty much intact. Enough to provide some shelter, anyway. We've already shifted the less-badly injured into several of them. Power's out in most, but it's still better than being out in the open."

"How long was I unconscious?" she asked sharply.

"Almost half an hour."

Bessany blanched. If she'd remained unconscious much longer, she might well have frozen to death. There must've been just enough heat trapped under that solid rubble to keep her alive long enough to wake up and shout for help. "If the power's off in most of our shelters, we'll need wood for building fires . . ."

"There are many trees down," Chilaili offered. "I had to climb over them to reach your nest. I heard the twist-wind from the top of the cliffs and knew it had passed over this place. I hurried, Bessany Weyman, as fast as I dared."

Bessany's throat tightened. She touched Chilaili's arm, shuddering as the wind whipped stinging snow through the broken walls of the recreation room. "Thank God you did. I'll ask why you're here later."

Chilaili gave Bessany her strange, head-bobbing nod. "Yes. It is more important to find the trapped ones first."

They dug through the rubble in teams, freeing more people, locating more coats and distributing them. Herve selected four men who had escaped with only minor cuts and bruises, put them into rescued cold-weather gear, roped them together for safety's sake, and sent them out with lights to bring in wood while the search for survivors went on. Chilaili was a godsend, lifting heavy slabs it would've taken three or four men to shift. They found some people unconscious, others badly injured and screaming with pain—and some who lay ominously still, crushed and broken or surrounded with sickening crimson stains where they'd bled out through arterial damage.

Bessany worked with shaking hands, trying not to look into the faces of friends who had died in the rubble. She concentrated on guiding or carrying the still-living toward shelter, helping the uninjured reach whichever side lab was closest and ferrying the badly injured to the med lab. Salvatore di Piero, their construction engineer, had rigged a temporary wall of thick plastic sheeting across the jagged hole torn in one corner of the latter.

Grigori Ivanov, their surgeon—dazed and bleeding from multiple cuts—was finally pulled free. He leaned against Herve Sinclair while Bessany bundled him into a coat, then Chilaili literally carried him into the warmth of the med lab. Bessany followed at their heels while the others continued searching the wreckage. Her hands and face were frozen and the wind whipped through her long hair like knives. She stumbled toward the med lab in a deep fog, telling herself she was more fortunate than most—she was on her feet and functional. And still alive. She couldn't bear to look at the bodies they'd placed in a snow-covered stack to one side, awaiting burial once the living had been cared for.

They slipped past the curtain of plastic sheeting and warmth enfolded them. The relief from just being out of the wind was a tonic. Salvatore was busy examining the walls, shoring up the ceiling in places where the plascrete had cracked. The wounded lay on beds, on examining tables, on the floor, many of them moaning or crying out in harsher tones. Chilaili set Dr. Ivanov gently on his feet and braced him with one powerful arm.

He leaned against her for long moments, not even questioning her presence. He struggled visibly to still the shaking of his hands. Then he straightened with a grim look in his eyes and raked his glance across the lab, taking in equipment and supplies that had been spared and the appalling number of injured. He said only, "Bessany, can you help me as triage nurse?"

She nodded woodenly, so tired she was reeling on her feet.

"Life-threatening injuries first, everything else second," Ivanov said, then waded in.

Bessany followed her instincts and checked the unconscious first, figuring that anyone who was still knocked out suffered potentially far more serious injury than those thrashing around and screaming. She lost track of time, moving from one critically injured colleague to another, calling urgently for compresses or Dr. Ivanov's surgical skill. Ivanov performed miracles, doing emergency surgery to stop internal hemorrhaging, while dazed volunteers splinted broken bones and bandaged the less severely wounded.

At some point, Bessany glanced up to see Chilaili squatting beside one of the equipment mechanics, whose leg lay at an alarming angle, an injury far enough down on the triage list, nobody had reached him yet. Chilaili felt carefully for the break, then slipped something into the man's mouth for him to bite down on and moved her big, clawed hands purposefully. She set the broken bone with one easy movement. The mechanic screamed; then Chilaili gently tied a splint in place and pulled a blanket around his shoulders, murmuring something soothing to the suffering man before moving on to the next person in need of care. People stared at the tall, powerful Tersae as she moved amongst them. It was so unlikely, seeing her here, treating the injured.

Bessany had to swallow tears. Unlikely only in context, she realized. Chilaili was a trained healer. She doubtless had enormous experience setting broken bones and treating shock and blood loss. The effects of shock were essentially the same in all warm-blooded animals and a broken bone was a broken bone, whether it was part of a horse, a human, or a Tersae huntress. The only part of her gentle ministrations that seemed so jarringly out of place was her willingness to help humans at all, when Chilaili's species had declared unilateral, total war against the colonies.

She's come to repay the debt for saving Sooleawa's life, Bessany realized, watching Chilaili crouch beside a pile of food stores along the wall, which somebody else had scavenged. She broke open cans with her bare claws. She handed out food to those too injured to walk, even sent someone out with basins to collect snow, to melt for drinking and cooking water.

Through a blur of exhaustion, Bessany found herself thinking, *My God, with Chilaili's help, we might just survive this.* Tears stung her eyelids again and clogged her throat. How many of them would have died in the rubble without Chilaili's strength to shift the heavy debris before they froze to death? She couldn't even hazard a guess. Bessany scrubbed her eyes fiercely with the backs of her hands, which only smeared blood across her face, some of it hers, most of it other people's. She tugged off the coat she'd forgotten she wore, pulled her shirt loose, and wiped blood and tears from her face with the hem. Her hands shook so violently, she could barely control them, and her knees had gone dangerously spongy.

Herve Sinclair touched her shoulder. "Bessany. We're past the worst now. Dr. Ivanov suggested you sit down, get some rest and something to eat."

She nodded. "All right. I won't argue."

The project director stared thoughtfully at Chilaili, who moved out into the teeth of the storm again to search for more supplies. "At some point, I'd very much like to know what she's doing here."

"So would I," Bessany agreed in a low, shaking voice. "I think I can guess her reasons, but we need more than guesswork. If I'm right, she's come to pay the debt for Sooleawa's life by warning us an attack is coming. Probably as soon as the weather clears."

Sinclair blanched. "We can't possibly fight, Bessany. Even if we had weapons . . ." He gestured at the broken walls. "We're simply not defensible. And evacuating is out of the question. The tornado smashed the hangar.

There's nothing left of the aircars, not even much rubble. Most of them were apparently sucked up and carried God alone knows how far." His voice shook. "From the look of things, the tornado barely grazed the recreation hall, or we'd all have been sucked out with them."

Bessany shuddered. "I don't suppose any of our communications gear survived?"

Herve shook his head. "We haven't found it yet, if it did. The SWIFT unit's completely gone, along with the room it was in. The field radios are missing, too. Our main radio transmitter is smashed and the tower's down, twisted into useless junk. We'll keep looking, but I'm not very optimistic."

God, we can't even call for help. . . .

Bessany swayed sharply, fighting waves of exhaustion.

"You're weaving on your feet," Herve said gently. "Come on, let's get you into one of the other shelters, get some food into you."

Bessany let him pull the coat around her shoulders again, let him steer her outside and across the rubble field to the geology lab. Seven refugees huddled around a blazing fire that had been built in one corner, next to a window cracked open slightly, just enough to let the smoke out. Elin Olsson presided over the fire, keeping it properly stoked. The petite geologist, blonde hair streaked with dark stains, greeted Bessany with a wan smile and scooted over enough to give her room to sit down. The elfin geologist handed her a ration pack with three of the high energy bars they carried while doing field research. Bessany ate one without tasting it and washed it down with cold water from a basin of melting snow.

As she sat beside the crackling fire, watching the flames dance across the carefully stacked wood, her own injuries finally made their presence felt. From scalp to toes, the ache of bruises and multiple stings where she'd sustained cuts and scrapes spoke of the abuse she'd suffered. Her hands were shaking and all she really wanted was to lie down and sleep for about a year.

Elin glanced up and met her gaze. "Bessany?"

"Yeah?"

She expected the geologist to ask about Chilaili. Not for the first time, Elin Olsson surprised her. "Do you think the military help the Concordiat promised will get to us in time?"

Before the Tersae attack us?

The unasked portion of that question reverberated between them. Bessany shook her head. "I don't know, Elin. I just don't know." She bit her lip. "I kept sending messages to my brother-in-law, but he never answered. After Alex's death . . ."

Elin, who knew the whole story, reached over to wrap a comforting arm around Bessany's shoulders. "That wasn't your fault, hon."

Bessany shook her head. "No. I know it wasn't. But John Weyman tried to contact me, afterward, and I never answered his messages. I couldn't. Just *couldn't*." She closed her eyes over burning salt water. "God, Elin, I was so stupid. . . . And now we really need his help, I'm afraid he's returning the compliment."

"I can't imagine he would deliberately ignore you, Bessany. Or any message from Thule, come to that. He's probably just out on the frontier, fighting the Deng invasion," Elin insisted quietly, "and hasn't even seen your messages. So don't blame yourself, okay? None of this is your fault."

Bessany sighed. Elin was doubtless right, of course. It wasn't her fault and John Weyman probably wasn't spitefully ignoring her. But she knew only too well that even when the promised military help finally arrived at Thule, there was very little chance that help would be directed toward *them*. The mines were the critical installations on Thule—not a battered group of scientists huddled in the wreckage of their research lab. She said in a low voice, "If they can get to us, they will. *If*." She lifted her gaze from the heart of the flames and met Elin Olsson's frightened glance. "But even if they do manage to bring a fighting force out here before we're overrun, this station is dead last on anybody's priority list for defense."

It was dreadful, watching the elfin geologist come face to face with that bleak assessment. They weren't defensible, wouldn't have been, even before the tornado. They couldn't evacuate, neither by air nor by ground, not with most of their equipment wrecked or simply missing. Walking out was impossible, not with as many seriously injured people as they now had. And Bessany was far too experienced even to hope the cavalry would come over the hill in time.

Chapter Eleven

"This is the goldangdest thing I've ever seen."

Hank Umlani, Rustenberg's Chief of Industrial Fabrication, stared at the plans Senator had provided, understandably scratching his bushy grey hair and frowning at the technical specs he held. The thing was disarmingly simple. So simple, it didn't look like much of anything, let alone a weapon.

Alessandra asked patiently, "Yes, but can you *make* it? With the equipment and supplies on hand?"

Umlani looked up, raking a weary glance across the warehouse where they stood, a warehouse which now held the entirety of Rustenberg's surviving resources, moved into one protected location inside the perimeter wall, in a depressingly short time. Crews of miners were hard at work around them, conducting a hasty inventory. Ginger Gianesco, Rustenberg's Ops Director, had not been able to supply them with anything remotely resembling a psychotronics technician, let alone a Bolo systems engineer, which had forced Alessandra and Senator to get creative in planning the town's long-term defense.

The first step had been to list on a master inventory every weapon the miners could field. The colonists had come up with a surprising variety of personal arms: several very useful modern rifles brought out to defend mining parties from predators, plus sonic stunners, 20 kilowatt laser zappers, hypersonic needle guns, an honest-to-God anesthesia rifle, even a reproduction single-shot Sharps breechloader, which a hobbyist had brought with him.

"Isn't that buffalo gun a little primitive?" Alessandra had asked dubiously.

The owner, a burly man in his forties, gave her a nasty grin. "Wasn't too primitive for three of them damn turkeys."

They'd even counted the two longbows kept in the meeting hall, along with the colony's other recreational equipment. Senator had protested, saying, "Longbow projectiles wouldn't even scratch my armor," then had desisted, suitably impressed, when one of the women put an arrow through a chunk of beef taken from the shelter's refrigeration unit, demonstrating its effectiveness at piercing protoplasm. Alessandra had sent out crews with the modern guns, putting Senator in charge of turning them into an automated defense system. She could hear his voice booming in the cold air, through the open door of the warehouse.

"A simple computer system is all we will need. Something that will tell the guns to shoot back at anything which fires at the wall. The automated guns will use a triangulation system with range-finding lasers to determine the exact distance to anything shooting at the wall. This will trigger the guns in the most optimal position to fire back. The computers you already have on hand are more than adequate to run this system . . ."

His automated system wouldn't stop a crazed, lone

Tersae with a satchel charge in its claws, but it would drop anything that fired a rifle, mortar, or missile. She'd also sent several parties of miners out into the icy darkness with hand lights and ropes to comb the fissures and narrow gorges surrounding the town, hunting for possible Tersae weapons caches and scouting out good spots to place remotely controlled ambushes.

Still others checked on the mining equipment and the oil refinery. And just in case evacuation became necessary, she'd also sent a search party out through the ruins, hunting up every surviving transport left in town. That, too, comprised a very short list: seven aircars used for two-person aerial surveying teams and three lumbering, automated ore carriers that would hold a lot of people, but wouldn't top more than ten kilometers an hour.

For God's sake, she prayed, *don't let us have to evacuate this town. Not in a hurry, anyway.* If she and Senator did their jobs properly, that wouldn't be necessary. But with Senator's malfunctions, she was hedging her bets every way possible. Alessandra fully expected more trouble, not much later than dawn. She just hoped one malfunctioning Bolo, one battle-rattled brigade captain, and a gaggle of exhausted colonists could put together the necessary defense works before then. Particularly since most of the colonists with military experience had already died.

She shook herself out of her grim thoughts and peered up at the burly fabrications engineer holding Senator's blueprints. His thick, calloused fingers were covered with the scars of his trade. She asked again, patiently, "Can you build this, Mr. Umlani?"

"Well, yeah," Umlani nodded, frowning down at the blueprints, "we've got the tools and the necessary materials to build these things, no problem. Simple as dickens, ain't it? We can even make the glass balls pretty quickly, I'd think, using the ore smelting equipment and ordinary sand. There's a whole hill of the stuff in the mine spoils. It's easy enough work, even the kids could handle it." He glanced up, curiosity lighting his dark eyes. "You say this thing really existed? Was used in battle, I mean?"

Alessandra smiled. "Indeed, it was. Senator found a mention of it in his military history archives. Dates back all the way to Old Terra's First World War, he said. It was fielded for a while alongside machine guns and poison gas. How many of them can you build? And how quickly?"

Umlani grinned, teeth white against the exhausted darkness of his face. "Lots and very."

"Good. Get cracking, if you please. The sooner they're built and in place, the better I'll feel. Particularly since the weather appears to be clearing out there. God knows how many warriors the Tersae will throw at us, once this freezing rain stops."

"Right." Umlani hurried away, bellowing for his fabrication technicians.

Alessandra hunted up Ginger Gianesco and found her handing out cups of coffee salvaged from the supplies as half-frozen miners came in from the work crews. Alessandra accepted a cup with a nod of thanks, then asked, "What can you tell me about the refinery?"

The operations director blinked in surprise and raked limp, silver hair back from her face. "What do you want to know about it?"

"Aside from why it's here at all, what've you been cracking the crude into? Diesel fuel? Gasoline? Heating oil?"

The older woman's face rearranged its series of wrinkles. "We built it to provide ourselves a cheap, local source of fuel. Oh, we don't need it now, but we're going to grow, or planned to, anyway, and it won't take much growth to outstrip the snap generators we brought along. Equipment like that is expensive to freight all the way out here." A grimace touched her mouth. "You wouldn't believe the hell we caught, putting in that refinery. There's a xeno-ecologist over at Eisenbrucke Station who sent her research assistant out to us a couple of months back, to set up wildlife monitors and conduct studies. I couldn't say what the xeno-ecologist's like, but that assistant of hers . . ."

Gianesco shook her head, eyes dark with pain. "Stupid, greenhorn kid," she said roughly, the tone of her voice belied by the shimmer of wetness in her eyes. "Brought himself out here with a brand-spanking-new degree and a bunch of crazy notions about not spoiling virgin wilderness. We didn't come out here to admire the birds and the bees, we came out here to mine saganium. And build a colony our kids will inherit. That boy threw an honest to God tantrum over the refinery. Didn't speak to anybody for weeks, after construction started, just glowered like we were mass murderers and muttered under his breath about industry raping yet another world."

"What happened to him?"

She blew unhappily across her coffee cup. "He spent most of his time communing with his data recorders. God knows what, exactly, he was looking for out there, but he obviously preferred it to *us*. Poor fool went into shock when the Tersae attacked. Literally couldn't believe it was happening." She stared bleakly into her cup. "He didn't survive the first attack wave."

Alessandra wasn't surprised. She'd seen the type before. Gentle, liberal, very young. Full of sincere and noble ideas. Dangerously naive. They died fast and messy when war broke out around their ears, the way it had on Thule. She frowned then, trying to pinpoint something Gianesco had said, something useful. Then she had it. *Wildlife monitors.*

"Did his equipment survive?"

Gianesco blinked. "Yes, I think it did." She consulted the inventory list on the handheld unit clipped to her belt. "Most of it, anyway. Yes, here it is."

"May I?" Alessandra held out one hand.

The operations director handed over the slim unit and Alessandra scanned the list, lips pursed thoughtfully. "I've been worried about how to spot the approach of war parties in those gullies out there, since Senator has only a limited number of aerial survey drones on board. Those model airplanes Harry Bingwa scrounged from the recreation workshop will help, since we can mount cameras in them, but the Tersae are likely to shoot those down as fast as we put them up. This," she tapped the palm-sized screen, "just might do the job. You said there was a map of the terrain immediately surrounding the town?"

Gianesco nodded. "It's a geological features map, pinpointing the richest saganium deposits in the region. We'll have to pull it up on the main computers, though. I don't have it loaded on my hand unit."

She led the way past crates and cartons of supplies and forlorn piles of personal goods scavenged from damaged houses and headed out through the open doors on the far side of the warehouse. A blast of icy wind caught them as they made their way across the frozen ground between the warehouse and the surviving meeting hall. The hall was crowded with refugees: people injured in the defense, volunteers trying to administer dwindling supplies of medications, harried mothers trying to cope with young children exposed to far too much trauma.

Gianesco stopped at their hastily rigged "war room" and tapped commands into the computer system they'd brought up from the underground bunker, installing it here as the colony's new command center. The map flashed onto the screen, showing narrow gulches, deep gorges, and snaking fissures spreading in every direction, as though Rustenberg were the center of a web spun by a spider on hallucinogens. Alessandra leaned down and jiggled controls, zooming the magnification. "Hmm . . . ordinary claymores and jump mines aren't going to work very well, are they?"

"Why not? And what's a 'jump mine'?"

"A mine that detects the approach of infantry and propels itself up to about here," she measured her own chest with one hand, "then detonates. Messy as hell. Effective, too, against unarmored personnel. Which I understand the Tersae are? Unarmored, I mean?"

Gianesco nodded. "None of the ones we've seen have worn anything but fur and weapons belts."

"Good. As to the other" —she tapped the screen with one fingernail— "the way these fissures twist and turn, an ordinary mine, even something relatively directional like a claymore, won't be very effective, because the blast won't go around these corners. We need something that will."

"Like what?" Gianesco frowned. "What kind of weapon turns corners?"

Alessandra smiled. "You might just be surprised. What kind of industrial gasses do you have on hand? Anything heavier than air will do."

Light began to dawn in the older woman's tired eyes. "Good lord, yes. Fuel-air explosions, down in those ravines . . ."

"Exactly," Alessandra grinned.

The look in Ginger Gianesco's eyes made Alessandra feel about eight feet tall. To see a woman go from bitter, exhausted hopelessness to the dawning realization that there was something her people could do, after all, besides cower behind the Bolo's malfunctioning guns, went a long way toward erasing the worst of the hell Alessandra had suffered against the Deng.

Gianesco flagged down one of the older kids detailed to courier jobs. "Jennifer, go find Hank and Amanda. Tell 'em we need to bleed off the main natural gas tank at the refinery, into every portable gas cylinder they can lay hands on."

"Yes, ma'am!" The girl sped off, vanishing through the doorway with a slam of the meeting hall doors that set the nearest little ones whimpering.

Alessandra thinned her lips, seeing that. She coldly hated the Tersae for creating the fear she could see shining in the children's wide eyes, trembling on unsteady little lips. She'd seen, as well, the bodies of children who'd died with guns and spotting scopes in their hands, defending the walls as their parents finished the desperate effort of pouring the last stretches of defensive perimeter. And she'd seen the eyes of the kids who'd survived, eyes that would've looked old and hard in a fifty-year-old's face. The Tersae would pay for what they'd done here. Pay *dearly*. She and Senator had only just got started on ways to make those furry bastards pay.

"What else can we do, Captain?" Gianesco asked quietly. "And how can we deliver the fuel-air cylinders to the targets?"

Alessandra frowned down at the map again, unsure how to answer the second question. "About that refinery. You never did mention what you're cracking the crude oil into."

"Gasoline, mostly, to power some of the smaller tools. It's still one of the cheapest fuels around, particularly on worlds with a decent supply of crude oil, which Thule has. Evidently," one corner of her mouth quirked, "the climate wasn't always so chilly."

"Good thing, too," Alessandra muttered. "I wonder . . ."

"*Commander?*" her Bolo asked through the comm link at her belt.

"Yes, Senator? What is it?"

"I have been listening to your conversation, Commander, while supervising the field crews. May I make a suggestion?"

"Name it."

"I've been studying the ore carriers, Commander," Senator went on. "Their design has suggested a delivery system for some of the fuel-air mixture cylinders you were just discussing. It will be necessary for me to leave the town relatively undefended, in order to locate and destroy the enemy's home base. The computer-controlled gun systems we are setting up along the wall tonight will not be effective for indirect-fire scenarios."

"Yes, I've been worried about that," Alessandra agreed. "What do you suggest?"

"We could rig a carbon-arm trebuchet from some of the mining equipment out here, piggyback it onto an ore carrier to deliver a payload to a predetermined selection of ravines, computer controlled and preprogrammed for distance to target and depth of the selected gully. A computer could determine where in the arc of the throwing arm the payload should be released. We could predetermine various places to park the trebuchet, to reach a number of predetermined targets. We might even be able to rig a computer-deployed parachute system to provide drag on the projectiles, so they drop more accurately into the ravines."

"That's good," Alessandra blinked in surprise. "That's *very* good. We'll put somebody on it. What else?"

"Ms. Gianesco, how much sugar do you have in storage?"

"*Sugar?*" The operations director blinked in astonishment.

"Yes, Ms. Gianesco. Refined sugar."

Alessandra saw abruptly what her Bolo had in mind. "My God, that's *wicked* . . ."

"Thank you, Commander. About that sugar?"

"Uh . . ." Gianesco was consulting her handheld unit. "Not a lot. Maybe fifty pounds."

"More than enough," the Bolo replied firmly. "We will need to begin immediately, Commander, to prepare the mixture in time to field it before the next attack."

"Right. And we'll need someone to haul the sugar out to the refinery."

Gianesco, expression baffled, flagged down another courier. Then she stared at Alessandra, eyes begging the question.

Alessandra grinned. "Ever hear of foo gas?"

The mining ops director frowned and shook her head. "Should I have? I've mined a lot of things over the last forty years, but I've never heard of that."

"Foo gas isn't a specific substance, it's more of a generic effect. It's what you get when you toss a burning liquid, like jellied gasoline, say, through a burning substance like white phosphorus. The jellied fuel ignites in a burning wave that fries anything in its path. Like, say, Tersae warriors in a gully."

"With no way to climb out," Gianesco breathed. "My God, that's horrible." A faint, dreadful smile touched her eyes. "The sugar gels the gasoline?"

"Very effectively."

Her eyes went hard as blue gunflints. "Good. Show me what to do."

Dawn was a grey sliver along the horizon when Alessandra walked the perimeter one last time, inspecting the new installations in person. Ginger Gianesco walked at her side, along with Hank Umlani, who

showed them his night's handiwork with a justifiable
flourish of pride.

"What is it?" Gianesco asked dubiously, staring at
the device Umlani had set into a mound of dirt and
rock about four feet high.

"It's elegant, that's what it is," Umlani grinned.

The flat, meter-wide metal disk didn't look like
much, even to Alessandra, let alone an effective
weapon. It sat quietly on a spindle that ran through
a hole in its center, with a simple conveyor mechanism
that arched over the top, ready to deliver its payload
to the waiting weapon.

"What's it supposed to do?" the operations director
frowned.

Umlani chuckled. "This bar" —he tapped a crosspiece fastened to the spindle, turning it so that it swept
in a flat circle around the metal platter— "spins at 100
revolutions per second." The end of the bar reached
almost to the edge of the platter, describing a meter-
wide circle as it turned. "At 100 revolutions per second, you get 60,000 revolutions a minute. At 60,000
RPM, the end of the bar will be moving at 314 meters
per second."

"Yes, but what does it *do?* And why is there a hole
in the end of the bar?"

Umlani reached into a coverall pocket and dropped
an ordinary glass marble onto the platter, near the
spindle in the center, his fingers simulating the action
of the conveyor mechanism. The glass sphere was
roughly made, with no polish of any sort, just a simple
orb that Hank Umlani's fabricators and Rustenberg's
children had churned out by the thousands during the
night. "When the bar spins," he said, moving the crosspiece slowly by hand again, "it bumps the marble like
so. Centrifugal force operates to keep the marble
moving in a straight line." As he turned the crosspiece,

the marble did just that, moving from the center of the platter out to the rim, walked along by the movement of the bar. "By the time it reaches the edge, it's moving at the same speed as the end of the bar. And 314 meters per second is *fast*, as fast as some guns throw a bullet."

Gianesco suddenly saw it. "The marble slips through the hole in the end of the bar! And goes flying off the edge! How accurate is this thing?"

Umlani chuckled again. "The Bolo says it's nothing like as accurate as an ordinary rifle, but it's plenty good enough for our purpose. We've put 'em in a circle all the way around the original edge of town, one every five meters. This'll fling a marble at a slight upward angle, so the projectile never goes higher than five feet or so off the ground. The marble drops in an ordinary ballistic parabola down to four feet off the ground again, out to a range of about 150, maybe 200 meters. When we activate the system, we'll end up with a glass curtain of death, one those damned birds will have to run through to get close enough to our wall to use satchel charges or small arms. Ought to be as effective as machine gun fire. Bolo says they were actually tested in battle, centuries back, but they were dropped from the arsenals because machine guns were more accurate."

Alessandra nodded. "They worked just fine in trench warfare, though, and that's pretty much what we've got here. Trench warfare." Alessandra gestured in the growing dawnlight toward the gullies and ravines. More nasty surprises waited silently in the shadows at the bottoms of Rustenberg's natural stone trenches.

Gianesco was about to ask another question when Senator interrupted. "Commander, our wildlife monitors have picked up enemy troop movements in the ravines. We face a heavy concentration of enemy warriors. I will cover your return to town."

Ginger Gianesco paled. Hank Umlani swore. Alessandra broke into a run across the icy ground. The civilians panted at her heels. Alessandra didn't bother looking over her shoulder. Senator would be watching and the last thing they needed was to put a foot wrong in the broad swath of rubble strewn like caltrops between themselves and the defended wall. A massive rumble shook the ground, then Senator bulked huge, gun snouts black against the pale grey dawn as he charged straight past them, interposing his bulk between them and some unknown—

The world shook.

And the whole sky erupted into the colors of hell.

They fell flat in the rubble, knocked down by the shock wave from the Bolo's twin Hellbores. Alessandra panted into the dirt and tightened her fingers around broken chunks of plascrete. *What the hell was shooting at us, for him to unlimber the Hellbores?* Whatever it was, it didn't shoot back. Alessandra scrambled to her feet and snatched the others up by the backs of their coveralls. *"Run!"*

They needed no second urging.

Chapter Twelve

I am anxious to be on the ground again.

As we drop from orbit, plunging toward Thule's turbulent surface, I see the curve of the planet's snowy shoulder in triple images, one from my own sensors, one from telemetry provided by the Darknight, and a third from her destroyer escort. The Darknight and the Vengeance will remain in orbit as long as needed, guarding our vulnerable backs from potential space-based attacks by whatever alien race is providing high-tech weaponry to the Tersae. The ships track deployment of the battle group as my fellow Dinochrome Brigade comrades scatter across Thule's four main continents. We drop from the blue-black edge of space into the blue-white haze of Thule's thermosphere, which is merely a thin scattering of molecules here, at an altitude of 150 kilometers.

The blizzard which has prevented Tersae attacks at Seta Point still rages, providentially, but the telemetry I receive from the CSS Vengeance includes weather-pattern projections which show the storm system clearing Seta Point within seven hours of our arrival. It is essential that we reach our duty station before the enemy can field a force to attack it. Our very arrival may well trigger the enemy into risking the blizzard to destroy the colony before we can arrive. Our descent carries us around Thule's hulking shoulder and down into night, which is spectacular as we pass through the ionosphere. The sight draws uncharacteristic commentary from my commander.

"Damn, that's beautiful . . ."

Curious as to what John sees, I limit my sensors to only those spectra perceived by humans. A blaze of stars backlights a sky-spanning display of aurora borealis. Wildly writhing curtains and ribbons of green and red light flicker and dance, swaying across the darkness, pierced here and there by the streaks and flashpoint bombs of a meteor shower.

It is, indeed, beautiful. I am deeply pleased, that John has noticed, leaving me to hope he will not withdraw into deep isolation again, as he did after his brother's death. It took so long for me to break down that isolation the last time, I feared for many months I would lose him as commander and friend. I am therefore grateful to the silent dance of ghostly light across Thule's night skies and regret the briefness of our transition through the dazzling display.

But the eleven-kilometer reading on my altimeter marks our abrupt transition into the storm-racked troposphere. We plunge into heavy cloud cover which effectively blinds my own sensors. It is unsettling to "see" clear air above me, through the eyes of the CSS Darknight, *while everything around me—and more critically, everything below—remains wrapped in the dense haze of night-darkened storm clouds.*

We suffer a jolting ride due to high wind speeds, with unstable wind shears and shifting gusts making lateral corrections from the lift platform's engines a constant necessity. My commander, who loathes combat drops as much as I detest confinement aboard naval transport ships, hums tunelessly under his breath and stares fixedly at the altimeter. "Anybody down there watching us?" *he asks tersely.*

"I have detected no scans on any of the standard wavelengths. If the enemy has seen us, they are using a technology completely alien to our experience."

John Weyman grunts noncommittally, using a tonal inflection I have learned, over the years, to translate roughly as "wouldn't surprise me, if they did." Given the information in our mission briefing, virtually everything about the enemy is unknown. It is an interesting way to begin a war. I comment, pragmatically, "Coming up on five thousand feet. Brace for braking thrusters."

My heavy lift sled fires its main engines, slowing our precipitous plunge through the storm. Blizzard conditions leave us totally blind and rock us violently. Temperatures hover at zero degrees Celsius, plus or minus three degrees on average. Wind chill factors drop the temperature another twenty degrees, making the storm lethal to any unsheltered human on the surface.

My thoughts stray to Bessany Weyman and the unknown cause of Eisenbrucke Station's communications blackout. I grow concerned that weather fierce enough to destroy the research station's radio and SWIFT units will have left the inhabitants exposed to fatal temperatures. Even discounting the risks of enemy attack, there may be trouble ahead if serious damage has occurred to the physical shelters at Eisenbrucke Station—or at Seta Point.

Given the look in John Weyman's eyes, my commander shares this worry.

The gusts ripping through my external sensor arrays are creating problems already, running the gamut from ice and slush buildup on sensor lenses, particularly those bearing the brunt of the wind, to wild harmonics that create sensor ghosts, static discharges, and false images.

I want down. Badly.

I pull in my main sensors, tucking them back into armored turtle cowlings, and deploy backup sensors instead, as a precaution. "One thousand feet," *I advise.* "Scanning terrain with radar. Matching terrain features with on-board maps." *I correlate data rapidly.* "We are five kilometers off target, John, north of Seta Point along the Whiteclaw River. Five hundred feet. Applying lateral thrust to avoid crossing the Whiteclaw on the ground."

"Good idea," *John nods agreement. According to survey data, the Whiteclaw River is a treacherous chute of white water along its upper reaches and still runs fast and deep where it spills out onto its alluvial plain, directly beneath us. The settlement five kilometers to the south has been built to mine alluvial deposits as close to the rugged mother lode as possible. Given the data from our mission briefing, plus input from my radar arrays, I do not relish the thought of trying to ford the Whiteclaw in a blizzard; the energy expenditure to avoid this while still airborne is well worth the trouble. I monitor our lateral progress carefully via radar.*

"Approaching the Whiteclaw River. Two hundred feet—"

Violent wind shear topples me turret-side down. We plummet like a stone, tipping and tilting crazily as the lift's engines scream, trying to right us again. I yank all retractable small-caliber weapons systems inboard to protect them. I can do nothing about fixed systems, including my Hellbore and mortars. I am canted at a one-hundred-six-degree angle when my turret plows into something solid. One corner bites deep, digging a jagged trench. I slam into the ground like a flipped beetle, stunned by a momentary overload from my pain sensors. A howl bursts from my stolid commander. We plow across frozen ground in a slide I can neither control nor halt. Top-side external sensor arrays—ignored in the rush to protect my weapons systems—rip loose from their mountings, scoured away by the wild skid.

The sickening slide ends abruptly when the ground vanishes beneath my turret. My war hull teeters, tips, and plunges downward, half rolling and half somersaulting as we fall straight into the foaming Whiteclaw. We strike the water like the Titanic diving for the deep. Water pours in through holes where backup sensor arrays have been torn out by the roots.

I close emergency hatches on the flooding conduits, desperate to minimize electrical damage to my systems and to keep the water from pouring through interior spaces by means of cable conduits and access crawlways. Another slam against a solid surface jars my war hull, then I come to rest on the river bottom, canted mostly on my back and deeply shaken.

John gasps into the comparative silence, his breaths ragged as he hangs upside down in the command chair, cushioned by the protective webbing used during combat drops. The hiss of a hypo-spray sounds from the autodoc built into the chair, feeding medication into his system. As the medicine takes effect, he begins to swear monotonously, spitting blood from a bitten mouth. He struggles to wipe his eyes clear as that blood trickles down past his nose and into his eyes and hair.

Hand shaking, he reaches unsteadily for the med-console, which pops open. Supplies have been webbed in as snugly as my commander, with commendable foresight on the part of my designers. He fumbles an elastobrace loose while muttering creatively at Thule's *inimical weather, then laboriously wraps a swollen elbow in the brace. I monitor his vitals, fearing shock and internal injuries, while attempting to ascertain damage to myself.*

We have, at least, reached the ground without encountering enemy fire.

"How bad is it?" *John mutters, fumbling the med-console closed again.*

"Your vitals are holding at acceptable levels—" *I begin.*

"Not me, you loveable idiot," *John mutters,* "how bad is the damage to *you*?"

Oh.

"Performing damage assessment. I have lost backup external sensors across the entire upper surface of my turret. Portside sensor cowlings are showing red-line. There is warping damage to some of the sensor hatch covers. I managed to retract small-caliber weapons systems before we hit. Checking outboard, larger-caliber systems. One rank of turret-mounted infinite repeater snouts has sustained minor deviations from true, measured down the long axis, although the deviations are well within battle-damage tolerances for continued operations."

My commander blinks, then asks, "Your guns are bent?"

"Not all of them," *I prevaricate.* "A rank of portside, nonretractable fifty caliber gatlings snapped off completely. They were my least robust external weapons, however," *I hasten to add,* "and their loss should not materially affect my ability to carry out our mission. The remainder of my nonretractable weapons have not been affected."

"Huh. Including your Hellbore?"

I scan, performing a pre- and post-crash comparison of angles and tolerances. "There is no deformation in the Hellbore barrel," *I am pleased to report.*

"Well, that's something." *John sighs.* "All right, next step. How badly jammed into this river bottom are we? Among other things, the human body wasn't designed to hang upside down for long periods of time."

Indeed, my commander's face is already turning an alarming shade of red as blood pools under the weight of gravity. I turn my attention rapidly to my predicament, since the sooner I solve mine, the sooner I will solve my commander's. I scan my surroundings, using what sensor arrays have survived the crash, mostly nestled in the protected spaces along my prow, starboard side, and stern. "The river bottom is narrower than I would like," *I relay,* "but there should be sufficient room to maneuver, if I am very careful. I am still locked into the lift platform, which should be of considerable help. The engines are still functional."

John manages a shaky grin. "Best news I've heard in the last five minutes. Okay, let's see if we can flip you right-side up."

The lift platform's engines are, of necessity, powerful, capable of lifting and maneuvering a 14,000-ton Bolo. I have come to rest mostly on my turret, but my portside is lower than my starboard, which will assist my task considerably. I apply thrust carefully to the portside lateral thrusters. The engines snarl and scream and my war hull shifts ponderously. I succeed in rolling completely onto my back. And there, I find myself stuck. The lateral thrusters, less powerful than the main lift engines, are unable to shift me any farther, without the rocky river bottom to push against. Chagrined, I am forced to admit the worsening of our predicament.

"I am sorry, John," *I apologize.*

My commander chews his lower lip thoughtfully, wincing slightly and wiping blood again. "Can you rotate your turret? If we bring your Hellbore in line with the very bottom of the river and fire it, the recoil concussion might jar us loose enough for the lift engines to flip us all the way over."

It is a good plan. I have landed with my Hellbore facing upstream, but angled so that it is pointed slightly downwards. The river is narrow enough that my prow—and therefore my Hellbore—lies within twelve meters of the far riverbank. I slid into the water prow foremost, somersaulted once, and came to rest in this position. If I can rotate my turret so that my Hellbore faces as far down as possible, the barrel will also swing farther towards the far bank. This will give me an extra boost, as the Hellbore discharges into more surface area of stone than water.

I attempt to rotate my turret, feeling the immense strain in my internal servos as they struggle to turn with the immense weight of my war hull plus lift platform resting against them, jamming my turret down into the rocky riverbed. The servos were not designed to function under these conditions. I run them dangerously into the red, but my turret groans and grinds its way slowly in a ponderous arc. I halt the attempt to allow overheating servomotors to cool, then begin again. "I have rotated my turret as much as I dare," I report. "Brace for Hellbore fire."

WHAM!

I rock against the blast and fire thrusters on the lift platform. My prow rises off the river bottom and I fire again. WHAM! The engines scream and I rotate my turret wildly, bringing the Hellbore around for optimal position as I rock onto the very edge of my treads. WHAM! I turn and fall with a ponderous crash and slosh. The instant my treads are lowermost, I fire all thrusters and the lift platform rises with an agonizing scream. We tip and tilt, then my damaged turret breaks through into snow-shrouded air.

Water surges and pours. Steam rises from the superheated river, which now boasts a radically altered shape. My treads clear the water and I fire rear thrusters, moving across the roiled and boiling surface of the Whiteclaw toward the blessedly solid rock of the far bank. I carefully avoid the deep bite where my guns have blasted that rock, melting it in spots. I angle, instead, toward a secure landing spot farther downstream. My weight crushes flat a heavy growth of dense shrubbery which lies between water's edge and a thick stand of riverine forest. If I were human, I would cheer. My commander, collapsing white-faced into the depths of the command chair, does, in fact, manage a weak hurrah. He grins into my nearest video pickup.

"You did it!"

"We did it," *I correct gently.* "It was your idea, John."

"Occasionally," *he chuckles,* "I do have good ones. Whooee, what a ride! All right, my battered friend, damage assessment, please."

Water continues to pour out of my war hull. Within one point three minutes of exposure to the blizzard, ice forms a solid coating over my entire hull, including main sensor hatch covers, external backup sensors, and gun barrels. The ice blocking my main sensor hatches will require time to melt and the coating across visible-light sensors on the backup systems leaves me blind in the visible-light spectra, but I am right-side up and mostly intact. For the moment, it is a worthwhile trade.

I flash schematics onto my forward data screen, showing my commander the extent of damage. "Thirty-nine percent of my turret sensors have been damaged. I do not have sufficient spares on board to replace more than thirty-seven percent of them and I would advise against making any repairs while weather conditions remain this severe." *Ordinarily, of course, I would have been brought up to full depot readiness before being deployed in a new combat drop, but I have seen three months of nonstop combat, much of it rugged, and there was no time to bring my on-board stores up to specs. The CSS Darknight's crew loaded as much replacement equipment as possible from ship's stores, but even their large inventory was spread thin, attempting to reoutfit no fewer than five combat-depleted Bolos.*

"What are the relative levels of damage in this schematic?"

I color-code the display. "Green sensors are fully functional. Orange warning lights indicate crash damage which limits functionality. Ninety-two percent of the orange-marked damage is attributable to sensors hatch covers that have been slightly warped, preventing the hatches from opening properly. This should be relatively easy to repair."

My commander snorts. "You mean something about this mission might actually be easy?"

The wan smile accompanying this question marks a return to my commander's usual droll sense of humor, pleasing me immensely. "Compared with the landing? Absolutely."

The wan smile becomes a genuine grin.

"Sensor arrays marked in yellow are fully functional, or rather, will be once thawed out. My entire war hull is now coated with ice, which has sufficiently blocked the indicated sensor arrays, they are of limited use. The visual-light camera lenses in particular have been affected, as the ice has rendered them temporarily opaque. I have initiated antifrost heating systems, but it will take time to clear them. Navigation will be possible, of course, using radar and infrared systems, but I will not be able to move at optimal speed until the camera systems are clear of ice. My turret servo-motors have suffered a twenty-three percent loss of function, due to the strain of breaking loose. I will not be able to turn my remaining turret-mounted weapons as quickly or reliably as usual."

"Understood. We've been dealt a lousy hand, for sure, but any crash you can walk—or limp—away from isn't *all* bad. All right, let's see if we can limp into Seta Point, shall we?"

I attempt to disengage from my lift platform and discover yet another casualty of the crash. The platform has suffered warping throughout its structure. I cannot disengage the autolocks. "John? We still have a problem."

"Oh, Lord, now what?"

I explain.

The last thing I expect is the rusty laugh my commander responds with. I stare at him, abruptly concerned for his health. He wipes tears with an awkward hand, then manages to wheeze, "What a pair we are, Rapier. All banged up and nowhere to go . . ."

"It will be very easy to pull loose, simply by engaging my drive engines, but getting back to the ship will be a problem, which is why I hesitated to act without consulting you."

John continues to chuckle. "At the moment, that's the least of our troubles. All right, Rapier. If we have to break it to get loose, then we have to break it. Somehow, I don't think they'll take it out of our pay."

I refrain from pointing out that Bolos do not earn pay, then engage my drive engines. It takes zero point three seconds to rip loose from badly bent moorings. I leave behind a tangled, mangled hunk of metal, one that has given its life nobly in service of mine and my commander's, and set out along the riverbank. I move parallel to the Whiteclaw, along which the Seta Point mines stretch, reflecting that the river is more than aptly named. It certainly has mauled me, as effectively as any clawed beast.

Perhaps the forcible jarring of our crash landing and subsequent escape from the river has knocked circuitry loose somewhere in my psychotronics, for I must work harder than usual to gather my scattered thoughts from the various remote system modules where they reside. Four point two minutes elapse before it occurs to me that I would pick up speed considerably if I were to move away from the river, where I am forced to plow through the edge of a dense riverine forest, grinding down trees and lower, dense undergrowth beneath my icy treads.

I consult on-board maps and aerial survey photos and alter course, breaking through the relatively narrow band of forest cover which hugs the route of the Whiteclaw. Beyond lies more open ground, where badlands have given way to alluvial plain, covered with tough grass which lies flattened, now, beneath a mantle of snow. The greatest obstacles here are deep snow-drifts and the frozen streambeds of small tributaries.

I pick up speed rapidly, crossing small tributary streams with a shattering of surface ice and a splash of dark water. I am anxious to reach my duty station, as my presence there will allow John to send scouting parties to Eisenbrucke Station by ground transport. If, of course, someone can be found to go. I hope—rather desperately—there will be someone at Seta Point willing to risk it, since neither my commander nor I are free to go, ourselves. If not . . . I hold onto my hope, reminding myself that humanity can be a remarkably brave and selfless species, when the situation warrants it.

John consults a side viewscreen where I have displayed a map of the region, superimposing our position *onto it. John nods to himself, then opens a radio frequency via controls on my command-chair console.*

"Seta Point, do you copy?"

A burst of static is followed by a human voice, one which sounds very young. "This is Seta Point. Who is this?"

"Lieutenant Colonel John Weyman, Third Dinochrome Brigade."

"Really?" This childlike squeal is followed by an excited shout. "Dad! Dad! It's a Bolo commander!"

A faint smile touches my commander's lips. A moment later, a deeper voice hails us, somewhat uncertainly. "This is Seta Point, Bill Hanson, speaking."

"Lieutenant Colonel John Weyman, here," *my commander responds.* "We're inbound along the Whiteclaw River, ETA your location in three minutes. We'd hoped to set down closer to your settlement, but the weather wasn't very cooperative. Our landing was a little more exciting than either of us would've preferred."

A rusty chuckle emerges from the speaker. "We're awfully grateful to that weather, Colonel Weyman. And most of us use more, ah, colorful words to describe it." *My commander shares the chuckle, then Bill Hanson says in a tone that betrays worry,* "I don't suppose you know what that godawful noise we heard a few minutes ago was? We thought the Tersae were attacking through the blizzard, after all. We sent out every man and woman who could scrape up a weapon to defend the edges of town. They picked me to man the radio, because I broke my leg, sliding on the ice."

My commander grimaces. "Sorry to hear that, Mr. Hanson. And that noise was us, I'm afraid. We suffered a very bad landing. Ended up turret-side down at the bottom of the Whiteclaw. We had to fire the Hellbore to jar ourselves loose. You can call everybody back inside, get 'em out of this weather."

"That'll be mighty welcome news," *Hanson responds.* "It's a bad night to be outside. Anything we can do, once you get here?"

"If you've got a medico, I'd welcome their help. I banged up an arm on landing."

"Roger that, and I'll put a fresh pot of coffee on, Colonel."

"I'll look forward to it. We'll see you in about two minutes. Weyman, out."

Two point one seven minutes later, Seta Point appears in my sensors, a radar ghost at the top of a bluff overlooking the Whiteclaw. The site must have been chosen with flooding in mind. This has, however, left the town unpleasantly exposed to the vagaries of Thulian weather and leaves the settlement dangerously vulnerable to enemy artillery fire. On the positive side, the openness of the terrain will make it harder for enemy infantry to approach without exposing themselves to murderous fire from my guns.

By the time we arrive, climbing a well-constructed, wide road to the top of the bluff, my visible-light sensors have warmed enough to melt the ice sheathing their lenses, allowing me to see where I am going far more clearly. I am glad of this, for we discover an immense crowd waiting for us. The entire settlement has come streaming to the edge of town, suited up against the snow and heavy, gusting winds.

I halt at a safe distance, unwilling to come closer on the icy ground for fear of a skid. My running lights make my towering prow clearly visible despite the snow-filled darkness—uptilted faces gape at my ice-shrouded duralloy war hull and gun snouts. Through my thawing external sensors, I hear the concerted gasp which rises from more than a thousand throats.

Civilian awe at seeing an ordinary Bolo never ceases to amaze me, even after fifteen years of active service.

I have speculated, sometimes, that there must be something of a religious, or at least superstitious, element to this reaction. Judging by my own experience, the human mind fears—in a primitive, subconscious fashion—that which is larger and more powerful than itself. Even when that something was fashioned by human hands and human ingenuity.

I find this very lonely.

My commander unhooks himself from the command chair and shrugs on cold weather gear stored in a bin at the back of my command compartment, moving gingerly and scowling at his swollen elbow. "Well," *he sighs philosophically, glancing into my forward camera,* "let's see what we can do, shall we? Maintain full Battle Reflex Alert and scout the whole perimeter of the settlement. Find out which areas of town are most vulnerable to attack. I'll see if I can find anything useful from the colony's stores to repair your sensor arrays, at least."

"Understood, John."

He climbs down and greets the welcoming committee, which elicits a wild cheer of welcome. The crowd moves toward a structure adequate to hold the entire population. It is time for John to initiate his council of war—and time for me to discover the exact shape and extent of the terrain I must defend. Satisfied that I have safely delivered my commander to our duty station, I carefully back up, turn, and tackle the next phase of my mission.

Chapter Thirteen

Wakiza trembled with cold as he huddled under the uncertain shelter of the trees, trying to keep the worst of the sleet from lashing him in the darkness. At fifteen summers, he was one of the youngest warriors of Hook-Beak Clan, a barely blooded hunter without a single raid against enemy clans to his credit.

Three times, he had watched in despair as the war parties were sent to destroy the human nest. And three times, those war parties had been driven back, failing to crush the hated creatures from the stars. When told that he would be assigned to the night watch for the fourth attempt, rather than the attack teams, he pleaded with the war leader for a better assignment, certain the end was near and afraid he might miss the final victory.

"Your time to die gloriously will come, Wakiza," Chesmu told him sternly. "For now, obey orders and keep silent. That is my final word."

Night watch.

Duty barely worthy of a newly hatched nestling.

Wakiza watched bitterly as more fortunate warriors crossed open ground unchallenged, entering the strange nest that lay—insanely—open to the winter sky. He watched with rising jealousy as the attack party blew holes through the defensive wall, all but unopposed by enemy fire. He felt useless—worse than useless—squatting here under a tree while the older warriors took all the glory for themselves. He had spent his entire fifteen summers aching to please the Ones Above, to show his creators that he was brave and swift and worthy, and now others were winning the battle he had so desperately longed to join—

The night split wide open with flame and noise.

A monstrous *thing* fell from the storm clouds, spitting death and venom.

Wakiza's beak fell open in shock. It was bigger than the entire clan's living cavern. Bigger than anything Wakiza had ever seen. Fire belched from it, lancing down through the sleet-filled darkness to ignite the weird, alien structures of the human nest. Flames roared high into the night skies, leaving Wakiza trembling on his belly against the frozen ground.

"It's a metal ogre!" he whispered.

He had not truly understood, until now.

Their best missiles detonated against it without visible effect. The thing kept coming, dropping down from the clouds, shooting its weapons in a fiery rain of death. It was unbelievably ruthless, destroying virtually the whole human nest in its zeal to kill every member of Hook-Beak Clan's attack parties. Not one of the warriors chosen to enter the enemy's nest came out again.

Wakiza turned and fled into the night, duty-bound to carry home word of the ogre's arrival. By the time he arrived at the living cavern, he was bleeding and dazed, slashed by thorny underbrush and several nasty tumbles down rocky gullies. He was shaking so hard, he could scarcely gasp out his message.

"The thing burned down everything outside the defended wall!" Wakiza chattered the words out through shudders that shook his thin, adolescent shoulders. The grizzled, aging war leader and the clan's *akule* exchanged dark glances as Wakiza added, "Never have I seen such ruthlessness! Nothing our warriors threw at it even scratched the thing. Please, Honored Chesmu, give me the chance to carry out vengeance for our slain brothers!"

Chesmu gripped Wakiza's shoulder under bruising fingers. "You shall have that chance, gladly. Come, there is much to be done before dawn."

They left the nest again under cover of darkness, although dawn was only an hour or so away. Sleet continued to fall, but the weather wise amongst their clan's warriors agreed that the storm would soon break, leaving clear, cold weather in its wake. That would only make it easier for the hated defenders to see them coming. There was not much time left, if they hoped to destroy the enemy and earn a place with the Ones Above for all eternity.

Wakiza brought up the rear of the war leader's own handpicked band. As they crept down into their chosen ravine, he was shocked at the wide swath of forest leveled during the night, depriving them of useful concealment. *It must have been the ogre,* he realized, awestruck. What else could have flattened so many trees and ground them into splinters underfoot in so short a time?

After a moment's frightened thought, however, he realized the loss of the forest cover probably mattered very little. Their war parties were spread out through dozens of twisting, narrow gorges that would allow them to creep so close, it would require only a short dash to reach the enemy's nest. Powerful the ogre might be, but it could not patrol every approach to their target.

Besides, the Ones Above had given them weapons capable of crippling and perhaps even killing the huge machine, if they could take the metal beast by surprise. When Wakiza had reported the failure of their missiles against it, Chesmu had ordered the deadliest weapons they possessed brought up from the war caches in the nest's lowest caverns. If all went well, this dawn, the metal ogre would be the one surprised and dismayed.

And shortly after that, dead.

Wakiza's heart thudded at the thought that *he* would have helped to kill it.

Grey light was just topping the upper edges of the deep ravine when he heard it, the sound of distant missiles igniting. His heart pounded wildly, listening. The attack had begun! He fought a terrible urge to scramble up the steep ravine wall to look as the deadliest of their weapons, two ogre-killing bombs strapped to a pair of missiles, raced toward the metal monster. He gripped his rifle in trembling hands, wanting to see—

The world erupted into a hell of sound and blazing, unearthly light. Wakiza screamed, falling flat against the rocky ground, which shook under his belly. An instant later, flame erupted from the head of the gorge, blasting toward them like an avalanche. Wakiza dropped his rifle and climbed straight up the rocky wall, one terrified eye rolling downward to see the war leader and warrior after warrior swept away, crisped in an instant. He lunged and scrabbled for claw and talon holds, felt the searing heat approaching, whimpered . . .

Then fell forward onto sleet-covered ground.

He snatched his feet up as the killing wave of fire

passed beneath him. He didn't dare look down into the ravine, where their best had just died horrible deaths without striking a single blow against the enemy. He looked up, instead, and saw gouts of flame spurting up from the edges of other deep ravines. Screams carried on the wind, screams that cut off with hideous abruptness. A distant movement caught his eye and he craned around to look.

Across the open ground between himself and the enemy's nest, beyond the wall the humans had put up, he could see something like a gigantic dark thorn. It rose up with shocking speed, flinging something across the wall, then it dipped again and vanished beneath the wall before reappearing to fling *another* something, which flew in a slightly different direction. Wakiza watched, hypnotized, as the nearer of the two things soared out toward a deep crack in the earth. A strange cloth of some kind bellied out abruptly from the top of it, halting its flight. It dropped with seeming gentleness into a ravine perhaps five seconds' fast sprint away—

A massive explosion ripped the dawn. Chips of stone and searing heat hurled their way skyward. Wakiza screamed again, cowering and hiding his head. When he lifted his shaken gaze again, trying to nerve himself to climb to his feet and run, he saw warriors pouring up over the lips of gullies and ravines which had not yet been torched by the enemy. They were racing across the open, rubble-strewn ground, shooting missiles at the distant walls or gripping rifles in the hopes of getting close enough to fire. They raced forward in three-second bursts, moving fast in relays across the open ground, shooting missiles and rifles to cover one another as they ran for the alien wall.

And as Wakiza stared in horrified fascination, those who shot missiles toward the enemy nest drew murderous fire from the wall, going down in a spray of blood and fur. Those who shot their rifles earned the same fate—but those who simply ran forward without shooting seemed invulnerable. Wakiza gulped and started to rise, thinking he would scavenge a rifle from one of the warriors already killed and carry it close to the wall before firing. Then he noticed a buzzing noise, like a thousand mound-stingers roused to homicidal fury.

Startled, he looked around for the telltale mounds and spotted a whole line of them, which he hadn't noticed in the darkness of the previous night. Surely the humans couldn't have found a way to turn the mindless mound-stingers into a weapon they could use at will? Despite the angry buzzing, he didn't see anything like the stinging cloud of insects which were often the last thing an unlucky hunter heard, if deep water to jump into was not close at hand when the mound-stingers' ire was roused.

The buzzing rose in crescendo—then one of the six warriors in the team running toward the nearest buzzing mound went down, struck by something Wakiza couldn't even *see*. The warrior screamed, writhing in agony where something had cut literally all the way through his body. Three more warriors went down within seconds, struck by the invisible mound-stinger weapon. The remaining two stared in such wild terror, trying to determine where the invisible weapon was coming from, distant rifle fire from the defended wall blew straight through their skulls. Wakiza froze in place, too horrified to move, convinced that if he rose from the icy ground, he, too, would go down, dying a shameful death without so much as a single weapon in his hands.

Overhead, a stiff-winged bird soared past with a high-pitched whine.

An instant later, the metal ogre's enormous bulk appeared from around the curve of the wall. An instant after that, explosions shook the ground all around him. Wakiza screamed and flung himself down into the ravine behind him, falling and scrabbling for handholds, then he landed with a bone-wrenching jar. The stink of cooked flesh was foul in his throat. Burned shapes huddled everywhere, charred lumps of flesh that still smoked in the grey dawnlight.

Wakiza fled, running wildly toward the end of the gully they'd entered so jovially just minutes previously. It was worse than suicide to fight the metal ogre, it was utter madness. He had to warn the nest, warn the *akule*, who could at least plead for help from the Ones Above. They needed help and stronger weapons and food for their little ones, who would surely go hungry in the deep winter snows, now that most of their skilled hunters had died on the battlefield. He ran until his breath was a raw, bleeding rasp in his lungs, skidded and slid and climbed across fallen timber and pounded as fast as his legs could carry him toward the uncertain safety of home. Once there, he burst into the clan's living cavern and gasped out his tortured message, collapsing into the *akule's* horrified arms.

"Dead . . . all dead . . . Chesmu and the others . . . please, *akule*, beg the Ones Above for help . . . nothing can stand against the metal ogre, *nothing* . . . without help, we shall all surely die . . ."

Under the *akule's* careful questioning, he gasped out everything he'd seen, described it in as much detail as he could recall through a numb haze of horror: the giant thorn that threw the massive bombs, the waves of fire in the gullies, the invisible mound-stingers, all of it. When he'd finished, the *akule* said gently, "You have done well, Wakiza. Very well. Rest now. Rest and recover your strength, for you will be sorely needed."

Wakiza closed his eyes, shuddering violently. Dimly, through the thundering in his ears, he heard the *akule's* voice in the Oracle chamber, begging their creators for help, for weapons to destroy the metal ogre, for anything the Ones Above could send. He relaxed, at last, no longer fighting the blackness of a dead faint as he realized he'd done it, he'd brought the warning in time.

For now, at least, the clan was safe.

Chapter Fourteen

Colonel Ruk na Graz glared morosely at the data screens which comprised one entire wall of his cramped office. He had resented this duty assignment from the day his posting had been ordered from the Homeworld. His uncle had fallen from the emperor's favor yet again, scuttling Ruk na Graz' own hopes for a successful military career. *Damn* that long-toothed, hot-tempered, loose-tongued old fool! If not for his uncle, Ruk na Graz would never have been reduced to commander of a dismal, airless hole bored into a cratered chunk of rock at the back of beyond.

He tapped clawtips in a pattern of irritated impatience against his desktop, hating almost as bitterly the orders which had just come from the Imperial palace on Melcon. Those orders kept his forces—such as they were—bottled up uselessly in garrison on this godsforsaken airless moon.

He could only watch in rising frustration as the enemy reinforced itself with ever more troop transports, ever more battle machines, while he was forbidden even to poke his muzzle into the open, much less strike a blow against the hated humans. Melcon, he had decided morosely, was rotten with incompetence and greed. A cowardly lunacy had permeated the Imperial palace, one that kept the border patrols from openly confronting the Empire's enemies, as honor demanded.

Why, in his grandfather's day, these arrogant, upstart humans would simply have been blasted from the sky the moment they dared appear in orbit above a Melcon-held world. Particularly one where such an important—and expensive—scientific experiment was under way.

But with a new emperor on the throne, Melcon now ordered the military forces on the borders of Melconian space to hide, to gather data in secret, to do nothing that would betray their presence to their new human neighbors. Safer for Melcon, perhaps, when dealing with enemies as potentially damaging as the humans, but such a fight was utterly without honor.

And now that dishonorable policy of secretive cowardice had landed squarely on his own desk. He glared at a printout of his latest orders, received just before the new human battle group had broken into the system from hyper-light drive. Ruk na Graz held a snarl rigidly behind his teeth, to prevent his aide de camp from hearing it, in the outer office.

"Under no circumstances," those orders read, "are you to allow the enemy to take prisoner any live populations of Tersae. The enemy must not gain access to information about Melcon through access to these experimental animals. The safety of the Empire and the Homeworld far outweigh the results of this experiment in biological manipulation, fruitful as it has been. If it becomes necessary to protect the secrecy of this project, execute destruct codes and evacuate the star system."

Lunacy!

"Execute destruct codes," they said. His muzzle wrinkled in bitter distaste. He didn't give a damn about the experimental animals, but it was such a wretched waste of Melconian time and effort, to simply euthanize the beasts before the experiment had reached its fullest maturity. Generations of Melconian scientists had poured their talents and genius into the creation of the Tersae, into the manipulation of their genetic code, gathering critical information on biological deformation in the process, information that would give Melcon the edge in *any* long-term conflict with her enemies.

From where he sat, at least, the humans looked more and more like the worst enemy Melcon had yet encountered. Intelligent, resourceful, capable of manufacturing weapons that were the equal of anything developed in Melcon's weapons laboratories, they were also doggedly tenacious. Everywhere humans had gone along the edges of Melconian space—or Melcon's uneasy border with the Deng—the humans had poured immense resources into holding onto balls of utterly worthless rock, valueless apart from the presence of human colonies.

A scowl lifted the jowls from his teeth. That tendency to fight for worthless bits of rock might apply elsewhere, but it was clear to Ruk na Graz that the humans had found *something* of immense value here, something they were mining by the shiploads. Whatever it was, it was valuable enough to send war machines in to defend the mines, and that spoke—to Ruk na Graz, at least—of critical war materiel. His increasingly urgent reports had been totally ignored, leaving him no choice but to watch from this carefully-hidden moon base while cargo transports jockeyed and maneuvered through the muck and debris of this misbegotten star system.

The Tersae were certainly far too stupid to figure out what the stuff might be and why the humans wanted it. The *only* thing the Tersae were good for—in this particular context—was delivering bullets and bombs. And they were so incredibly brainless, they blew themselves up more often than not, dying "gloriously" for their makers. Ruk na Graz snorted. They didn't even know how to die properly. If not for the waste of so many Melconian lifetimes spent creating and manipulating them, he'd almost have enjoyed issuing the destruct codes.

A low buzzer interrupted his bitter ruminations. "What?" he asked harshly.

"Forgive the intrusion, Colonel Graz, but Science Leader Vrim is asking to see you."

Ruk na Graz bit back the angry words on his tongue. "Send him in," he growled.

"Yes, Colonel Graz."

The door opened and Grell na Vrim entered, muzzle respectfully lowered. The Science Leader had gone grey around the jowls, having spent most of his career on this moon base or conducting field research down on the surface. Vrim had not been pleased by the order halting all such field trips until the human threat had been satisfactorily neutralized. If the Science Leader had come to demand yet again that he rescind that order . . .

Ruk na Graz waited for the aging scientist to halt in front of his desk before speaking.

"Yes, Science Leader?"

Holding some sort of printout tucked under one arm, Grell na Vrim met his gaze squarely, anger visible in the set of his ears. "Is the rumor true, Colonel? Has the Homeworld ordered the destruction of the Tersae?"

Ah . . .

"It's no rumor, Science Leader." He tossed the print-out across his desk.

Vrim read it, clamping his ears flat to his skull. "This is an outrage!"

"I agree."

"Then—?" Hope flared in the tone of his voice and the brief lifting of his ears.

"I will do whatever is necessary, Science Leader, to protect the Empire and the Homeworld from threat."

"But—" Vrim closed his mouth again with an audible snap of his teeth. "Yes. Of course. May a lowly scientist ask if we are expected to sacrifice our own lives, as well, protecting the Homeworld's secrets?"

Strength still blazed in those eyes, the strength of a zealot dedicated to his mission. Ruk na Graz was unable to disguise the sympathetic twitch of his ears. Vrim was no soldier and did not bring the same expectations to his work that a soldier would have, facing those orders. The Science Leader saw only the ruin of his life's work in that sordid little printout—and rightly feared the destruction of his life, as well.

"I sincerely hope not," Ruk na Graz said quietly, giving the most honest answer he could, for he respected the Science Leader, although he would never dare admit it to a mere civilian. "That would be a far greater waste, in my opinion, than the loss of a few thousand flightless, furry birds. To lose good Melconian lives, protecting the secrets surrounding those stupid beasts . . ." He shook his head in frustration. "Given the strength of the human incursion into this system, they are clearly determined to fight as long and as hard as necessary to inhabit that wretched ball of ice. I would advise you and your people to start packing. The Homeworld will not allow me to fight for this star system, so the best we can do is make a run for it in a fast transport ship while the humans are distracted."

"Distracted?" Vrim asked, openly puzzled.

"That is my worry," Ruk na Graz growled. "Yours is getting your people and as much of your research data as possible ready for emergency evacuation."

"Yes, Colonel," the Science Leader muttered. He brought out his own printout, then. "We have received a transmission from one of the Tersae clans." He handed it across.

Ruk na Graz frowned at the transcribed message. "Invisible mound-stingers? What in the seventeen moons are they talking about?"

Vrim shrugged. "I don't know. I was hoping you might have some idea, since I don't know much about weapons systems."

Another scowl lifted Ruk na Graz' jowls. "I've never heard of anything remotely like this. Buzzing mounds and invisible weapons that cut holes through a solid body? If this were a military installation, at least I'd have access to a decent laboratory of weapons technicians, to try figuring it out." He tossed the printout onto his desk, so disgusted he couldn't even find words to express it.

"Will you honor their request for more weapons?" Grell na Vrim asked.

"Are you *mad*?" Ruk gasped. "We won't even *answer* this ridiculous communication! The *last* thing we can afford is to attract the attention of the human ships in orbit." Dark suspicion flared. "For the gods' own sake, don't tell me you've already sent a reply?"

"No, no, of course not," the aging Science Leader hastened to reassure. "I wouldn't consider such a thing during a state of war, not without consulting you first. Which is why I came, of course."

"Of course." He swept a hand toward the pitiful, pleading printout. "Add that to your data, Science Leader, then start your people downloading and packing."

"Yes, Colonel Graz. At once, Colonel Graz. Your support is so *deeply* appreciated, Colonel Graz." The aging scientist stalked out of his office, ears flat again with anger.

Ruk na Graz sighed. Such an unutterably *stupid* waste.

He turned his gaze back to the data screens once more and glared at the blips of light representing the human military vessels in orbit. He hated the idea of tucking tail and running without a fight. Hated it almost as much as he hated the humans. Unless he was very much mistaken, this was going to be a long and shameful war. And the fools on Melcon were robbing him of the right to strike the first blow.

Chapter Fifteen

PROXIMITY ALERT!

My sensors detect two fusion bombs, piggybacked onto a pair of guided missiles, fired directly toward my war hull. I charge forward, horrified, passing my commander and the two civilians with her, interposing my bulk between them and the incoming missiles. I have zero point zero two seconds to decide which of my malfunctioning weapons to fire, knowing there is a high probability I will miss my targets. My Hellbores are the only weapons I possess which have a broad-enough field of fire to destroy the bombs even if my aim is slightly off.

I fire twin Hellbore blasts point-blank at the incoming bombs.

I rock on my treads. The overpressure knocks my commander and the miners flat. Both incoming bombs vanish in a hellish flare of light. Radioactive isotopes scatter across my war hull and the three humans lying flat behind me. The bombs have not detonated, merely spilled their contents, which was my intended purpose.

My commander snatches up her companions and shouts at them to run. They stagger forward while I scan for more incoming missiles. Seeing none, I check telemetry from the wildlife monitoring cameras we have set up and determine the moment is ripe. Further delay will only lessen the effectiveness of the blow I am about to strike.

I send out a radio pulse, signaling the detonation systems in the trenches.

Explosions and the weird, chopped-off screams of the enemy drift on the grey morning air. I retreat toward my commander and pivot so that my access ladder is directly beside her and the civilians. "Commander, all three of you have been exposed to dangerous levels of radioactive isotopes from the fusion bombs I have destroyed. Please strip off contaminated clothing and come aboard at once, to begin chelating treatments in my command compartment."

Alessandra DiMario snarls, "Strip, dammit!" *even as she wrenches at the zips and fasteners of her uniform.* "There are observation couches with autodocs built into them, up there. Move!"

They strip to the skin, then climb, moving very fast, indeed. I turn jets of water on them, spraying them down to rinse away as much of the residue as possible—while blessing my designers for building such a feature into my external chassis, anticipating potential need for battlefield decontamination. I open my command compartment hatch and the civilians tumble inside, half climbing and half sliding down, dripping water and shaking with cold from the frigid wind which has been blowing across their drenched skin and hair. I dial up the heat in the command compartment, turning fans onto high, while Alessandra shoves them into the observation couches and slaps restraints into place. I swing autodocs over them and commence treatment even as my commander throws herself into the command chair and engages restraints. I have already closed my command hatch by the time her own autodoc sends medication racing into her bloodstream, countering the effects of radiation exposure and chelating the isotopes already absorbed.

The battle is well under way as I swing my attention and my guns toward the enemy. The carbon-arm trebuchet operates with surprising efficiency, reloaded by waiting miners the instant the arm swings back down to loading height. As the enemy comes surging up out of the ravines and gullies, fleeing the death waiting for them there, the deadly rain from our marble throwers and automated gun systems begins to wreak a terrible havoc.

I fire at targets which appear to pose the greatest threat, attempting to control the wild inaccuracies of my guidance and control systems. I now understand what it would be like to be stricken with palsy. Human lives are at risk and I cannot control my own weapons systems. I charge forward, firing massively, rather than accurately, and know savage satisfaction when enemy warriors go down before my guns. Other warriors, weaponless and bloodied, turn to flee from my roaring treads and mortar fire.

"They're running!" The gasp of surprise breaks from Ginger Gianesco.

The enemy is, indeed, running. In blind, terrified desperation. The Tersae attack groups have been so badly shaken, even their suicide squads, far to the fore in their efforts to gain the wall, now turn to flee. The defenders shoot them down ruthlessly, firing into broad, fur covered backs which make easy targets for the enraged miners.

"Shall I pursue or consolidate defense efforts here?" I ask as the surviving Tersae warriors vanish into the

cover of what little forest I have allowed to remain standing. "Odds are approximately 98.7 percent that they will make directly for home. If they lead us to their base camp, we could render it inoperative, accomplishing our long-term goals quickly. We might also be able to secure undamaged samples of the technology they have been using to conduct the war."

My commander turns slightly in her command chair to catch the eye of Rustenberg's Operations Director behind her. "Do you have the medical facilities to treat exposure to radiation?"

Ginger Gianesco thins her lips. "Not anything like a full clinic, I'm afraid. And we didn't come out here prepared to mine radioactives, so we're shy on some of what we ought to have. But there's enough to keep us going until there's time for full treatment, somewhere. I've treated radiation sickness in other mining operations, so I'm no neophyte."

"In that case, I'd suggest we drop you off here. There's no telling what we're going to run into, out there. Your people need you here, both of you."

"Thank you for everything you've done, Captain," *Gianesco says with a catch in her voice.* "More than I can say."

"Our pleasure, Director. Let's get you out of here, so Senator and I can go finish off the job properly." *I rush across the rubble field to pivot and stop next to the defended wall. A ragged cheer rises from the defenders. I am both surprised and honored by the salute. Ginger Gianesco and Hank Umlani unstrap from their couches as I remove the autodocs.*

My commander does her best to reassure them. "Senator's autodoc systems have given you the critical first treatment. We'll do our best to finish this up fast, so we can get you back into the autodocs as soon as possible. There are spare coveralls in a compartment behind your couches, by the way," *she adds with a slight smile. All three humans are as naked as newborn infants. Our passengers respond with rusty chuckles.*

As they slither into coveralls and climb toward my hatch, I bid them farewell. "It has been an honor to serve with you."

Ginger Gianesco hesitates for three heartbeats in the exit hatch. "You come back and tell us about it, Senator, you hear me?"

I am deeply touched. "I will do my best, Ms. Gianesco."

She nods sharply. "That's all anyone can ask. Thank you, Senator."

They climb swiftly down, stepping from my war hull to the top of the wall, where they are welcomed by their own. I close the hatch, pausing just long enough for my commander to finish slipping on her own coverall. As she returns to my command chair, I back away carefully, pivot, and charge across the open rubble field once more. I have tasted blood. Before this business is done, I will do a great deal more than simply taste it. My commander watches my forward viewscreen through narrowed eyes as my sensors track telltale heat signatures through the trees ahead.

"Still running hard, aren't they? Good. Follow 'em, but not too closely."

"Understood, Commander." *I launch an aerial drone, having kept them in reserve for just such a contingency. The drone races skyward, scanning the terrain ahead and monitoring the crashing, terrified progress of our prey. I detect thirteen heat signatures in a cluster, with a fourteenth far ahead of the others.* "Looks like somebody panicked and ran sooner than the rest," *my commander says drolly.*

"If we cut to the east of these trees," *I flash a superimposed map over the images from the drone,* "I

can pursue without having to grind down timber to
follow. Smashing down trees will make a great deal
more noise and might well cause the enemy to veer
course from their home base. I have sufficient aerial
drones on board to track them through the remaining forest cover, even if the enemy recovers enough
sense to begin shooting them down."

"Good plan. Do it."

*I turn to the east, circling the stand of trees, which
allows the panic-stricken enemy to believe they have
eluded me. They slow slightly in their headlong rush,
staggering and gasping, offering one another assistance
as battlefield injuries make themselves felt. I realize for
the first time that substantial size differences exist
among the individuals, with some topping a full eight
feet in height and others reaching no higher than an
average human female, nearly a meter shorter than the
tallest individuals. As I ponder possible explanations
for these differences, I am deeply startled to receive
a command-frequency hail from near orbit.*

"CSS *Darknight* to all Bolo units in the field, file
VSR, please."

"Good God!" *Alessandra stares.* "The *Darknight*?
That's a heavy cruiser!"

I respond to the request for VSR. "Unit SPQ/R-561
of the line, reporting. Captain Alessandra DiMario,
commanding."

"DiMario here," *my commander takes over the VSR.*
"We are engaged in pursuit of enemy forces" *—she
glances at a side screen for the distance—* "zero point
nine kilometers east of Rustenberg. We have repelled
a substantial attack here and are tracking survivors to
their home base. If you can spare a medical shuttle,
Rustenberg's Operations Director and Chief of Fabrications could use a full course of antiradiation treatments. We had a near miss with a couple of fusion

bombs. If Senator hadn't destroyed them, there'd be nothing left of Rustenberg but slag."

"Understood, Captain," *a crisp female voice responds.* "We'll send a team down as soon as we can. We've brought five more Bolo units with us, which we've fielded to undefended colonies. If you need help, we're in parking orbit with the destroyer CSS *Vengeance.* We'll watch your backs from up here, in case whatever's arming those birds decides to intervene. *Darknight* out."

"Roger that, and thanks. DiMario out." *My commander frowns, tapping her fingers against the padded console under her hand.* "Now there's an ugly thought," *she mutters.* "I really want a look at whatever those things have stockpiled in their base camp. And where the devil are the Tersae keeping that camp? Does your drone see any heat signatures that would indicate an aboveground encampment large enough to support as many personnel as we've already killed?"

I widen the range of the drone's sensors, which have been focused tightly on the fleeing Tersae. "No, Commander, there are no heat plumes besides Rustenberg's within a fifteen-kilometer radius of the drone. Shall I boost it to a higher altitude?"

"No, launch a second drone. I don't want to lose sight of those things, which we could do if they jump into a narrow ravine and take shelter under an overhang or in a cave somewhere, while the drone's looking for heat plumes."

I launch a second drone, boosting it to a higher altitude. There are still no visible heat plumes besides Rustenberg's. "I have scanned a fifty-kilometer radius, with negative results. Any shelter the Tersae are heading for must be underground, to shield the heat of campfires this thoroughly. If," *I add thoughtfully,* "the Tersae require cooked food or campfires for warmth."

"Huh," *my commander grunts.* "With those beaks of theirs, they could well eat raw meat. And I suppose it's possible they wouldn't need shelter or warmth to survive a Thulian winter. Presumably most of the wildlife gets along just fine. But whatever their tolerance for winter weather, they're using advanced technology and *that* wouldn't fare too well if left out in freezing rain or blizzard conditions. I think you're right, Senator, they've got an underground hidey-hole."

I study the geological map provided by Rustenberg's Operations Director, but it reveals too little about subterranean features to be of substantial use. I monitor data feed from both drones, watching the straggling enemy as it limps toward home. Having swung wide around the stand of trees which has given the enemy a false sense of security, I slow to a crawl and parallel enemy progress toward their unknown destination.

The lone Tersae survivor running far in advance of the others vanishes into a ravine. A heat plume rises abruptly in a visible beacon. I send the drone lower, angling its cameras to peer into the shadowed depths. The narrow ravine hides the opening to a cavern of unknown dimensions. A well-fitted cover has been stretched across the entrance. It was the opening of this cover that sent the heat plume skyward.

We have found the enemy's base camp.

Two point zero three minutes later, I detect a strong radio signal originating from the ravine. Startled, I lock on and hear a burst of alien chatter. My commander leans forward, expression intent.

"If I had to place a bet," *she mutters,* "I'd say they're yelling for help."

"Agreed, Commander. The signal is both powerful and directional, aimed at something in orbit."

My commander hails the CSS Darknight. "*Darknight,* DiMario here. We are picking up a Tersae radio transmission aimed at an orbital target. Do you hear the signal?"

"Roger and affirmative, we've got it." *A brief pause ensues.* "It's tripped a relay system inside an orbiting satellite. We're warping orbit to attempt capture."

"Roger that, *Darknight*. We'll apprise you of further developments on the ground."

The cluster of Tersae warriors following the front-runner has reached the same steep-sided ravine, climbing down by means of a rough trail hacked out of native rock. My commander speaks softly. "All right, Senator, it's payback time. Let's go."

Savage satisfaction floods my ego-gestalt circuitry, skittering weirdly through the tangle of jury-rigged connections between older and newer psychotronic systems. As I rev up my drive engines to battle speed, I hope that my malfunctioning systems hold together long enough to destroy the enemy and take its base camp intact for the intel specialists. Then I slash my way into the forest with a ponderous crash of falling timber and close in for the kill.

Chapter Sixteen

Wakiza had not yet recovered his own strength when the other survivors, shaking and exhausted, crawled into the warmth and safety of the winter nest. Moments later, they all jerked upright again at the sound of distant crashing through the forest. The stone of the cavern floor began to rumble underfoot, as the earth had done when the great metal ogre had charged toward them.

"The ogre!" Wakiza gasped. "It's coming!"

Exhausted, wounded warriors exchanged sick looks of fear, then staggered up again, snatching up weapons in shaking hands. Cries of fright rose on all sides from the women and little ones. The *akule*'s voice rose authoritatively. "Get the little ones into the deepest cavern! Anyone capable of holding a weapon, arm yourself and move out, quickly. We must stop the ogre before it reaches the nest!"

Already, half-grown boys were struggling to carry out the last of the missiles from the weapons-cache cavern. Wakiza hoisted a missile to his shoulder, grabbed

up a replacement for the rifle he'd lost, and rushed
out into the cold morning, climbing the path up from
the bottom of the ravine. The ground shook underfoot.
A hideous, terrifying growl filled the air, while the snap
and crash of full-grown trees sounded loud as gunfire
in the distance.

Wakiza began to run, sobbing for breath as the rest
of the surviving warriors joined him. A glance behind
showed him a ragged line of women, pupils wide with
terror, carrying rifles and struggling to control their
panic. Rage formed a hot and stone-hard knot in his
breast. That it should come to this! Arming women to
defend the very nest! A whisper at the back of his skull,
that this threat to clan and nestlings was no less than
what they, themselves, had sought to inflict on the
humans, was a breath of sacrilege through his mind.
He snarled at the fleeting guilt that thought stirred to
life and ran through the trees, weapons clutched tightly
in his grip. Now was not the time to debate the wisdom of actions long since taken.

The ogre's snarl had reached deafening proportions
when he saw the great metal hulk of the thing towering higher than the trees. Wakiza dropped to brace
one knee against the frozen ground, taking aim with
his one missile. He took careful aim at the wicked gun
snouts high above him, then slapped the plunger on
his missile. A blast of heat scorched his shoulder as
the weapon flew toward its target. Wakiza rolled and
ran, not even waiting to see if the missile struck, flinging himself prone behind an outcropping of rock. Fire
belched through the trees and the shock wave of a
massive explosion shook the ground.

Then he was up and running again, trying to get
around to the side of the metal monster as it kept
coming, invincible, unstoppable. He caught sight of
other warriors firing missiles, saw terrified women

dropping to their knees, fumbling with weapons they had only the vaguest notions of how to fire. The ogre's gun snouts belched flame and death. Trees crashed all around, cut off like twigs by the ogre's guns. Screams of pain and terror echoed through the forest. Wakiza fired his rifle at the thing, hating with a maddened red haze. Guns higher off the ground than three fully grown warriors spat at him. He threw himself prone as flame and explosions erupted everywhere around him.

And still it kept coming. Missiles detonated against its sides without effect.

Sobbing in terror and frustration, Wakiza wondered with a despairing howl, *Why have the Ones Above forsaken us? Can't they hear our frantic pleadings? Have they no eyes to see our distress?* They were alone in this glade of death, abandoned to the monstrous shape of the enemy's guns, with no hope remaining. All that remained was to die in defense of home and nestlings. Wakiza hurled himself forward, screaming out his hatred as the only antidote to terror.

Chapter Seventeen

I run a gauntlet of enemy fire.

Their missiles, fired at point-blank ranges, pass my malfunctioning gun systems with devastating ease, wreaking havoc with my forward sensor arrays and small-arms systems. My commander grits her teeth as we grind forward, slashing out as best we can with poorly aimed salvos from my infinite repeaters and chain guns. The enemy falls sporadically, crushed under my treads when I pass over those who fall wounded in front of my prow. Many of those opposing us fire awkwardly, as though they do not know how to use the weapons in their hands.

"They're throwing everything they've got into the defense," *my commander says in a hushed voice.* "Look at the difference in size and personal decorations. Those are Tersae females down there."

I believe my commander to be correct.

Slaughtering females who are all but helpless is distasteful, but the enemy has shown no mercy to human females and children. I press forward through the scattered defenders, determined to neutralize the threat from this base camp. The deep-fissured ravine appears through a thin screen of remaining trees. I grind them down and angle my guns to fire into the deep cavern at the bottom.

Ion-bolt infinite repeaters bark and snarl, whipping through the flimsy covering across the cavern entrance, vaporizing it and part of the rock with it. Weird, alien screams rise from beneath the stone overhang. Mortars streak upwards toward my hull, half of them detonating against the rocky walls of the ravine. The remainder arc high overhead. I angle my upper turret guns toward them, knocking down five of the seven incoming rounds. The remaining two detonate against my turret. Pain spreads through damaged sensor arrays. I fire VLS missiles and more ion bolts into the ravine, chewing away at the stone of the cavern entrance. Smoke and rocky debris choke the air.

Surviving enemy ground forces rush forward from behind me and along my flanks, firing ineffectually with rifles and grenades. I scatter antipersonnel mines and devote my main attention to taking the base camp. Another blast from ion-bolt infinite repeaters smashes into the cavern entrance and a massive chunk of rock shifts and falls, collapsing down from the ceiling. Screams erupt inside the cavern once again. The enemy does not return fire. Zero point eight minutes after the partial collapse of the cavern roof, Tersae begin staggering from the cavern entrance. I take aim with antipersonnel systems . . .

Then pause, startled.

The Tersae hold no weapons. But neither are they attempting to surrender.

They are fleeing something terrible within their own cavern. Those staggering into the open are falling, *twitching horribly. Blood appears, oozing from body cavities, pouring from beneath skin and fur.*

"Omigod," *Alessandra breaths, her voice raw with horror.* "Something's broken open a container of chemical war agents! Or maybe biologicals." *Her voice goes dark with rage.* "Those goddamned bastards gave biochemical warfare compounds to *stone-age savages!*"

I notice with a chill of horror through all my systems that the few surviving Tersae who have been trailing me, firing rifles into my rear armor, have begun to stagger, already falling down and writhing in massive spasms. There is no time for consulting anyone, even my commander. I fire Hellbores into the ravine, again and again, turning the entire cavern to molten slag in my efforts to destroy as much of the unknown biological or chemical agent as possible before it can spread.

"Warn Rustenberg to evacuate," *I say.* "I've done what I can to contain most of the spill inside that cavern, Commander, but I can't destroy the compound that's already escaped. Rustenberg is directly in the wind-dispersal pattern."

Her hand shakes as she reaches for the controls on her command chair. "How long do they have and how far do they have to run?"

I check wind speed and direction. "Seven minutes, Commander. They need to reach a point forty kilometers due north within seven minutes."

"My God," *she chokes out,* "they'll never do it in time." *She slaps controls.* "DiMario here. Evacuate Rustenberg immediately; repeat, *evacuate Rustenberg immediately!* The Tersae have released an unknown biochemical warfare agent into the atmosphere. You are at critical risk. You have seven minutes to reach a safe zone forty kilometers due north of Rustenberg."

The familiar voice of the Operations Director gasps

across the connection, "Gianesco here. We don't have enough transports to evacuate everyone!" *She then snarls at someone else, voice swinging away from her comm link,* "Dammit, move those children faster!"

Another voice breaks into the conversation, a terse female voice. "Lieutenant Carter here, en route to Rustenberg aboard a *Darknight* transport shuttle. We dropped from orbit three minutes ago. We're jettisoning medical equipment to make room for evacuees. We're ETA your location two minutes at maximum speed."

"How many can you take out?" *Ginger Gianesco's voice is ragged, raw.*

"Seventy adults, maximum, inside the shuttle, and that's stripping her to the deckplates. Lieutenant Commander Lundquist is doing that right now. If you can pack people into one of those big ore containers, we have the engine capacity to lift it out with us."

"We'll cram 'em in 'til they can't breathe," *the Operations Director vows.* "Set down at the mineworks, we'll be waiting there with everyone we can't ship out in our own aircars. Gianesco out."

There is nothing further my commander and I can do for the civilians we have come here to protect. We are too far from Rustenberg to reach it, even at maximum speed, and even if we could reach the town in time, my war hull is thoroughly contaminated. Indeed, my commander is now trapped in the command compartment. I watch that realization dawn in her eyes, see the terror rise with cruel devastation as memory of lying trapped inside another Bolo breaks through her awareness.

"I am with you, Commander," *I say gently.* "This time, you are not alone."

Her breath is ragged as she nods. "Yes. I know. Thank you, Senator. I'll be . . . fine."

Her shiver belies her words, but she holds onto the

shreds of her composure, eyes closed, lips trembling as she wages an internal battle to rival the one we have just come through. I sit beside the blasted cavern, surrounded by the enemy's dead, and hate the unknown creatures who have wrought this devastation. Whoever, whatever, wherever they are, they must be made to pay. The contaminated wind whistles across my turret, racing toward Rustenberg and the desperate refugees trying to flee. Oh, yes, this unknown enemy must be made to pay.

Most dearly, indeed.

Chapter Eighteen

"John!" *I hail my commander through the comm link, urgently.* "Trouble at Rustenberg!"

I relay the messages I have picked up from the Darknight's *descending shuttle and from Unit SPQ/R-561 and his commander. I forward a second VSR outbound from Unit SPQ/R-561.*

"—preliminary data indicate a type of rapidly acting neurotoxin. I have taken tissue samples for analysis. I have also discovered the carcasses of a flightless bird species which shares a probable 99 percent matching genetic material with the Tersae. The timing of their deaths indicates a high probability that these animals also died within three minutes of contact. All Units of the Line, be advised to use extreme caution when attacking any Tersae home base."

My commander snarls a curse through the comm link. This is, indeed, dire news. Not only are the colonists at Rustenberg at serious risk, it will be difficult to effectively neutralize the Tersae as a fighting force without the ability to attack their camps. My commander, voice rasping with tension, speaks brusquely. "I'm coming aboard, Rapier. Get your duralloy backside up this bluff, stat. And get me a link to General McIntyre. Patch it through the *Darknight,* if you have to, but get him."

I establish the contact while racing up the wide road to the top of the bluff. I am forced to relay through the Darknight, *as General McIntyre's duty station is on a continent on the opposite side of the planet. The General's response is terse.*

"McIntyre here. This better be good, Weyman, we've got one hell of a crisis under way."

"Request permission to depart Seta Point for Eisenbrucke Station immediately, sir. If the Tersae have biochemical weaponry, that research station is now our top priority. We need the scientists there, badly. It would take days to get another research team here—and with a weapon like SPQ/R-561 just described, we may not *have* days."

"God, I hate it when you're right, Colonel. How soon can you be there?"

"Rapier?"

"If we encounter no significant obstacles, we could reach Eisenbrucke Station within thirty minutes."

"Then get moving," *General McIntyre responds crisply.*

"Roger that. *Darknight*, has this damned weather cleared Eisenbrucke yet?"

The communications officer aboard the naval transport responds negatively as I reach the top of the bluff and slew around to a halt, waiting for my commander's arrival. "Afraid not, Colonel. They're deeper into the storm front than Seta Point and still under thick cloud cover."

"I was afraid of that." *My commander's voice is breathy with the sound of running. He appears through the swirl of falling snow, moving fast. Several Seta Point civilians run with him while John issues final instructions for the town's defense in our absence. My commander clasps hands with the town's operations director, who wishes him luck.*

"Thanks," *my commander responds grimly.* "I have an awful feeling we're going to need it."

My commander hauls himself up the ladder, climbing awkwardly with his elbow locked in a brace. I pop my hatch open and John clambers aboard, sliding down into the command chair.

"Go."

I turn cautiously while civilians stumble back to a safer distance, then launch myself down the slick road at the greatest speed I can safely make. Once we reach the flat river plain, I open up my engines, crossing the alluvial flatness at maximum sustainable battle speed, aware that I will be forced to slow the pace once into the badlands which surround Eisenbrucke Station. The ride jolts my commander badly, but there is nothing I can do to cushion him that the command chair is not already doing.

"Are there any maps of cavern systems on this ice ball?" *my commander asks abruptly.*

"No, John. The initial surveys conducted by the planetary scouts were not comprehensive enough for that. If the Thule Research Expedition has filed such reports, they were not available to Sector Command. The scientists have only been in place three months and may not have filed any reports at all." *I consider another possible avenue of inquiry.* "We could request the Ministry of Mineral Resources to check their archives. Given their sponsorship of the expedition as well as the colonies, they would be the agency most likely to receive such reports, if they exist."

"God, what a helluva way to run a war. We're thirty

minutes away and the only way to ask is to send a SWIFT message all the way to the Inner Worlds. All right, do it. Relay through the *Darknight*, Code Delta Zulu One. And query Sector Command, while you're at it. Just on the unlikely chance Bessany overcame her hatred long enough to try contacting me."

I wince at the bitterness in my commander's voice as I send the communiqués, requesting the Darknight *to expedite under the most urgent code a field officer can use to obtain critical data. It will take time for us to receive answers, even using SWIFT transmission. I leave the flat alluvial plain behind and climb into the badlands, angling toward Eisenbrucke Station at reduced speed.*

The blinding snow worsens as we press deeper into the storm. High winds engulf my war hull, whistling past at speeds gusting in excess of 75 kilometers per hour. I am forced to a slow crawl, using radar to probe my way ahead, blinded in all my other sensors by the white-out conditions of the blizzard.

Eleven point three minutes after the CSS Darknight *sent our messages via SWIFT, we receive a response from the Ministry of Mineral Resources. The team at Eisenbrucke Station has, indeed, filed reports. There is no mention of cavern systems in any of them. But the reports forwarded by Bessany Weyman leave my commander pale with rage.*

"My God!" *he explodes.* "What in *hell* were those bureaucratic jackasses doing, sitting on these?"

Thirty-seven seconds later, we receive the response from Sector Command, and it is even worse. Bessany Weyman has attempted to contact my commander. Five times. Her reports, full copies of those sent to the Ministry of Mineral Resources, include further notations indicating copies have also been sent to the Ministry of Xenology. None of her messages were forwarded to our duty station at the front lines of the Deng conflict. The reason for this is as simple as it is devastating: Bessany Weyman, as widowed sister-in-law, lacks the status of immediate family. Her messages therefore languished in a no-man's land of electronic limbo.

John Weyman is unable to speak for nineteen point zero seven seconds after receiving these messages, the most recent of which were sent just after the Tersae attacks began, imploring John to make someone listen to her. When he is capable of speech, my commander whispers in a terrible voice, "Get General McIntyre again. Get him on the line and forward these reports to him, stat."

I comply instantly, appalled by the blunders which have left Bessany Weyman's urgent messages spooled in limbo at Sector Command and utterly disregarded by the Ministries of Mineral Resources and Xenology.

"McIntyre here. What is it, Colonel?"

"We got trouble, General. Oh, Christ, we got trouble. I'm sending you the reports Eisenbrucke Station filed, by priority bounce."

"Eisenbrucke Station filed reports? On the Tersae?" *General McIntyre's question is sharp.*

"Damn right, they did. The xeno-ecologist is my sister-in-law, General. She made contact with the Tersae three *months* ago and started filing immediate reports, which she copied to me at Sector Command. If anybody at either Ministry had actually read them, those reports would've been sent all the way to Central Command, covered with red flags. And nobody at Sector bothered to forward them to me on Sherman's World."

General McIntyre has a creative vocabulary. Even after fifteen years with John Weyman, I am deeply impressed. I do not fully understand the human compulsion to alter their language usage when under stress, but I have become conversant with much of this stress-induced vocabulary. General McIntyre puts my own meager knowledge to shame as he fires off commands to his adjutant to send a blistering message to the Minister of Xenology, demanding immediate and full analysis of Bessany Weyman's reports.

"Mother Bear," *he mutters,* "it's going to take time to plough through this stuff."

"I know," *my commander agrees in a grim and angry tone.*

"Get to Eisenbrucke as fast as possible, Colonel, and let's hope to God those people are still alive. McIntyre out."

John breaks off the transmission and begins to read. I compress the messages and play them for myself at higher speed, looking for critical information at a much faster rate than the human mind can absorb such data. Even so, I have not yet digested the lengthy reports, which are quite astonishing, before we reach the edge of the valley sheltering Eisenbrucke Station. I probe carefully with radar, looking for the ramp which our records show was constructed for egress of heavy equipment. I find it within zero point five seconds of arrival.

"I have located the ramp. ETA Eisenbrucke Station, three minutes."

My commander nods, pale with tension. He continues to read, which is currently the best use of his time, since we can see nothing through the blowing snow. I inch down the ramp, two hundred feet above the valley floor. I am deeply uneasy, for my treads are wider than the ramp, making the turns harrowing even without high winds buffeting my war hull. We lurch and grind our way downward, crumbling the edge and sliding on the occasional patch of thick ice which has accumulated in the corners of the sloping turns. My commander's knuckles show white where he grips the armrests of his command chair. He has stopped reading. When I reach level ground at last, I am nearly euphoric with the joy of having made it down without sliding off and crushing my commander. We have already crash-landed once on Thule. I do not wish to repeat the experience.

"My radar is picking up a great deal of debris," *I am forced to inform him almost immediately.*

"What kind?" *His voice goes hoarse with stress.*

I probe ahead as my treads grind across the first scattered remains of what appears to have been a substantial stand of trees. "Something has taken down a broad swath of the forest in this valley. This does not appear to be battle damage. I pick up no chemical signatures from high explosives. I do not detect the burn scars typical of energy weapons. If forced to guess, I would say these trees were hit by a violent wind force. There is a great deal of twisting damage to the trunks my treads are passing across."

"Twisting damage?" *my commander echoes.* "As in a twister? A tornado?"

"The type of damage is consistent with tornadic winds, yes."

"What about the research compound?" *he asks grimly.*

My radar signals bounce off the compound's buildings, which are one hundred twenty-seven meters away. "The compound is partially intact," *I say, trying to put as much positive spin on the situation as I can manage, for my commander's sake. Several buildings have been completely flattened and others appear to be entirely missing.* "I do not believe the Tersae can be responsible for what happened in this valley."

"No," *John mutters, studying the radar echoes on*

my forward data screen. "But a *tornado?*" *He scrubs his face with unsteady hands.* "Any signs of life at all?"

"I detect several strong heat sources in various buildings," *I respond hopefully,* "and there are active power emissions from the research station's power plant." *I continue to scan, speeding up to reach the broken compound more quickly. I detect motion and a moving heat source emerging from one of the damaged buildings. It clearly originates from a biological life form. It is too large to be human. I grieve. I rage. I target the hated heat source.* "Enemy sighted," *I am forced to say.* "Shall I engage?"

A terrible sound breaks from my commander's throat. Then, raggedly, "No. I want the bastards alive."

"Understood, Commander."

I rush forward to engage the Tersae who have come like carrion crows to fight over the remains. In the idiom of Old Earth, the time has come to go crow hunting.

Chapter Nineteen

Ginger Gianesco had never scrambled so hard in her life.

The few transports they had left were either far too small or far too slow. The big ore transports would never make a forty-kilometer dash in seven minutes, not with a top speed of ten KPH. And the aircars . . .

"Pack the smallest children into those scout cars!" she shouted into her radio, which relayed her instructions through loudspeakers that were part of the meeting hall's emergency system. The mob of refugees crowded aside, making way for anyone with children. "Move it, people!" When the volunteer packing the first aircar in line tried to close the hatch with only five kids aboard, Ginger snatched it open again. "Pack 'em in tighter, dammit! I don't care if they can breathe or not, stuff 'em in and redline those engines, but get 'em *full*!"

She could hear Hank Umlani talking to the pilot of the descending medical shuttle by radio, asking what kind of harness to rig on the ore carrier they'd be packing full of nearly everyone in town. *Hank's problem,* she told herself harshly. Confused, frightened children were pulled, shoved, stuffed into the aircars, toddlers and infants passed over by frantic mothers.

"I need teenagers with pilot ratings! Stat!"

She found seven skinny kids, thirteen and fourteen years old, to pilot the aircars, saving the space an adult pilot would've taken up. They used the space savings to pack extra little ones into the cockpit. Five children, six, seven, ten children crammed into cabin space designed for two adults and a minimum of equipment. Seven surviving aircars, a hundred kids under the age of fifteen. The numbers were against them. Ruthlessly, Ginger dragged out of line anybody older than twelve.

"Go!" she shouted as each car was filled to capacity.

Engines whined, protesting the overload as the aircars lifted, one by one, over the wall and sped northward. Ginger didn't have time to watch them go. "Adults and teens, to the refinery! The *Darknight* shuttle's going to airlift the rest of us out in an ore freightbox. Go, go, go!"

People ran, slid on icy patches, carried those too injured to run on their own, hauling them through the gap in the defensive wall where the Bolo had knocked a hole in it. Ginger ran through the shelters, the meeting hall, the warehouse, checking to be certain everyone was out.

They were.

She arrived at the refinery with a burning stitch down her side. Hank Umlani had already divided the arrivals: teens and anyone under 5' 5" in line for the medical shuttle, everybody else into an empty freightbox. A team of five worked feverishly under Hank's direction, rigging steel cables for a cargo sling. The cargo freightbox was an immense steel oblong, designed to haul a full ton of refined saganium ore for transfer to an orbital ore freighter. It boasted hinged doors at the top for easy loading at Rustenberg's refinery and a hopper-type door at one end, which could be tilted over the hopper of an off-world fabrications plant, dumping the refined ore directly into the smelting furnaces.

That hopper door made an emergency entrance for the crowd of refugees.

"No shoving," Ginger shouted as the line threatened to disintegrate into shambles. "We've still got time." The line settled down, moving faster once order had been reestablished. Reassured that loading was going as smoothly as possible, Ginger craned her neck skyward. She spotted it within seconds, the flare of light that marked the *Darknight*'s incoming shuttle. Ginger checked her watch. Four minutes, twelve seconds to reach safety . . .

The shuttle fired braking engines at a terrifyingly low altitude, rocking visibly. The pilot fought the bucking craft, having waited until the last possible second to reduce speed. They came in at an angle and set down four yards from the line of teenagers, at exactly T-minus-four minutes. Pneumatic doors opened with a hiss. A uniformed officer jumped down and beckoned urgently.

"Go!" Ginger shouted. "No shoving, but keep moving! Go!"

Seventy people, the shuttle pilot had said. By packing in teens and the shortest adults, they crammed in eighty, loading them in one minute forty-three seconds. The officer—introduced over one shoulder as "Lieutenant Commander Gerhard Lundquist, Assistant Ship's Surgeon"—called out, "Okay, Carter, we're loaded up. I'll help 'em hook up that cargo carrier."

Ginger led him toward the cable crew at a dead run. "Hank! You got those cables ready?"

"That's a roger, but we're not fully loaded yet."

"Hook 'em up now, we can't wait 'til the loading's done!"

Hank's crew dragged the long loops of cable back to the shuttle, where the ship's surgeon helped fasten them to cargo hooks fore and aft. The team had the cables hooked and secured in sixty-eight seconds flat. Loading proceeded unbroken, moving at a frenzied pace. The cargo bin had already swallowed more than five hundred people, jammed in standing on the floor, even on one another's shoulders. Ginger helped push in the last three-hundred-plus refugees, ignoring cries of pain as elbow, knees, and feet jabbed, knocked, and stepped on tender regions. Hank shoved in his assistants last, then bodily lifted Ginger onto someone's shoulders—several someones, judging from the bony projections shifting under her hips and shoulderblades. Hank was shouting at the surgeon, "Somebody's gotta latch this shut and drop the bars from the outside!"

"Get in—I'll take care of it!"

As Ginger craned her neck around to look, Hank sucked in his nonexistent gut and slid between several sets of feet. The big steel hopper doors swung ponderously shut with a massive, reverberating clang. The heavy bars slammed down, pegging the doors into place. Ginger counted off the seconds on her glowing wrist chrono's dial, waiting for the shuttle's liftoff. Her radio sputtered. She heard the surgeon snarling at the pilot, "Go, dammit! I knew the risk when I signed on. There's not room back there for a housefly and you know damned well we've got kids jammed so tight into the pilot's compartment, you'll need a crowbar to get 'em out. Go!"

Omigod . . .

The shuttle's engines whined savagely. There was one godawful jerk as the cargo carrier shifted. Gasps and cries of pain bounced off steel walls. Then they swayed into the air, tilting slightly in the way of cargo slung beneath an airborne transport. They picked up speed. They were moving fast already and kept accelerating. Ginger desperately tried not to think about that young surgeon back there, who had just volunteered for suicide, if the unknown war agent was as deadly to humans as it was to Tersae. Her vision didn't want to focus properly.

Think about what we accomplished, she told herself fiercely. Seventy-seven kids out in Rustenberg's aircars. Eighty more in the shuttle. Another eight hundred twelve adults and teens stacked like cordwood under Ginger's battered, bruised backside. All racing potential death through the clouds.

They had sixty-two seconds to travel forty kilometers.

And unless the gods were very kind, that courageous surgeon had only sixty-two seconds left to live.

Chapter Twenty

If Bessany hadn't been in the med lab again, one corner of which still boasted a temporary covering to keep out the snow, she might not have heard it in time. As it was, she became aware of the approaching noise just after Chilaili left the room, heading out to fetch more wood for the cookfires. Bessany jerked her head up and listened. Something enormous was approaching across the ruins of the forest, moving at a high rate of speed and grinding whole tree trunks under an immense weight, crushing them with a snapping, grating sound. After an instant of total befuddlement, she realized what it must be. A chill of horror raced down her spine.

"Chilaili!" She broke and ran, shouting at the Tersae who would, by now, be in the approaching Bolo's gunsights. *"Chilaili!"* Bessany skidded outside, slipped and slid through the snow to where the Tersae had stopped, swivelling her head in puzzlement from the noise of the approaching war machine to Bessany's wide-eyed, coatless rush forward.

"What—?" the Tersae began.

"*Get down!*" Bessany shouted, hurtling herself between the *katori* and the massive weapon bearing down on them from the blizzard. It was going to fire, any second now . . . Wicked gun snouts appeared through the blinding white whirl of snow, towering above them. Antipersonnel guns were trained straight at them.

"*Don't shoot!*" Bessany screamed at it, flinging out both hands in a hopeless gesture. It ground to a halt less than five meters away and sat motionless while Bessany's deafening heartbeats slammed against her chest. She couldn't even see all of it, just part of the prow with its bristling weapons and the fronts of its immense treads. "Chilaili," she gasped out, "as you love life, *don't move*! Don't even breathe!"

She heard a hatch opening somewhere above, which startled her, heard the clatter of feet on metal. Then a man appeared through the wind-driven snow and ice, rushing forward, a wicked-looking gun in one hand. An instant later, she stared up into the very last face she had expected to see coming toward her out of a Thulian blizzard. Her eyes widened and her mouth fell open, but no sound emerged past the squeaking constriction in her throat.

"My God," John Weyman breathed, "you're *alive* . . ."

A jumble of emotions slammed through Bessany, wild relief fighting for space with shame and embarrassment. The raking claws of nightmare would never have descended on her if she'd simply believed this man in the first place. She struggled to find her voice. "You came. You must have read my reports. . . ."

"Yes," he said grimly. "I've read them, all right. Some of them. About twenty minutes ago."

"Twenty minutes?" she echoed, baffled. An absent shudder caught her, chattering her teeth in the biting, subzero wind. "But—"

"Later," he said gruffly. "You're freezing and so am I."

He turned toward the med lab—and halted in his tracks.

Chilaili hadn't moved. Wasn't breathing, either. She was staring, pupils dilated with shock, at the Bolo's towering war hull. Bessany didn't like the look on John Weyman's face. "Please ask your Bolo not to shoot Chilaili."

"Are there any more of those things here?" His gaze never even flickered from Chilaili and his grip on the pistol was so tight, she wondered why the bones of his hand hadn't cracked.

"No, there aren't any more Tersae here," she bit out. "And they're not 'things.' They have names. This," she gestured brusquely, "is Chilaili. My friend."

A muscle jumped in his jaw. "Rapier," he growled, gaze still glued to Chilaili, "please do not shoot the prisoner. Not until I've had a chance to interrogate it, anyway."

"You really are Alexander's brother, aren't you?" Bessany snarled.

John Weyman's face ran deathly white in the glare of light pouring from the med lab. Bessany was so recklessly angry, she didn't even care. "Chilaili," she snapped, "forget about more wood for the cookfires. We'll bring it in later. Let's get inside before I freeze to death." She strode toward the med lab, fists clenched.

The tall *katori* took a hesitant step to follow, head cocked sideways to keep one eye rolling backwards toward the Bolo's bristling guns. Herve Sinclair blocked their way, gaping up at the Bolo. Bessany shoved roughly past. "Herve, please ask everyone to come in for a meeting. We've just officially been rescued. The Bolo's commander will want to debrief everyone."

"Is it safe?" he asked uncertainly.

John Weyman's voice came as an impatient growl behind her. "Of course it's safe. Rapier doesn't shoot humans." The slight emphasis on the last word brought Bessany around again, glaring. Chilaili had moved cautiously to one side, putting Bessany between herself and the massive machine outside. And, coincidentally, its commander.

"Bessany—" he began, pushing past Herve to stalk toward her.

"No," she gritted out. One hand came up involuntarily, halting him in much the same way as her outflung hands had stopped the Bolo. "Not yet. We're scattered in half-a-dozen lab buildings. The Navy waited three months to answer my reports, so you can cool your heels for another five minutes, until we're all here. You really need to hear what we have to say."

That muscle jumped again in his jaw. "Yes. I do. More than you can possibly guess."

Their gazes locked, striking sparks in the silence. Stone-hard muscles flexed in his jaw and his long, lean hands. The muzzle of the gun swung slightly at that movement, scaring Bessany. Then he surprised her. He ran one of those tense hands through his hair, brushing away melting snow, and let go an unhappy sigh.

"All right," he said, voice low. "We may not have spoken since that damned wedding, but you've never given me any reason to mistrust you. And God knows, my family put you through enough hell, we owe you a break or fifty. I'll give you, and it" —he glanced pointedly at the Tersae behind her— "the benefit of the doubt. For now."

Bessany drew a long, shaky breath. "Thank you," she said quietly. "And Chilaili is not an 'it.' She's a master healer and she's my friend. Please treat her with the courtesy she deserves."

His mouth tightened into a thin, white line. "I'm trying," he said roughly. "Given standing orders on those—creatures—you should be damned glad we didn't fire on sight. Just for the record, were they," he darted a cold look at Chilaili, "responsible for the damage here?"

"No. A tornado hit us. According to Chilaili, we picked the worst spot on Thule to build this lab. An assessment I fully support. And just for the record," Bessany muttered, tucking both hands under her armpits to warm them, "why did it take you so long to read my reports?"

"We've been in the field, on the front lines of the Deng invasion," he said with a growl. "Sector Command never forwarded your messages. Much as it galls to say it, you don't fall into the immediate-family category. So a very junior communications technician dumped every one of your messages into a holding queue. I found out twenty minutes ago, when I queried Sector Command and the Ministry of Mineral Resources for any reports out of Eisenbrucke Station."

"But . . ." she stared, aghast, "surely the Ministries sent *some* kind of message to the head of Sector Command? If not Mineral Resources, surely Xenology did?"

Anger sparked through his eyes. "No. I bounced copies immediately to General McIntyre, here on Thule. If anyone at Sector had seen them, McIntyre would have known. He was as shocked as I was."

The staggering scale of bureaucratic bungling left Bessany ashen.

John said bitterly, "I suspect the only messages Mineral Resources bothered to read were those directly involving saganium. God only knows what Xenology's excuse is."

"And here I was, stuck out here, thinking—" She reddened, unable to hold his gaze. From the set of his mouth and the look in his shadowed eyes, John Weyman knew *exactly* what she had been about to say.

"It's all right, Bessany," he said quietly. " I can imagine only too well what you've been thinking. Given what you went through with Alex, I don't blame you a bit." He fell silent then, studying the med lab with quiet intensity, taking in every detail, from the cracked and braced ceiling to the badly injured men and women in every bed they'd been able to salvage. Even so, some of them had been tucked into makeshift pallets on the floor.

A brooding frown hovered around his mouth, but he didn't ask questions, waiting for the others to arrive. He kept his gun in his hand, however, and seemed electrically aware of Chilaili, who had remained utterly and prudently silent. Bessany noticed, for the first time, a medical brace around his elbow and wondered how he'd come to be injured. If the Tersae were behind it, he wouldn't be the only human, by a long shot, with a score to settle.

People were arriving through the snow, wearing hastily donned coats or wrapped in blankets, most of them whispering in awed tones about the Bolo parked outside. When they'd all gathered, jamming themselves into every possible empty space in the room, John broke the hushed, expectant silence. "I'm Lieutenant Colonel John Weyman, Third Dinochrome Brigade. And in case you're wondering about the name, Bessany is my sister-in-law."

He cleared his throat slightly, his expression reflecting considerable chagrin. The scandal of his brother's death had been reported from one end of human space to the other, so he had to be wondering what she might have told her colleagues, what deeply intimate and damaging details she might've shared about his relatives.

He went on doggedly, despite the curious stares.

"Recent events have bumped you people to the number one defensive priority on Thule. That's why I'm here with my Bolo, rather than mounting defense over the mines at Seta Point."

"Recent events?" Herve Sinclair echoed. "What can possibly have happened to make *us* so important?"

John's blue eyes were chips of ice. "I hope to hell your biochemists and their lab equipment have survived, because the Tersae have stockpiled a very nasty chemical—or maybe biological—weapon. They released it during a battle near Rustenberg. The town's been evacuated."

A dreadful silence crashed down. Every gaze, including Bessany's, swung toward Chilaili. The tall *katori* was watching John Weyman, head tipped sideways and swinging slightly in that maddening head motion so typical of the Tersae.

John said harshly, "I'm hoping you people can find a way to protect the colonists against this stuff, because it's deadly. It acts like a hemorrhagic neurotoxin and it kills within minutes. It was released during an attack on one of the Tersae's underground camps. The stuff wiped out the whole population within three minutes. And it killed a whole flock of those birdlike things that resemble them, in the forest nearby."

Bessany blanched. A whole nest, wiped out? *And* a flock of their genetic ancestors? How could the Tersae's creators have given something like that to creatures who barely understood the most basic items of advanced technology? It was one thing to give them rifles and bombs, which only warriors would be put at risk, trying to use. But to give them something like a biochemical weapon that would destroy a whole clan, if accidentally released . . .

She glanced at Chilaili—then stared, while the hair on the nape of her neck stood starkly erect. John's words had clearly baffled the tall *katori*. Bessany had seen enough of the Tersae's facial expressions during the past three months to read that look with utter certainty. Chilaili had not the slightest idea what John was talking about. *They don't know they have it,* Bessany realized with a ragged pounding of her pulse. *My God, they've stockpiled a deadly biochemical weapon and they don't even know they have it.*

Even as that realization sank in, Chilaili turned a puzzled eye on Bessany, begging the question with a silent look. Bessany drew a deep breath, trying to gather her scattered wits. She had to say something and she didn't want to blurt out her suspicions. Not yet. She needed time to think about this, to see all the ramifications. A few minutes, at least. She finally latched onto a way to break the awkward silence. "To begin this properly, Chilaili, I must first tell you that John Weyman is the brother, the nestmate, of my life-mate, who is now dead." There, she'd managed to say that in an almost normal tone of voice.

The Tersae's pupils dilated slightly with surprise. She swung her head back toward John.

"I am honored to know you, John Weyman. I have deep respect for Bessany Weyman. Your nestmate chose wisely, to seek her as life-mate." She hesitated, while John's eyes widened at hearing Terran standard coming from the tall alien's oddly shaped beak, then Chilaili asked, "The great ogre responds to your commands?" One clawed hand gestured cautiously toward the temporary wall and the Bolo beyond it.

"What do you know about Bolos?" John asked harshly.

Chilaili blinked. "This is how the ogres are called? We know very little of them. The Ones Above warned us against the humans' metal ogres, but I had not believed such a thing could be so large."

John narrowed his eyes. Drew a breath. Paused, glancing at Bessany, then said carefully, "Tell me about the Ones Above."

"They created us," Chilaili said at once. "And now they are trying to destroy us."

John opened his mouth, then stopped. A peculiar expression flickered through his eyes and halted whatever he'd been about to say. "They're what?"

"They are trying to destroy us. It is why I came through the snow and the wind to Bessany Weyman's nest. I am desperate to halt this war before it destroys my clan and the other clans, the whole of my people. Without the help of humans like Bessany Weyman, we are doomed. Either you will win this war and destroy us, or we will drive you back to the stars—which I do not think likely—and the Ones Above will destroy us. In all the wide world, there is only one human we could turn to. So I came, to beg her help. And also," she added with forthright simplicity, "to pay the life-debt I owe her for saving my only daughter's life. If I cannot stop this war, I have at least brought the warning there will be an attack."

John stared at Chilaili for a full ten seconds without making any sound at all, while his eyes reflected the sudden reordering of long-held assumptions about the nature—and identity—of their enemy. "I think," he finally said, swinging his gaze toward Bessany, "you had better tell me the whole story of what's happened here."

She let go her breath in a long, silent sigh, unaware until that moment that she'd been holding it so rigidly. Speaking very quietly, she told him. He listened intently as each person in the room told their own parts of the story, in turn. Surprise dawned in his eyes and continued to grow, like the sun rising above a glacier. And as he continued to listen, some of the ice began to melt from those chilly blue eyes. His gaze drifted again and again to Chilaili, expression baffled as the researchers and technicians talked of Chilaili digging them out of the rubble, teaching them how to keep campfires going while they looked for enough spare parts to hook the various labs back into the power plant, how to cook food over a bed of hot coals, how the Tersae had set broken bones, treated injuries and shock, changed wound dressings, and brought in snow to melt for drinking and cooking and wash water for the injured.

By the time the last of them had spoken, the worst of the harsh suspicion had gone from his eyes. Caution remained, clearly visible in his expression, but he no longer looked at Chilaili like something he'd have preferred to shoot out of hand and question later—if she survived the first salvo. When the last technician had finished speaking, he frowned thoughtfully. "I don't think I have to tell you how surprising all of this is. Given the ferocity of Tersae attacks elsewhere, I'd have bet money this wasn't even possible. Frankly, it's giving me some fairly weird ideas."

He roused himself from his distracting thoughts with obvious difficulty. "If I might suggest it, this med lab isn't large enough for all of us and the patients in here need quiet and rest. I'd like a brief tour of the facilities that survived the tornado, please. Then I need a meeting with Bessany, Herve Sinclair, Dr. Ivanov, and anybody with a biochemistry background. And Chilaili," he added with a glance toward the Tersae. "We have a great deal to thrash through, yet."

Sinclair nodded. "Of course, Colonel."

"All right, let me get my cold-weather gear. I'll meet you back here in five."

Bessany watched him hurry through the snow and vanish up the side of his Bolo. As she turned back into the room to retrieve her own coat, she wondered what, exactly, his weird ideas might be. Was it possible that Alexander Weyman's brother actually saw the potential for alliance that Bessany had already seen? Had seen, in fact, as early as that first wild night in the thunderstorm? An alliance she had begged various ministries and military agencies to consider in her reports? She glanced at Chilaili, who stood carefully out of the way as people left the med lab. Then stared, while shock like icewater raced through her veins.

John had left Chilaili unguarded.

Just to get a coat.

Her heart thumped in a sudden heavy rhythm of hope, so unexpected it caused a physical pain. Maybe he'd done so only because he knew the Bolo could take out the whole building if Chilaili tried anything. But maybe—just maybe—he really had decided to give Chilaili a chance? Bessany closed her eyes for a long moment. She knew what was at stake here, possibly better than John did, because she had already deduced things about Chilaili's makers that he couldn't possibly know yet, if he'd had her reports for only twenty minutes.

Given what she already knew, that news about the biochemical weapon had shaken her. Badly. The fact that Chilaili had no idea the stuff existed had shaken her even worse. She knew John didn't believe yet, in Chilaili's ignorance, but Bessany was absolutely certain. Nor could she imagine a clan *katori* being kept totally unaware of it, if anyone at all in the clan knew it existed. Not with the survival of the whole clan at stake, once the genie was out of the bottle. And if the Tersae genuinely didn't know they possessed such a thing . . .

What in *hell* was it doing in their winter nests?

Chapter Twenty-one

Lieutenant Commander Gerhard Lundquist wasn't dead. And that astonished him.

Gerhard didn't have to check his wrist chrono to know that the fallout from the Bolo's destruction of the Tersae base camp had reached Rustenberg. He'd been standing in the dust cloud for ten minutes, now. And he was still alive. *Maybe,* he gulped, *it just takes longer for humans to die of the stuff?*

He finally pulled out his comm link and radioed the shuttle he'd helped pack full of terrified refugees. "This is Lieutenant Commander Lundquist. Are you there, Carter?"

The comm link sputtered. *"Gerhard?"*

He grinned. "Hi, Patty. Yeah, it's me."

"Why the hell aren't you dead?"

"Search me." He managed a wan chuckle. "Literally, I suspect, once the biochemists get their hands on my corpuscles. Look, according to what the Bolo said, I ought to be dead by now, but I don't even feel sick. And I'm standing right in the thick of the dust cloud. I figured there wasn't any point in hiding, so I just decided to get it over with. I've been breathing the stuff for, uh," he glanced at his chrono again, "eleven and a half minutes now. By the way," he asked, stomach fluttering slightly despite the fact that he was—as of yet—unharmed, "did everybody get out of the kill zone in time?"

"Barely, but yes. We're forty-five klicks out, sitting in a deep ravine, out of the worst of the wind. Hold tight, Gerhard. I'm patching you through to General McIntyre, via the *Darknight*."

A gravelly voice boomed from the comm link. "McIntyre here. What the devil d'you think you're doing, Lundquist, not dying on schedule?"

Gerhard blinked, startled speechless.

"That's a joke, Commander," the general's voice rumbled. "And a poor one, my apology. But you've given us a nasty little problem, y'see, staying healthy when you ought to be flopping around like one of those oversized chickens."

"Yes, sir, I know. Believe me, I know only too well. I'm a ship's surgeon."

"Now there's a piece of luck we hadn't counted on. I'm routing Unit SPQ/R-561 back to your location. I want blood samples, tissue samples, urine samples, hell, I want samples of everything it's *possible* to sample. We need to know if all humans are immune to this bio-weapon or if you're a confounded freak. No insult intended."

Gerhard grinned. "None taken, sir."

"Good. Report anything out of the ordinary. Notify your medical colleagues on the *Darknight* and the Bolo's commander. Captain Alessandra DiMario will be working with you for the duration. We've got another Bolo team en route to Eisenbrucke. If the research team is still alive, you'll have some help on this."

"Any help at all is welcome, General. Meanwhile, I'll see if the evacuees left behind any medical gear, to get started on those samples. I'm afraid we jettisoned our equipment during drop, to coax extra speed from the engines."

"Good job, that, by the way. Notify me the instant you have any hard data to report. McIntyre out."

The comm link sputtered, then Gerhard's own commander hailed him. "Captain Harrelson here. I second the general's opinion on that rescue effort. Good work, Lundquist. Very good work. And I'm real glad of the chance to tell you that."

"Not half as glad as I am to hear it," he chuckled. "In all the rush, did anyone think to ask for replacement supplies? We still have two key administrators with hard-radiation exposure. They need treatment, stat."

"Understood. We'll drop a medical team with a new batch of supplies on another shuttle."

"Deeply obliged, Captain."

"Get to work then. I want a full report, so don't you dare go dying on us before you finish it, you hear me?"

"Yes, ma'am. You want it, you got it."

"Good. Harrelson out."

He clipped his comm link to his uniform belt, then started hunting through the evacuated town, settling on a big warehouse as the likeliest spot to search. He found jumbled piles of personal belongings, foodstuffs, tools, ammunition for various weapons, equipment whose purposes were beyond him, clothing, all manner of miscellany. A computer someone had left running in the scramble hummed softly in the silence. Gerhard's footsteps echoed as he hurried across and scrolled through the data screens. The open file proved to be a master inventory of the seemingly random heaps. He found the entry he needed just a few screens down.

"Meeting hall," he muttered aloud, just to hear

something besides the sound of the wind through the open warehouse doors. "Recreation cabinet. Huh. I wonder which building the meeting hall is?"

He found it three minutes later by checking the largest structures first. Two minutes after that, he was sorting through a hodgepodge of medical supplies, badly depleted by the sheer volume of Rustenberg's wounded. Fortunately, the shortages were mostly in wound dressings, pain-killers, antibiotics, and surgical supplies like saline and sutures. He found plenty of hypodermic syringes and specimen containers.

It took very little time to fill the various cups, vials, and plastic bags, although it was more awkward than he'd thought, trying to draw blood one-handed. "They don't teach *this* in medical school," he muttered under his breath, wincing slightly. He'd just finished jotting down a list of metabolism tests he would need—providing he hadn't died before it was time to conduct them—when he heard a low rumble in the distance. Gerhard looked up, startled, then realized what it must be. "The Bolo's coming!"

He hurried outside, heading in the direction of the noise, and clambered up a sturdy section of scaffolding to peer over the town's defensive wall. He'd been so busy, he hadn't been able to peek at the five Bolos tucked into the *Darknight*'s immense cargo bay. He'd never seen a Bolo, not up close and personal.

By the time it was a few hundred meters away, he was gaping. "My God, that thing's huge!" The closer it came, the bigger it loomed, until it blotted out the light like an immense metal cloud above his head. The engine noise changed pitch and the rumbling of the wall under his hands and the scaffolding under his feet changed as well, then the machine stopped. Gun snouts jutted out above Gerhard's head, protruding over the top of the wall, it had come so close.

An amplified voice, sounding female, spoke from its depths. "You look pretty healthy to me."

Gerhard grinned. "Sorry if that disappoints you."

"Not at all," the voice chuckled with a smooth, rich sound like sun-warmed honey. He wondered if she were as beautiful as her voice. "I'm Alessandra DiMario, commanding Unit SPQ/R-561. And this," she added, "is Senator."

He gave the Bolo a salute. "Lieutenant Commander Gerhard Lundquist, sir, ma'am, at your service."

A different voice, distinctly male with a metallic burr around the edges, greeted him. "It is good to meet you, Commander Lundquist."

"The pleasure is definitely mine," Gerhard said with genuine feeling. Not only was he talking to a Bolo, he was fizzing with the sheer exuberance of still being alive. "I've got a batch of samples ready, by the way. When I heard you coming, I rushed outside without them. I can bring them out."

"No need," Alessandra DiMario reassured him. "Just climb down and lead the way. We'll come through the hole we punched in the wall last night and follow you."

Gerhard, he smiled giddily as he scrambled down, *today is just your lucky day.*

To which the back of his brain whispered, *Yeah—ain't it great?*

He certainly wasn't going to argue the point.

Chapter Twenty-two

"Maintain Battle Reflex Alert," John told Rapier as he wriggled into his cold-weather gear. "I'm not expecting any serious trouble until this blizzard clears, but what one Tersae could do, others can duplicate. And I'm certainly not ready to trust Chilaili *carte blanche*, no matter what Bessany and the rest of those scientists say. I sure as hell don't trust her clan."

"Understood, Commander."

John nodded and rejoined the science team, confident in Rapier's ability to warn them or deal with any trouble that might threaten from the clifftops. Their tour of the battered research outpost didn't take long. They carried heavy flashlights to pierce the snow-filled gloom. Herve Sinclair and Dr. Ivanov acted as guides, pointing out each surviving, damaged, or missing structure, while Chilaili broke trail through the deep snow. Even the Tersae had donned a layer of furs for added warmth, but her bare feet—or talons—were apparently impervious to the cold.

Bessany stayed at John's side, a silent ghost shivering

in the blasts of wind. Her long, dark hair whipped across her face where strands had escaped her parka hood. They made a surprisingly quick circuit, due mostly to the fact that so much of the station—which had never been large, in the first place—was simply gone.

John kept one hand near the side arm strapped to his hip at all times, but the Tersae gave them no trouble, not even any furtive moves. The tornado had—thank God—spared the biochem lab, along with all of its equipment and data. Bessany's records had survived, too, another small miracle, since the room right next to her lab had been smashed to rubble.

John chose the biochem lab for their meeting site, since it was too small for refugees to take shelter there. The power was off, so they set their flashlights on top of cabinets and high-tech equipment the power outage had rendered temporarily silent. The room was so cold, their breath steamed.

"Is there any way to get the power back on, in here?"

"Probably," Herve Sinclair frowned, "if we could find enough cable to reconnect it to our power plant. We've been digging under the snow to find broken connections, trying to restore power to the shelters. I'm afraid we haven't had much luck finding cable. Our maintenance warehouse was scoured clean, right down to the foundations. We managed to cannibalize enough cable from damaged labs and living quarters to bring the shelters back on-line, but there wasn't enough to do small labs like this one."

John nodded. "That's one problem easily solved, anyway. Rapier carries spare power cable for just this kind of emergency. Put a crew to work looking for the broken ends and we can splice into your power plant within minutes." He spoke into his comm link. "Rapier, open your rear portside cargo bin, please. Herve Sinclair will be coming out with a crew for that power cable."

"Understood, Commander."

Sinclair, pausing on his way out, directed a wan smile at the comm link. "You can't know how good it is, being rescued. We'd all but given up hope." That said, he vanished into the swirl of snow. Dr. Ivanov volunteered to fetch Alison Collingwood, their biochemist, and her technician, Arnie Kravitz.

The moment they were gone, John turned to the Tersae. "All right, Chilaili," he said quietly, "I've been very patient, but it's time you answered a few questions."

"What do you wish to know, John Weyman?"

It was positively uncanny, hearing human speech coming out of a mouth not even remotely designed for it. The effect reminded John strongly of trained parrots, a disturbing image under the circumstances. The deep shadows cast by their narrow flashlight beams only heightened the strangeness. "For starters," he narrowed his eyes, "tell me everything you know about this biochemical weapon."

"I do not understand. I was deeply confused by your words, earlier. Please explain what a 'biochemical weapon' is."

Bessany spoke a shade too quickly, before John could answer. "You remember that time we talked about what causes illness, don't you, Chilaili?"

"The tiny living things you spoke of?" she asked, swinging her gaze around to peer at Bessany. The alien cocked her head downwards, since Bessany was nearly a full meter shorter than the Tersae. "Yes, I remember very well. I have tried to teach the clan the things you said, to keep these tiny living things from harming us. We wash everything more frequently now, and when I care for the injured and the sick, I wash my fingers and claws with very hot water, carefully boiled. There has been less sickness, since we began this."

"I'm glad, Chilaili," Bessany said with conviction. "Very glad. A biochemical weapon is a tiny thing—sometimes alive, sometimes not—that causes illness. One so terrible, everything exposed to it dies. If someone knows how, they can take things that are merely dangerous, things that might only make you very sick, and change them into something deadly."

The Tersae's pupils dilated. "As the Ones Above altered us?"

Chills ran down John's spine.

"Yes, Chilaili," Bessany nodded. "Exactly like that."

"But the Ones Above have never given us such a thing."

"You're sure?" John asked sharply.

The Tersae turned that eerie gaze on him once more, causing alien shadows to leap across the walls. "I am a master *katori*, John Weyman. I would know such a thing. It is my duty to heal my clan of *any* illness. Such a thing would put the whole clan at risk, so I would *have* to know." The Tersae hesitated a moment then, as though struck by a sudden thought. Even John could read the sudden uncertainty in that alien face, those alien eyes.

"What is it, Chilaili?" Bessany asked gently.

"My mother died when I was fifteen summers old, the same age Sooleawa is now. She was killed while hunting. It is possible my mother died before she had the chance to tell me of such a thing. But," an odd sigh gusted past her beak, "my father's mother *believed* I was fully trained. She had spent much time with my mother, assisting her, for my mother's mother died young, also, which left the clan with only one *katori* to treat the sick and the injured. It is why she thought my mother would have taken great care to teach me all that she knew, because she had lost her own mother so young."

"So it's possible your mother didn't tell you?" John asked.

"That is possible, yes. Or that my mother's mother may have known, and died before *she* could pass on the knowledge. But I cannot believe that only a clan's *katori* would have known such a thing existed. Such an important weapon would *have* to be known, not only to the *katori*, but also to the war leader and the *akule*."

"The what?" John frowned.

"He- or She-Who-Looks-Up."

"The priest or priestess who speaks the words of the Oracle," Bessany translated. "From what Chilaili and Sooleawa have told me, the Oracle is some kind of radio transmitter/receiver. The Ones Above speak through them and the clans can ask their creators questions."

Another chill touched John's spine.

Chilaili was nodding, in grotesque parody of a human gesture. "Yes, this is so, John Weyman. The Ones Above always speak to us through the Oracles. We have never seen their faces directly, only flat images of them. We have never seen the wondrous machines they build to fly between the stars. The weapons they gave us were stored long ago in the deepest caverns of the winter nests. Could such a weapon survive for so many years?"

John did not like what he was hearing. "Yes," he growled, "it could. Possibly for hundreds of years."

Chilaili's pupils dilated. "That is frightening," she whispered. She *was* frightened, too. Even John could see it. Her hands were shaking and her voice was unsteady. "Our grandmothers' grandmothers might not have known had such a thing been left so many years ago. But surely a clan's *akule*, at least, would know?

And the *akule* would be honor-bound to reveal the secret to the *katori* and the *viho*, the war leader. It would endanger the clan, not to tell them."

Chilaili's fright shook John, dispelling his suspicions far more effectively than any protestations of innocence. "What about the other clans?" he asked. "Might *they* have something like this? Or do you talk to anyone outside your clan?"

The Tersae clicked her beak softly. "Yes, I have spoken with the *katori* of other clans. We trade widely when the clans are not warring with one another. There are often summer meetings of the *katori* from neighboring clans, to share ideas and new discoveries. What we *katori* speak of amongst ourselves is just as serious as this 'biochemical' weapon, yet not one of the other *katori* has mentioned such a thing."

"Chilaili," Bessany asked, "in these wars between clans, would the war leaders use weapons given them by the Ones Above to fight each other?"

She clicked her beak again, more rapidly this time, giving John a strong sense that Chilaili was in distress. "It is forbidden," the Tersae whispered, glancing uneasily toward the ceiling as if afraid her gods would overhear, "but in my mother's grandmother's day, it is said a terrible war full of bitter hatred broke out between two clans far to the south. It quickly became *altsoba*, total war."

"Total war?" John echoed. "Like your war against the humans?"

"Yes," Chilaili said with devastating simplicity.

"Tell me more about this *altsoba*. The one in your mother's grandmother's day."

"Before the fighting was done, the two clans had used *all* the weapons given them by the Ones Above. Weapons that explode with terrible noise and force, weapons that fly through the air very quickly, weapons that throw lethal projectiles. Both clans were destroyed. The worst of the bombs left nothing but great holes in the earth where the winter nests had been, holes as large as this valley, where nothing would grow for years afterward. When I was still a nestling, the clan's *akule* used stories about this war to instill proper awe toward the power of the Ones Above and their weapons. But none of the tales told of this *altsoba* mention anything like a living weapon that kills within a few heartbeats. I cannot believe that a clan pushed to the edge of survival would fail to use this terrible weapon against an enemy, if the clan knew it existed."

"From the sound of it," John said roughly, "that's exactly what they did at Rustenberg."

Chilaili had no answer for that.

Bessany was frowning. "We've been incommunicado, with the radios missing, so I don't know what's happening with the rest of the colonies, but it seems to me other clans would have used this stuff before now, if they thought it would kill us."

John rubbed the back of his neck under his parka. "Not necessarily," he was forced to admit. "Not if they knew it might kill them, too. Damn, what a prickly puzzle."

Bessany narrowed her eyes. "Chilaili, would a clan ask the Ones Above for guidance before using such a weapon? And would the Ones Above answer them?"

John shot his sister-in-law an intent stare. Unit SPQ/R-561 had picked up a radio transmission just before the release of that neurotoxin, something he hadn't mentioned to anyone here. Chilaili's head swung around to peer at her. "A clan's *akule* might well seek permission for the *viho* to use such a deadly weapon, or ask for guidance to avoid destroying the clan when using it. But the Ones Above have not spoken since this war began. The last message our clan received before I left the nest cavern was the command to kill the devils from the stars. The blizzard had already begun by then, and we could not leave."

Bessany frowned. "This is something I've never asked, Chilaili, but how often do the Ones Above speak through the Oracles? And what do they talk about, when they speak?"

John followed her logic instantly. If Chilaili's creators spoke infrequently, on very general subjects, then the Oracle might well be nothing more than a long-distance communications system similar to SWIFT, capable of reaching across interstellar distances. But if they spoke frequently, on matters of day-to-day import, there had to be a base of operations somewhere in this star system, probably on one of the moons. And the more he thought about *that*, the less he liked it.

"The Ones Above speak to the *akules* several times during the wheel of the year," Chilaili answered readily enough. "They remind us of our duty to them or tell us of new laws we must obey. Sometimes they warn us of impending danger. They have spoken twice to Icewing Clan about great stones which were about to fall from the sky. Each time, the clan sought safety underground, although such a thing has never happened during my life. My father's grandmother was a child when the last great stone fell. The clan nearly starved that winter. Everyone would have perished had the warning not come in time, allowing the clan to take shelter in the deepest cavern in our territory."

"A meteorite warning system?" John glanced at Bessany.

"It makes sense," she shrugged, although there was a hard edge to her voice. "It's clear they view the Tersae as lab rats. A big meteorite would wreak havoc with a sizeable investment of time, money, and scientific resources. This is the biggest eugenics experiment I've ever heard of and it's obviously been under way for generations."

"God, yes." The cold finger that had touched John's spine repeatedly during the past few minutes left his whole body chilled this time. An experiment lasting multiple generations spoke to a massive, disturbing level of government support. And that scared him. Badly. *My God,* he wondered, staring at Chilaili, *what have we stumbled across here?*

"All right," he muttered, "I'll grant you the importance of a meteorite warning system to protect their research. But is the surveillance carried out by live technicians? Or an automated computer system?" He frowned. "And if they're using live technicians, are they still in the system somewhere? Or did they abandon their base quietly and slip away through all the muck out there, when our first military forces arrived? Or have they sent a courier," he blanched at the sudden thought, "to bring in reinforcements?"

Bessany eyes widened. "You mean we could find ourselves under attack? By an alien war fleet coming in from hyper-light?"

"Yes. We could. I don't like this, Bessany. I *really* don't like this. They're watching us, Bessany. Whether they're still in the system or operating automated equipment from a safe interstellar distance, they're watching us. Gathering data on how we fight, how we react, how we think. And that bothers the hell out of me."

"What bothers me," Bessany muttered, "is this hemorrhagic neurotoxin. If Chilaili's makers didn't give it to the clans to use against 'devils from the stars'—" Her eyes suddenly widened. "Oh, my God . . ."

"*What?*"

"Chilaili," she whispered, voice shaking, "tell John about the threats your *akule* used to force Icewing Clan to obey. To attack Seta Point, I mean, and this station, once the weather had cleared."

Chilaili blinked. "The Ones Above demand total obedience. The *akule* reminded us of this. I was not the only one arguing against the attack. Many Mothers and Grandmothers want nothing more to do with the Ones Above. They are murdering us slowly, by altering our chicks inside their eggshells. They are making the males more violent, more suicidal. The *akule* was afraid when the Grandmothers spoke of defying our makers, for his greatest desire is to protect the clan to which his life-mate was born. He gave up his own clan to mate with Zaltana, our last *akule*. Since her death five winters ago, he has worked ceaselessly to protect . . ."

Chilaili's voice trailed off, prompting Bessany to ask, "What is it, Chilaili? What's occurred to you?"

"Only that in twenty seasons together, they produced no chicks. Not one. Is it possible the Ones Above have caused this somehow?"

Bessany sucked down a hissing lungful of air. "God, yes. If they've gengineered each clan to be fertile only with members of their own birth clan . . ." She met John's gaze. "Don't you see it? The Tersae are in serious genetic trouble. And I mean *serious*. This war could wipe out the whole species. All it would take would be to drop the gene pool of each clan below the critical recovery threshold. The Tersae's creators *have* to know that. Yet they've ordered the Tersae to stop at nothing to kill us."

"My God, Bessany, what kind of monstrous things are we dealing with here?"

"Why do you think I kept sending those urgent messages?" She pressed fingertips to her eyes, rasped out, "I could see some of this even *before* Chilaili came here to warn me. But this . . . My God, this changes everything, the whole scale of the war, the stakes we're fighting for, the level of ruthlessness we're up against."

John groaned aloud over the disaster of those unforwarded, unread, unholy reports. When he got back to Sector Command, heads were going to roll. He'd see to it they *bounced*, all the way down those impressive stone steps. "What, exactly, were these threats the *akule* used?" he asked grimly.

Chilaili, whose puzzled expressions were becoming rapidly more fathomable, said, "The Ones Above long ago warned the clans that disobedience would be severely punished. A clan that defies the will of the Ones Above will be totally destroyed. The only clans which ever dared such disobedience, the ones that used the weapons meant for the star devils against one another, *were* destroyed. Perhaps by one another, perhaps by the Ones Above, as the *akule* insists in his teaching parables. I cannot say for sure. But the *akule* spoke the truth, when he reminded us that the Ones Above will turn their most powerful weapons against us, if we disobey."

The snow outside had more color than Bessany's face. Her voice shook. "I'm an idiot, John, not to have seen it sooner. All the clues point to it."

"Point to *what*?" he demanded, not quite seeing where she was going with this—although he was quite sure he wasn't going to like it.

"That neurotoxin wasn't developed as a weapon against some hypothetical enemy from the stars. If Chilaili's right, it's been sitting in the ground for hundreds of years, so it predates any possible human contact with the Tersae's creators. Not only that, there's no guarantee that a neurotoxin deadly to one species would even make another species sneeze, so it wouldn't make sense to create a weapon out of a neurotoxin unless you knew the biochemistry of the target you planned to kill."

"If it wasn't developed to kill humanity, then—" His

eyes widened as he saw it. *"It's meant to kill the Tersae!"* John stared at his sister-in-law. Felt the skin along his back crawl. Eugenics experiments, a doomsday neurotoxin to wipe out the experimental animals . . .

Names from ancient history slipped into his mind, terrifying names like Mengele, Treblinka, Auschwitz. Worse yet, what did the experimenters plan to do with the information they were gathering? A planetwide study in deliberate genetic deformation of an intelligent, self-aware species had all kinds of ugly implications attached to it, very few of them connected to mere scientific curiosity.

Before he could pursue those implications any further, Rapier hailed him with a code that meant incoming priority message, top secret and scrambled. John swore aloud. "Excuse me, but I've got a coded transmission coming in." He stepped outside and touched controls on the comm link. "Go ahead, Rapier."

"We have received a transmission from Unit SPQ/R-561, John. Lieutenant Commander Lundquist, assistant ship's surgeon, stayed in Rustenberg to make room for children being airlifted out. He is still alive and shows no signs of illness. Unit SPQ/R-561 is conducting analyses of tissue samples. General McIntyre has instructed him to relay the results to the research team here."

"Dear God. Bessany could be right. Download those analysis results to a data disk. I'll come up for it."

Six minutes later, he walked back into the biochem lab. Herve Sinclair and Dr. Ivanov had returned with Alison Collingwood and Arnie Kravitz. Bessany said, "I've told them our hypothesis . . ." Her voice trailed off. "What is it?"

"It looks like you were right. We've got a survivor at Rustenberg. A ship's surgeon who gave up his seat to make room for some kids. I want to know why he's still alive." He handed the data disk to Dr. Collingwood. "The Bolo at Rustenberg's already working on tissue analyses. These are the preliminary results."

The biochemist took the disk with a dazed expression just as the power came up. Lights glowed in the overhead panels and equipment hummed to life. "We're going to need heat in here," she said. "And God knows how many of our chemicals have been ruined from freezing."

"Put together a list of what you need. We'll requisition it from the *Darknight* and the *Vengeance*. I'll see what Rapier has in the way of heating units, tucked away in his cargo bins."

"Thank you. Very much." She shook off the dazed air. "Let's get cracking, Arnie. Inventory the supplies, please, while I check the equipment."

Time to let them work uninterrupted, John nodded to himself. He'd only be in the way, now. He caught Bessany's eye, tipping his head toward the door. "Want to help me scrounge for those heating units?" She glanced at Chilaili and he sighed. "Bring her along."

Rapier had moved closer to the lab, to make the job of stringing cable easier. A rear cargo bin stood open, where Sinclair's crew had retrieved the power cables. "You're getting snow up your backside, Rapier," he said into the teeth of the wind, since they were well within pickup range of the Bolo's external sensors.

"There is nothing in my portside aft cargo bin that will be damaged by a little snow," the Bolo responded drolly, his voice booming above the sound of the wind. "If you're looking for heating units, you'll find them clipped at the back of that same compartment. I left the hatch open, since you mentioned wanting them."

John grinned. "That's what I like about you, Rapier. You're the most thoughtful fellow I know."

The Tersae was staring at the immense machine,

open-beaked with astonishment. "The ogre speaks for itself?"

John and Bessany exchanged glances.

Bessany answered first. "Yes, Chilaili. A Bolo is much more than just a machine. Bolos are as self-aware, intelligent, and self-directing as you and I are."

Chilaili's beak opened again, but no sound emerged for several seconds. She blinked repeatedly, her alien eyes dilated in shock that even John could read. "But—" she began, then halted again. "I do not think even the Ones Above can realize this. They spoke of the ogres as great machines, with bombs and missiles like the ones they gave us. The Ones Above instructed the clans carefully, if the humans brought the ogres to this world. We were to kill the commanders, if possible, to cripple the machines and render them helpless."

"That's very interesting," John said quietly, while a sudden spark of excitement flared. It was an advantage, however slim. John was beginning to think any advantage at all would prove critical, because he could see a much larger war brewing in their immediate future. "Extremely interesting, in fact. Let's get those heating units rigged, shall we?"

It didn't take long to retrieve and carry them inside, where Bessany set them up with brisk efficiency. Satisfied, John excused himself to finish reading Bessany's reports. He was anxious now, to glean every speck of information possible from them.

He climbed up and settled himself in the command chair, calling up the first of his sister-in-law's field reports. "When I've finished going over these," he told Rapier, "I'll want your opinion. You may see something I'd miss."

"Understood, Commander. Routing to main data screen. If I may speak freely?"

"Of course, Rapier. You never have to ask permission to say what's on your mind, you know that."

"I only wanted to say," the Bolo's voice came out very softly, indeed, "how grateful I am that I was created by *humans*."

John's throat closed. "You're welcome."

Humanity had never been paid a higher compliment.

Chapter Twenty-three

I must speak to Chilaili.

When Bessany Weyman and the Tersae emerge from the biochem lab, I ask Chilaili to return to my portside aft cargo hold, which is more than spacious enough for the tall Tersae to find a comfortable seat. It will provide a sheltered, private place to talk. My commander's diminutive sister-in-law, however, glares up at my war hull, her scowl fiercely protective. "I won't let you imprison her."

"You are welcome to join the conversation," *I seek to reassure her.* "Indeed, I would welcome your insights, Dr. Weyman. There is much I am trying to understand."

This appears to mollify her. She nods and gestures Chilaili ahead of her. They climb into the cargo bin, which is fully climate controlled, since I often transport perishable items and delicate equipment needed by beleaguered civilian populations.

"I am going to close the hatch partway, to keep the heat inside," *I explain, moving the hatch cover until*

*it lacks but three point zero one inches from being
closed. Heat builds satisfactorily as I turn up the fans
which warm the cargo bin. The Tersae has tilted her
head sideways and back, peering upward at the
grillwork of the cargo-hold speaker. I cannot read the
emotion which passes across the Tersae's face. A sim-
ian may pull back its lips in the same fashion humans
do when they smile, but among simians, this expression does not indicate friendliness.*

"The humans created you?" *she asks.*

"Yes, that is correct."

*I do not expect the question she asks. With a brief
glance at Bessany Weyman, as though apologizing in
advance, she startles both of us.* "Do you fear them?"

"No, Chilaili. I wish only to protect my makers. It
is my mission, my purpose. It is why I was created."

"It would be good," *Chilaili says in a low voice,* "to
know why you had been created."

*The simple truth in her words is devastating. Do all
biological life-forms feel this unutterably lonely
confusion?*

"All my life," *Chilaili says softly,* "I have wondered
if I have a soul. I am a created thing. Alive, but artificial. If I understand the teachings of the Ones Above,
as they have come down through my Grandmothers,
only the Ones Above who created us possess souls. Yet
I see evidence—strong evidence—that this is not true."
*Chilaili turns her head to peer down at her human
friend.* "If your kind have no souls, then there is no
such thing as a soul and the ones who created me are
nothing more than howling beasts."

Bessany's eyes grow wet.

The Tersae whispers, "I need to believe that there
is at least some tiny piece of me that is worth more
than the flesh and blood and bone they created."

Bessany's fingers are unsteady as she places a

trembling hand on her friend's arm. "As you trusted me enough to come through this blizzard with your warning, Chilaili, trust me on this. You *do* have a soul. A very beautiful one."

A large, taloned hand comes to rest on Bessany's. "You are distressed. I did not mean this."

I hesitate, uncertain whether this is the proper time to broach my concern, but can see no gain in further delay. I harbor an intense desire to help this child of the enemy—and Chilaili's status as the only source of information we have about her unknown creators is only part of the reason for it.

"I am concerned about the future of the Tersae," *I say carefully.* "It is possible my commander could persuade his superiors to spare the clans' total destruction, if we could find a way to persuade the Tersae to defy the Ones Above by halting this war. Can you tell me anything, Chilaili, that might help us accomplish this?"

The Tersae stares up at my grillwork speaker. So does Bessany Weyman, whose expression evinces considerable astonishment. This is not surprising, considering my own purpose as an engine of war. I attempt to explain. "If I can find a way to halt this war and protect human lives, minimizing the need for future military intervention here, while at the same time protecting the Tersae from destruction, I will have accomplished far more than winning a few battle honors while protecting a few saganium mines."

Bessany Weyman's eyes grow wet again.

Chilaili stares at my speaker grill for eleven point nine seconds before speaking. "You would do this? For my clan?" *The disbelief in her voice is, perhaps, not surprising.*

"Yes, Chilaili. I would. If it is possible to do so without compromising my mission."

A deep sigh escapes the tall alien huddled beside her human friend, then Chilaili begins to speak. "Our oldest teaching stories say the Ones Above came to this world long ago, but we have never known why. Perhaps they are curious about the worlds which circle the stars. Or perhaps they only wish to hold power over them, as each clan of the Tersae holds power over its home range and covets the territory of others. The Ones Above told us how we were fashioned, to instill proper reverence and obedience. I gave these things willingly, even joyfully, until the damage to our eggs and the violence in our males became too serious to ignore.

"The command to put our eggs into the blessing chambers, which were unknown in my mother's childhood, came through the Oracle. My mother said the clan returned to the winter nest one season, just after I was hatched, to find the blessing chamber in its place, put there in our absence during the summer gathering season. The Oracle gave the command to put our eggs into it that winter."

Bessany frowns. "Then they have to be somewhere in this star system, don't they? To install equipment like that in every clan's winter nest, they've got to have some kind of base of operations, even if it's only infrequently manned."

I ask, "Is the *akule* the only member of the clan allowed to listen to the Oracle?"

"That is the custom, yes. There are certain rituals only the *akules* know, rituals that allow them to operate the Oracle properly and safely."

Bessany asks thoughtfully, "Do your creators use a language only the *akule* knows, or do the Ones Above speak the same language as the Tersae?"

Chilaili hesitates before answering. "Many seasons ago, when I was very young, I overheard the *akule* who tended the Oracle then. Zaltana was speaking with the

Ones Above, from the holy chamber reserved for the Oracle, which is where *akule* lives. The Ones Above spoke the same words we do, much of the time, although there were things said which I did not recognize as any words I had ever heard before. Of course, I was very young. Not above five years out of the nest. But I remember it vividly."

"Because you heard the voices of the Ones Above?"

"Yes, partly. To hear the voices of our creators . . . It was exciting. Frightening, as well, because it was taboo. And I remember because the *akule* was young and beautiful, very kind and sweet-natured. She had fallen deeply in love with the third son of an *akule* from the clan nearest our own. They had met while hunting in the area where the ranges of both clans overlapped. Zaltana was begging the Ones Above for permission to become life-mates with the male she loved so desperately. When they granted her request, I felt great joy, for it made her so happy. She had always been kind to me."

"I wonder why they said yes," *Bessany wonders aloud, her voice tinged with bitterness.* "If they knew she couldn't produce children with him, then they knew your clan wouldn't have an heir to the office of *akule*, which would be a critical loss for a clan." *She shakes her head, frowning.* "God only knows what they were thinking. Or planning. It's even possible," *she says grimly,* "that they knew it didn't matter. Either they genuinely don't care whether one clan survives or dies, or they're planning to end the experiment soon."

I do not like either proposed scenario. The latter hypothesis is particularly disturbing in terms of potential time constraints, but my main thoughts tend in a different direction altogether. "Did you actually see this Oracle, Chilaili?"

"No. Not then. But when our clan leaves its winter

nest, we always take the Oracle with us, so I have seen it many times since. It is the only gift of the Ones Above that the clan never travels without. The blessing chamber is too large to carry with us during the warm months and we would not need it during the summer, in any case. Winter is the time of mating and breeding, when we are safely sheltered belowground. But we always take the Oracle, for we never know when the Ones Above may wish to speak to us. Or when we may need to call them and plead for help or guidance."

I conclude that if the Ones Above decide to destroy an entire clan for disobedience or some other reason and plan to use the neurotoxin to accomplish it, they have only two options: They must either wait until that clan returns to its winter nest or the clans must carry the neurotoxin receptacle with them.

The Oracles, treated with reverence and care, are clearly the receptacle of choice.

This would certainly explain the release of the neurotoxin at Rustenberg. A direct hit on a permanent, underground shelter would be almost guaranteed to rupture the containment vessel, if not by a direct hit, then by the fall of rock which would crush the casing and release whatever was inside. The more I ponder it, the more certain I become.

Bessany Weyman has seen it as well. "It's in the Oracles, isn't it?" *she breathes aloud.*

"I cannot imagine a more logical containment vessel." *I begin to wonder if there would be a way to neutralize this threat by sealing off any openings or release mechanisms in the Oracle's casing. If this could be accomplished, it would allow the Tersae to act without fear of immediate retaliation. And the ability to act freely might be enough to persuade Icewing Clan, at least, to break off relations with the Ones Above and ally themselves with humanity. At the very least, it would stop the attacks against Seta Point and Eisenbrucke Station before any lives are lost on either side.*

I ask Chilaili her opinion of this theory.

She considers carefully for fifty-eight point three full seconds of silence. "I don't know if it would be enough," *she replies at last, with commendable honesty.* "There are many Grandmothers on the Council who would gladly declare independence of the Ones Above. Their only desire is to safeguard our eggs from further tampering. But the males? They are accustomed to obeying the edicts of the Council, but we have never tried to order the males to do something that violates the orders of the Ones Above. I do not know if it would work." *Her voice registers deep distress.*

This certainly complicates the issue, but I believe I see a way out. "Chilaili, would you be willing to teach me your language?"

The Tersae blinks, pupils dilating in a response I am learning to equate with surprise. "I will try, but Bessany Weyman was unable to reproduce many of the necessary sounds." *She glances apologetically down at her human friend.*

Bessany smiles. "Bolos are not limited in the same way."

Chilaili gives her eerie, head-bobbing nod. "If you wish, I will teach you."

"May we begin now, please? Time may be very short. The storm front is nearly past, which means clear weather is nearly upon us."

She does not ask why I wish to learn, which is just as well. I am not certain she will like what I have in mind. If, at the last moment, Chilaili balks, I will at least have gained a working knowledge of the enemy's language. And if Chilaili does not balk, perhaps we will have gained a very great deal more, indeed.

Chapter Twenty-four

Dr. Alison Collingwood had been hard at work for ten straight hours when she confirmed it. Bleary eyed with exhaustion, suffering cricks and cramps in her neck and back, she straightened up with a soft groan and ran both hands through her hair, dragging the lank mess back from her face. It had taken the combined computing power of two Bolos, Bessany Weyman's xeno-ecological genetic testing equipment, added to her own, blood and tissue samples from Chilaili and samples gathered by the Bolo at Rustenberg from Lieutenant Commander Lundquist and from the carcasses of dead birds which comprised the Tersae's ancestral stock, plus samples of the neurotoxin put through tests she had requested Senator to conduct; but she finally had the answer.

Stumbling slightly over her own feet, she told her assistant, "Good work, Arnie. Fabulous work," and emerged from the biochem lab where they'd been closeted for so long. When she stepped outside, Alison was surprised by the ominously clear daylight air. The sky was crystalline, the sunlight so bright it hurt, reflected in diamond-point sparkles off the snow. The Bolo, parked just outside the lab, greeted her at once.

"Good afternoon, Dr. Collingwood. Do you have news?"

She nodded wearily. "We've got it, Rapier. Humans aren't at risk."

A hatch opened high overhead and Lieutenant Colonel Weyman appeared, moving fast as he skinned down the ladder without touching the rungs. Bessany Weyman and the rest of the station's personnel—those not confined to the infirmary—came running through the snow, alerted by the Bolo's booming voice. Chilaili, too, appeared from somewhere behind the Bolo.

"You're certain?" the Bolo's commander asked the moment he reached the ground.

"Yes. Completely. The damned thing's diabolical. And so is whoever developed it. Bessany, you were right. Not only was that neurotoxin created specifically to kill the Tersae, it had to be gengineered at the same time the Tersae were developed."

"What do you mean?" Colonel Weyman asked with a frown.

Alison thinned her lips. "The neurotoxin attacks a specific neuropeptide receptor site and triggers a chain reaction through the cells, killing the host horribly within minutes. Humans don't have that particular neuropeptide or its receptor sites. When I asked Senator to test the neurotoxin on tissue from live, uninfected ancestral stock, the stuff invaded within seconds. When exposed to human tissue, the stuff was completely inert. No molecular action at all."

"That doesn't necessarily mean it was gengineered specifically for the Tersae. Any number of wild species on Thule could be affected."

She shook her head. "No, they wouldn't. Bessany's

taken specimens from a whole range of species similar to the Tersae over the last three months. Only one of them has this neurotransmitter."

Bessany scowled. "That's the one they used as ancestral stock then." She glanced at her tall brother-in-law. "If Alison didn't find that neuropeptide in the other samples, it's because it's not there. There are biochemicals in muscles that aren't found in the gut, for example, and there are neuropeptides unique to the brain. So for every species I tranked with the dart gun, I took bone and marrow samples, brain tissue, muscle and gut samples. I scraped talons and claws, sampled myelin sheaths, and clipped small nerve samples. I was *thorough.*"

Alison nodded. "So was I. Believe me, I was. I tested every one of those samples, checked and triple checked the results, had both Bolos do the same. Humans are not at risk from this stuff."

Tension drained visibly as Lieutenant Colonel Weyman rubbed the bridge of his nose. "Thank God," he said quietly. "Good work, Dr. Collingwood. You too," he nodded toward her assistant, who had come stumbling out of the lab to join them. "All right, the first thing we do is tell the refugees from Rustenberg they can go home, get them out of this freezing weather."

"Those refugees may not be at risk," Bessany said bleakly, "but Chilaili is. And Sooleawa. And every other Tersae who might be persuaded to switch allegiance. Given the way this war's going, with the clans losing so heavily, the Ones Above may decide to destroy them, just to keep us from getting our hands on any live prisoners. If we don't help them, the Tersae don't have a prayer. And everyone at this station owes Chilaili that much, at least: a simple shot at survival."

"I agree, completely," the Bolo's commander frowned, "but I don't see any way to stop that neurotoxin, if the

Ones Above decide to send the signal that releases it. Unless . . ." he paused, a startled look blossoming in his eyes.

"What?" Bessany asked urgently.

"We can't stop them from releasing the stuff without some way to clog the release valve so it can't disperse, and even that's no guarantee that some of it won't get out. But what if we could block their neuro-peptide receptor sites?"

Alison's jaw dropped, even as she kicked herself for not thinking of it first. "Good God. Develop an inert analog?"

He nodded. "Exactly. *Can* you?"

"I don't know," Alison said, a trifle breathlessly. "I don't know, but it's worth trying."

"There's still a delivery problem," he mused, brows hooked downward. "We'd have to get it into their living quarters, which won't be easy."

"There's not a problem with Icewing Clan," Bessany insisted. "Chilaili could take it right into the nest."

Everyone swung around to look at the Tersae.

"I do not understand," Chilaili said. "What is this 'analog' you speak of making?"

Bessany answered. "We want to create a substance that would prevent the weapon in the Oracle from harming you. Like an antidote to poison. Even if the Oracle released the poison, if you had breathed the substance we created *first*, the poison wouldn't harm you." She glanced at Alison. "How far in advance would we need to release the analog, to protect them?"

Alison held up her hands. "I don't know. Best guess, an hour? Unless those tissues are saturated, the neuro-toxin would get through."

Lieutenant Colonel Weyman nodded. "I'll talk to Rapier about possible delivery systems we can cobble together. If we can protect your clan," he asked Chilaili, "can you convince them to renounce allegiance to the Ones Above? To try an alliance with humans? Or at least call off the attacks on Seta Point and Eisenbrucke?"

Alien eyes blinked in the harsh sunlight. "We will risk much, to save the eggs from further tampering. But I think the Council would have to witness a direct attempt by the Ones Above to kill us, to convince them we should seek alliance with humans."

The Bolo spoke up. "I have an idea about that, Commander. I am convinced the Oracles are both the source of the neurotoxin and the means by which to effect a reversal in the loyalties of the Tersae. If Dr. Collingwood is able to develop a compound to block the neuropeptide receptors, then we have a way of preserving the Tersae. I believe I have come up with a way to persuade Icewing Clan to transfer its loyalties. If Chilaili agrees to try my experiment with her clan, and if you can persuade General McIntyre that we have much to gain, with relatively little risk to human personnel, I would suggest conducting a trial run the moment Dr. Collingwood's analog is ready."

"What, exactly, do you have in mind?"

"I intend," the Bolo said with just a trace of smugness in his voice, "to subvert the Oracles . . ."

Chapter Twenty-five

Alessandra wasn't used to seeing the face of the enemy. As she read through Bessany Weyman's reports, copies of which Lieutenant Colonel Weyman had forwarded at her request, gooseflesh prickled and eerie sensations ran electrically down her spine at odd, unpredictable moments. Photographs of Chilaili and Sooleawa, along with detailed accounts of their beliefs and customs, gave these particular enemies starkly individual faces. And names. And dreams, hopes, fears. Everything, in short, that made an anonymous creature vividly real. What Alessandra found in Dr. Weyman's reports made it difficult to reconcile these particular Tersae with the fanatical killers Alessandra had fought three times now, since landing.

Among other things, she recognized honor when she saw it. And she hadn't expected to find it *here*.

Alessandra drummed her fingertips on the console of Senator's command chair, frowning at the data screen and shrugging herself into a slightly more comfortable position under the long arm of the autodoc. Senator was still busy pumping medication into her system and would be for some time to come. Alessandra was fully capable of admitting how difficult it was to remain objective when the Tersae had fired fusion bombs at her. Things like that made war rather personal. But she was also honest enough to know there was more to her uneasiness than that.

For Alessandra's entire career, the opposition had remained anonymous. Certainly, she'd never thought of the Deng as anything but a collective mass of ugly protoplasm labeled "enemy." The war with the Tersae had been very different from combat against the Deng, yet the Tersae had remained curiously unreal, shadows on a data screen. It was, perhaps, merely a feature of mechanized warfare, fighting at a level of psychological, if not geographical, distance from the enemy, but Alessandra had never before actually *looked* into an enemy's face.

Until now.

It didn't help Alessandra's peace of mind to know that Chilaili had saved human lives at Eisenbrucke Station. That suggested—strongly—that at least some of Alessandra's emotional reactions to the Tersae involved demonizing, a common-enough occurrence during war, to be sure, but one that made negotiated settlements harder to accomplish. Of course, there were some enemies with whom negotiated settlements were so impossible, the mere attempt was tantamount to suicide.

Chilaili is one individual, she told herself. *One very small, unimportant individual, paying back a personal debt and nothing more. This doesn't change the rest of the war. Negotiated settlements with a pack of fanatical killers is about as likely as Senator learning to fly without a lift sled.*

Chilaili's actions at Eisenbrucke did not change what

other Tersae had done at Rustenberg or the other mining colonies, one of which had been totally obliterated before the colonists even knew they were at war. The one thing Chilaili *might* change was what humanity knew about the Tersae's creators. Alessandra scrolled back through Dr. Weyman's reports, not even certain what it was, precisely, that she was looking for, but whatever it was, she wasn't finding it. And that bothered her. She was still brooding over it when Senator said, "We have an incoming message, Commander, on maximum security scramble."

"Let's hear it." Almost any distraction was welcome, at this point. She was going stir-crazy, trapped in this command compartment with no idea how much longer she'd have to wait.

The speaker crackled. "Captain DiMario, do you copy, over?"

Lieutenant Colonel Weyman's voice had become very familiar, during the last few hours. "DiMario here. What is it, Colonel?"

"We're sending Rustenberg's refugees home. Humans are not at risk. If nothing else, you can climb out of your Bolo, now."

A wave of giddy relief passed through her. "Thank God, all the way around. We'll put candles in the windows for those poor folks."

"I'm sure they'll welcome the sight. Now, you've gone through Dr. Weyman's reports?"

"Yes, sir. Twice."

"Good, because we've got ourselves a 'situation,' here."

She heard the emphasis, even through the speaker. "A 'situation,' sir?" she asked cautiously.

"We need Lundquist's help again. Dr. Collingwood is trying to create an analog to the neurotoxin. Something that will block neuropeptide receptor sites in Tersae tissue."

Alessandra's mouth fell open. "For God's own sake, *why*? I mean, why would we want to interfere with something that kills the enemy *for* us? That stuff may be horrible, but so is butchering helpless children! Have you *seen* the eyes of the survivors who fled Rustenberg? I really don't understand why we should block something that will do the job we came here to do, without risk to human lives."

Clipped anger shot through the speaker. "Genocide's an ugly word, Captain."

"You're goddamned right, it is! And I don't like being on the receiving end of it!"

"Neither do the Tersae. And you and I, Captain, are *not* the ones dishing it out. *That's* the little situation I mentioned."

All the arguments Alessandra had been marshaling to trot out in logical order piled up in the back of her throat. "What do you mean?"

He told her. In gruesome detail. And that explanation triggered a shocked reordering of everything Alessandra thought she'd known about the Tersae— which was a fair amount, after reading Bessany Weyman's reports. As Alessandra listened, a cold sickness began to clutch at her. She'd never had children, but her sister had. It was far too easy to imagine the way she'd feel if something had held *their* lives under that kind of gun.

The explosive conflict that unleashed, between sudden sympathy and preexisting cold hatred, left Alessandra floundering in a brutal riptide of emotions. She genuinely didn't think she could ever forget what the Tersae had done, or the shocked anguish that burned in young children's eyes like cold flame. Murdered innocence was only a small step removed from murder, period. Certainly, the suffering went on longer, when the victims survived.

But much could be forgiven a species whose children were held hostage.

Weyman's voice jolted her out of a hazy state of shock. "Any questions, Captain?"

Several thousand, she thought dazedly. Not one of which affected her immediate duty. "No, sir. I'll start work with Lundquist immediately. Same routine as before? Coordinate research efforts through both Bolos?"

"Precisely. If you and Lundquist need anything—and I mean *anything*—holler."

"Thank you, sir," she said quietly. "We'll get right on it."

"Good. Keep me posted. Weyman out."

Alessandra broke the connection and sat motionless in her command chair for several moments, trying to reorder her chaotic thoughts. They swooped and circled like carrion kites, coming back again and again to the unknown creatures who had set up this vast, planetary experiment. John Weyman's voice echoed through those whirling thoughts: *Genocide's an ugly word* . . .

Yes, it was. A filthy, ugly little word. She wanted to loathe the Tersae's creators as much as she'd hated the Tersae until a few moments ago. It should have been desperately easy to hate the "Ones Above." But it wasn't, because a contrary corner of her mind whispered, with forceful insistence, *Are we any better?* And the reason she asked it was the guilt which had been preying on her mind ever since that moment on the battlefield, when Unit DNY had died.

Today, Alessandra sat inside another sentient machine, a thinking and feeling entity that was undeniably alive, one her own species had created, just as this unknown alien had created the Tersae. The Bolo she sat inside, right now, busily pumping life-saving

drugs into her system, had been pronounced obsolete—
and therefore slated for destruction—by the Corps of
Psychotronic Engineers. The Corps had shown Senator no more pity, assigning him casually to oblivion,
than the Ones Above had shown, reducing the Tersae
to the status of lab rats, sacrificed at alien whim. It
was only Senator's extraordinary good fortune that the
Deng War had come along, pulling him out of mothballs for an upgrade, before the Corps had gotten
around to frying his action/command core.

Humanity had developed the Bolos specifically to
die in the place of human soldiers. Bolos were thinking, feeling individuals. They loved life as much as she
loved her own. They loved their duty—so much so, they
delighted in the chance to demonstrate their worthiness and fulfill their destiny. A Bolo would charge
gleefully into battle, delighted by the chance to prove
itself capable of defending its beloved creators. Even
when those creators gave orders that led to their deaths.

How did that differ from suicidal Tersae rushing into
battle to die for *their* creators?

In many ways, Bolos were actually *less* free than the
Tersae, who were able to hunt and pursue pleasure in
their own time and in their own way. A Bolo was
allowed no independent action outside a battlefield.
Except for a few obsolete units scattered here and
there as heavy farm and mining equipment, a Bolo had
no way to exist other than as a platform of war. Until
very recently, a Bolo had not even been permitted the
full use of its multipartite mind outside the battlefield,
for fear a machine carrying that much firepower, a
machine able to think clearly and complexly during long
stretches of peacetime, might start to entertain dangerous thoughts.

Self-aware, self-directing, able to appreciate music
and literature and the sweet agony of friendship, Bolos

were strictly bound to one purpose and never allowed to stray outside it, literally on pain of death. A Bolo that broke its programming to take action outside the allowable parameters was condemned as a rogue and executed, without mercy, without hope of reprieve.

There was no sidestepping it. Humanity held the same sword above a Bolo's head as the sword held above the Tersae: obey or die. Worse yet for a Bolo: obey *and* die. Where did the difference lie? In the creator's hands?

She held hers up, staring at them as though they belonged to someone—some*thing*—else. No, she realized slowly, frowning at her fingers as though seeing them for the first time, the difference didn't lie in the hands. It lay in the mind. A Bolo was not just cannon fodder; it was far more than a lab animal to be sacrificed, with no more compunction than a biology student felt, drowning live worms in formaldehyde. A lab rat never knew why it was to be killed; but a Bolo *always* knew. Knew it and accepted it and went to that death gladly, demonstrating courage worthy of the best humanity had produced from its own biological heart.

She didn't make the mistake of anthropomorphizing them. Bolos were *not* human. But there wasn't a Bolo commander alive who didn't recognize the essential humanness of a Bolo's mind, of its soul, perhaps, standing as mirror image to the minds and souls that had created it. That was what inspired a commander's unstinting friendship—and loyalty—that marked such relationships. It was the kinship of minds that created such wrenching grief when a Bolo passed out of existence. It was like the death of a child or a soulmate, leaving an ache far worse than a mere empty hollow in one's life. In a way, a Bolo became immortal when it died, as immortal as the great heroes of old, the Leonidases who, in their living and their dying, became far more than merely human.

Such sacrifices would be honored as long as the Brigade—or human hearts—endured. Her own lost friend, Unit DNY, would be sung of by soldiers who understood, by cadets who would understand only too soon, by youngsters with shining eyes, who understood only that something precious had died, and far too soon.

As Alessandra gazed at Senator's command compartment, his antique walls and data panels, she saw her Bolo with eyes that were finally clear again. And what she saw made Alessandra realize the most important thing she had ever come to understand. She had watched Senator struggle to overcome handicaps perpetrated on him by ham-handed technicians. Had watched him prevail anyway, with a rising sense of awe at the steady flow of brilliant solutions he fielded, one after another, to make up for those handicaps. Having finally recognized what had been there, all along, to see, Alessandra knew quite abruptly that she would fight like a cornered hellcat for his right to survive.

"Senator," she said softly, releasing her command chair's harness and sliding into a clean uniform, "I don't think I ever told you, but you're one *hell* of a fine Bolo. And come hell or high water, I'll make sure you get the chance to stay that way. I'll get a shipload of psychotronic engineers out here to fix you, even if I have to light fires under every brass butt from Sector HQ to Central Command. You've earned it. So don't you go getting any damnfool notions about joining any mothballs, you hear me?"

"Yes, Comma—" The Bolo paused. Said instead, "Yes, Alessandra."

She smiled. "I like the sound of that."

Very softly, her Bolo said, "So do I, Alessandra. Thank you."

No other words were necessary.

Chapter Twenty-six

After fifteen hours of brutal work by Eisenbrucke Station's biochemistry team, John Weyman watched Dr. Collingwood load a specially-rigged aerosol canister which would release her newly created compound into Icewing Clan's nest. "I've suspended it in a colorless, odorless gas," she explained, "since the clan will need to breathe it for an hour without knowing it."

They had tested the analog as best they could, with tissue taken from Chilaili and airlifted out to Rustenberg, for exposure to the neurotoxin. And while the tests went perfectly, tissue was not a whole organism and they were gambling with the fate of a sentient species.

Unfortunately, neither John nor anybody else could see any other way to proceed.

John made certain Chilaili knew how to operate the device, then packed it into the Navy shuttle that had flown back from Rustenberg, along with a smoke grenade and a can of spray sealant, the kind used to repair micro-meteor hull breaches in Navy ships, couriered down from the *Darknight*.

The rest of Eisenbrucke's personnel had already been airlifted out, aboard civilian aircars from Seta Point, flying low to the ground under the protection of Rapier's long-range guns. The last civilian transport was ready to ferry Dr. Collingwood, her assistant, and Bessany out to Seta Point, but Bessany—with characteristic stubbornness—refused to board. "No," she insisted. "I'm going with you and Chilaili."

"If something goes wrong—"

"You'll need a xenology expert. Or Chilaili will need a friend. Or both."

He gave up trying and simply helped her climb into Lieutenant Carter's shuttle.

Their transport was well armed with antimissile systems, freeing Rapier for the part he would play in the upcoming charade. The Bolo had already headed out, needing a good head start, since he couldn't travel as fast through broken terrain as an airborne craft could fly across it. Rapier wouldn't need to get as close as they would, but John wanted him relatively near, in case things went seriously sour. John gave Lieutenant Carter one of Elin Olsson's geological survey maps, on which he'd indicated the point where Icewing's war party had first been spotted, their heat signatures pulsing brightly against the snow.

"This," he tapped the marked location, "has to be pretty much dead on target for their winter nest. I want you to bring us in fairly close, then drop us here." He tapped a second marked location. "We'll hike the rest of the way, so the shuttle doesn't attract attention."

Carter flashed a brief smile. "Piece of cake. Lots simpler than airlifting out nearly a thousand people in seven minutes. All right, let's rock and roll."

John vowed to make sure Lieutenant Carter received a whopping commendation.

He pulled himself into the cockpit, settling in the

copilot's seat, while Carter switched on the engines and ran swiftly through her preflight check. John glanced into the back, where Bessany sat next to Chilaili. The Tersae was scrunched into an acceleration couch far too small for her frame. The pack she'd brought with her through the blizzard sat at her feet.

"We're going to lift off in a couple of minutes, Chilaili. If you get airsick—queasy enough to throw up—there's a special sack in a pocket next to your right hand."

"Thank you, John Weyman," she said, her voice a deep rumble from being bent double to fit into the couch. She turned her gaze to the window, staring out across the ruins of the research station. Given her grip on the couch's armrests, she was terrified and trying not to show it.

He was suddenly very glad Bessany had insisted on coming along.

Carter said, "All right, everybody, hang onto your lunch. We're set to go."

She throttled up the engines and lifted out of the little valley. John caught a glimpse of the "bridge" which had given the doomed station its name, a glittering span of solid ice, beautiful, treacherous, deadly. Like everything else about Thule. Then the shuttle banked, they picked up speed, and Carter shot her craft out across the forest at treetop level.

After a moment, Chilaili asked in a strained voice, "May I know why we fly in the wrong direction to reach my nest?"

"I'd rather not end up in a dogfight with any missiles," Carter said. "I want to set you down fast and get out again without being spotted. The last thing we want is to alert your nest. And we don't dare risk blowing you and that analog up in the air, if your war party sees us and decides to shoot."

"Ah . . . thank you."

"You're welcome." The pilot glanced at John, eyes glinting as if to say, "This'll be one to tell my grandkids," but said nothing, concentrating on flying as close to the treetops as possible. A journey that had taken Chilaili a full, bruising day, struggling through the blizzard, took the Navy shuttle fifteen minutes, even allowing for the long loop to come in from the opposite direction. Carter spotted the clearing marked on the map and settled her craft gently between tall stands of coniferlike trees that whipped and swayed in the backblast.

"Good luck, Colonel!" Carter called as John popped the hatch and slithered down to the ground, joined a moment later by Chilaili and Bessany. They waded through deep snowdrifts to reach the cover of the trees, so Carter would have clear space for takeoff. *I ought to have my head examined,* John thought with a sudden jerk of his pulse as the shuttle lifted off and vanished over the trees. *There's a whole lot of lonesome out here.* He hadn't felt this vulnerable in years, having grown accustomed to riding into battle with fourteen thousand tons of duralloy war hull between himself and fast, messy death.

Bessany's expression as she glanced into his eyes told him she knew exactly how he felt.

"Come," Chilaili said quietly. "My nest lies this way."

They followed wordlessly as Chilaili moved rapidly through the trees, staying well inside the cover of forest where the drifts weren't as deep. Seeing Chilaili in her native environment was vastly different from seeing her at the research station or scrunched into a Navy shuttle. Her movements were freer and easier, her stride longer, her gaze more alert as she swung her head gently from side to side, gauging distances and guiding them unerringly into the easiest paths.

For a full, grueling hour, they plowed through snow-drifts, navigated tangled underbrush, and cut around steep-walled gorges where frozen waterfalls glittered with all the raw beauty of wild water solidified into natural sculpture. Their painfully slow progress sent John's respect soaring, realizing just what it meant that Chilaili had struggled through this same deadly landscape in a howling blizzard.

When Chilaili noticed their flagging pace, she adjusted her longer stride, for which John was intensely grateful. He was in good athletic shape—the Brigade required it—but he wasn't anywhere near the equal of an eight-foot-tall, winter-hardened Tersae huntress, adapted for this climate and accustomed to its rigors. Bessany showed definite signs of strain, despite three months of heavy fieldwork. Adding to their discomfort, the temperature was dropping sharply, now they were on the back side of the storm system.

Breathing the bitterly cold air was like sucking down knifeblades with each breath. When the gauge on his survival gear registered five degrees below zero, John pulled full-face protective masks from his pack and handed one to Bessany. She flashed him a game smile and pulled it on under the hood of her parka. John's mask rubbed his chilled skin painfully at first, but as his face warmed up beneath the protective fabric, some of the misery abated with the warmth. He steadfastly refused to think about Rapier's toasty warm command compartment.

The character of the land changed as they neared Chilaili's winter nest. The deep basalt flows and the weathered gorges cutting through them, so prevalent in the region immediately surrounding Eisenbrucke Station, gave way to a gentler topography of limestone outcroppings, sinkholes, and ravines worn through the softer rock by running water. They crossed frozen streams, treading carefully on the ice where sharp, broken branches and water-rounded boulders jutted up through the frozen surface. Chilaili had to help them scramble up steep, snow-covered stream banks more than once, careful not to dig her claws into their wrists.

By the time Chilaili began to slow down, picking her way with great care, John was panting and Bessany was in visible distress. At length, Chilaili held up one large, furred hand and they halted. She slithered forward on her belly, motioning them to join her. John crept up beside her and Bessany slid forward next to him. They found themselves peering down into a narrow defile, no more than five meters across at its greatest width and nearly fifteen meters deep. At the bottom, he could see a dark, shadowed place where a cave opened out from the steep limestone cliff. A few tall, spindly conifers grew up from the bottom, providing enough coverage that the narrow crack in the earth probably wasn't very noticeable, even from the air. It was a fiendishly effective spot to hide a clan's winter nest.

Chilaili gestured for them to move back, away from the lip of the overhang. He nodded, scooting on his belly in the snow. Bessany and Chilaili did the same, then the Tersae touched the side of her head, where a tiny, hidden earphone rested inside her aural canal. She would be able to hear anything John, Bessany, or Rapier said to her. Chilaili pulled an elaborate cloak from her pack and touched a tiny camera lens hidden amongst the animal talons and teeth, strips of fur, and what looked like bunches of dried herbs. The camera was so small, John couldn't see it and he knew exactly where to look.

John slid equipment out of his own pack, testing his own earphone and tapping the microphone in the hood of his parka to be sure she was receiving him properly. Bessany did the same and Chilaili nodded. They double-checked the signal from Chilaili's camera to be sure his palm unit was picking up a clear picture, then he handed over the analog canister, along with the spray sealant and a smoke grenade. The Tersae tucked them into pouches they'd rigged on her weapons belt, hidden beneath the voluminous folds of her cloak.

Chilaili covered his hand briefly with her own, whether to offer reassurance or to draw courage from the contact, he wasn't sure, since her hand was shaking violently. She repeated the gesture with Bessany, who gave her a quick smile. Chilaili's alien eyes flickered briefly with some strong emotion he couldn't read, then she rose and moved swiftly away through the trees, cloak billowing.

John traced her progress on the tiny screen on his palm unit. She climbed down a path which had been swept clean of snow, taking great care with her handholds on the limestone walls, and reached bottom safely without being challenged. She pushed aside a snugly fitted screen, allowing a wafting scent of woodsmoke and alien cooking odors to drift up through the cold air. John's pulse thudded raggedly in his ears. Bessany reached over and gripped his gloved hand.

For good or ill, there was no backing out now.

Chapter Twenty-seven

Chilaili was afraid.

She hadn't been this frightened since the day her mother's mangled body had been carried home. The responsibility which had descended so crushingly on her young shoulders that day was as nothing compared with the weight of responsibility she carried now. If she failed . . .

Then it would be a very short failure.

The moment she stepped past the screen, Chilaili was engulfed by shrieking hatchlings. They danced joyously around her, welcoming her home with shrill cries, so overjoyed by her return, they overcame their awe of the *katori* cloak. Smiling and patting heads with her free hand, she took advantage of the outcry she'd known would greet her return. Chilaili angled the nozzle of the largest canister she carried to project slightly beyond the edge of her cloak. She drew a deep, ragged breath—and plunged the release mechanism.

The hiss was completely drowned out by the yelling hatchlings. Chilaili waded into the main living cavern, spewing the stuff into the air as she walked. An invisible cloud spread out above the heads of the little ones, forcibly ejected by the humans' special container—such a fragile barrier between all she loved and hideous death. The canister turned cold against her fur, then the hissing stopped. An instant later, Sooleawa threw herself into Chilaili's arms.

"Mother!" she cried, trembling violently. "I've been so afraid! When you didn't come and didn't come . . ."

"Hush, precious one," she soothed, taking her daughter's face in both hands and smoothing her fur. "I'm home now."

But not, her mind whispered, *safely. Honored Great-Grandmothers, watch over us . . .*

Sooleawa smiled, then Chilaili greeted the clan's ruling Grandmothers, the mothers heavy with eggs not yet laid, and the huntresses who would not be leaving for at least another day, to attack an empty research station. In the shadows, the males too old to go to war greeted her with pleasure, nodding from where they sat brooding their daughters' and granddaughters' eggs. Given her long absence, they doubtless looked forward to the poultices and tisanes she would prepare to soothe their aching bones and stiffened muscles.

Even the *akule* greeted her with simple, warm joy. "We feared the worst, Chilaili," he said earnestly, taking her hands briefly in his. "Trying to travel through such a storm . . . Thank the Ones Above, you are safe. The ritual went well?"

She nodded, not trusting her voice to speak the lie.

"All is well, then. The war party set out for the larger human nest nearly a full day ago. If the Ones Above look kindly on them, they will reach that nest within another two days and destroy it."

Chilaili nodded again, still unable to speak. The

humans and their ogre—their Bolo, she corrected herself—could have killed the entire war party at any time, without ever coming close enough for the warriors to fire a single shot or lob a single bomb in self-defense. Insanity, to fight such an enemy. The canisters under her cloak—one empty, two waiting for the right moment—were so heavy, they dragged at her spirit as well as the pouches she had slipped them into.

"Sooleawa," she said tiredly, "could you bring me a cup of something hot to drink? I'm chilled clear through."

"Of course, Mother!"

The girl scampered off and Chilaili turned in a slow circle, allowing the humans a good view of the cavern through the device hidden on her cloak. "There are too many empty hearths," she said quietly, glancing from one living space to the next, each family's spot marked by the outlines of cooking hearths and sleeping furs. "Never have we sent so many of our clan to battle." She shook her head and let out a deep and weary sigh. "Is there news from other clans?"

Great-Grandmother Anevay gestured for Chilaili to sit beside her. She sank down onto a pile of sleeping furs arranged next to the old woman's hearth. Anevay offered her a bowl of savory *wurpa* stew, smoking hot from the fire.

"Yes, *katori*," she said as Chilaili began to eat, "there *is* news from the other clans. Grim news, all of it. We have not dared use our Oracle. The *akule* has heard explosions and screams through ours, every time a clan has used theirs to plead for help. These devils we fight are merciless." The ancient matriarch shook her head sadly. "You were right, Chilaili, to warn us that we fight an enemy more deadly than we could comprehend. But in all honesty, what else can we do?"

Chilaili couldn't answer that question.

Not yet.

"The Ones Above have not spoken at all, then?" she asked.

"No," Kestejoo sighed, joining them. "We have not heard their voices since the beginning of the war."

The *akule* looked as tired as she felt. In his own way, Chilaili realized, he felt the burden of this war as heavily as she did. She feared what he would do when the Bolo launched the second phase of their desperate plan. Fortunately, Sooleawa returned with a steaming cupful of *ijwa* tea, distracting her from that worry. Chilaili sipped gratefully, although the sloshing liquid revealed the shameful unsteadiness of her hands.

"You're trembling, Chilaili," Kestejoo said worriedly. "Are you all right?"

She nodded. "I have fasted for many days, is all. And the trip back through the deep snow was exhausting." That, at least, was honest enough. "The stew and the tea will restore my strength."

They did help, in fact. The taste of *wurpa* stew and mellow *ijwa* tea soothed her jangled nerves with their simple familiarity, reminding her that she was home for however long a time remained to them. The humans had shared their food unstintingly, but she had found human fare unsettling in its strangeness. It was so good to be back amongst her own kind, to see her beloved daughter's face, it was all she could do to swallow past the constriction in her throat.

She sat and listened to Sooleawa's bright chatter and Anevay's humorous account of the days she'd been away, sharing all the silly squabbles between nestlings, passing along the complaints and aches of the older grandmothers and grandfathers. Squealing laughter rang cheerfully from the little ones as they played chase and stalk through the living cavern. Their world was bright and happy again with the safe return of their *katori*. For them, the war was a faraway tale that had not yet touched their lives directly.

All too soon, that would change.

Chilaili sipped her tea and nibbled at her stew and silently counted down the passing minutes. An hour, the humans had said. During the days spent with them, she had learned to judge very accurately the span of time they referred to as one hour. When that deadline passed with nothing but silence, her hands grew unsteady again and her pulse jumped. *Soon*, she groaned to herself. It had to be *soon*.

Sooleawa had just brought another cupful of tea when the Oracle's incoming-message alarm sounded. It echoed shrilly from the little cavern where the *akule* tended the device. Even though she had been expecting it—or perhaps *because* she had—Chilaili started violently, sloshing hot tea across her hand. She swore viciously, even as the *akule* lunged to his feet and ran for the Oracle Chamber. Chilaili's hand throbbed where the tea had scalded her palm pads. Her heartbeat thundered. John Weyman's voice whispered in her ear, "Get ready, Chilaili. This is it."

And hard on the heels of that alien whisper came Bessany Weyman's: "Courage, my friend."

"Mother?" Sooleawa asked worriedly, noticing Chilaili's sudden distress.

Chilaili shook her head and gave her daughter a wan smile. Hands shaking violently, she fumbled the canister of sealant and the heavy, round smoke grenade out of their pouches, then turned her head toward the Oracle Chamber. A moment later, the *akule* reappeared, looking shaken. "Will someone help me carry the Oracle, please?"

"Carry it?" Great-Grandmother Anevay asked sharply. "Carry it where?"

"Into the living cavern. The Ones Above have commanded me to bring the Oracle out, so everyone can hear."

A murmur of surprise ran through the cavern. Several huntresses followed the *akule* back into the Oracle chamber. Chilaili heard a scraping sound, several grunts, then the sound of claws on rock as they returned. The Oracle was far larger, Chilaili now realized, than it needed to be if the only purpose it served was communication. Compared with the equipment the humans used to speak over vast distances, the Oracle was enormous. It required four adults to carry it.

John Weyman's voice muttered in her ear, "Good God, that thing's huge. What do they have concealed in there?"

"At a guess," Bessany Weyman's voice rasped out a whispered answer, "data recorders of some kind, with enough computer storage space to hold several decades' worth of accumulated information. Visual as well as audio, given the size of that thing. I wonder how often they harvest the data? And how?"

The Bolo, hooked into the communications equipment Chilaili and the humans carried—and therefore able to see and hear through the device on Chilaili's cloak—spoke up.

"I'm picking up faint electronic signals originating from the Oracle and a dozen other points throughout the cavern. These probably indicate hidden cameras in every chamber of this cavern complex, transmitting via low-power signals to the data recorders in the Oracle casing. The clan is closely observed at all times. And, of course," the machine added with devastating simplicity, "the Oracle contains enough neurotoxin to kill the entire clan."

Chilaili shuddered. And realized for the first time, with a sickening sense of what might have happened, that the defiance they had discussed the night of the Council's vote could easily have triggered the Ones Above into destroying them.

"Anybody see a neurotoxin delivery system on that thing?" John Weyman asked tersely.

"Not without a more detailed look at it," Rapier replied. "Chilaili, can you get closer?"

She didn't want to go near the abomination, but it would kill her just as dead from across the cavern as it would standing right next to it, so Chilaili rose to her feet. "Sooleawa," she said in a low voice, "stay beside me. I want you to see the Oracle clearly. This is a moment never to be forgotten."

A vast understatement . . .

And if the humans' antidote didn't work, if the deadly neurotoxin poisoned them, after all, she would kill Sooleawa with her own hands. It would be far kinder to kill her child with a swiftly broken neck than to let her suffer the death John Weyman had described in such horrifying detail. The hatchlings were crowding forward, wide-eyed with wonder as the huntresses set the Oracle down on a natural rock platform along the cavern wall. Chilaili stepped close enough to give the humans and their machine a long, clear look at the device. It sat stolidly in its place, squat and malignant. She hated the sight of it.

The Bolo spoke abruptly into her earpiece.

"There is no logical communications or data recording purpose I can fathom for the protrusion at the right-hand side of this device, near the upper edge. I believe it to be the nozzle of an aerosol delivery system. Watch this nozzle closely, Chilaili, during the next few minutes. If I am correct, this is where the Oracle will attempt to release the neurotoxin."

Chilaili found the spot the Bolo was describing and riveted her gaze to it.

If there is any mercy left in the world, don't let us die—

The Oracle began to speak.

"My beloved children," it said, using the carefully prepared message Chilaili had helped the Bolo draft, "listen well, for I have tidings of great distress."

The adults exchanged worried glances while the children crept to their mothers and huddled close. The silence in the living cavern was so complete, Chilaili could hear the distant drip of water from the inner caverns. Even the hatchlings listened in overawed silence.

"Generations ago, my children, I created you. I took mindless beasts from the wild, gave them intelligence, gave them understanding of languages and laws. Once I had created you, beloved children, I returned you to these wild forests. I left tools to improve your lives, weapons to defend yourselves, and especially I left the Oracles, to call for help if you needed it. These gifts I gave freely and with love, because I cared so deeply for you. It was painfully difficult to leave you here, but you needed to grow in your own way. It was in my mind to return when you had grown wise enough to fully understand my gifts. When you were ready, I hoped you might fly at my side between the stars.

"But in my absence, a terrible thing has happened. Unknown to me, my brother returned to your world. He has been ill for a very long time, dangerously ill in his mind and his soul. He has done a terrible evil to all of you, which I have just discovered. My sorrow is boundless, for he has filled your innocent hearts with hatred. He has poisoned your chicks, especially your male chicks, twisting their minds to match his own. And he has caused you to wage a dreadful war against creatures who never meant harm to you or to me. This war with the humans has nearly destroyed you, my children, *and it was never necessary*."

Shocked sounds broke from every throat. Even the nestlings whimpered in fright, some of them too young to understand the words, but fully aware of the adults' distress. At Chilaili's side, poor Kestejoo was trembling, gaze locked on the Oracle he had tended so diligently for so long, his expression wavering between sick horror and disbelief.

The Oracle spoke again. "But even this is not the worst of his evil, my children. In his twisted madness, he has placed a dreadful weapon inside each Oracle. A weapon that is meant to destroy all of you, to hide the sin of what he has done, so you could not speak, should I discover his crimes. Already, an entire clan has been destroyed by this weapon, killed horribly. Even the chicks died within minutes. I grieve for them, my children. And I grieve for you, because this is the last time you will ever hear my voice. You must destroy the Oracle now, so that no evil creature will ever again pose as your creator or harm you through a device I meant to help you. And you must stop this insane war with the creatures my brother has wrongly called devils. You must stop the war immediately and beg them for peace, for they are creatures of honor and will not harm those who honestly seek friendship with them."

In her ear, the Bolo said, "The Oracle has commenced some kind of automated transmission—"

Chilaili lunged forward, simultaneously hurling down the smoke grenade and bringing up the sealant. There was a sharp explosion behind her, releasing a cloud of yellowish, stinging smoke. Chilaili shouted, "Breathe in the fumes! As you love life, *breathe deeply!*"

She'd just reached the Oracle when a different voice came from it, a cold voice, full of cruel indifference. "You have sinned, Icewing Clan. You will now die."

Screams erupted behind her—terror-stricken, shrill—tearing throats and shredding nerves. Chilaili plunged the control valve under her fingers to release the sealant. Hands shaking, she sprayed and sprayed the place on the right-hand side of the Oracle. Hunter vision narrowed the entire universe down to that one tiny, deadly spot. The Oracle was humming, giving out a high-pitched whine from somewhere deep inside, as though something were spinning or moving—or trying to. The projection under the humans' hard-drying sealant was vibrating. She sprayed it again and again, hating it blackly, hating the death it was trying to spew out. The entire right side of the Oracle disappeared under a coating so thick it resembled solid rock.

She did not stop until the canister was empty.

When the stream of sealant failed at last, her legs threatened to buckle under her.

But a wave of panic-stricken movement behind her caught Chilaili's attention. A surge away from the Oracle threatened to become an avalanche, sweeping more than two hundred terrified women, children, and stiff-limbed old men toward the narrow cavern entrance.

"Have no fear!" Chilaili shouted. "Hear me! There is no danger! I swear this, as master *katori* of Icewing Clan!" Her voice, at least, was one they had trusted for many winters. Even stumbling half blind through the thick, yellow smoke, they heard that trusted voice calling them back, reassuring them.

The huntresses stopped first, forming a dam against which terrified children and trembling old ones broke and foamed like waves in a storm-lashed lake. They slowed and paused, coughing and trembling. "This yellow smoke," Chilaili waved one hand at the pall of acrid fumes drifting through the cavern, "has kept you safe from the Twisted One's poison!" It was a lie, but a small one. At such a moment, dramatics were necessary, a fact she knew only too well as a master healer. Half of any cure was the patient's simple belief. The clan would never have believed in something they could neither see nor smell.

The nestlings would have nightmares for weeks.

But they were still alive.

"Good work, Chilaili," the Bolo's voice spoke into her ear. "Very, very good work. I detect a cessation of activity inside the Oracle. It has either shut itself off again or burned out the mechanism attempting to break through the sealant. If you had not sprayed such a thick coating, that aerosol nozzle might well have broken loose and released the neurotoxin. Clearly, the Oracle contained a dead-man switch programmed to activate on a timer in the event of outside electronic tampering. . . ."

Chilaili couldn't take in another word the machine was saying. Now that the worst of the terror had passed, she sank to her knees, trembling violently, so sick with reaction she needed to spew onto the floor. Sooleawa crawled toward her, eyes streaming, voice hoarse.

"Mother? Are you ill? Did The Twisted One's poison touch you?"

She shook her head. "No, child," she managed to gasp out. "No. I'm just shaken with mortal fright."

"What happened? What was that awful stuff you shouted at us to breathe?"

"An antidote . . . to the poison hidden inside the Oracle," she whispered.

An anguished cry sounded behind her. Chilaili lifted her head sharply. The *akule* was down on the cavern floor as well, wheezing and coughing. The look in his eyes was dreadful. That look of betrayal ran so deep, it had shattered something critical to his sanity. He shook violently on hands and knees, rocking and swaying like a terrified and confused hatchling.

"Kestejoo?" she asked softly.

A terrible sound broke from his throat. Then he whimpered, "Gods and ancestors, Chilaili, what have I done? Sending us to war against the humans, worshiping that . . . that false and evil *thing* . . ." A wrenching sob broke loose. "*I have spent my whole life worshiping a lie!*"

Chilaili's heart broke, witnessing his distress. He had already lost so much.

To lose his god, as well . . .

He lifted a wildly haunted gaze and stared into Chilaili's eyes. "How?" he whispered, voice ragged, on the edge of fractured sanity. "How did you know? How could you possibly have known?"

"Because the Ones Above—the *True* Ones Above— told me. I have been with them these past three days. With them and with the ones we have wronged, the humans."

The *akule* simply stared, perhaps unable to take in even one more shock.

Anevay croaked out hoarsely, "*Together?*"

Chilaili nodded, unwilling to speak another direct lie. "I have learned their speech," she said instead, rolling a warning eye at Sooleawa. "They are honorable creatures, Great-Grandmother. If we stop the attack on their nests, if we help them stop the war with the other clans, they will protect us, as they have done just now. It was the humans who made the antidote to the poison concealed inside the Oracle." She managed a wry smile. "It is even possible that one day we may even call them friends."

The *akule's* voice shook. "How can you even speak the word friend, when we have tried so hard to destroy them? Surely they wish us all hideously dead!" The unspoken "In their place, I would" hung on the air like the yellow pall of smoke.

Chilaili sat back on her heels, gestured at that smoke. "Let me tell you what happened, my gentle and respected friend. One of their great metal ogres attacked a winter nest. That was how the poison in the Oracle was discovered. The Oracle was broken open in the attack. The poison spilled out into the air . . ." She shuddered. "Every Tersae and every beast in the forest from which we were fashioned died, within the span of time it would take to walk to the entrance to our winter nest and climb up to the top of the bluff. They died with blood pouring from their skin, their eyes, their tongues—"

Several of the children began to wail again.

"I am sorry," Chilaili whispered. "But you must understand how hideous a death the Evil One Above planned for us. The humans and the True Ones Above found the antidote to this terrible poison. Then the humans brought me here, in one of their flying machines, so I could reach the clan in time. I ask you, Kestejoo, would *we* have acted to save the lives of *their* hatchlings, had our places been reversed?"

The *akule*'s gaze dropped to his hands. He shook his head.

Chilaili gentled her voice. "You have asked if we can call the humans friends? Yes, I believe we can. And the only way to begin, respected *akule*, is to stop being their enemies."

"Yes," he whispered, eyes slightly less wild. "If what you say is true—and how can it be anything else?— then the clans of the Tersae have wronged them, dreadfully." He stopped rocking like a crazed child. "Thank the—" His voice caught and he started rocking again, a motion filled with misery. "At least," he said carefully, instead, "there is still time to prevent Icewing Clan from committing the same wrong." He drew a deep breath, coughing slightly as the smoke stung, then rose on unsteady feet. "I will go, myself, to bring the war party home again. They might not listen to you, perhaps, but they will certainly listen to *me*." He tipped his head to stare at the Oracle, misshapen now, and silent. "And I will tell them to leave their weapons in the snow."

"I will go with you, Kestejoo," she said softly, rising to her feet as well. "There is someone I want you to meet . . ."

As she led the way out into the sunshine, where two humans and a machine waited, Chilaili's only fear—and it was a sharp one, as they left the cavern and climbed up the steep path—was that somehow, the attempt to stop their males from attacking Seta Point would go wrong. Like Kestejoo, she wanted to offer up a prayer.

And like Kestejoo, she had no idea who—or what—to pray to.

Chapter Twenty-eight

Ruk na Graz stared at the display screen numbly, gazing at his own destruction.

It had taken several moments for the import of the data to sink in. One of the Oracles had started to transmit an "I am tampered with" duress code, along with a rogue transmission channelled through it. The unit had then simply dropped off-line, blocked in mid-transmission by sophisticated electronic jamming from a ground-based source. Once he'd realized what that meant—that the humans knew the Oracles existed and had literally taken one over with their own broadcast *in Tersae sub-dialect*—it was far too late to prevent the damage.

The continued jamming had prevented his technicians from accessing on-site camera systems to see what was happening down there. Ultimately, of course, it didn't matter. It was enough to know that something was jamming the Oracle's signal. If the humans knew enough to do that, they knew far too much. It was disaster of the first magnitude. Utter shame and disgrace . . .

How had the humans learned about the Oracles? Presumably the same way they'd learned to speak the Melconian sub-dialect the Tersae had been taught. One of the damned experimental animals had done the unthinkable: it had defected. Ruk na Graz wanted to howl his rage and frustration. He bit down on it until he had his ragged temper under tenuous control, then snarled at his aide, "Get Science Leader Vrim in here! *Now!*"

Vrim arrived three minutes later, panting from the exertion of his hasty journey. "War Leader?" he gasped out.

"One of your filthy experimental creatures has defected to the humans." Ruk na Graz shoved a transcript of the Oracle's final broadcast into the aging scientist's shocked hands. "Would you care to explain *how?*"

Vrim's ears went desperately flat against his skull. "This is terrible," he whispered, "just dreadful. Merciful ancestors, we never dreamed their grumbles would lead to *this* . . ."

"*What grumbles?*" Ruk na Graz roared to his feet, slamming his fists against the desktop.

The Science Leader flinched. "We've been hearing complaints from most of the clans over this business of deforming the males' genetic material through the blessing chambers—"

Ruk na Graz stared, unsure whether to snarl or simply shoot the fool. "You heard seditious talk," he whispered in a dreadful rage, *"and didn't bother to report it?"*

"It was valid data!" Vrim cried. "Don't you see? We were trying to understand the social ramifications of their discovery that the damage to their eggs in the blessing chambers was causing the violent trend in their young males! We didn't expect them to make that connection at all. The sociological data have been utterly fascinating. If we'd reported it right away, we'd have lost the chance to fully study it, because the military caste might have shut the whole thing down in knee-jerk reaction.

"We just never dreamed they could do anything *about* it. Except grumble, of course, and hold back a few of their eggs. We've spent generations inculcating a pathological fear of 'devils from the stars.' That ethnocentric conditioning should have worked to prevent this." He rattled the transcript in his hands. "You're sure one of them has actually *defected?* The humans could simply have taken live prisoners—"

"That hijacked broadcast was made in fluent, properly inflected Melconian," Ruk na Graz snarled. "Not pidgin. Not a few random words cobbled together from the babblings of terrified prisoners. Either one of those damned animals has taught the humans its language or it crafted the message *for* the humans. Or possibly both. Your failure to report the Tersae's discovery of genetic tampering, not to mention widespread sedition over it, has put the entire Melconian Empire at risk! Do you begin to comprehend everything the humans now have access to?"

Vrim was shaking, eyes wide and panic-stricken. "I-I'm sorry, War Leader, I just didn't realize the danger—"

"Then realize this! We have no choice but to evacuate immediately. This project ends *now*, whether you like it or not. And unless I am very much mistaken, the Emperor will order us both to suicide, when we return home. Now, get out. And take your gods-cursed data with you!"

The aging scientist fled, whimpering.

Ruk na Graz was pondering which of a ghastly list of things to do next when a technician from the monitoring center arrived, trembling and gulping. "War Leader . . ." he began, voice shaking.

"Out with it!"

"The communications relay satellite . . . the humans have captured it. Taken it aboard their warship. Several hours ago, we think. We didn't realize it until just now, when the emergency broadcast from the compromised Oracle was relayed through it. The relay showed it seriously out of position, inside the human vessel. . . ."

Ruk na Graz sat down slowly, unable to say anything at all for several seconds. He finally asked, in a terrible, strained whisper, "Why in the seventeen moons didn't you order it to self-destruct?"

The technician gabbled out, "We—we can't. It's so antiquated, War Leader, it has no destruction mechanism on board."

Worse and worse . . .

So far as he knew—and he prayed to all his ancestors, to let it be true—the satellite hadn't been programmed with Melcon's home coordinates, since its use had been strictly limited to in-system signal relay. But the enemy now had access to the master codes of the Melconian Empire's entire military communications system and the frequencies used by both civilian and military agencies. These humans were clever beasts. After what they'd done already, he could imagine only too clearly what they would accomplish, with that much information about Melcon.

They must not capture this moon base.

In it were star charts, military and trade routes, a thousand useful details to an enemy bent on conquest. If the humans figured out how to operate that captured satellite, they could send a pulse that this base would automatically answer, giving away their location instantly. Paw shaking, he called up the program necessary to initiate the auto-destruct sequence, then pressed the intercom buzzer to summon his personal aide.

"Yes, Colonel?"

"Order the immediate evacuation of this base. Personnel *only*. If it cannot be carried in one bag, it must be left behind and destroyed. I want this base cleared within one hour. *One hour*, do you understand that, pup? I have already set the auto-destruct program in motion. This base will be blown to its component atoms a quarter hour after that deadline. And disable the entire communications system before the humans figure out how to sound us out. *Move*, pup!"

Ears pinned flat to his skull in distress, the shaken young aide ran. An instant later, the emergency intercom blared the news. Between strident pulses of the alarm siren, he could hear shouts and shrill wails of protest. The sound of ignominious defeat . . . He made himself move very deliberately, downloading copies of his most critical files, dumping the data cubes into a carryall, abandoning even the holos of his wife and pups, which occupied a cherished corner of his desk. Their escape ship must be stripped for running. He would see his family soon enough as it was, right before his court-martial.

The last thing he did before leaving was key in the Oracles' auto-destruct code, which the moon base's powerful transmitter would send planetwide seconds before the base blew itself to hell. He snarled as he punched in the command, his last official act as Military Leader of a failed project. Then he stalked into the corridor and headed for the transport that would take him home to die. At least the damned experimental beasts would precede him by a good, long margin.

Humanity could not get their stubby hands on more Tersae if he'd already destroyed them.

Given even one planet cracker, he could have destroyed the humans, as well.

Chapter Twenty-nine

Tension dragged at Bessany's nerves.

She and John Weyman had pulled off their face masks, despite the bitter cold, stuffing them into pockets for this critical meeting. Bessany glanced at her brother-in-law and read tension in the set of his jaw. He kept his hand hovering near his side arm, without actually resting his fingers on the grip.

"John," she said in a low voice, "I don't have the words to thank you enough. I wish . . ."

He glanced down into her eyes, surprise dawning in his own. "You wish what?"

She swallowed hard. "That I'd listened to you, that day. That I'd met you first."

A look of mingled pain and pleasure ran through his eyes, shadowed eyes that had seen entirely too much of the former and not nearly enough of the latter. Speaking very softly, he said, "So do I." He pressed her gloved fingers in his and added, "Maybe we can start being friends?"

She nodded, scarcely trusting her voice. "I'd like

that," she managed, blinking back wetness. Then Chilaili appeared through the drifted snow, accompanied by a taller, more gracile Tersae, and Bessany jerked her attention back to this critically important first meeting. She recognized the Tersae with Chilaili at once, having watched on John's hand-unit viewscreen as Chilaili greeted this individual. This was the *akule*, the Tersae who would know more about the Ones Above than any other in Chilaili's clan. There were subtle differences in the shape of his beak, the patterns on his fur, the color of his eyes that marked him as belonging to another bloodline, an outsider who had adopted Icewing Clan out of love. Chilaili looked short beside the taller, slimmer Kestejoo—and short was not an adjective Bessany had ever associated with Chilaili before.

The Tersae were quite near before Bessany realized the *akule* was trembling. A sudden wave of pity swept through her, driving away Bessany's own nervousness. She was facing an unknown alien; he was facing a devil, moments after losing his god. Chilaili paused three long paces away and spoke quietly, in her own language. Bessany caught some of what the *katori* said, but Rapier translated directly into the tiny receiver tucked into her ear.

"Kestejoo, these are the humans who saved our clan. This is Bessany Weyman and the nestmate of her lifemate, John Weyman. The humans' metal ogre, their Bolo, answers the commands of John Weyman."

Kestejoo trembled more violently.

"Bessany Weyman," Chilaili switched to Terran standard, "John Weyman, this is Kestejoo, *akule* to Icewing Clan."

Bessany had long since learned the proper Tersae greeting from Chilaili. She had worked hard during the last several hours on pronunciation. She took one step forward, holding out her hands, and murmured the ritual greeting. "May the ancestors smile upon you, Kestejoo."

His pupils dilated with shock. He darted a swift, terrified glance at Chilaili, who made a little head-bobbing motion, then he took a slow step forward and stretched out his own hands. They shook like leaves in a high wind. Behind her, Bessany sensed more than saw the sudden tension coiling through her brother-in-law, but Kestejoo merely touched her outstretched palms with his own and whispered the greeting in return. His voice was deep, pleasant to the ear, and the pads on his palms and fingertips were surprisingly soft. Far softer, in fact, than Chilaili's, which belonged, after all, to a seasoned huntress.

"I am sorry," Bessany said carefully. "I do not speak your words well. I will ask Chilaili to speak our words to you."

She had to listen closely to catch the answer, due in part, she suspected, to slight dialectic differences that gave Kestejoo a different accent. "I will honor your words and listen carefully."

Rapier's translation in her ear helped.

Kestejoo spoke again, more rapidly, and Chilaili translated. "We must stop our clan's war party, but they have traveled more than a day's march ahead. It will be difficult to catch them."

John stepped forward, causing Kestejoo to flinch slightly, despite nearly a meter difference in their heights. "We have a machine that can take us to them much faster than any of us can run through snow. We will take you close, then let you walk ahead, to meet them alone."

Chilaili translated and Kestejoo nodded. "Yes. That would be best. Where is this machine?" he added, glancing toward the forest.

John pulled out his comm link. "Rapier, how close are you now?"

"Within three kilometers, Commander, due south."

Kestejoo rolled one worried eye toward the voice emerging from the comm link.

"You're the xeno-ecologist," John glanced at Bessany. "Do we hike out to meet Rapier or bring him in close enough to terrify the entire clan?"

"Let's bring him in. It's one thing for Chilaili to tell the clan that we're willing to form an alliance; it's another thing entirely to see a Bolo up close and personal and not have it shoot at you."

Her brother-in-law gave her a wan smile. "Mmm, yes, I see your point. All right, Rapier, join us, please."

"At once, Commander."

"Perhaps we should go to a small clearing near here?" Chilaili suggested. "I would not want the little ones to panic and run off the lip of the ravine when the Bolo comes."

"Why don't you just have them come up after Rapier gets here?"

Chilaili nodded gravely. "Yes. We will do this." She turned to Kestejoo and translated.

A few moments later, a distant rumble and a sound like popcorn in a kettle reached them, rising rapidly in volume as the immense Bolo came crashing through the forest. The sound of splintering trees rose to a wild crescendo. The earth shook under Rapier's mighty treads, then the top of his war turret appeared above the trees. Powerful muscles in Chilaili's arm, hardened by years of hunting, bulged as she gripped Kestejoo's wrist, preventing him from bolting.

The *akule* was trembling wildly, pupils dilated in terror as Rapier ground down trees like kindling. His prow emerged through a white spray as snow-covered trees went down in front of him like a weirdly reversed wake behind an oceangoing ship. Rapier's guns bristled ominously against the dazzling, sunlit sky.

The Bolo came to a halt five meters away, a beached battleship on moveable treads.

"May the ancestors smile on you, Kestejoo, Chilaili," the machine boomed—in Tersae.

Kestejoo let go a strangled, wildly terrified sound, then stared at Chilaili when she returned the greeting. "May the ancestors smile on you, Bolo Rapier." She turned to Kestejoo then and spoke too rapidly for Bessany to follow the words. Rapier translated into her earpiece.

"The machine has acted with great honor since the day I first saw it, Kestejoo," she was saying in a low, urgent voice. "It could have destroyed our war party at any time after they left the nest, without even showing itself, but it has not done so. You see, it does not fire upon us."

"It—it is so—I had not dreamed so vast a thing could—" Kestejoo paused, panting visibly. "And the Evil One Above wanted us to *fight* such a thing?"

"Yes," Chilaili said gently. "He did. Come, Kestejoo. Come and meet the Bolo machine."

She drew him forward on trembling legs. Bessany stayed back, giving John the high sign, as well. They watched in silence as Chilaili led the *akule* toward the Bolo's treads, which towered above even the Tersae. As Chilaili touched the Bolo and coaxed Kestejoo to do the same, John murmured, "Now there is a brave man."

Bessany nodded. "Extremely."

It took them ten minutes, but Chilaili coaxed the rest of the clan out into the snow, to meet the Bolo. Cries of terror lifted and some of the little ones clung to their mothers, but Chilaili got them all to the top of the bluff. The Bolo greeted them softly, speaking

Terran standard and allowing Chilaili to translate, which surprised Bessany until she realized Rapier was taking no chances that anyone would recognize his voice as the same one which had come through the Oracle.

Touching the Bolo's treads became a weirdly poignant ritual, enacted again and again as the clan came forward in faltering groups of two and three. Sooleawa walked past Bessany at one point, leading two little ones by the hand. She dipped her head infinitesimally in greeting as they passed, meeting Bessany's eye with a long look of wonder. By the time the last of the clan had completed the ritual, even Kestejoo had begun to lose the worst of his fear. Bessany was actually starting to feel good about this—

"Commander," the Bolo said urgently, startling cries of fear from the watching crowd. "I am receiving transmissions from Units of the Line across Thule. Oracle signals have been traced from fifteen locations, responding to some sort of coded burst from a far-orbit source. Explosions on one of the smaller moons were detected seconds after the transmission. There has been a massive, planetwide neurotoxin release. The nearest neurotoxin release will put Icewing Clan's war party in the wind dispersal pattern within forty-five minutes."

Blood drained from Bessany's face. "Oh, my God." She felt like somebody had just punched her. Then the full implications of Rapier's words hit home. "John!" She clutched his arm in both hands. "That war party has the only adult male Tersae left on this whole goddamned world! Without them, the gene pool is too small to sustain the species!"

John was snarling into his comm link, "This is Lieutenant Colonel Weyman! Emergency priority! We need an airdrop of neurotoxin analog as fast as you can rendezvous! Carter, scramble your butt *now!*"

He was already running toward Rapier, shouting over one shoulder, "Bessany, get Chilaili and Kestejoo into the command compartment with us. It's gonna be one *hell* of a jolting ride. They'd be bashed to death in that cargo hold."

Chilaili was staring at Bessany in deep shock. "Tell me it is not true?" she whispered, voice breaking with agony. At her shoulder, Sooleawa was gulping in visible distress, having understood the Bolo's words perfectly.

"It's true," Bessany said roughly. Tears stung. "There's no time, Chilaili! If you and Kestejoo can't persuade those males to lay down their weapons and let us give them the analog . . ."

The *katori* whirled and gasped out the dire news. Screams and wails rose on the frozen wind. Several older Tersae actually collapsed in the snow, moaning and tearing at their head-fur. Sooleawa broke from the group and ran, vanishing down the path that led to the living cavern. Above them, Rapier's voice boomed into the icy air, speaking in urgent Tersae.

"Icewing Clan, if it can be done, we will save them. Chilaili, you must come *now.*"

Chilaili dragged the stunned Kestejoo forward, shoving him bodily onto the ladder. Sooleawa reappeared, screaming, "Mother! Wait!" The girl was running through the shocked clan, carrying something that looked like oddly shaped snowshoes. She had brought two sets. "You will need them, Mother, to move quickly through deep snow! And you'll *have* to go on foot, partway, or the war party will fire on the ogre!"

Chilaili hugged her daughter hard as Bessany shoved Kestejoo up the ladder rungs; then they were all climbing toward the command compartment. Both Tersae had to suck in their bellies and scrunch their shoulders to fit through the command hatch, but they made it. John pushed them hurriedly toward the observation couches as they tumbled down the ladder. There were, thank God, three of those couches. Bessany's half-swallowed her slight frame. The Tersae barely fit, wedged in like ticks in a narrow crack. John snapped restraints in place on all three couches and shouted at Rapier, "Go! Go!"

The Bolo was moving even as John flung himself into the command chair and slapped controls that webbed him in. The Bolo pivoted with a ponderous, yawing movement, then started forward. They picked up speed. Rapidly. The ride grew rough, got rougher, and was soon nearly unendurable.

"We're running at emergency speed," John flung over one shoulder, "so it's gonna be a little bumpy. Rapier, get me aerial feed, stat."

"Launching aerial drone."

The forward data screen came to life with a dizzying blur of motion as the drone's camera raced skyward. Chilaili and Kestejoo gasped. The stink of terrified Tersae hung on the air.

"Posting orbital feed from the *Darknight* to Lateral Two. The *Darknight* has had the war party in continuous view. Superimposing over Elin Olsson's geological maps."

The data screen above Bessany's right shoulder flared into life, showing Elin's familiar maps. A small red blob appeared on it, marking the location of Icewing Clan's males.

"Carter here," the shuttle pilot's voice crackled over the speaker. "Outbound with two full canisters of analog and two of those yellow smoke bombs. I've got extra sealant, too, just in case."

"Roger and good work," John said crisply. "Home in on the signal from Rapier's aerial drone. We'll get in as close as we dare, then send Chilaili and Kestejoo forward with the analog. Rapier, get me Dr. Collingwood. They'll have left Eisenbrucke by now. Try Seta Point."

"Call initiated."

Less than one minute later, an exhausted voice came on the line. "Alison Collingwood."

"Lieutenant Colonel Weyman. We're outbound to deliver analog to—" He paused, flung a question over his shoulder. "Chilaili, how many males are in that war party?"

"Twenty times eight."

"—a hundred sixty adult males. Can we dose 'em in the open or do they need to be in a confined space?"

"Confined is a lot more certain."

"Damn. I was afraid of that. Rapier, analyze those geological maps. See if you can find a good-sized cave somewhere near that war party."

"At once, Commander. Located. There is a small-ish cavern located two point nine kilometers southwest of their present location. If the map is accurately marked, it should be adequate to hold them."

"Elin's maps are accurate," Bessany put in. "Trust me on that."

"Locate the entrance with that drone, Rapier, so we can guide 'em in."

"Yes, Commander."

"How far away are we? From the war party?"

"Seventy-five point zero one kilometers. At maximum sustained sprint speed of one hundred forty-eight kilometers per hour, it will take point five zero six hours to reach the war party. This will give us less than fifteen minutes to convince the war party to drop weapons, reach shelter, and administer the analog."

"That's not enough time!" Bessany gasped. It had taken a full hour's exposure to safeguard the females and children—and even that was no guarantee, since Chilaili had blocked the Oracle's release valve.

"It's all the time we've got," John snarled. "Rapier, how many Tersae can you cram into your cargo holds, based on Kestejoo's size?"

Chilaili's voice quavered out, "Kestejoo is smaller than males born to Icewing Clan."

"Thank you, Chilaili," Rapier responded. "If we emptied all cargo holds, I might be able to put sixty males inside my war hull, but I do not believe it will be possible to empty them in time. The Navy shuttle could hold the same number, although it would be cramped. Lieutenant Carter could flood her craft with the analog from one canister, while rising up out of the neurotoxin wave front. Carter could keep them in orbit, if necessary, until their tissues have fully absorbed the analog. The other canister can be discharged in the cave."

"Good plan, Rapier. Damned fine plan. How deep is that cavern?"

"Unknown, Commander. Depth is not indicated, only lateral dimensions."

"John," Bessany said, wincing as a bad jounce jarred her teeth together, "Elin's original data files contain 3-D imaging. I know she did some subterranean mapping in 3-D, I just don't know how extensive it was."

"Contacting Seta Point," Rapier said at once.

Two minutes later, Elin Olsson was gasping into Seta Point's transmitter, clearly having run all the way. "This is Elin Olsson."

"Lieutenant Colonel Weyman here. Rapier's transmitting one of your geological maps with a particular cavern marked. Do you have a 3-D image of this region?"

"I'll have to drag out my data files. I'll be back." They could hear the slap of her feet as she ran. There was a ghastly, endless wait, then the sound of a door crashing back reached them and Elin said, "Got 'em.

Let's see which area you've marked." Another, shorter pause followed. Then she said, "Oh, God, that's right at the edge of my test zone. Let me drag out the downloads I made . . ." They waited yet again, while human and Tersae fear sweat mingled to form an acrid, metallic stench. Then Elin gasped out, "Got it. Yes, I have a 3-D rendering. I'm sending it now."

Seconds later, a new image flickered to life on Lateral Three. The cavern was small in cross-section, as seen from above in two dimensions, but it ran deep. Really deep. And it narrowed wickedly at one spot, where they might be able to erect a barrier to lower the amount of neurotoxin that got in. Bessany's breath sobbed out in wild relief. "It may be deep enough, John. And look, we can rig a barrier of some kind, there, at that narrow spot."

"We'll try it," John said grimly. "Dr. Collingwood, do you have any indications on the persistence of this neurotoxin?"

"No, I'm afraid not. The samples we've worked with haven't shown any sign of degrading."

"God alone knows how long that stuff will persist, then. At least we had Lundquist crank out mass quantities of that stuff. I want every shuttle en route with canisters to turn around and rendezvous with me. We may need to keep Chilaili's entire clan dosed for weeks to come. Hell, maybe months. If it persists long enough, we may have to evacuate the whole clan off-world."

A sobbing sound broke from Chilaili.

Kestejoo, when she translated, just moaned, beak clacking softly in distress.

"Commander," Rapier asked abruptly, "how soon after ordering me to rendezvous at the winter nest did you hear my approach?"

"Within seconds."

"Then I dare not come any closer than four

kilometers to the war party unless a way can be found to muffle the sound of my approach. We cannot afford to excite them into firing on me, since we would never persuade them to lay down their weapons in time, afterward. Sooleawa anticipated this problem, in fact, when she brought the snowshoes to Chilaili. I am calculating possible alternate routes." Silence fell again, stretching Bessany's nerves taut. "Possible alternate route located." A green line appeared at a tangent to the racing red line of their current trajectory. "By routing through this valley, we can use rock walls to reduce the distance the noise will travel and bring us to within two point five kilometers. This will add three point zero five minutes to my transit time."

"Do it. It'll shave time off the final dash Chilaili and Kestejoo have to make through deep snow."

"Changing course."

The view on the forward data screen swung dizzily, then they were charging ahead on the new line, which still flashed green ahead of them and changed to red as they followed the new course. "Rapier, get Carter on the horn again," John said tersely.

The speaker crackled. "Carter here."

John relayed the altered plan.

"Sixty adult Tersae?" the pilot responded. "It's a good thing I'm still stripped for emergency running, isn't it? We'd never have fit 'em all in, otherwise."

"Roger that. I'm transmitting the rendezvous point, Lieutenant. We'll meet in a valley two-and-a-half klicks from the Tersae war party. You'll need to approach low and fast. Can you get in without being spotted?"

A grim chuckle reached them. "I can outrace the devil, Colonel, but God alone knows if I can sneak up on an armed Tersae war party. Okay, I've got the map—jeezus, that's wicked terrain. I'll swing around at treetop level and come in from the far end of the valley. That'll at least put me lower than the ground, relative to their position."

"Roger, that sounds like the best shot we have. See you at the rendezvous point."

"That's a rog, Colonel. Carter out."

The command compartment fell tensely silent as Rapier crashed through the rugged terrain at top speed. How long could the Bolo maintain this pace without straining his engines? Bessany had no idea. They literally leaped across narrow ravines, moving so fast, falling was never an option. Larger valleys forced them to dodge and weave, but Rapier seemed to have laid out his course in advance, using Elin's terrain maps as a guide, for their speed never faltered and they remained steadily on schedule as kilometer after kilometer churned away beneath his treads.

Bessany realized she was gripping the armrests of her observer's couch so hard she couldn't feel her fingers. When she tried to move her hands, they refused to budge. So she savaged her lip instead and stole a worried glance at the Tersae beside her. Chilaili's expression was ghastly. If the Ones Above had appeared at that moment, Bessany devoutly believed Chilaili would have ripped their furry heads off their stocky necks with her bare hands.

Bessany would have helped. Gladly.

A whole planet poisoned. A whole sentient species wiped off its snow-covered face.

Then they were skidding through the final turn, running down the last leg of the wriggling green line. Rapier dropped speed to a relative crawl to reduce the noise he was making. The Bolo navigated around stands of trees, rather than plowing straight through them. The angle of the command compartment shifted, tilting as Rapier descended a precipitous slope. They jolted their way toward the valley floor, descending at a spot shallow enough to let them enter without Rapier having to blast a ramp out of the walls with his guns—doubtless one reason the Bolo had chosen this particular valley. The aerial drone running ahead of them came to a halt above a narrow crack in the earth, then sank slowly down into the fissure, revealing the entrance to the cave they'd chosen.

"All right, people," John muttered, "there's the entrance. Looks big enough to get 'em through, thank God. Chilaili, you need to decide which members of that war party will shelter inside Carter's shuttle and which ones will have to take their chances in the cavern."

"We will place the oldest males inside the shuttle," Chilaili answered at once. "The younger ones have been damaged more intensely. We cannot afford to rely solely on the bloodlines of hotheaded, suicidal youngsters. The Evil One Above did his work well," she added bitterly. "I have seven sons who will shelter in that cavern. The youngest three have already killed two of their older brothers in senseless challenge . . ."

Bessany bit her lip, needing the sharp flare of pain to control her unsteady breaths. Then a long, low blur raced across the viewscreen, startling a gasp from Bessany and both Tersae. A Navy shuttle settled to earth at the upper end of the valley. Carter had made it without a single shot fired. Bessany started breathing again. *Maybe*, she chanted under her breath, *maybe* . . .

Rapier ground to a halt less than two meters from Carter's shuttle. The pilot was already out of her craft, holding two carrysacks with the precious canisters. "Everybody out," John barked.

Bessany fumbled with unfamiliar restraint catches. A swift glance at the chronometer sent her pulse skittering. They had twelve minutes to save a species.

Chapter Thirty

Chilaili had never scrambled so fast in her life.

John Weyman had already reached the ground and vanished into one of the cargo holds by the time Chilaili climbed down the long ladder. He emerged again holding a thick bundle.

"Use this to block the cavern where the passage narrows," he said tersely. "Spread it across the opening and use Carter's sealant to glue it in place against the rock. Kestejoo will have to seal off the whole edge, all the way around." He thrust both items into a carrysack and handed them to Kestejoo.

"I will explain on the way," Chilaili told the *akule*, whose eyes betrayed his frightened uncertainty.

Bessany Weyman thrust another item into Kestejoo's carrysack. "It's a portable light," she explained, glancing at Chilaili. "For the cave. Tell Kestejoo to push the big black button and the light will come on."

As Chilaili translated, John Weyman said, "Good luck, both of you. Carter has the canisters. Go."

She and Kestejoo sprinted toward the shuttle Chilaili

had ridden in such a short time ago. Lieutenant Carter
shoved one satchel at Chilaili, the other at Kestejoo.
"You'd better take one, too, Chilaili, in case you can't
get back to the Bolo in time. You've still got your
earplug? Good. I've put sealant and sensors in both
packs, so Rapier can monitor neurotoxin levels wherever you are. Go!"

Chilaili flung her thanks over one shoulder, already
running hard. She and Kestejoo climbed rapidly up a
rough stone slope and reached the top unscathed. They
strapped on their snow-webs, then pelted southward
at a mile-eating run, slogging across the crusted surface of the drifts rather than floundering through them
at a crawl. As they ran, Chilaili gasped out critical
instructions Kestejoo would need. She showed him how
to push the plungers on both the canister and the
smoke bomb and demonstrated how to use the spray
sealant. They covered the first mile in only three
minutes, but wooded terrain in the second mile slowed
them down. Branches and tangled snags of vines caught
at the snow-webs. *We'll never make it in time,* Chilaili
groaned, *not unless they turn around and meet us
partway.*

She drew a deep breath and sent the clan's distress
call rolling across the snow, a low-pitched cry that
would travel for miles. Kestejoo glanced at her, startled,
then realized what she was attempting and added his
own urgent cry. They staggered forward, sending out
the repeated distress calls, and finally broke into the
open again.

A broad, trampled swath of snow marked the war
party's trail; they had passed just minutes previously,
from the look of the snow. Then Chilaili's heart lifted.
"There!"

The whole war party had turned around and was
racing back to meet them. "Thank . . . the . . .

ancestors . . ." Kestejoo gasped out. He was holding his side, clearly in pain from the sustained effort. The moment the war party was close enough to hear, Kestejoo shouted, "We are betrayed! We have but minutes to live!"

Yiska, fur greying with age but still powerful—he'd fought off several challenges just this turn of the season alone—pushed through to the front of the crowd. "What do you mean, Kestejoo? How are we betrayed? Why do we have only minutes to live?"

Kestejoo gabbled out their dire news: the warning from the True Ones Above, the Council's desperate alliance with the humans, the attempt by the Evil One Above to kill the entire clan. He finished up with the worst news of all. "The Evil One Above has murdered the other clans, *viho*. *All* of them, everywhere in the world! The poison is loose on the wind, blowing toward us as we speak. The True Ones Above and the humans have given us the antidote, but we must be inside a shelter we can seal off. Even then, there is a risk that some of us will die, but it is the best chance we have."

Shocked curses spread through the war party.

Chilaili shouted to be heard. "The sixty oldest warriors must come with me, to shelter with the humans. There is not room for everyone in the humans' machine, so Kestejoo will lead the rest of you to a cave near here. Another human machine is hovering over it to point the way." She pointed to a flash of sunlight, where the airborne "drone" could just be seen above the treetops.

Tohopka, one of the youngest warriors, pushed roughly forward. "I say it is a trick! A trick of the devils from the stars! We must not listen, must not believe these lies!"

Kestejoo roared forward, boxing Tohopka's ears

soundly. "How *dare* you question the *akule?* I heard the voice of the Evil One Above come through the Oracle, giving the order to release the poison. *Everyone* in the clan heard it. Without the humans, we would all be dead! The Council has formally declared alliance with the humans as our only prayer of survival. If you wish to die in the snow, with blood pouring from your skin and eyes and nose, you are free to do so. But do not destroy the whole clan with your stupidity!"

The young warrior, momentarily stunned, recovered his wits with a roar. He launched a murderous blow full of wicked claws—

—and Chilaili slammed a fist into his belly and flung him headlong into the snow. "As I am *katori*," she snarled, "do that again and I will kill you myself! *There is no time! Die, if you like! But I will not let you kill our entire race!*"

Yiska broke the shocked hush. "The sixty oldest warriors, go with Chilaili. *Now.* The rest of you, follow Kestejoo."

Mutters of rebellion raced through the ranks. Her own youngest sons were snarling defiance. "It is better to die than make alliance with devils!"

Old Nahiossi, whose weapons hand bore only three fingers from an ancient wound, growled, "Only a fool dies without purpose. The Spirit Warrior of our ancestors has watched over us this day, guiding the humans to help us. I thank Hania for his mercy. Kestejoo, go. Let whoever chooses to follow go with you. *Go.*"

Kestejoo began to run. The vast majority of warriors, solidly in their middle years, went with him, dropping their weapons to lighten their burden. Chilaili's four oldest sons joined them. She faced down her three youngest, standing rebelliously with their age-mates. "I gave you life, sons of my nest, taught you all that I could. But if you have learned nothing of wisdom, you are no sons of mine."

The eldest of the three muttered, "I may or may not trust a foreign-born *akule* and I may never trust the humans, but our mother does not lie." He dropped his weapons and sprinted after Kestejoo. A moment later, several of the younger warriors followed, including Chilaili's second-youngest son. The third stood his ground with nine of his friends.

Chilaili said softly, "I will not sing your names in the eulogies, for there is no bravery in a foolish death." She turned her back and began to run. The oldest warriors of the clan joined her, led by Yiska himself.

"I hope," he growled, "that your trust in the humans is not misplaced."

Chilaili didn't bother to answer. She needed her breath for running. Ten fools out of a hundred and sixty warriors. Far fewer losses than she'd dared to hope. If only they reached safety in time. If only the analog worked properly. If only . . .

She tried, frantically, to reckon the number of minutes that had passed, how much time they'd lost arguing with doomed, hotheaded fools. She decided, despairingly, that she had no idea how much time was left—and drew comfort from the silence of the tiny radio in her ear. *They will warn us, if the poison catches us before we reach shelter, they will warn us, I have to believe they will.*

They burst through the stand of timber to run the final mile—and found Lieutenant Carter's shuttle parked just beyond the trees, every hatch standing wide open. Carter was standing in the snow beside it, shouting, "Hurry, Chilaili! You're down to less than two minutes!"

Chilaili let go a sob of thanks and shouted, "Climb into the machine! Hurry!"

The warriors paused, staring.

"Move!" Chilaili snarled. "We have less than two minutes!"

Warriors stumbled forward, piling into the shuttle. Sixty of them, heavily muscled, tall, trying to scrunch down into the only available space. Chilaili shoved Yiska into the last narrow place left. Carter dogged the hatch closed. "Into the copilot's seat, Chilaili," the human shouted, running for the pilot's hatch on the opposite side. Chilaili dragged herself in through the open hatch and slammed the heavy door shut. Carter scrambled into her own place and shut the final hatch. "Now, Chilaili! Release that analog now!" Carter was yanking at the craft's controls, tugging a device over her face as the craft tilted and roared into the air.

Chilaili snatched out the canister of analog and pushed the plunger, spewing its contents into the shuttle. "I've released the antidote," she shouted over her shoulder, pushing the control on the smoke bomb as well, to provide the critical visual element necessary to *belief.*

"Breathe as deeply as you can!"

Yellow smoke mingled with the invisible antidote, setting them to coughing. The device on Carter's face protected the pilot's nose and eyes from the stinging smoke. The smell of terror was as thick and choking as the smoke.

"I'm trying to climb above the neurotoxin plume," Carter said through her protective mask. "Rapier, what's the count?"

"You are fifteen seconds away from contamination. Fourteen . . . thirteen . . . twelve . . ."

Uncontrollable shivers hit as the Bolo counted down the seconds. Crowded into a small space, aware that this time, the poison had already been released, the terror was far deeper than before. *Please,* she prayed silently, unable to think beyond that one word. *Please* . . .

Relentless as a flash flood, the Bolo's voice counted down the seconds to doom, using their own language so they could all follow the words. "Chilaili, you are five seconds from contamination. The cavern is already inside the contamination zone. You are three seconds from contamination . . . two . . . one . . ." A tiny pause, while all of them held their breaths in mortal fright and Carter continued climbing at a steep angle. Then: "You are contaminated. Monitoring parts per billion." Another ghastly pause came. "I detect a low level of neurotoxin in the shuttle, holding steady at three parts per billion. Contamination in the cavern has reached twenty parts per billion and continues to climb. Shuttle levels are holding steady. I have initiated countdown to onset of symptoms based on Unit SPQ/R-561's observations at the Rustenberg nest site. One minute thirty-nine seconds to estimated onset of poisoning effects at the cavern. Two minutes twenty seconds to onset in the shuttle."

Yiska, voice hoarse, called out from the cargo space behind her. "Chilaili? What do the humans say?"

"We are breathing the neurotoxin," Chilaili said, coughing as the smoke continued to irritate her throat. "The cavern has been contaminated, too. All we can do is wait to see if the antidote will work." Her voice quavered badly.

A low moan rolled forward, as even the most hardened of the warriors groaned in fright. It was one thing to die gloriously in battle—and quite another to die in convulsions from poison. Each passing minute took years to complete. As they neared the moment when they would all *know*, Yiska broke the dreadful silence.

"Chilaili," he said, voice low, "you have chosen wisely, leading us into this alliance with humans. I would not have thought it possible, even an hour ago. Whatever happens, know that you have the deepest respect a warrior can bestow." A low murmur of agreement rose from the other warriors.

Chilaili's heart overflowed with the things she wanted to say, but the tightness in her throat kept the words bottled up. So she clutched at the armrests of her seat and stared blankly at the blue sky, and simply waited. And waited. And waited longer still. Then the Bolo spoke once more.

"The cavern has passed the earliest calculated moment of onset. I detect no sound of distress through the comm link embedded in the neurotoxin monitor. Chilaili, the shuttle is now forty seconds from earliest onset. I will continue to monitor contamination levels."

Hope flared, an agony in heart and spirit. Time spun out, inexorable, yet none of them collapsed, none of them bled from skin or eyes, no one seemed to be ill at all. Chilaili's pulse thundered inside her skull, hammered at her throat.

"I detect no sound of distress from the cavern," the Bolo said again.

Bessany Weyman's voice came through the radio. "Why aren't they getting sick? There wasn't time to saturate their tissues with the analog."

Alison Collingwood's voice answered thoughtfully. "The concentrations in the shuttle, even in the cavern, are a lot lower than they are in the general atmosphere. Since they are breathing in the analog, I suspect there's a minor war going on at the receptor sites. The neurotoxin molecules have to compete with inert analog molecules for possession of every cell. The neurotoxin may require a certain threshold, body-wide, before it reaches critical toxicity. In combination, those factors might be enough to protect them. All we can do is cross our fingers and wait."

Chilaili didn't understand all the words the human had spoken, but she'd caught enough of it to translate for the others. "We may be all right?" Yiska asked, voice hushed.

"We aren't dead yet," Chilaili answered. "No one is." The dreadful tension gripping her had begun to drain away, slowly, as genuine hope took hold.

"Chilaili," Carter said softly, "look out the windows."

She did—and gasped.

There was no longer blue sky overhead. It had gone dark as night, with a blaze of stars visible. Below, a thin blue-white haze curved away beneath them. And below that, Chilaili gaped at the awe-striking sight of their homeworld, glittering where sunlight struck the snow. She could see dark patches and long, snaking scars that at first made no sense, then she made the connection between the dark green color of the patchy places and the dark green of the conifer forests she knew so well. If those were the forests, then the long, wrinkled scars were *mountains*. The staggering scale of it took her breath away. In the distance, where the world fell away in a mysterious curve, she could see immense stretches of a beautiful blue color.

"Wh-what is the blue?"

"The ocean, Chilaili," Carter said gently. "You've never seen the ocean, have you?"

She shook her head, staring.

"You may be up here only for an hour or so, while that analog saturates everyone's tissues, but for an hour, Chilaili, welcome to the stars."

Chilaili's throat closed up again. She tried three times to find her voice, then whispered, "Can you see, Yiska? Through the clear places in the machine? We're flying among the stars. And the whole world is below our feet."

Icewing Clan had fulfilled the destiny promised the

strongest, wisest, best clan. For one, short hour they would fly amongst the stars. Chilaili wept at the price paid for that hollow honor.

And soon—very soon—she must look into Bessany Weyman's alien eyes and give her friend the sole thing she could offer in return for their lives: one final, critical thing the humans *must* be made to understand.

Find our creators, she would say, *find them in their hidden homes amongst the stars. Then kill them. All of them.*

After what the humans had done, this day, Chilaili's makers would not rest until they had destroyed humanity, on every world her new friends called home.

Her thoughts, as cold and silent as the stars, held the ominous ring of prophecy.

DAVID WEBER

Buy Honor Harrington at your local bookstore or at www.baen.com

On Basilisk Station	(HC) 57793-X /	$18.00	☐
	(PB) 72163-1 /	$7.99	☐
The Honor of the Queen	72172-0 /	$7.99	☐
The Short Victorious War	(PB) 87596-5 /	$6.99	☐
The Short Victorious War	(HC) 7434-3551-6 /	$14.00	☐
Field of Dishonor	87624-4 /	$6.99	☐
Flag in Exile	(HC) 31980-9 /	$10.00	☐
	(PB) 87681-3 /	$7.99	☐
Honor Among Enemies	(HC) 87723-2 /	$21.00	☐
	(PB) 87783-6 /	$7.99	☐
In Enemy Hands	(HC) 87793-3 /	$22.00	☐
	(PB) 57770-0 /	$7.99	☐
Echoes of Honor	(HC) 87892-1 /	$24.00	☐
	(PB) 57833-2 /	$7.99	☐
Ashes of Victory	(HC) 57854-5 /	$25.00	☐
	(PB) 31977-9 /	$7.99	☐
War of Honor (Oct 02)	7434-3545-1 /	$26.00	☐
More Than Honor (anthology)	87857-3 /	$6.99	☐
Worlds of Honor (anthology)	57855-3 /	$6.99	☐
Changer of Worlds (anthology)	(HC) 31975-2 /	$25.00	☐
Changer of Worlds	(PB) 0-7434-3520-6 /	$7.99	☐

For more books by David Weber,
ask for our free catalog, or visit www.baen.com

TIME SCOUTS CAN DO

In the early part of the 21st century disaster struck—an experiment went wrong, bad wrong. The Accident almost destroyed the universe, and ripples in time washed over the Earth. Soon, the people of the depopulated post-disaster Earth learned that things were going to be a little different.... They'd be able to travel into the past, utilizing remnant time strings. It took brave pioneers to map the time gates: you can zap yourself out of existence with a careless jump, to say nothing of getting killed by some rowdy downtimer who doesn't like people who can't speak his language. So elaborate rules are evolved and Time Travel stations become big business.

But wild and wooly pioneers aren't the most likely people to follow rules... Which makes for great adventures as Time Scouts Kit Carson, Skeeter Jackson, and Margo Carson explore Jack the Ripper's London, the Wild West of the '49 Gold Rush, Edo Japan, the Roman Empire and more.

꧁꧂

"Engaging, fast moving, historically literate, and filled with Asprin's expertise on the techniques and philosophy of personal combat, this is first-class action SF."　　*—Booklist*

"The characters ... are appealing and their adventures exciting ..."　　*—Science Fiction Chronicle*

꧁꧂

The Time Scout series
by Robert Asprin & Linda Evans

Time Scout	87698-8	$5.99	___
Wagers of Sin	87730-5	$5.99	___
Ripping Time	57867-7	$6.99	___
The House that Jack Built	31965-5	$6.99	___
For King & Country (HC, Aug 02)	7434-3539-7	$24.00	___

If not available through your local bookstore send this coupon and a check or money order for the cover price(s) + $1.50 s/h to Baen Books, Dept. BA, P.O. Box 1403, Riverdale, NY 10471. Delivery can take up to eight weeks.

NAME: _____

ADDRESS: _____

_____

I have enclosed a check or money order in the amount of $ _____